CALL
BACK

Other books by Denise Grover Swank:

Magnolia Steele Mystery
Center Stage
Act Two
Call Back
Curtain Call (October 2017)

Rose Gardner Investigations
Family Jewels
Trailer Trash
For the Birds

Rose Gardner Mystery
Twenty-Eight and a Half Wishes
Twenty-Nine and a Half Reasons
Thirty and a Half Excuses
Falling to Pieces (novella)
Thirty-One and a Half Regrets
Thirty-Two and a Half Complications
Picking up the Pieces (novella)
Thirty-Three and a Half Shenanigans
Rose and Helena Save Christmas (novella)
Ripple of Secrets (novella)
Thirty-Four and a Half Predicaments
Thirty-Four and a Half Predicaments Bonus Chapters
Thirty-Five and a Half Conspiracies
Thirty-Six and a Half Motives
Sins of the Father (novella)

The Wedding Pact
The Substitute
The Player
The Gambler
The Valentine (short story)

Bachelor Brotherhood
Only You
Until You

denisegroverswank.com

CALL
BACK

A Magnolia Steele Mystery
Book Three

Denise Grover Swank

chapter one

O h, my God. You're Magnolia Steele," a woman said from behind me, her voice shaking with excitement.

It was my first day back to work at Rebellious Rose Boutique in historic downtown Franklin, Tennessee, since the attack. A murderer had viciously beaten me in my apartment three days before, and I was still sporting visible bruises, although they were mostly camouflaged with makeup. I'd been hesitant about returning to work, but I needed the little money my sales clerk job paid. So, sure, I'd expected to deal with customers' reactions to my domestic violence look, but I hadn't prepared myself for being recognized by name, although I wasn't sure why not. Only four weeks ago, I'd acquired national attention for exposing my breasts in an epic meltdown on the opening night of my debut as a star in a Broadway musical.

I spun around to face her, plastering a smile on my face. "Can I help you?"

The woman was in her early twenties, which didn't surprise me since my new fame seemed to have come from all the YouTube videos of my *performance*, and not the theatre world. "It *is* you!"

"We're having a sale on cookbooks," I said with a forced smile, ignoring her comment. "Twenty percent off."

"Will you sign it?" she asked with a giggle.

"She'd be delighted to," a man said from the front of the store. I shot him a glare when I recognized his voice. "She'll even personalize it."

Colt Austin, Middle Tennessee's resident womanizer, had just walked into the shop.

Great. What was he up to?

Colt was an exceptionally good-looking man, and he knew it. With his short dark-blond hair, crystal blue eyes, and the two dimples that appeared whenever he smiled, he enthralled almost every woman who crossed his path. Even I had a hard time escaping his spell, and I was immune to most men's charm.

I gave him a patient smile. "I'm sure she doesn't want *that.*"

Colt walked up to me and wrapped an arm around my upper back, his hand squeezing my shoulder. I tried not to flinch at the contact—my bruises were worse than I liked to let on, and Colt didn't know how many there were.

"Don't be so modest, Magnolia." He flashed his bad-boy smile at the woman, and her attention momentarily shifted focus, not that I was surprised. Colt garnered attention from women of every age and marital status.

"Oh, my gosh," the woman said as a dreamy expression crossed her face. "Are you a country music star?"

"Not yet, darlin'," he said with a wink. "But I'm workin' on it. Why, Maggie and I had a performance just last Friday night. I'm trying to convince her into another one. Maybe you'd like to come?"

I shoved an elbow into Colt's side, and he dropped his hold. Taking advantage of my freedom, I moved closer to the display. "We don't have any performances planned in the near future. Now, about those cookbooks . . ."

"I'll take two," the woman said, practically bouncing with excitement as she glanced from me to Colt, unsure which of us deserved her attention more.

"Which ones?" I asked as I picked up a thick book. "Here's one featuring Southern cooking, and another on bread—"

"Sure, those two, I don't care," she said, keeping her gaze on Colt. "I just want you to sign them. And him too."

Colt's grin spread, and I rolled my eyes. His already impossible ego would become unfathomable. "I'd be delighted," he said.

I grabbed the two books and headed toward the register, ignoring Colt's amused grin.

I'd kill him later. With no witnesses.

Alvin, my boss and the owner of the boutique, tried to interest our excitable customer in an apron and some cooking utensils, but she shook her head, still starstruck. "Just the cookbooks and their autographs."

I started to ring her up as Colt shimmied closer to her. He leaned his elbow on the counter as he peered into her flushed face. "You from around here, darlin'?"

Her face turned even redder, and she stammered, "Uh . . ."

"Why, Colt Austin," I said in an accusatory tone, planting a hand on my hip. "Are you flirting with that girl *right in front of me?*"

The dreaminess left the young woman's face. "Oh, my goodness. Is he your *boyfriend?*" She shook her head. "Of course he would be," she said, somewhere between mournful and reverential. "*He's* gorgeous. *You're* gorgeous . . ."

I couldn't stop the smile that lifted my lips. The police hadn't let me back into my torn-up apartment yet, and my sister-in-law, Belinda, had loaned me some of her clothes. The cream, vintage-style dress with yellow and pink rosebuds did great things for my complexion.

Momentary confusion had flickered in Colt's eyes, but it was quickly replaced by playfulness. "You know what we have isn't exclusive, Maggie Mae. And I can't help it if this beautiful young woman has captured my attention."

She practically swooned, and I wondered what he was up to. Colt was a charmer, but he didn't usually lay it on this thick with other women around me, not that I cared . . . well, mostly. We weren't together, after all, just friends.

"That will be thirty-six dollars and ninety-seven cents," I said.

"For two cookbooks?" she asked in dismay.

"They're *Southern Living* approved," I said, picking one up and tapping the seal on the corner.

"Oh, well, I'll just take one."

"Which one?"

"I don't care. It's not like I'll actually *use* it. The cheapest one." She turned to Colt. "Do you have many performances? I'd love to see one."

He graced her with a lazy grin. "I'm usually a solo artist, but me and Maggie have sung together a couple of times. We have an agent interested in signing us. He thinks we could be big."

I shot him a look that reminded him that was never going to happen, even though I felt a bit guilty over it, even though the prospect made me a little wistful. Colt had been trying to break into the country music scene for years, and the one night we'd performed together at the Kincaid had brought an agent knocking on his door, but only if we were a package deal, something I wasn't interested in. I'd spent enough time in the limelight following my Broadway disgrace. I was interested in lying low for a while.

Especially since my own personal stalker had been keeping an eye on me since my return to Franklin. But I'd made the Nashville news after my attack on Saturday night, so it could be argued I wasn't much good at lying low.

"Eighteen dollars and sixty-three cents," I said.

The woman dug out a twenty-dollar bill and handed it to me as she continued to watch Colt. "Would you sing something for me now?"

He chuckled. "Right now? I'm sure Alvin wouldn't approve of me disrupting his business."

Alvin had been standing to the side, taking in everything, but now he moved closer with a beaming smile.

"I have a guitar in the back. How about you and Magnolia sing together? I'm sure she's missing the stage."

Colt gave me a lackadaisical smile, but I could see the pleading in his eyes.

I *was* missing the stage, and I had loved singing with Colt, maybe a little too much, but I hated to give him false hope. Still, Alvin had been an amazingly understanding boss in the short time I'd worked for him, so I hated to refuse him. "Sure."

The woman squealed.

I refrained from rolling my eyes. "Who would you like the cookbook made out to?"

"Trina."

The cookbook author would probably be less than grateful that a washed-up Broadway star and a wannabe country singer were signing her bible on bread, but at least I was making a sale. I grabbed a pen and wrote in swooping script, *Always chase your dreams*—something I'd come up with after accepting the role of Scarlett in *Fireflies at Dawn*, my first starring Broadway role—and then signed my name, Magnolia Steele, and a heart below it.

I lifted the book and handed it to Colt. Our eyes locked and I was surprised by the gratitude I saw there. For agreeing to sing with him? But he looked away before I could get a good read. He scribbled something below my signature, then handed the cookbook back to Trina as Alvin emerged from the back with a guitar.

"Where in the hell did you get this?" Colt asked in awe. "That's a vintage Gibson."

I couldn't help wondering the same. While Alvin's store had a mixture of new and vintage items, there wasn't a single musical instrument.

He shrugged as he handed it to Colt. "It was mixed up in a batch of antiques I got last week. I've been trying to figure out what to do with it."

Colt took the guitar and strummed a few chords, then tightened the strings to tune the instrument.

Alvin pulled a stool out from behind the counter and dragged it to the front door.

"Alvin?" I asked, starting to feel uneasy. "What are you doing?"

"Setting up." He disappeared out the front door, reappearing in the front window as he placed the stool front and center.

I smelled a rat.

I narrowed my eyes as I turned to Colt, about to accuse him of being part of this, but it was obvious Alvin had caught him by surprise. Otherwise, he would have brought his own guitar. No, it would seem my enterprising boss had cooked up a unique way to draw attention to his store, not that anyone other than Trina was likely to see the connection between cookbooks and country music.

His smile as wide as his face, Alvin came bustling back in, only to immediately leave with another stool. At least we'd both get a seat.

When he finished tuning, Colt glanced up at me with a twinkle in his eyes. "Showtime."

Even though I was irritated to be roped into this, I couldn't ignore the butterflies of excitement in my stomach.

Colt held the door open for Trina and I, then perched on the stool and strummed a few chords. Still a little reluctant, I sat down beside him. Trina stood facing us, so excited she was practically jumping up and down, our fan base of one.

"What do you want to do?" Colt asked. "Our set from Friday night?"

Part of me didn't want to sing at all. Four weeks ago, I'd been onstage in New York City, living my dream. Now I was a street performer.

But the entertainer in me won out. "Sure."

He started Lady Antebellum's "Need You Now," the first song we'd sung together last week, a few nights before our debut at the Kincaid. I chose not to reflect on the fact that he'd pulled me onstage to sing as a distraction after I stumbled upon Walter Frey's dead body—the second murder victim I'd found since moving back to Franklin. The first time, I'd ended up as a person of interest in the police investigation, and Colt had—rightly—deduced I was terrified of it happening again.

I started singing the first verse of the song. Colt quickly joined in, and I lost myself in the music. In less than a minute, Colt and I were singing the chorus to each other, and my heart felt lighter than it had in days.

I could almost forget that I'd nearly been killed by a Nashville dentist, Geraldo Lopez, the man who had likely murdered my father.

I could forget that nearly a million dollars' worth of gold had been stolen from my apartment—gold my father had possibly embezzled from one of his financial clients.

I could forget that I was staying with Brady Bennett, a Franklin police detective who had let me sleep in his bed for the past three nights. Or that he had neither pushed my boundaries nor asked anything of me.

I could forget that I'd arranged to meet Walter Frey the night of his murder. He and my father had set up a meeting the night of my father's disappearance, and I'd hoped to ask him about it. Instead, he'd been murdered outside of the bar where he was supposed to meet *me*—something Brady hadn't included in the report on Frey's murder.

I could forget that Brady's best friend, Owen, another Franklin detective, had likely hidden facts about Walter Frey's death. And that he'd lied about the events leading up to Dr. Lopez's death. He'd saved me, but he was hiding something.

I could forget that my brother Roy had a deep violent streak and not only hated me, but he was beating his sweet wife, Belinda.

I could forget that my mother was dying from cancer—a fact that, at her request, I had hidden from nearly everyone around me.

Most of all, I could forget that ten years ago I'd run away from my high school graduation party, sought shelter from the rain in an abandoned house, and found myself in the middle of a real-life nightmare. A man had murdered a woman in front of me, and he'd carved a mark into my leg with a hunting knife so I would never forget the price of telling. And I hadn't—I'd suppressed memories of the traumatic event so thoroughly they'd only begun to resurface after my return to Franklin.

I could even forget that my attacker was still watching me, texting me on occasion to remind me of the importance of keeping everything that had happened in that dark, dank basement a secret.

All that was here in this moment was me, Colt, and the music—and I felt like I could breathe for the first time in days. We sang for thirty minutes, gathering a huge crowd on the sidewalk before we were done, and Alvin knew what he was doing apparently, because more customers went into the boutique during our performance than in the whole, admittedly short, time I'd worked there.

So I was feeling pretty good until I looked up and saw a man in the back of the crowd with a baseball cap pulled low to partially hide his face. He was facing me, and while I couldn't see his eyes, a slow smile lifted the corners of his mouth when he realized I'd noticed him. It wasn't the kind of smile I was used to getting from men—there was something menacing about it. Knowing.

My heart skipped a beat and the hairs on the back of my neck stood on end. Could he be the man who'd held me captive ten years ago? *He'd* worn a hood, and I'd never gotten a good look at his face.

Without thinking, I started toward him, but another man was headed toward me, and the expression on his face told me I was about to meet with another kind of reckoning.

Detective Owen Frasier.

chapter two

C olt noticed Owen moments after I did. Putting his hand on my shoulder and leaning into my ear, he asked, "Want me to get rid of him?"

I was still too shaken by the man in the baseball hat, who'd already slipped away, to ask Colt how he knew Owen. He'd encountered Brady a few times—most of them unpleasant—but as far as I knew, he'd only seen Owen at the Kincaid last Friday night, standing next to me. Hell, I'd barely spent any time with Owen myself.

"No. I need to talk to him." I'd been expecting Owen to come looking for me. It was part of the reason I'd asked Brady to let me stay with him after my apartment was declared a crime scene. It had seemed unlikely Owen would force a confrontation, especially an unpleasant one, in front of his best friend. But I'd had enough time to collect myself. I could face him now.

Colt kept his hand on my shoulder as he addressed the crowd. "Thanks for listening, y'all, but Maggie and me are gonna call it a day. Be sure to head inside and check out the fine display of vintage and newer household items, and you sure don't want to miss Alvin's cookbook sale—twenty percent off!"

It sounded a lot like a prepared spiel, which made me wonder again if I had been set up. But I had bigger fish to fry—like the detective heading straight for me.

Steeling my back, I met him at the front of the crowd. "Detective Frasier, what a pleasant surprise. What are you doing here?"

A few of the women who'd lingered after the performance were casting envious glances in our direction. I'd gone from singing with one devastatingly handsome man to talking with another gorgeous one. Owen was tall, dark, and handsome, but the apprehension in his eyes made me wary.

"I was downtown for lunch and decided to see what all the commotion was about."

I motioned to the store behind me. "Just Alvin trying to drum up a little business."

"Did he have a permit for that?"

"Did he need one?"

He didn't answer, his gaze landing on Colt, who'd been cornered by a couple of women. "I confess, I'd also planned to drop by and see you."

I wasn't surprised, but I wasn't pleased either. "And how did you know I'd be here?"

"Brady." His gaze turned back to mine. "Got a minute to chat?"

"Sure," I said breezily, as if nothing was amiss.

"How about we walk down to Starbucks and get some coffee?"

It was an understatement to say I didn't trust Owen, but Starbucks was about as public as it got, which meant I should be safe. "Okay. Let me go tell Alvin."

"I think he knows you're leaving," Owen said, motioning to the window.

Sure enough, Alvin was standing behind the window, watching me with a worried look. I lifted my hand in a short wave, then pointed down the street.

Alvin nodded, still looking concerned, but business was booming a little too much for him to keep his attention on me.

"You seem to have a way with men," Owen said dryly.

I grinned, pretending not to notice the barb beneath his words. "Well, I'm not sure about *that*."

"You've got Brady under your spell."

I laughed. "I assure you, I'm incapable of holding *anyone* under a spell—otherwise, I wouldn't be working at a boutique in downtown Franklin. I'd be back in New York onstage."

"See, I think you *could* be back in New York, yet you're still here." His tone held a challenge. "Why?"

I glanced up at him, letting my smile fade. "Do you want to have this discussion here on the sidewalk?"

"No. Definitely not."

Something in his tone made my heart thud against my ribcage. Owen had lied in his report about the events leading up to Geraldo Lopez's death, and I hadn't contradicted him. I'd claimed my memories of the shooting were a blur, but Owen had watched me intently while I gave my report, and I suspected he knew I wasn't telling the truth. If so, he was right—I'd been alert and aware for the shooting, and I knew Owen had shot Dr. Lopez to stop him from saying something.

Was Owen going to call me on it now?

A warm smile spread across his face, but wariness filled his eyes. "Let's get our coffee and sit before we talk."

We walked silently to the coffee shop. He paid for both of our drinks and then suggested we sit outside at the ice cream shop tables across the street.

As soon as we were settled at one of the folding tables, he asked, "How are you holding up after everything?"

I took a sip of my coffee and lifted one shoulder into a slight shrug. "Okay. Still sore, but I'm getting better."

"Brady says you're having nightmares."

My eyes widened in shock. "Brady's been talking to you about me?"

He gave me a sympathetic smile. "Not really. I pressed him. I suggested you see a trauma counselor, but he insisted you were fine."

Brady had never mentioned the possibility to me, not that I would have gone. "And the subject of my nightmares came up during your conversation?"

He rested his hand on the table and leaned closer. "No. I asked him a few questions about you. The sort of thing I'd do to check up on a trauma victim. You know, 'How's Magnolia? Is she having any anxiety? Any nightmares?' When he didn't deny the nightmares, I figured you were probably plagued by them." He looked into my eyes. "You were beaten and nearly killed, Magnolia. Then your attacker was shot to death in front of you. By *me*. It was a traumatic experience for both of us. There's no shame in being anxious."

I set my coffee cup on the table. "I'm fine."

"Sometimes it helps to talk about an experience like that, and I know you're not talking to Brady, which seems a little odd."

The hairs on the back of my neck stood on end again. "I'm a private person."

"Private enough that you took off ten years ago without a single word to anyone?"

I resisted the urge to cross my arms over my chest, instead forcing myself to look steady and unaffected. "I hurt my mother terribly when I took off to become an actress, and now that I'm back, I'm trying to make amends for my thoughtlessness."

"I'm sorry. I didn't mean to bring up any painful memories," he said, his face shifting into a sympathetic mask. I'd seen worse acting on a few Off-Off Broadway productions. "Since you and Brady are becoming closer, I thought I would offer to be a friendly ear. You and I shared the experience, so I thought it might be easier for you to talk to me."

I struggled to control my fear. "I already gave my statement."

"Oh, I know," he said kindly. "This is off the record. Friend to friend."

The corners of my mouth tilted up into a smile, and I tried to relax my cheek muscles to make it look more natural. "That's very kind of you, but I think I've processed the situation."

"This isn't easy for me to admit," he said, looking down at his coffee cup before returning his gaze to me. "But I need to talk about it too."

"Maybe *you* should be the one seeing a trauma counselor," I said in a teasing tone.

"I thought it might be better to talk to you. That's why support groups work so well. You can share your feelings with someone who understands."

He held my gaze, and I could see he wasn't just going to let this go. Maybe it would be in my best interest to reiterate that I was sticking with his version of the story.

"That's probably a good idea." I broke eye contact, wanting to look demure, and picked up my cup again. "But I don't like talking about it, much less thinking about it."

"I understand. But talking about it will probably help with the nightmares." He paused. "You said Lopez wanted something, but you didn't know what. Has that become any clearer since Saturday night?"

I took a sip of coffee, forcing it down my tightened throat. *Play a role.* I was a clueless victim. "No. He just kept asking where *it* was, and when I asked what he was talking about, he said I already knew." I *was* lying, but I was playing my role so well I almost believed it. However, the look on Owen's face suggested he wasn't buying it.

"I don't understand why he'd go to so much trouble to attack you if you didn't have it."

"I don't even know what *it* could be."

"That's what you said the other night, but you also suggested he might have been after the money that went missing when your father disappeared." His eyes locked on mine. "Have you considered it might not be money?"

I blinked, feigning confusion. I was pretty damn sure he knew it was gold and was trying to get me to admit it. "What could it possibly be? A safety deposit key like Brady suggested?"

"No. Something else."

"I don't know. I was just a kid when Daddy left."

"You were fourteen," he said, watching me closely. "Brady said you and your father were very close."

I tilted my head. "Sounds like you and Brady have been talking about me more than you let on."

He ignored my statement. "Your father didn't tell you?"

"Why would he? Looking back, I'm sure he tried to keep as much from me as he could."

"So why would Lopez think you had it?"

"Because he was desperate? He had to be to fake his own kidnapping and kill people." I narrowed my eyes. "I thought this wasn't an interrogation."

He looked momentarily startled, but the next second he sat back and smiled. "Sorry. Habit."

"If you question your girlfriends like that, it's no wonder you're currently single," I said with a playful grin. I truly deserved a Tony nomination for this performance.

He laughed, but it sounded forced. "There's probably truth in that."

Since he was so hell-bent on continuing our chat, I decided to go on the offensive. "How did you get to my apartment so quickly that night?" I asked. "I'd just called Brady before Dr. Lopez broke in my door. Then the next thing I knew, you were there to save me."

He shrugged. "The police station isn't too far from your house."

According to Brady, Owen hadn't been on duty that night, which only made me more suspicious. "Thank goodness you showed up, or I might be dead."

"Just doing my job."

"Well," I said sincerely, "Thank you."

He nodded. "But you know full well what happened when I shot Lopez. Why didn't you tell Brady?"

I hesitated, wondering how to answer.

His face became a blank slate. "Let's make a deal, okay? Let's be as honest with each other as we're able to be."

I tilted my head—the qualifier he'd tacked on worked to my advantage, but it also worked to his. If he stuck to the arrangement, at least I could trust he wasn't lying to me. But could I really trust that? I'd have to hear him out and decide later. "Okay."

"Why are you staying at Brady's apartment?"

That wasn't the question I'd expected from him. "Because you said I couldn't stay in my apartment while you were collecting evidence."

"Why not stay with your mother?"

I studied him for a moment, then gave him a demure smile. "My mother and I don't get along very well, which is why I'm working at Alvin's boutique and not full-time in her catering kitchen." While all of that was kind of true, it wasn't the real answer to his question. I didn't want to put my mother in danger.

"So you're using him."

This conversation was not going the way I'd thought it would. "I'm not using Brady."

"I know for a fact that you're not sleeping with him."

"*Excuse me?*" I asked, outraged. "He told you that?"

"He didn't have to. I know." He squirmed in his seat, suddenly looking like he regretted starting this conversation. "There are other ways of knowing, Magnolia. I've been friends with him for eight years, and it's my job to read people."

"I like Brady. A lot. However, I just jumped out of a disastrous relationship in New York, and it's not fair to him if I jump into something before I have it all sorted out."

"So why are you staying with him?"

"Honestly?" I asked, holding his gaze. "He makes me feel safe. Safer than I've felt in a long time. It seems to me that Brady's a big boy and can handle himself, so tell me why you really want to know."

He was quiet for a moment. "He's a sucker for a damsel in distress, and we both know you're caught up in something bigger—much bigger than a dead dentist. Brady needs to stay the hell away from it."

His admission caught me by surprise. "And you think I'll drag him into it if I stay."

"I know you will."

And suddenly I had confirmation that I'd only scratched the surface of what my father had gotten mixed up in. Something Owen clearly knew a thing or two about.

"And you?" I said. "You're involved."

"Yes, I know more than I've let on," he said, scanning the street. "But I knew you did too when you didn't contradict my version of how Lopez went down."

"Do you know what he was looking for?" I asked.

His mouth tipped into an amused smirk. "Do *you?*"

I held his gaze. "Fair enough."

"You're going to keep digging," he said flatly.

I could lie, but I saw no reason to hide the truth from him. I wasn't some super sleuth who could fly under the radar. He was likely to find out what I was up to sooner or later.

After the inauspicious end to my meeting with Walter Frey, I'd started digging into the mystery of my father's disappearance. For each answer I'd found, I'd surfaced a dozen new questions. One of those Pandora's boxes was the plaster dog I'd given my daddy years before. I'd rescued it from the family garage, only to find those gold bars hidden inside, along with a note telling me to trust no one. At first, I'd presumed he'd hidden it fourteen years ago, right before his disappearance, but Colt's friend had run the serial numbers, and three of the bars had been made four years after he vanished. There was more to be dug up, and I wasn't stopping until I uncovered it all. "Yes."

"I'd like to point out that it would be incredibly stupid and dangerous for you to keep meddling. There are people who don't want their private business exposed."

That gave me pause. I'd already realized how deadly this game was, but most of the key players were now dead, weren't they? "I know the police version of my father's disappearance is wrong. And I have proof."

"And you learned this from Geraldo Lopez?"

"I have multiple sources, Owen."

"Sources like Sydney Crowley? Shannon Morrissey's sister?" He grinned, but it wasn't kind. "You really suck at this. You're not even trying to hide what you're doing."

"I never claimed to be a detective."

His expression turned grim. "All the more reason for you to stay out of it."

"I'm doing this to find out what really happened to my father. What's your involvement?"

"I'm a police detective," he said in a derisive tone. "Isn't that reason enough?"

"To be delving into a fourteen-year-old mystery? And keeping it from your best friend?" I asked in disbelief, then shook my head. "No. It's because your uncle was involved in my father's case." His uncle had been accused of being a dirty cop over his handling of the case. Was Owen trying to prove his uncle was innocent, like Brady had insinuated, or was he after the gold?

His eyes widened slightly. Perhaps he was surprised that I, with my shoddy detective skills, had made the connection. I wasn't about to let him know that Brady had drawn the dots together too.

"You said you're digging into this to find out what happened to your father," he said. "Are you sure you really want to know? What if he wasn't as clean as you think he was?"

I'd already asked myself that question more times than I could count over the last few days. "I could ask the same about your uncle."

His face flushed with anger. "Your father's integrity may be in question, but my uncle was a good cop."

25

"Then why do you care if I keep digging? Scared I'll find out something about your uncle that you don't want known? You've been on the force for eight years, so forgive me if I find it coincidental that you're only now trying to prove his innocence—after I was the one who pried the case open again."

"Don't flatter yourself, Magnolia," he said dryly. "Finding a couple of dead bodies doesn't make you a crack investigator."

I shifted in my seat. "That reminds me of something. When I found Walter Frey, he had a cell phone and a note in his hand. But Brady said there was no mention of either of those things in the police report. In fact, the report says he didn't have a cell phone at all. You took them, didn't you?"

Walter Frey hadn't wanted to meet me at the bar that night. I'd pressured him into it, and I still felt somewhat responsible for his death. After finding his body, I'd leaned in close to see if he was still alive. That was when I saw those things in his hand. Given the reason for our meeting, I'd deduced that the list was composed of people for me to either talk to or investigate. Geraldo Lopez was the only name I'd recognized offhand, and I'd made an appointment at his office using an alias. The rest was recent, and rather unpleasant, history.

I'd also seen two partial names on the list. Christopher Merritt, I'd discovered, was an accountant who'd disappeared just like my father had, only years later. The last entry ended in *–ogers*. I had no idea who it could be, but I planned to find out.

Owen stared at me, not contradicting my accusation, so I had to assume he *had* taken the list and the phone.

"You're not warning me to protect me. Or Brady, for that matter," I said, lowering my gaze to my hand on the table. "You're worried about what I'm going to turn up."

"Who says there's anything to turn up? Maybe I'm trying to keep you from getting arrested for interfering with an investigation."

I gave him a wry smile. "What investigation? My father's disappearance case is closed. And so is Walter Frey's, now that we know Dr. Lopez killed him." I decided to be blunt. "I like how you threw everyone off the trail by saying Mr. Frey was robbed."

An ugly look spread across his face. "Are you accusing me of interfering with an investigation?"

"We both know Walter Frey wasn't robbed. But he *was* part of your uncle's investigation into my father's disappearance, and you didn't want to draw any attention to that."

Owen's face reddened. "You got what you wanted— proof your father didn't run away with his mistress. Time to let it go."

"There's more. A lot more."

"Stay out of it, Magnolia. I can't be responsible for what happens to you if you continue to push."

"No," I said as a new truth hit me. "I suspect that's true, or you wouldn't be warning me at all." While I knew I should be worried about my safety, at the moment I was more worried about dragging the people I cared about into the middle of it. "But we both know you lied about killing

Lopez. You were covering up your involvement in something."

He looked startled for a second before he managed to conceal his reaction. "Magnolia, this is bigger than your father's disappearance. Just accept that he's gone and move on with your life—without Brady." He stood. "Your apartment's been released. You're free to move back in, but if you're smart, you'll move back to New York and leave this all behind."

chapter three

When I reentered the shop, I thought I saw the guy with the baseball cap again, but this man was shorter and broader than the guy I'd seen in the crowd. I shook my head. I was getting paranoid.

Colt had left, but he'd sent a text asking me to let him know when I got off work. We'd drummed up a nice crowd for the store, and the effect had snowballed—people passing by kept stopping in to see why so many people were there. I ended up staying an hour past the end of my shift, not that I was complaining. I was flat broke. Again.

I called Colt as I walked out the back door.

"What did he want?" he asked without preamble.

"Don't you want to know who *he* was?"

"I already do. Owen Frasier, the Franklin police detective who was with Bennett at the Kincaid Friday night. The guy in charge of Frey's murder. Now what did he want?"

Sure, Colt had seen Owen and me together at the bar, but that didn't explain why he knew him by name. "I don't want to talk about it over the phone. I'm headed to my apartment to pick up some things."

"So you're gonna keep shacking up with Detective Hot Stuff?" he asked, sounding disgusted.

I decided to ignore his question, feeling guilty enough about staying with Brady. "Are you going to meet me there or not?"

"See you in ten minutes," he said before he hung up.

My phone rang again before I could put it down. I cringed when I saw it was my sister-in-law Belinda.

Although we'd texted several times over the past few days, I hadn't seen her since Saturday night, after my attack. Earlier that evening, she'd put on an Arts Council fundraiser. I'd helped cater the event for Momma's business, and Steve Morrissey had confronted me there, angry that I'd sent a policeman to talk to him about Geraldo Lopez's disappearance. For the rest of the evening, Belinda had stuck by my side like glue. She had given me a solid alibi around the time of Morrissey's death, which seemed a little . . . convenient. Even stranger, she'd told me that my brother was at a dinner in downtown Nashville, but I was almost certain I'd seen him lurking in the shadows outside of the fundraiser. My gut told me that my sister-in-law knew something about Morrissey's death and that my brother might be involved. I needed to talk to her about it, but I wasn't quite sure how, and everything else had unfurled from there . . .

She'd texted earlier today, and I'd promised to call her when I finished at the store.

"Hey," I answered, trying to sound breezy as I started my car and pulled out of the parking lot. "Sorry I haven't called yet, but I just got off work. We had a huge crowd today."

"I hear you and Colt put on a performance." I wasn't surprised to hear the disapproval in her voice. She'd made it clear that she thought I should steer clear of him.

"Alvin coerced us into it."

"I heard you were a hit."

Belinda's wedding planner business was only a couple of blocks from the store, and word traveled fast downtown. "We drew a bit of a crowd."

"How are you? I've been so worried about you," she said. "Especially since Brady wouldn't let me see you."

"It wasn't that he wouldn't *let* you," I said as I turned down the street of my apartment. "I was sleeping. Besides, I tried to call you later, but you were meeting with clients."

"What are you doing tonight? Roy's working late, so I thought maybe we could get dinner."

"Oh," I said. "Brady said he'd be home by six."

She was silent for a beat. "So you're still staying with Brady?"

"For the time being," I said. "Detective Frasier came by the store earlier and told me that my apartment has been released as a crime scene. I'm headed there now to pick up some things to take to Brady's."

"Doesn't it freak you out to go back there?"

Yes, but I wasn't sure I wanted to admit that. "I'm only going up for a few minutes. Besides, Colt will be there."

"For someone who's living with Brady, you're spending an awful lot of time with Colt." From anyone else

31

it would have sounded judgmental, but Belinda sounded more like she was worried I'd get hurt.

"I know how it looks, but I'm not sleeping with Brady. I'm just staying there."

"I thought you liked him."

"I do, but I'm just not ready yet."

"Because of Colt?"

"Colt and I are just friends, Belinda. You know that."

"Colt doesn't have any female friends."

"Well, he's friends with me," I said, sounding more defensive than I would have liked.

"I'm sorry. I'm not trying to sound like your momma."

I laughed. "No worries there. Momma would have been a lot more blunt. I know your warning comes from love, but there's nothing to worry about. Rushing into a relationship with Brady seems like a bad idea, and there's absolutely nothing to worry about with Colt. I'm not stupid enough to become one more woman in his revolving door."

"I know you're not, but it's my job as your sister-in-law to worry about you."

I smiled, my heart feeling full. Out of all the people I'd gotten close to since coming back to Franklin, I valued my relationship with Belinda the most. "You have no idea how much that means to me. Thank you." I paused to swallow the lump in my throat. "I wish I could have dinner with you, but maybe we could have lunch tomorrow instead."

"I have lunch with a client. I know you're not a morning person, but what about breakfast?"

"I have to be at Ava's to clean her house at eight thirty."

"Surely you don't have to clean her house if you aren't even staying there."

I snorted. "Have you *met* Ava Milton? Of course I do, but I want to see you, so are you willing to meet at seven thirty?"

"Yeah," she said, her voice cracking slightly. "I miss you, Magnolia."

"I miss you too. I'll see you tomorrow." I hung up as the house came into view up ahead.

I was glad I'd had the call to distract me, because I wasn't as nervous as I'd expected to be when I pulled into the driveway.

The crime tape was gone when I parked my car in front of my second-floor garage apartment. I hadn't been back since Brady had whisked me away to his place late Saturday night. I'd left with only the clothes I was wearing and my cell phone.

But now that I was here, I was beginning to have second thoughts about going back up there. I'd almost been killed in this place. It had taken me years to get over the trauma I'd suffered in the basement of that abandoned house in the woods ten years ago. Even though the memories hadn't returned to me until recently, the experience had scarred me in every way possible.

The problem was that I *needed* this apartment, however little I wanted it. I couldn't stay with Brady indefinitely. It was out of the question to move back in with my mother, given that I planned to keep digging into my father's disappearance—and God knew how unlikely it was that Ava Milton would let me out of my six-month lease without charging me an arm and a leg.

I got out of the car and wasn't surprised when the screen door instantly opened at the back of the house. Ava Milton, my landlady, stuck her nose in everything and knew all about my comings and goings. She'd made it abundantly clear that she wanted a quiet tenant, so I was sure to get an earful considering her house had essentially become a *Law & Order* episode last Saturday night.

"Magnolia Steele," she said in a stern voice. "You're back."

I spun around to face her. "Detective Frasier came to see me at the shop today to tell me the apartment had been released. I thought I'd check it out."

She stepped through the door and walked toward me. The look on her face told me I was in trouble. "He told me the same thing. We'll walk through the place together and assess the damage."

A horrifying new thought occurred to me: I wouldn't put it past her to hold me responsible and make me pay to repair the damages. That was money I didn't have.

She headed up the staircase to my apartment, leaving me to follow. When we got to the top, she stopped and stared at the door. "This will have to be completely replaced," she said in a snippy tone.

Since the wood around the lock on the door and the door frame had been fragmented by bullets, I saw no reason to disagree.

She pushed the door open and took several steps inside, but I stayed in the opening, taking in the damage that had been done to the open-floor-plan, one-bedroom apartment.

The living room furniture had been shoved around, and there was a shattered lamp on the floor that had apparently gotten broken in the scuffle—or the ensuing investigation. The utility closet door in the kitchen was open, and cleaning products were strewn across the kitchen floor. Otherwise, the only sign that a man had been murdered here was the sickeningly large stain on the hardwood floors.

"That will likely need to be replaced," Ava said.

"But I can move back in before it's done, can't I?"

She turned back to look at me. "You want to move into an apartment with a bloodstained floor?"

I shuddered. "No, but I don't know how long I'll be where I'm currently staying."

"You don't want to stay with your boyfriend?" she asked with narrowed eyes. Her tone made it clear she didn't approve of me staying with him. I hadn't told her where I was staying, but I wasn't surprised she knew.

"He's not my boyfriend. He's just a friend. But he's interested in more, and I'm not ready to go there yet." Why was I telling her this? She was the biggest busybody in town—the last person I wanted to let in on my personal tribulations.

"Well, you can't move back in before the door's replaced," she said. "And the soonest that can happen is tomorrow."

"How about after that?"

She watched me for a moment, then motioned for me to walk back outside. I had to admit that looking at the bloodstain was giving me the creeps. How was I going to live here? The memories were bad enough without the physical evidence of what had happened here. Maybe I could find a throw rug big enough to cover it.

But she'd made no mention of charging me for the floor or the door, so maybe I'd get out of it.

When we reached the bottom of the stairs, she turned to face me. "I still expect you to clean my house tomorrow morning."

"I hadn't forgotten. I'll be here, Miss Ava."

Her face softened, and she studied me for several seconds. Just when I thought she was about to say something comforting, her eyes hardened again. "Eight thirty sharp. Don't be late, or I'll tack a late fee on to the cost of the repairs."

And there it was.

"Miss Ava, I have no idea how much it will cost to repair those things, but I barely have a penny to my name."

"Then you'll do extra work for me. I have plenty of projects to keep you busy. Are you working at the boutique or for your mother tomorrow?"

"Not at the boutique," I said reluctantly. "But I work for the catering business at four."

"Then plan on showing up at eight thirty and staying until you need to leave for your second job."

Part of me thought about telling her no, but right now she had me between a rock and a hard place. "Yes, ma'am."

I saw Colt walking up the drive out of the corner of my eye. He grinned as he approached. "If it isn't my two favorite ladies." He stopped next to us and turned his dazzling smile on my landlord. "Good afternoon, Miss Ava."

She shot him a dark look. "Don't you go trying to flatter me, Colton."

"Flatter you?" he asked in a teasing tone. "I only speak the truth."

Their eyes locked for a brief moment, and her mouth pursed before she turned and headed for her back door. "Eight thirty sharp, Magnolia."

"I'll be here."

Colt and I watched her walk inside, and I wondered once again how they were tied together. According to Colt, he'd done some work for Ava two years ago, but he refused to even hint at what he'd done, and my landlord would only say he was a *loyal resource*. Momma's best friend Tilly had insinuated there'd been plenty of late-night meetings, but I refused to believe they'd had a sexual affair. The more I learned about Ava Milton, the more I believed she'd consulted him for something seedy.

Colt waited for the door to close before he turned to me, his smile falling. "What did Frasier say?"

How much did I want to tell Colt? Though I was reluctant to trust anyone, I was beginning to feel way out of my league. I needed an ally, and Colt had proven that he was there for me. His dark past had made him streetwise enough to be helpful. He'd moved Daddy's plaster dog into my apartment for me, and we'd discovered the gold together—only, I'd kept my father's note to myself. Colt had connections and he'd written down the serial numbers stamped into the gold bars and brought the list to one of his friends along with one of the bars. If not for Colt, I wouldn't know about the three bars that had been made after Daddy's disappearance. How much more helpful would he be if I told him everything?

I offered him a tight smile. "Let's go upstairs."

He nodded and we headed up to my apartment. He pushed in the partially open door and walked in, then stood in the middle and did a slow scan of the room.

I stood in the doorway, still not able to make myself walk all the way in. This did not bode well for my prospects of successfully moving back in. "Owen said—"

His back was to me, but he swung around and said, sounding angry, "I don't want to hear about your afternoon with another man, Magnolia. You know how jealous I get, and it's bad enough you're shacking up with the other cop."

My mouth dropped open. What was he talking about?

"I changed my mind," he said. "I'm starving. Let's go get something to eat." Then he headed toward me and grabbed my hand, twining our fingers together as he closed the door behind us and then led the way down the stairs.

"Colt—"

"Get in your car, Maggie." He stopped next to the driver's door and opened it for me. The tightness in his voice scared me, so I did as he ordered. He walked around to the passenger side and climbed inside.

"What just happened?" I asked as soon as the doors were shut.

"Someone has bugged your apartment."

"What?" I gave a slight shake of my head, sure I'd heard him wrong. "How could you possibly know that from standing in the center of the room?"

"I saw a camera in the bookcase. It's pretty well hidden, but if you know where to look, it's easy to spot."

"Wait. You were looking?"

"Someone wants the gold, Maggie, and they think you have it. It makes sense they'd bug your place to find out where it is."

"Who would do that?"

"You tell me," he said in an accusatory tone.

"Not Brady. He doesn't know anything. Besides, we haven't discussed when I'm moving back into the apartment, so why would he bug this place? But it could be Owen, especially since he was so insistent I leave Brady's apartment and come back to my own."

"And what else did Detective Frasier have to say earlier?"

"He's worried that I'm using Brady and will hurt him."

Colt snorted. "Were you painting each other's nails when he said it?"

I scowled. "No. While I *do* believe Owen's worried about him, there's more to it. He made no secret of the fact that he knew Dr. Lopez was looking for something. Neither of us mentioned the word gold, but I'm sure he knows. The question is how?"

"We have to assume we're all on the same page," Colt said.

"Agreed."

"I wasn't lying when I said I was hungry," Colt said. "Let's head over to Puckett's and talk there."

My mouth gaped. "Are you crazy? You want to discuss this in public? *Downtown?* You need to refocus your priorities. We have to debug my apartment. If there's one camera, there's more."

"No. We're going to leave them there."

"*Are you kidding me?*"

"No." He turned to face me. "Maggie, listen. If we take the cameras out, they'll know we're onto them. We can purposely mislead them. Give them false information. If they act on it, we might be able to figure out who's behind it."

I shuddered. "Maybe so, but I can't live there knowing someone's watching me."

"Then we'll set them up right away. But for now, we'll go get something to eat and figure out where to go from here."

I frowned, then checked the time on my phone: 3:45.

"Got a hot date?"

My head jerked up, surprised by his jealous tone. "Brady said he'd be home around six."

"Is he expecting a hot meal when he gets home?"

I shot him a look. "What the hell has gotten into you?"

"I just don't see why you're doing this."

"Doing what? Staying with Brady? I already explained it to you. He makes me feel safe."

"It's more than that, and you know it, Mags. You're playing a dangerous game. Owen's dirty. How can you be sure his best friend isn't part of it? What if Owen's warnings are just to throw you off so you'll trust Brady?"

"It doesn't matter if I trust Brady or not, because, for the millionth time, I'm. Not. Telling. Him. Anything."

"You say that now . . ."

"What am I supposed to do? There's a camera in my apartment, and I can't go to Momma's. I'd leave if I could, but I'm stuck." But even as I said the words, I didn't altogether believe them. I'd liked staying with Brady a little too much. I'd let myself pretend I could have a quiet, domestic Franklin life, even though I knew it wasn't true.

"I know you are." He sounded resigned. "Start the car. Let's go."

I convinced him to pick up a sandwich from the deli instead, and we drove to Pinkerton Park and sat on top of a picnic table while we watched several preschoolers on the playground. I told him about my conversation with Owen, then waited.

"So what do you want to do?" he asked as he licked mayonnaise from his finger.

"Keep digging."

"Why?"

I was silent for a moment. "I don't know."

"You need a better reason than 'I don't know.' Frasier's right. This whole situation seems pretty damn dangerous."

"I want the truth, Colt . . . I need it."

"You know the truth, Mags. Lopez killed your father."

Except I wasn't so sure I believed that anymore— there was so much it didn't explain. I narrowed my eyes. "Why are *you* doing this? What's in it for you?"

He turned to look at me. "Honestly? I want a cut of the gold."

"With the exception of the bar you have, the gold is gone. All of it. Even the last bag. Someone took it from my purse in the catering van on Saturday night."

His eyes flew wide open. "They stole your purse?"

"No, they stole the gold and my father's gun. They left my wallet."

"Shit." He ran his hand over his head. "Which means they knew what they were looking for. You're sure Lopez didn't take it?"

"No. He was looking for it when I found him in my apartment. And if he'd stolen it out of my purse after I purposely sent him there to get it, I doubt he would have come back to beat the real location out of me."

"You told him where it was?"

"He was going to kill me. Plus, Steve Morrissey's body had just been found and the place was crawling with cops. I was hoping they'd see him breaking into the catering vans and arrest him."

His brow lowered and he grudgingly said, "Good thinking."

"Thank you," I said in a snotty tone. "Give me a *little* credit."

"How about Morrissey?" he asked, losing his attitude. "Maybe he found the gold before Lopez shot him."

"I don't know. Maybe—although I don't know how he'd know my purse was in the van. And if Morrissey found it, wouldn't Lopez find it on him when he killed him? But I'm positive Lopez stole the rest of the gold from my apartment. The timing was right. He staged his disappearance around lunchtime on Friday, and the break-in happened that afternoon."

"So we find the gold Lopez stole; then we sell it and split the profits. You just leave the rest of it alone."

"Colt, there's something I need to tell you about the gold."

"You know where it is?" he asked in a mocking hopeful tone.

"No, I wish." I leaned over my legs and took a moment, worried Colt would be pissed that I hadn't told him this right away. Or that it might be a mistake to tell him at all. "When you broke the dog statue, I found a note mixed in with all the filler paper."

"*What?*" His eyes pierced into me. "What did it say?"

"It was addressed to me," I said slowly. "It was from my father."

"Your father left you a million dollars in a plaster dog?" Anger washed over his face. "Did you know that when you found the damn statue in your mother's garage? You just used that sob story about how it looked like the statue you gave your father, might be the same one, so I'd haul it to your apartment?"

"No, Colt! I swear!" I protested. "I had no idea the gold was in there until it broke."

Strangely enough, that seemed to appease him. "Okay."

"Let me get this straight," I said, getting irritated. "You were pissed when you thought I knew about the gold, but you don't care that I kept the note from you?"

"Yeah, because in the first instance, you would have been using me. But in the second, you were just withholding information you weren't ready to share. It's all about intent." His eyes lacked their usual glint of humor. "You have your secrets and I have mine. We've respected that about each other. I see no reason to change it now."

I didn't know much about his past beyond that he wasn't proud of it. That it had cost him the only real relationship he'd ever had. Belinda had told me that he'd been arrested for grand larceny, but the charges had been dropped and the records were sealed. That had given me a moment of pause. Ultimately, though, I'd come to the conclusion that even if I didn't always trust my own instincts, I trusted my mother's. Trust didn't come easily to her, and she trusted Colt implicitly.

"The note told me to trust no one, which is part of the reason I didn't show it to you." I paused. "Colt, the note I found with the gold was left by my father, but you said some of the serial numbers were issued four years after his disappearance."

He watched me for several seconds. "You think Lopez lied about killing him? That he's alive?"

"Lopez never specifically said he killed him, but he *did* admit to killing Morrissey and others."

"You're reaching, Mags. Don't you think Lopez would have asked you where your father was?"

"No, he was more interested in the gold. Besides, I'd already gone to him looking for information about my father's disappearance. He knew I had no idea where he was." I put my hand on Colt's knee. "Even if my dad's . . . gone, I don't think he died the year he disappeared. I think he was still around four years later to put the gold in that dog."

"The gold was *minted* four years after your father's disappearance. It could have been put in that dog a month ago, for all we know. Roy put the statue in the garage. Maybe he hid it in there for safekeeping."

"With a note from my dad? Roy would have destroyed it on principle alone. He hates me because he thinks our father loved me more, not to mention I can't see Roy leaving a million in gold in a plaster dog in my mother's garage. But how did Roy even get ahold of the statue? Last I knew, it was in my daddy's office when the police confiscated everything. Belinda said the furniture in Momma's garage belongs to Roy's old friend who moved abroad, but if that's true, why did we find Christopher Merritt's notepad in there?"

Colt shook his head and leaned over his legs and stared out onto the playground for several seconds. Finally, he sighed and sat up. He grabbed my shoulders and turned both of our bodies so that we were facing each other. "Maggie, as much as it pains me to admit that Owen Frasier and I agree on something, we do agree on this—if you continue looking into this, it could get you killed."

I tilted my head in suspicion. "How do you know Owen?"

Surprise flickered in his eyes, but he quickly covered it with annoyance. "He's a Franklin police detective. With my past, I made sure to keep tabs on the detectives in this town."

I didn't quite buy it, but I'd accept it for now.

"But you're evading my point. Look, I think we should just find the gold, hold on to it until your mother . . ." He grimaced. "Um . . . is no longer working at the Belles . . . and then take off for some non-extraditing tropical country. Like Vietnam."

"Vietnam?"

He shrugged. "I hear the beaches in central Vietnam are gorgeous, and it's cheap to live there."

My eyebrows rose. "Together?"

A sly grin spread across his face. "I'm not proposing marriage or anything like that, but we get along well. We could go as friends . . . or more." He winked.

Colt was a good-looking man, and Lord knew he could pour on the charm. The thought of lying on a tropical beach with him made me hot in places that had no business reacting to him. My head told me that Colt Austin was trouble with a capital T—good for a fling and nothing more. Still, something about him tugged at me. My ex-boyfriend had stolen all my money, ruined my career, and made me homeless, but I suspected Colt would do him one better. He was capable of stealing my heart.

I laughed, playing off his suggestion. "Let's just find the gold; then we'll figure out what to do with it. And yes, I'm going to keep digging into what happened to my father, and Geraldo Lopez knew more than he told me."

"Geraldo Lopez is dead, Maggie. He's not going to tell us anything. Dead men don't talk."

"Not necessarily true."

He snorted. "You planning a séance?"

"No, but he surely left clues. Christopher Merritt was an accountant, Walter Frey was a real estate attorney, and it wasn't a secret they'd worked on Steve Morrissey's finances with my dad. If you think about it, Geraldo Lopez was the odd man out. He was a dentist. How did he get involved?" I held his gaze. "There's at least one more person who might know something."

I told him about the note I'd seen in Frey's hand and that last, maddeningly incomplete name. Another potential source—"—ogers."

A strange look came over Colt's face, and I was sure I wasn't convincing him. "You don't have to help me with this," I said. "I can do it on my own. I already have been."

Determination covered his face. "No. Lopez almost killed you. You need a partner. I'm going to help."

"Why?"

"The gold, of course," he answered, a little too quickly.

"So help me find the gold and be done with the rest."

He slowly shook his head.

"You and I are two peas in a pod, Colt. We put ourselves above everything and everyone. If I'm going to trust you, you have to have a reason for helping, and I need to know what it is."

He lifted his hand to my cheek, tracing my cheekbone with his index finger. "I just want to make sure you're safe. Let's leave it at that, okay?"

My breath caught at the tenderness in his touch and his eyes, and alarms went off in my head. I could not get involved with Colt Austin. He was more dangerous than Brady. Besides, I wanted to be with Brady, right? He could offer me the normal, safe life I craved. But I found myself nodding.

He smiled, but there was something sad in it as he leaned in to kiss my forehead and then hopped off the picnic table. "Let's go. You still need to change into your apron and pearls so you can greet your man when he walks through the front door."

chapter four

We drove back to my apartment, and I was so freaked out about the cameras I convinced Colt to go back in with me while I picked up a change of clothes for the next day. When I parked in the driveway, I rested my hand on the steering wheel for a moment. "We didn't come up with a plan to set up whoever's watching me. Hell, we didn't plan anything at all."

"What's your schedule tomorrow?"

"I'm cleaning Miss Ava's house in the morning and then working for the Belles in the afternoon at four."

"First course of action should be getting the gold back. I'll do some digging to see what I can find out about Geraldo Lopez. Then we'll come up with a plan tomorrow when you're done with Miss Ava."

I scowled. "Miss Ava plans to keep me busy all day, working off the expenses for the damages to the apartment."

"Then I'll come by Ava's and we'll wing it. In the meantime, I'll do a little digging of my own."

I shot him a glare. "Don't go finding the gold without me."

"Now, Maggie . . ."

"I'm serious. If you find something we need to tackle tonight or tomorrow morning, text me, and I'll get away."

The amused look on his face suggested he didn't believe it, and I didn't feel like arguing the point.

"One more thing . . ." My stomach clenched. "I understand the rationale for keeping the cameras, but it freaks me out. While we're in there, can you try to figure out where all of them are?"

His hand covered mine, warm and comforting. "Yeah. And we'll come up with a plan to set them up tomorrow, okay? This is just temporary."

I nodded.

We headed up the stairs, and this time I actually made it past the doorway. I tried not to look down as I skirted the bloodstained section of the floor and slipped into my bedroom. Colt went into the kitchen and started opening cabinets.

"You got anything to eat in this place?" he asked.

"You just ate!" I protested, even though he was using it as an excuse to search.

"I'm a growin' boy." More cabinets banged shut.

I grabbed a small bag off the shelf in my closet and tossed it onto my disheveled bed. Before returning to attack me, Lopez had searched my apartment for the gold and left a mess behind. I hadn't found time to clean it up afterward, and the reminder of what had happened sickened me. Nothing much was broken, though, just tossed around.

Colt appeared in the doorway. "I found a box of raisins in the kitchen but not much else."

I hated raisins, so there wasn't a single raisin in this apartment. That had to be code that he'd found another camera. "What about the books you were looking for?"

"Only the two."

Three cameras in one open living room and kitchen? That seemed like overkill.

Colt walked into the room and picked up a handful of clothes and tossed them onto the bed. "How about we take fifteen minutes and make a stab at cleaning this mess up?"

I didn't want to stay in here fifteen seconds, but I realized what he was doing—he'd just created an excuse to look for cameras in my room. Besides, the mess needed to be cleaned sooner or later.

"Yeah. Thanks." I grabbed a pair of yoga pants and a T-shirt off the floor and tossed them into the bag while Colt continued picking up the clothes off the floor.

He started hanging a few of my dresses in the closet and took the opportunity to snoop around. Snagging a black, lacy bra off my dresser, he let it hang from his index finger. "It's been a while since I've seen you in this."

My heart sank. Colt had never seen me in my underwear. But I had a part to play. "How many weeks has it been?"

"Weeks? Plural?" he scoffed. "More like one."

One camera. In my bedroom. "I need to get my toothpaste out of the bathroom."

He tossed my bra onto the bed. "I'll get it for you."

I continued folding a stack of T-shirts, trying to hide my shaking hands. Colt was back less than a minute later, a tube of toothpaste in his hand. He dropped it into my bag, then grabbed my arm and pulled me to his chest, tucking my head under his chin. "I only found the one tube of toothpaste."

I stiffened, but he held me close, stroking my back. One camera. In my bathroom.

They were everywhere.

"I miss you," he said as he leaned back and looked into my eyes. "Leave Brady and we can move in here together."

I stared at him in disbelief.

"We're good together," he continued. "Sex with you is the best I've ever had. Tell me you'll think about it."

What was he doing? But he'd obviously come up with a plan on the fly. Those improv classes were coming in handy. "Okay. I'll think about it."

He lowered his mouth to my cheek, trailing a hot line of kisses down my face and neck as his hand slid behind my back and started to pull down the zipper of my dress.

I closed my eyes, taken by surprise by the fire racing through my blood, but then I remembered we were being watched, something of which Colt was firmly aware. He was doing this for a reason—how far did he plan to go? But as soon as he started to push my dress over my shoulders, I jerked away and pulled it back up. "No. I can't."

He put his hands on my shoulders and spun me around before he zipped up my dress, slipping his arms around my waist and over my stomach. Butterflies fluttered in my gut as he pressed his chest to my back and whispered in my ear, "I'm here when you need me." Then he kissed the top of my head and released me. "Let's go."

I nodded and then picked up my bag, trying to disguise how much his demonstration had unsettled me—then again, whatever Colt was trying to do, my reaction would help sell it.

But who was the audience? Suddenly it struck me. *That* was the reason for his performance. If Owen and/or Brady had planted the cameras, I'd likely find out right away. And while I approved of his method, I was unsettled by my reaction. I'd had plenty of make-out scenes in plays before, and I'd never once reacted the way I just had with Colt. I dismissed it as the result of being caught off guard.

Colt took my bag and then ushered me to the door. I saw my laptop on the island and grabbed it before he practically pushed me over the threshold and down the steps. He opened the car door and waited for me to get in before he squatted next to the open door. "Sorry about what happened upstairs. If Frasier's behind the cameras, he'll probably confront you sooner rather than later. I would have warned you, but . . . the whole place is bugged. Whoever put the cameras in can see *everything*. Even in your bathroom."

I shook my head, feeling overwhelmed. "I caught on to what you were doing pretty quick." A new thought hit me, and I felt like I was on the verge of throwing up. "Oh,

God. Were they there last week? Did they see me in the shower? Changing?"

He grabbed my hand and squeezed. "No, Mags. The police would have found them during their investigation. Those cameras were put in *after* they finished, which makes Frasier all the more likely to be the culprit."

I nodded, still feeling violated.

"No matter what, you can't stay there until we figure out who planted them."

"Yeah. Thanks."

"Do you feel safe spending the night with Bennett?"

I thought about how understanding and sweet Brady had been since my attack. He'd even carried me to the ambulance to get checked out. No, I couldn't believe that man would ever hurt me. "Yeah."

"It kills me to say this, but I think you should keep staying with him. Indefinitely."

After my reaction to Colt a few minutes ago, I was more confused than ever about staying with Brady. "I'll think about it."

He shut my door, then stood to the side and watched me while I backed out of the driveway.

It was barely five, which meant I could do some research before Brady got home by six. Besides Colt's ploy, we hadn't made much progress, and I had a feeling we didn't have a lot of time.

I parked in Brady's parking garage, stuffed my laptop into my bag, and then pulled my pepper spray out of my purse, ready to defend myself if someone was waiting for me. There were shadows lurking in the corners but nothing more substantial. After shoving the straps to my duffel bag and my purse over my shoulder, I pretty much bolted from the car to the elevator bank.

Brady had given me a key, so once I got to the third floor, I let myself into his unit and locked the door behind me.

I had less than an hour to search the internet for information. There was a desk area in his kitchen, and a quick search yielded a paper and a pen for note-taking. I grabbed a glass of water from the kitchen and settled onto the sofa, tucking an afghan around my laptop. Brady had given me the Wi-Fi password for my phone, so I logged in to his network.

The first thing I did was search for my father's name, and it shocked me how many hits popped up on the screen, especially since the internet hadn't been as much of a behemoth back then. I knew my father had been active in the community—particularly supporting non-profits, but I'd had no idea he was so active in the music industry. There was photo after photo of him at various music events, often standing next to music artists, both legendary—Garth Brooks, Alan Jackson, Reba McEntyre, Trisha Yearwood—and singers who'd never made it past their one hit song—Clint Duncan, Sarah Murphy, Todd Drum. The latter crew hadn't retained their fame, but they'd been seen as rising stars when the photos were taken.

My mouth dropped when I found a photo of Daddy arm and arm with my former nemesis, Max Goodwin, shyster talent agent, and his partner in crime, entertainment attorney Neil Fulton. The two of them had been murdered weeks ago.

I sat back on the sofa, grappling with this new information and what it could mean. Were Max Goodwin and Neil Fulton's murders connected to this conspiracy my father had been mixed up in? Amy Danvers, former assistant to country superstar Luke Powell, had been blamed for their deaths. She'd killed herself, or so the police had decided, and left behind a note admitting to everything. Could that have been a setup?

I grabbed my phone and texted Colt.

I think there's a connection to the Goodwin and Fulton murders and my father. I'll tell you more tomorrow.

I needed to see the guest list to Luke Powell's release party. Max Goodwin had been murdered at the party, and since I had quickly become the police department's number one person of interest, Belinda had gotten the list from Amy to help us look for other suspects. Neil Fulton had been murdered at Luke's home days later.

The Amy solution had never seemed like much of a solution at all to me, but I'd bought it, mostly, because everyone else had accepted it.

I opened a new browser tab and searched for Brian Steele + Max Goodwin. A long list of results popped up.

Why the hell had my father been involved with that sleazeball?

I started digging through the results. Most were random results, generated because my father and Max had attended many of the same events, but there was a post on the second page about Brian Steele and Max Goodwin and a singer named Tripp Tucker. According to Tripp, his team had wronged him, and he'd filed a lawsuit against a slew of people two years before my father's disappearance. His gripe with Max wasn't surprising—the agent had left behind a long string of disgruntled clients and wannabe clients—but he'd also filed suit against my father, alleging he'd lost what little money Tripp had made in an investment gone wrong. Neil Fulton had represented Max and Daddy, along with Christopher Merritt, the accountant, and Walter Frey, the real estate attorney.

Bingo.

The article mentioned the Jackson Project, so I bookmarked the post and performed a new search. Another slew of posts popped up, and the top result's title was "Ambitious Real Estate Venture Goes Belly Up." A company by the name of Winterhaven had started the project and then brought in investors. My father's name wasn't mentioned, but Walter Frey's name caught my eye.

I knew Daddy had a working relationship with Walter Frey and Christopher Merritt, but how far back did it go, and how involved had it been?

I leaned over my laptop and opened the next result, titled, "Winterhaven to Profit off the Collapse of Real Estate Project." Before I got beyond the first lines, I heard the door open behind me. Bolting upright, I spun around to see Brady walking through the front door.

It always made me smile to see him. He looked like a Boy Scout all grown up—tall and broad-chested and wholesome-looking, with wavy brown hair. He smiled back at me. "You're a welcome sight to come home to."

Brady made me feel things I wasn't used to feeling. Safe. Protected. Appreciated. I kept waiting for the proverbial shoe to drop because everyone had an agenda.

Everyone wanted something. But I had to wonder if I'd just become too jaded.

"Hey," I said softly and closed my laptop lid as he walked over and sat down next to me. "How was your day?"

His eyes filled with tenderness. "I'm the one who should be asking you. It was your first day back to work. I hope you didn't overdo it."

"I got a little tired, but nothing I couldn't handle. It helped that I only worked at the boutique today."

"I heard you put on a sidewalk concert with Colt."

I studied his face for signs of disapproval. Brady had made no secret of his dislike of my friend, but he looked pleased.

"How did you hear that?" I asked.

"I told you, I have eyes and ears everywhere." He grinned. "But in this case, it was Owen."

I struggled to hide my surprise. "Owen?"

"Yeah, he said he was downtown and stopped to listen. He also said you had quite a crowd."

Unless Brady was a hell of a good actor, he had no knowledge of my performance with Colt in my apartment a couple of hours ago. Maybe he just hadn't gotten around to viewing it yet, but I couldn't let my head go there. I needed to believe Brady was one of the good guys.

I turned on the sofa to face him, pulling the afghan higher on my lap. "It was Alvin's doing, and I suspect it was his attempt to gather more customers. It worked because we were packed all afternoon." I hesitated, then asked, "What else did Owen say?"

"That you sounded great. Maybe even better than when he heard you at the Kincaid." He took my hand and held it between his own. "You've acquired a new fan."

I couldn't hold back the wry grin that lifted the corners of my mouth. I wasn't surprised that was how Owen was selling it. "He stayed long enough to talk to me afterward."

His eyes widened. "He didn't mention that."

"He wanted to let me know that my apartment has been cleared," I said, testing him out. Sure, he'd welcomed me into his home a few days ago, and he'd held me at night when I couldn't sleep, but we'd only shared one kiss—the night we met, four weeks ago now. Brady was a red-blooded man, and he was bound to be frustrated. It occurred to me that maybe he wanted me to go but was too nice to actually kick me out.

His smile faded. "You can't go back yet. The door's been busted in, and the floor . . ." His gaze held mine. "Your landlord has quite a few things to address before you can move back in."

Relief washed through me, but I found myself saying, "Ava says she's replacing the door tomorrow."

"And the floor? She can't get that fixed in a day. I suspect that stain won't come out. It will either need to be refinished or replaced."

"I can throw a rug over it in the meantime."

"Why?" he asked. "You can stay with me, Maggie. This is working out, don't you think?"

"But why would you want me to stay?" I asked in genuine surprise. "I'm more like a roommate than anything else, and I'm not even paying rent."

"I like knowing that you're here—safe."

"But Geraldo Lopez is dead, so the threat has been eliminated," I said, even though I knew that wasn't true. As far as the police were concerned, the case was closed.

"I still like having you here."

I smiled and answered truthfully, "I like being here." And I did, but the time I'd spent with him hadn't been realistic. He'd taken two days' personal leave to stay with me, and we'd done nothing but watch movies and play board games. That wasn't real life. Besides, staying with him didn't necessarily make me safe.

"So stay," he said.

I stared into his warm brown eyes and wondered why I was holding back. Was I getting in my own way again?

He lifted his hand to cup my cheek, and I closed my eyes as his lips brushed mine. When I didn't pull away, he grew bolder. His tongue swept across my bottom lip, and I wrapped my hands around the back of his neck, opening myself to him. I let myself forget about the bad things in my life and focused on the good that was right here in front of me.

Brady lifted his head and grinned. "I've been wanting to do that since I saw you again last week."

"Standing over Walter Frey's dead body?" I asked. My mind was scrambling to catch up with what I'd just done. Kissing Brady complicated everything.

He cringed slightly. "Okay, not at that exact moment, but soon after. When I saw you singing with Colt."

It surprised me that he'd so casually mentioned Colt. He'd acted jealous before, and no wonder—Colt had helped me cover up a slip about the text messages I'd been getting from my stalker by pretending to be my mystery texter. He'd sent a message falsely insinuating that we were sleeping together; Brady had seen it, believed it.

"Did you get home early?" I glanced at my phone to check the time and was surprised to see it was close to six. "I was going to make dinner."

"You must have lost track of time. You looked involved in whatever you were working on."

I smiled but offered no explanation.

After several seconds of silence, he said, "I have a present for you."

"Really?" I couldn't help getting excited.

He pulled a small jewelry box out of his pocket. "Now, I know how this looks, but I promise it's not a big deal. I just saw it and thought of you."

He handed it to me and I lifted the lid, nervous over what I'd find, but I was pleased to see a metal magnolia blossom pendant attached to a simple chain. "Oh, Brady. It's beautiful."

"You really like it?"

"I love it." I pulled it out of the box and undid the clasp.

In a silent choreography that made me smile, Brady took the necklace from me, I held up my hair, and he fastened the chain around my neck. He turned me around to face him, fingering the pendant and then lifting his gaze to mine.

We stared into each other's eyes for several seconds. Was this what a normal relationship was like? Was this what marriage and love felt like?

I was still smiling, and Brady grinned back at me. "How about we go out to dinner? If you're not too exhausted from today."

"I worked a five-hour shift. That seems far from taxing."

"You were beaten pretty badly, Maggie. You're still healing."

"I'm fine," I said, pushing off the afghan. "But I'd like to freshen up before we go."

"Okay." He stood and offered me his hand, then pulled me up. "Any preference where we eat?"

"You're more familiar with what's good than I am. You decide while I get ready."

I headed down the hall to Brady's room and checked my reflection in his bathroom mirror. I didn't look too bad, just tired, so I added more under-eye concealer and freshened my lipstick. When I stepped back into the hallway, the sound of Brady's voice stopped me in my tracks.

"This isn't a coincidence, Owen. What are the chances of this happening again?" He paused for several seconds, then said, "You face your demons, and I'll face my own."

I crept closer and saw Brady sitting at his kitchen table in front of his open laptop. He glanced up and his eyes locked with mine. His back stiffened. "We'll talk about this more later," he said, hanging up without giving Owen a chance to respond.

What had they been talking about?

"You ready?" he asked as he stood. He smiled, but he wasn't himself.

"Yeah. I would have changed, but I've worn everything else Belinda lent me, and I just grabbed some work clothes from my place for when I clean Ava's house tomorrow."

He looked startled. "You stopped by your place?"

"Yeah, after work. I needed to talk to Ava about when I could move back in. I told you I talked to her."

"I thought maybe you called." He looked like he was forcing himself to relax. "I wanted to be with you when you went for the first time. I know it had to be hard."

I shrugged as I walked over to my purse. "It was hard when Ava and I took a look at all the damage, but it wasn't so bad when I went back to get my clothes." I almost told him that Colt had been with me, but decided to leave well enough alone.

I was silent as we walked to his car, wondering what demons Owen was facing. His uncle's possible corruption? Or was it something more recent? Maybe me? Owen had made it clear to me that he wanted me to move out of Brady's apartment. If he'd set up those cameras, he either hadn't seen the footage yet, or he'd decided to deal with it in another way. I didn't look forward to finding out which.

Forty-five minutes later, we were sitting at a high-top table in the bar of a hip new restaurant in the Belle Meade area. Since there was a thirty-minute wait for a table, we'd decided to have a drink in the bar. I was telling Brady several stories about my new boss, Alvin, when I heard a familiar voice behind me.

"Magnolia Steele, fancy meeting you twice in a few weeks."

I knew who it was before I even turned around. My father's former partner, and my brother's current boss.

"Mr. James," I said. "What a coincidence." I glanced around. "Going solo tonight?"

"I'm here at a business dinner. And I've told you a million times to call me Bill." He looked momentarily stunned when he glanced at Brady. "Detective Bennett."

Brady gave a slight nod. "Mr. James. I'm surprised you remember me."

"It's not every day a Franklin police detective visits me in my Nashville office, or at all, I might add. I'm only sorry I couldn't be more helpful." After Walter Frey's murder, I'd told Brady about my suspicions regarding my father's disappearance. He'd questioned several of the people who'd known my father best—Bill James included.

Brady smiled, but it looked more polite than friendly. "You were more helpful than you know."

Bill turned his attention to me, and his gaze fell to my chest before lifting slightly. "What a beautiful necklace."

I absently lifted my hand to finger it. "Thank you."

He hesitated and his expression turned sympathetic. "Magnolia, I was shocked to hear about your run-in with Geraldo Lopez. I had always suspected there was something . . . off about him. I'm only sorry you got dragged into the middle of it."

"Thank you."

"After everything that got tossed around by the press about Lopez and his involvement with your father, well, I'm sure you have a lot of questions . . ." He paused and shifted his weight. "What the press is insinuating . . . I want you to know that wasn't the man I knew, and I'm sure that wasn't the man you remember." A warm smile lit up his eyes. "Would you be open to meeting for lunch or dinner sometime and swapping stories about your father? I know how close you were to him, and while he committed some terrible acts, maybe we could both remember the good things, not the bad."

Brady said he hadn't gotten anything out of Bill James, but most people were guarded with cops. "Thank you," I said gratefully, even though the man creeped me out for some reason. Maybe because Momma had never seemed to like him. "I'd like that."

"Good. That's great." He reached into his coat and pulled out a business card. "My cell phone number's on there. Call me tomorrow and we'll make the arrangements."

"Thanks," I said as I took the card and glanced at it. His cell number was handwritten in blue ink on the back. "I'm looking forward to it."

Mr. James smiled and nodded before he headed back toward the dining area. Brady turned in his seat to watch him.

"I don't think you should meet with him."

His stern tone caught me by surprise. "Why not?"

"I don't trust him."

"But you said you didn't get anything out of him when you went to see him about my father."

"This has nothing to do with your father's disappearance."

That gave me pause. "Then what does it have to do with?"

He turned to face me, looking serious. "Maggie, in the short time I've known you, I've hardly made any requests of you, but I'm asking this—please don't meet with him."

"But—"

"No questions. Please. Just know that I don't trust him."

I really wanted to meet with my father's partner. I found it hard to believe my father could have embezzled from clients and found himself in the thick of bad land investments without his eagle-eyed partner noticing a thing. Whatever Bill James wanted from me, I wanted answers from him, and if I played the part of a dippy actress, he might just give them to me. Still, Brady was worried, and I couldn't ignore that. I wasn't going to do anything stupid, especially since Owen was watching me so closely. I'd figure out another way. "Okay."

He pushed out a breath and his entire body relaxed. "Thank you."

"Why does he make you so anxious?"

"Let's just say I have a few suspicions about him and leave it at that."

"Do you think he's dangerous?"

He watched me. "Please don't meet with him," he repeated.

"I said okay." Did that mean he was dangerous or not? Was he being evasive because this was related to police business?

Brady drained his wine glass, then flagged down the bartender. "I don't feel like eating here anymore. Would you mind going somewhere else?"

"Sure. Of course." Brady's intent had been to steer me away from Bill, but he'd only piqued my curiosity.

chapter five

We found another restaurant in Belle Meade, but Brady was quiet and tense. After we ordered our food, I reached across the table and grabbed his hand, startling him out of his thoughts.

"Contrary to your perception of me," I said quietly, "I'm not fragile, either emotionally or physically, and I can be a good listener. Why don't you tell me what's bothering you? I can handle it." Was Bill James connected to the issue Brady had been discussing with Owen? I wasn't sure I believed that Brady's suspicions of the man had nothing to do with my father.

He turned his hand over and clasped mine. "I never said you were fragile."

"No, but the way you've treated me . . . you've been so nice . . ."

"That's because I like you. I've made no secret of that. If you decide you just want to be friends, I'll accept that, but we both know there's a connection between us, and I won't lie and say I won't be disappointed if you decide to ignore it. But our kiss . . ." His troubled gaze held mine. "I don't want you to feel like you're obligated in any way."

"I don't."

"I wanted you to stay with me because I was worried about you. It wasn't some sneaky attempt to get you to sleep with me."

I gave him a soft smile. "I know. I kissed you back because it felt right. No other reason."

Relief washed over his face.

"Is that what's bothering you?" It didn't seem likely. His agitation had started with his phone call—and increased after we saw Bill James.

"Partially." He grabbed his water glass and took a big drink before setting it down. "No more work talk. Tell me a story about your work in the theatre world."

I was dying to know more, but knew he'd never tell me—at least not if I came at it straight on—so I launched into a story about an off-Broadway play I'd been in. The director, a man with early-onset dementia, had kept changing the blocking.

"On opening night, he changed it again, except the only person he told was the lead actress. There was a scene where she was supposed to do a trust fall, only the actor wasn't in the right place to catch her, so she fell right off the stage into the audience."

"Oh, no. Was she okay?"

"The audience wasn't your typical audience—the play was *way* off Broadway—and they thought it was part of the show. They caught her with their hands, and she crowd surfed for a good half-minute."

He grinned. "You're kidding."

I shook my head and laughed. "Nope. Word got out and the next night we had a crowd waiting for the crowd-surfing scene, but the director had changed it again. Regrettably—or not—the play only lasted a week."

"And how many plays have you done?"

"Good question . . . maybe forty? Forty-five? Some died in rehearsal and never made it to the stage. Mostly ensemble parts in the beginning. I worked my way up."

"How many Broadway plays?"

"Four. Once I hit Broadway three years ago, I quit my waitressing job."

"Did you always know you wanted to be an actress?" he asked.

Talking about my past was dangerous—it would inevitably lead to questions, and Colt was right. Since Brady was a cop, he'd notice any inconsistencies in my story. But I found myself trusting Brady more and more. Would it be so bad to tell him more? "No. I thought I wanted to marry my high school sweetheart, Tanner McKee, and become a teacher here in Franklin."

"When did you change your mind?"

Dangerous ground, Magnolia. "I decided life was too short and I needed an adventure before I settled down," I lied, then decided to tell him a small truth to corroborate my story. "So I took off for New York City the day after my high school graduation."

"How did your mother take it?"

"Not well. She barely spoke to me for years afterward, and my brother never forgave me."

"Sounds like it must have been awkward when you came home for visits."

I could lie, but I decided against it. It was easier to get tripped up by lies than the truth, and I could make this one work. "I never came home until the day of Luke Powell's party."

He did a double take. "You're kidding. Not once in ten years?"

"It was hard to get away. Most waitressing gigs don't have paid vacations."

"Still, ten years . . ."

"That must be hard for you to believe because you're so close to your family," I said. "My family fell apart when my daddy disappeared."

He frowned. "I'm sorry."

I shrugged. "It is what it is."

We spent the rest of dinner sharing stories. While I stuck to New York tales, he told me about growing up with his brother and sister. By the time the waiter brought our bill, I almost felt like a somewhat functional person. Brady Bennett really did seem like a steady kind of guy. The kind you'd be lucky to build a life with.

And damned if I didn't like imagining myself in that pretty picture.

"It's early," Brady said as we walked to his car. "Do want to see if we can catch a movie?"

I stopped and looked up at him, unsure about the decision I was considering. Was it so wrong to be impulsive just this once? "Can we go back to your place?"

"Are you tired?" he asked, worry filling his eyes. "Is everything okay?"

I gave him a soft smile. "For the first time in a very long time, everything is perfect." My life was in shambles, but tonight there was no place I'd rather be than with Brady. He almost made me believe there was a better, more normal life waiting for me outside of the craziness that had engulfed mine—and if I just stuck close to him, I might get there someday.

I placed my hands on his chest and reached up to kiss him. He kissed me back, then lifted his head and grinned. "Magnolia Steele, you are a woman full of surprises."

"I have plenty more," I said playfully, but anxiety prickled at me. How would Brady react when he found out all the secrets I'd been keeping? Based on what I knew of him, he'd not only be understanding, he'd want to help me.

We were quiet most of the way back to his apartment, and my mind drifted back to the cameras planted in my apartment. If Owen *was* the cameraman, what would he do if I started something with Brady? Would it hurt their friendship? I tried to feel some guilt over that, but if Owen had really stooped that low, maybe Brady deserved a better friend.

Brady snagged my hand as we walked through the parking garage to the elevator, and he was quiet until we were in his apartment. Once he locked the door, he turned to me, looking uncertain. "Do you want to watch a movie or something?"

"No." I closed the distance between us and kissed him. A spark ignited deep in my gut as I slid my arms around his back and pressed myself against him, needing him closer.

His mouth tore from mine and he searched my eyes. "Are you sure, Maggie?"

No. This was the stupidest thing I'd done in a long time, but I wanted this. *Needed* this. I needed to know that I could have a life with someone good. That my existence didn't have to be defined by fear. "Yes."

He kissed me again, threading his hand into my hair and tilting back my head as his tongue coaxed mine.

I matched his urgency, blindly searching for the buttons of his dress shirt. I had several undone when Brady lifted his head and searched my face. "I want you, Magnolia, but only if this is what you want. If you have any hesitations, tell me. We've been taking this slow. We can go back to slow."

I shook my head. "I don't want to take it slow. I want you."

He kissed me again, pushing me backward down the hall to his room.

Colt suddenly came to mind, uninvited. How could I be doing this now, after the way I'd reacted to him this afternoon? But I assured myself that I'd been playing a role in our trick to fool the cameraman. I wanted to be with Brady, not Colt, and this was the best way to purge the scene from my apartment from my head.

Brady stopped next to his bed and reached around my back to pull down my zipper. The cool air hit the bare skin of my back, making me shiver.

Brady pushed my dress over my shoulders and down my arms, and it dropped to the floor at my feet.

I reached for his shirt, made quick work of the rest of his buttons, and then pulled his shirt free so I had full access to his chest. After resting my hands a moment on his pecs, I let them wander down his hard abs to the waistband of his pants. It took a few movements, but I soon had his pants and underwear pushed down below his hips.

Brady kicked off his shoes, stepped out of his pants. He unhooked my bra, then pulled me down to the bed and kissed me. His mouth lowered to my chest as his hand slipped into my panties. My back arched and I gasped as his tongue teased my nipple while his hand slid between my folds. Soon I was writhing beneath him.

"I want you now," I moaned.

"But—"

"*Now.*"

He leaned over to his nightstand and opened the drawer to get a condom as I tugged off my panties. He rolled on the condom before turning back and covered my body with his.

I wrapped a leg around his back and lifted my hips as he entered me. He kissed me again as he thrust, and I grabbed his butt to pull him closer, needing him deeper as I climbed higher and higher. This man was what I needed—to feel safe and cherished—two feelings I'd never felt with any other man.

I gasped out his name as I came, clinging to him as he pushed deeper several more times before he gave one last thrust. He collapsed next to me, holding me close as we caught our breath.

"That was . . . fast," he said.

I rolled to my side to face him. To my surprise, tears were burning my eyes. "I'm sorry," I said.

He looked alarmed. "Do you regret this?"

"No. It's just . . ." I chuckled as I wiped a tear from my eye. "You must be having major regrets, thinking I'm one of those women who cries after sex, but I promise you that I'm not."

He grinned. "I just bring out the tears?"

"I don't know how to explain it. I'm just so overwhelmed . . ."

"Good overwhelmed or bad?"

"Good," I said, looking into his eyes. "You make me feel things I never expected to feel. Thank you."

"Oh, Maggie." He leaned over and cupped my cheek, kissing me with more passion than I would have expected after sex.

I wrapped my hands around his neck and held him close as I kissed him back.

He lifted his head and smiled. The happiness radiating from him was infectious, and I smiled back. This felt good; this felt *normal*.

Brady settled next to me again and rested his fingertips on my stomach, making lazy figure eights. "Are you working for your mother tomorrow?"

"Yeah. I'm cleaning Miss Ava's house, then working for Momma and Tilly starting at four. I won't be done until late because the event is up in Nashville."

"But you'll come here when you're done?" he asked as his hand moved over my hip, wandering to my thigh.

I was about to answer him when his hand abruptly stopped, and I realized he'd just traced my scar.

His body stiffened slightly as he propped himself onto his elbow to study it.

I'd been so stupid. Of course Brady would notice my scar. Most of my previous boyfriends had commented on it, but they'd all accepted my excuse—that it was the relic of a freak childhood accident involving my cousin and a cookie cutter. Of course, most of my exes were self-centered assholes, purposefully selected because they wouldn't pry, wouldn't go too deep. I suspected Brady would want to know all the details. He'd question anything that sounded unbelievable.

"Don't look at it." I covered the mark with my hand. It was ugly and it wasn't small. The two-inch long backward C had been carved high up on my thigh, and the slash through it had been deep enough that any doctor would have insisted on stitches. But when I woke up in the woods behind my house the night of my graduation—after *it* happened—I'd been too confused and disoriented to realize I'd been cut so badly. The next morning, my focus had been on fleeing Franklin.

"What happened?" His voice was tight and his body had tensed even more.

"Just a stupid childhood injury."

Brady sat up and leaned over to get a better look, trying to gently move my hand to the side, but I fought him.

His gaze lifted to mine. "I just want to see it."

"It's ugly. I hate it."

A soft smile washed over his face. "It's part of you and you're beautiful. Just let me look at it. Please?"

I sat up and moved my back up against his pillows and headboard. Feeling self-conscious and vulnerable, I reached down and pulled the sheet up to cover myself, clutching it to my breasts. "Why?"

"So I know more about you." He lifted his leg and pointed to a white pockmark on his left calf. "My brother accidently shot me with a nail gun when I was twelve."

"Oh, my God. How old was *he*?"

"Ten. It was an accident, but I've never let him live it down. How'd you get yours?"

"I told you. A childhood accident."

"I know, but *how*?"

"A cookie cutter."

"Now I really want to see it." He shifted to get a better vantage point and then shifted the sheet to expose my right thigh. Looking up at me to gauge my reaction, he asked, "Okay?"

He'd think it odd if I continued to fight him on it. I nodded slightly.

His finger lightly traced the mark. "No stitches?"

"What?" I asked in surprise.

"It looks like it was deep, but I don't see any stitch marks, and the straight line is a little wider, suggesting it didn't close properly."

I grabbed the sheet and pulled it back over my leg. "I thought you were a police officer, not a doctor."

I expected him to start a tug-of-war over the sheet, but he turned and sat up, cross-legged. "I have enough experience in forensics to know a thing or two," he said, his eyes meeting mine.

"I'm not a dead body, Brady," I snapped, but it didn't seem to faze him.

"No," he said in a husky voice. "You are far from it. Just making observations. I'm sorry if you were uncomfortable."

I didn't answer.

"Why didn't you get stitches?"

"You've met my mother."

"Yeah, and while she came across as harsh, I can't imagine her letting something like that go unattended. How old were you when it happened?"

I couldn't let him think my mother had been neglectful. If I'd gotten a cut as deep as this one as a child, my mother would have had me in an ER before I so much as got a drop of blood on the floor. "I was a teenager. I don't think she realized how bad it was."

His eyes turned serious. "That's an odd scar for a cookie cutter, Maggie. How did you really get it?"

"I'm not examining the scar on your leg to make sure it matches the diameter of a nail," I said in an ugly tone. "Am I a suspect?"

"What?" he asked in disbelief. "No."

"Then why all the questions?"

"Is it really so hard for you to believe that someone could just care about you? No agenda?"

"Yes." I hadn't meant to say it, but it was true.

He inched closer and sadness washed over his face. "Who hurt you so badly that you don't believe you can be loved?"

I jolted off the bed, tugging the sheet with me. "And now you're a psychologist. Just a jack-of-all-trades, huh?"

Brady watched me with his eagle eyes. "No, but I know when someone's been hurt, and your wounds go deep, Magnolia Steele."

"This is just a fling, Brady. So let's just keep to the superficial stuff, okay?"

I'd said it to hurt him, and the look in his eyes told me I'd succeeded. A momentary wave of guilt washed over me, but he was too smart for my own good, and he cared too much.

"This isn't a fling," he said softly. "But if that's how you need to define it to give us a chance, I can live with that." He climbed off the bed and stood in front of me. "No more talk about your scar. You can tell me what happened when you're ready. Okay?"

I nodded. Stupidly, I didn't want to give him up yet. "Okay."

"I'm going to take a shower. Want to join me?" When I hesitated, he added, "I won't look at your scar."

"Okay."

I knew he'd be unable to stop himself, and I was right. It was like telling someone not to look at a train wreck— you just couldn't help yourself. But I didn't call him on it. He'd already studied it enough to ask questions I couldn't answer. What did it matter now? Besides, he became far more concerned with the dark bruises and welts covering my back and the backs of my arms.

"I should have made you go to the hospital," he said, sounding guilty.

I looked up at him, narrowing my eyes. "Let's get one thing straight. You will never be able to make me do anything. You might ask and I might agree, but you can't *make* me."

His eyes clouded. "I'm sorry. It was a bad choice of words, but I feel like I didn't stress how important it was."

"You made your stance on going to the hospital very clear, and I made mine clear as well. I'm feeling better, and the bruises hurt a lot less."

The tension between us thickened, and I could tell that Brady was worried he'd say the wrong thing again. I brushed my teeth, put on a pair of pajamas Belinda had sent me, and then climbed back into bed, lying on my side.

Brady climbed in next to me. "I'm sorry," he whispered in my ear.

It was hard staying angry with him when he was trying to be so considerate. I rolled over to face him. "I'm sorry too."

He leaned down and brushed his lips lightly against mine. "You can stay here as long as you'd like, but I hope it's for a very long time."

I didn't answer, still unsure of what I was going to do. I had much bigger issues to deal with than my love life.

chapter six

I was startled awake by a ringing cell phone.

"Bennett," Brady's voice barked in the darkness. He listened for several long seconds before saying, "I'll be right there." He sat up and pushed back the covers.

"Is everything okay?" I asked, still groggy from sleep.

"I got called in to handle a case." He hesitated and then leaned over me. "I know you're supposed to work for Ava Milton today, but ask her if you can put it off."

I sat up, feeling anxious as I faced him in the darkness. "Why?"

"This case I'm headed to . . . I'd just feel better if you were locked up in my apartment."

"Is there something I should know?"

He paused. "No."

"Like I told you, Brady, I'm not weak. I can handle whatever you tell me."

"I know, but after everything you've been through . . . just hang out here today."

"What's going on? First you asked me to stay away from Bill James. Now you want me to spend the day in your apartment. You owe me some kind of explanation."

"Just trust me."

"That might have worked with all your previous girlfriends, but it won't fly with me. While your concern is sweet, I'm a big girl and can handle myself." I gave him a slight shove. "Now go do your job. We'll talk about this later."

He looked torn. "Will you check in with me when you leave? And a couple of times throughout the day?"

"Brady, what happened? What kind of case are you headed to?"

"I can't tell you, but if you won't stay here all day, please promise me you'll be careful."

"I promise. Now go."

Brady got out of bed and headed into his bathroom. I reached for my phone on the nightstand, only to realize I'd left it in my purse.

Moving in here, staying with him, it had made me stupid. So had my desire to pretend that my world was anything less than a nightmare. I needed to move out, but if Brady's case had him spooked, it had me even more spooked.

I was in the living room, looking for my purse, when Brady emerged from the bedroom wearing a frown.

"I'm sorry I woke you. It's four, so you still have a chance to get a few hours' sleep."

"I'll go back to bed, but I realized I never charged my phone." I offered him a smile as I dug it out of my purse. "It needs to be charged if you want me to check in with you. And don't apologize for going to do your job. It's important."

"Full disclosure," he said, stepping in front of me, "this happens more often than you might like."

"I can live with it. Now go."

He gave me a kiss and headed for the door. "Lock the deadbolt after I leave and call me on my cell if you come across anything suspicious today. Anything at all."

I closed the door behind him and locked the doorknob and the deadbolt before lifting my phone with a shaky hand. There was a text waiting for me on the home screen. My legs gave out and I collapsed onto the floor when I read the message from a blocked number—a text that had been sent about an hour before by my stalker.

You've been a very bad girl, Magnolia.

What did that mean? It took several tries to send a response.

I haven't told anyone.

I was surprised when he answered back within seconds.

Not even your boyfriend?

I sucked in a breath as tears flooded my eyes. I considered protesting that Brady wasn't my boyfriend, but that was a minor issue.

I haven't told ANYONE.

I didn't wait long for a response.

Keep it that way. I left you a present to help you remember.

Terrified, I started to cry as I called my mother.

"Magnolia?" she asked, sounding like I'd woken her from a deep sleep. "Is everything okay?"

I took a breath to pull myself together. How did I explain this call? I suspected there was no way to hide my tear-filled voice, so I decided to go with a semi-truthful explanation. "I had a nightmare that something happened to you," I said, surprised when a sob followed. She might be okay now, but very soon she would be gone, one way or the other. "I just got you back, Momma. I don't want to lose you."

"Oh, Magnolia," she said softly. "I'll always be with you."

I leaned over my legs as a new sob stole my breath. "It's not the same."

"I know, but it's the best we have."

I tried to get control of my emotions. My mother was the one who was dying, and I was crying like a baby.

"Why don't we go out to lunch this afternoon?" she asked.

My surprise at her request ebbed my tears. "Really?"

"Does it seem that crazy of an idea?"

"No. It's just that we haven't done anything just the two of us since I came back."

"That's my fault," she said. "But I want to fix things. Before it's too late."

"I want to fix things too."

"So lunch today," she said, sounding hopeful. "How about we go to Puckett's? We can meet and then walk to the catering kitchen together."

"Yeah. I'd like that," I said. I knew Ava had plans for me, but I'd tell her I was leaving at lunchtime. If she didn't like it, I'd quit and move out of the apartment. I wasn't sure where I'd go, but I'd figure out something. "I'm sorry I called and woke you."

"I'm glad you did. It's nice to know you still need me."

She hung up and it was a stark reminder that I'd still need her even after she was gone.

Momma might be safe, but I still needed to check on Belinda. It was way too early to call her, so I sent a text.

I know it's the middle of the night, but I felt a powerful need to check on you. Text me when you can.

After I sent the message, I worried that my brother would see it and punish Belinda. I should have waited to text her, but the week before, my stalker had sent me a photo of her—paired with a threat. What if he'd hurt Belinda to punish me?

Then someone else came to mind—someone the stalker might target. If he knew I was staying with Brady, he probably knew about Colt. I liked to think that Colt could take care of himself, but what if he was caught off guard?

When you get this, please let me know you got it. I'll explain later.

I had no idea what excuse I'd give him for texting, but I was too worried to care. I'd think of something later.

I made a cup of tea since I was way too keyed up to go back to sleep. What had my stalker meant by his threat? The last time he'd decided to send me a reminder, I'd found a dead cat on my doorstep, carved with the same mark he'd left on my leg. Would he escalate this time? I was worried about Belinda, but as much as I detested my brother, I had to believe he wouldn't let anything happen to his wife in the middle of the night.

Lack of sleep didn't keep me from circling around the problem again and again, questioning everything I thought I knew. Was it too dangerous for me to continue seeing Brady, or should I take a chance and tell him about my stalker? About what I'd seen all those years ago? But could he protect the people I cared about?

Taking my tea to the sofa, I grabbed my laptop and pulled the afghan over me like I had the day before. Brady had interrupted me last time, but now I had hours before I needed to meet Belinda for breakfast.

I decided to do a search for the failed land development project. Jackson Project was an outdoor shopping mall and condominium complex that had been intended for a location in northeast downtown Nashville. The project had faced opposition from the start because it planned to clear out everything and build fresh, destroying several historical homes in the process. Winterhaven, the corporation in charge, had gotten approval to bulldoze the homes, but it soon emerged they'd only obtained permission through bribery. The project halted before anything had been built, and all the investors' money had been used for legal expenses.

Next I did a search for Winterhaven and discovered that Max Goodwin had been a board member, and Walter Frey had been the CFO, but I saw no mention of my father's name.

Wasn't it enough that he'd been involved in selling shares?

I'd started to look up more about Winterhaven when my phone dinged with a text from Belinda.

I'm fine. Still on for breakfast?

I closed my eyes, dizzy with relief. She was okay. I composed myself and texted back.

Yes. See you then.

I glanced at the time on my phone—5:30. I still had an hour before I needed to get ready to leave. And I wouldn't expect to hear from Colt for another couple of hours.

I stood up and stretched the cramping muscles in my back. I'd just spent an hour looking up a corporation with a failed land investment nearly twenty years ago. Was I wasting my time? But I couldn't ignore the fact that my father had ties to a lot of dead men—too many for it to be a coincidence.

I continued searching, discovering that Winterhaven had dissolved after the land project, and even though the company had shown a profit, they'd paid off their board of directors, filed for bankruptcy, and closed. Multiple lawsuits had been filed and settled out of court.

I shifted my focus to Neil Fulton. He'd been in his early sixties at the time of his murder, with a long history of representing recording studios. At the end of his career, he'd helped Max Goodwin win multiple lawsuits filed by disgruntled clients. I suspected whatever trouble Daddy had been mixed up in dated back to the Jackson Project.

How was I going to dig into *that*?

chapter seven

Belinda was already sitting at a table when I arrived at the restaurant, and she greeted me with a weary smile. She looked like she hadn't gotten much sleep the night before, but then again, neither had I. Despite her obvious fatigue, she still looked better put together than most women I knew. She wore a pale aqua dress, and her hair was held back from her face with pearl-encrusted pins.

She rose when she saw me and pulled me into a hug.

The waitress stopped at our table, took our drink and breakfast orders, and then headed back to the kitchen.

"Have you seen your momma in the last few days?" she asked.

"No," I said, surprised it was the first thing she brought up. "I've talked to her a few times, but haven't seen her since I went to Brady's."

Belinda frowned. "She's not looking that great, Magnolia. I'm really worried about her."

I was sure the stress of my recent attack hadn't helped with her health issues. "Has she been to the doctor?"

"No, Tilly says she refuses to go."

Did she think the end was coming sooner rather than later? Was that why she wanted to meet for lunch? A knot formed in the pit of my stomach.

Guilt flashed in Belinda's eyes. Then she leaned forward and asked in a quiet voice, "How are you doing? I know it has to hurt that there are rumors floating around about your father again."

I wasn't surprised she'd asked. Only a week ago, she'd heard me tell Colt I was sure my father hadn't run off with Shannon Morrissey and her husband's money, like everyone had believed—that he had been murdered instead. "I'm not content to leave things where they are," I said. "I'm still digging."

She looked startled. "Digging into *what?*"

"I found out that Daddy had a connection to Max Goodwin *and* Neil Fulton."

"Your father was a financial planner who dealt with very wealthy clients. It's not surprising he knew them."

Her comment gave me pause. Belinda and Amy had been friends, so I'd expected her to react differently to this piece of news. I'd thought she would be eager for the chance to clear her friend's name. "Don't you think it's the slightest bit weird? Maybe this means Amy didn't kill them."

Belinda fingered the handle of her fork. "Of course she killed them. She wrote a note."

"But don't you think there could be a link between—"

Her gaze jerked up, and I was surprised by the cold look in her eyes. "Amy killed them."

We stared at each other for a couple of seconds before her expression softened and tears filled her eyes. "Trust me, it's hard for me to believe she did it, but there's no point in chasing windmills, Magnolia. Besides, delving into your father's disappearance nearly got you killed. You need to trust the police on this."

"I'm sorry."

She offered me a wavering smile. "No, *I'm* sorry. I understand your need to find answers, but you have to accept that Amy killed them."

This did not bode well for my plan to ask her for a copy of the guest list to Luke Powell's party, not to mention asking her again about the man hiding in the shadows who looked like my brother.

"But there's more," I said. "I also found out that he had a bunch of clients who invested in a failed land development project in north Nashville. There were lawsuits filed against him."

"That's why he had liability insurance," she said, her gaze holding mine, as though she was trying to hypnotize me into letting this go.

"How do you know so much about it?" I asked.

"Roy. He's practically taken over your father's job."

Yes, he had, which meant . . .

"Is Roy into something crooked too?"

The color washed out of her face. "Magnolia, you need to leave this alone."

I'd asked as an offhanded comment. I'd never expected her to confirm it. But it made so much sense—

Roy's attempts to drive me out of town, including the fifty-thousand-dollar bribe he'd offered me, and his violent rampage at my apartment after Brady had gone to his office asking questions about the past.

"Do you know how hard I've had to work to be taken seriously at my firm?" he'd asked. "I had to practically beg Bill to hire me, and I've had to work my ass off to get him to trust me. Three years, Magnolia, three fucking years I've kissed that man's ass."

In response to my suggestion that he find another job, he'd said, "I don't want to work anywhere else. I want to work at JS Investments, and you are ruining everything, Magnolia. Just like you've *always* ruined everything."

Somehow Roy had convinced Bill James to let him step into Daddy's shoes. But more horrifying than that was the fact that sweet Belinda seemed to know all about it—worse, she was protecting him.

Belinda clasped my hand, her fingers digging in. "Promise me you'll leave this alone."

Only a few days ago, I'd gotten angry with her for staying with my brother despite his obvious abuse. Holy crap. How had I not seen it? Roy wouldn't let her go because she could destroy him. "If you know that Roy is doing illegal things, you could go to prison too," I said. "But if he's questioned by police, they can't make you testify."

Her eyes filled with panic.

I squeezed her hand. "I can help you, Belinda. Brady's a police officer. We'll get you away from Roy and keep you safe."

"No!" she said, jerking her hand from mine. "I'm exactly where I want to be. I told you I have an exit plan. I asked you to trust me, and you told me you would. Has that changed?"

She'd said as much to me last week, after I'd confronted her about my brother's obvious abuse. I had to wonder about her exit strategy. Was she collecting evidence to use against Roy? "No," I said. "I still trust you." But that only meant I wouldn't hound her to leave Roy. I had no plans to stop investigating—if anything, it strengthened my resolution to keep going.

Relief washed over her and she reached over and squeezed my hand. "Thank you."

"But if you change your mind—"

"*I won't.*"

I had to force myself to smile. Belinda was one of the few friends I had here in Franklin, and in the short time I'd known her, I'd become very attached. I couldn't stand the thought of losing her.

"What a lovely necklace," she said. "Is it new? I don't remember seeing you wear it."

"Brady gave it to me last night."

She was surprisingly quiet.

"Do you have a wedding this weekend?" I asked.

"On Friday," she said, looking grateful for the change in subject. "But I'm going to a masquerade ball on Saturday."

"In Nashville?"

"No. Here in Franklin. It's a fundraiser for Middle Tennessee Children's Charity. They raise money to help lower income children. The guest list is impressive."

"Oh," I said, recognizing the name of the charity. "The Belles are catering that event. I didn't realize it was a masquerade ball. In April? Aren't those usually in October?"

"They have masquerade balls in New Orleans during Mardi Gras," she said, picking up her cup of coffee. "So why not?"

When we walked outside the restaurant, Belinda pulled me into a tight hug. "Why don't you take some time off? Maybe go visit a friend for a long weekend? What about your friend traveling with *Wicked*? Isn't she in Minneapolis right now?"

I pulled away to study her face. "Omaha, and what are you talking about? Why?"

"It's just that you've been through so much the month you've been home. Maybe you should get away and breathe a little before you come back and deal with your momma's imminent passing." She cringed. "I'm sorry. That was tactless."

I shook my head. "No. It's true. She's dying. Which is exactly why I can't go anywhere. I need to be here."

She hugged me again. "I love you, Magnolia," she whispered in my ear. "I just want you to be safe." Then she abruptly dropped her hold, spun on her feet, and hurried off in the direction of her wedding planning office.

I straightened my back as I watched her run away from me. She didn't have to handle my brother alone. She was my family now. I'd help her even if she didn't think she wanted help.

I'd parked my car behind the catering office, so I walked the few blocks to Ava's and then headed around the house. When I rapped on the back door, Ava opened it before I had to knock a second time.

"Magnolia Steele," she said in a brisk tone. "You're full of surprises."

"Because I'm not late?"

Her lips twitched with the hint of a smile, but her grim expression quickly slipped back into place. "At least you're dressed appropriately." Then her eyes narrowed. "Except for your necklace. Don't you find it crass to wear the very thing you were named after?"

"No," I said, reaching for it. "It was a gift and it's beautiful. And it's not like it's gaudy. It's barely a half-inch in diameter."

She studied me for a second before a pleased look filled her eyes. "Your choice."

Was that a test?

She grabbed a plastic tote of cleaning supplies and thrust it at me. "I expect you to have the living room and dining room dusted and the wood floors on the first floor cleaned within an hour and a half, and then I have another job for you."

I stared at her in surprise. "You don't want me to clean the powder room or the kitchen?"

"Did I stutter?"

"No, but—"

"You may get started now. I'll be upstairs if you need me," she said, walking toward the staircase. "But I see no reason why you should need me. Even a simpleton could clean a house without special instructions." Then I heard her footfalls on the stairs.

I couldn't help grinning. Somehow I'd gotten used to the cranky woman and actually found her antics amusing, although I suspected that might change after I told her I needed to leave by one forty-five to eat lunch with my mother.

The great thing about cleaning was it was a mindless job, giving me lots of time to come up with a plan for how to continue my investigation. I didn't want Belinda to know what I was up to, so it seemed safest to focus on the past. Maybe Momma would be willing to talk about Daddy now that Morrissey and Lopez were no longer threats.

I still hadn't heard from Colt, but I told myself not to worry yet. He was probably still sleeping.

I had dusted the living and dining rooms—which took longer than expected, given all the knickknacks—and started mopping the floor when I heard banging at the front door. I cast a glance upstairs, briefly wondering if I should tell Ava. I didn't know if she'd want me to answer it, but the increasingly persistent knocking made up my mind for me.

I opened the door, shocked to see Brady's stern face.

"Brady," I gasped.

He reached out and tugged me to his chest. "You just scared the shit out of me."

I pulled loose and looked up at him. "What are you talking about?"

"I've been calling and texting you for over an hour, and you never answered."

I pointed my thumb behind me toward the kitchen. "I left my phone in my purse. I didn't think Miss Ava would want me carrying my phone around."

"Magnolia's correct," Ava said from behind me, making me jump a little. "She's here to clean my house, not dawdle on the phone."

"This is police business," Brady said, his jaw tight.

"Oh, is it?" Ava asked in a haughty tone. "Are you here about Emily Johnson's murder?"

"*What?*" I breathed out as my vision blackened and my knees started to buckle.

Brady quickly caught me, holding me to his chest. "Maggie."

I tried to answer, but I was too shocked to respond. Emily and I had been nemeses in high school, but she'd become friends with my mother after I left town, filling the void in her life. As a favor to my mother, she'd served as my attorney while I was a person of interest in the Max Goodwin case. She'd suspected there was more to my story of why I'd abandoned Franklin after graduation, but she hadn't gotten any further than suspecting.

I remembered the text I'd received in the middle of the night.

I left you a present to help you remember.

My stalker had done this. He'd killed Emily. Because of me.

Brady was keeping me upright, and Ava was watching the whole scene with her eagle- sharp eyes. I needed to pull myself together.

I glanced up into Brady's worried eyes. "Is it true?"

He gave Ava a sharp frown before turning his attention back to me. "Yes. But I wanted to tell you myself. I know she was your attorney when you were questioned about Goodwin's murder."

My legs felt strong enough to bear my weight, so I pulled free, wrapping my arms around my chest in an attempt to hold myself together. "Her murder was the case you were called out for this morning."

"Yes."

I gave a sharp nod. Was that why he'd acted so strangely this morning? "What happened?"

"I'm sorry. I can't tell you any details." At least he sounded apologetic about it.

"*Where* did it happen?"

When he didn't respond, Ava piped up. "She was murdered in her apartment. Her neighbor saw her dog in the hallway, scratching at the door and trying to get back in. She knocked on the door to find out why the dog was loose at three in the morning, but the door swung open. Emily was dead in the kitchen. Blood everywhere."

A new wave of queasiness washed over me.

"Ms. Milton," Brady said in a stern tone.

"What?" she asked, looking pleased with herself. "You may not be able to tell her the official facts, but I'm at liberty to tell her what I know."

"It's hearsay," he said, narrowing his eyes.

"And yet it's true. I don't spread gossip, Detective Bennett. I only tell the facts."

Brady didn't contradict her, so I knew what she'd said was the truth.

I felt lightheaded again, but I tried not to look as horrified as I felt. I'd done this. I'd killed Emily Johnson.

I sat down on the edge of the sofa, knowing that Ava would probably have a fit over me sitting on her furniture, but it was better than passing out on the floor. So many questions raced through my head, but I couldn't risk asking Brady any of them. What if he made the connection? I glanced up at him, surprised by the worry in his eyes, and wondered if I should tell him everything I knew. About that night ten years ago, and the texts I'd been receiving ever since my return to Franklin. But I had nothing concrete to tell the police. Was I really willing to gamble the lives of the people I cared about? My stalker had sent me a photo of Belinda last week, along with a not-so-subtle threat, so I was damn lucky she was still alive.

Brady was watching me like a hawk, looking like he was ready to swoop in and hug me again, but I had the overwhelming urge to do this on my own.

"Thanks for coming to tell me," I said as I stood. Then I shot a dark look at Ava since she'd technically been the one to break the news—and none too gently. But nothing else in my life had been gentle. Why expect gentleness now? "I need to get back to work."

His eyes hooded. "I didn't *just* come to tell you about her death. I'm here to convince you to spend the rest of the day at my apartment."

"Why?"

"There's a murderer on the loose, Maggie." But the look he gave me let me know he thought I had a particular reason to worry.

I looked back at Ava, who still stood at the bottom of the stairs. "I need to talk to Brady for a moment. I'll be back in a few minutes, and you can dock the time I spend talking to him." I didn't wait for an answer, just shoved Brady through the open front door onto the porch and closed the door behind me.

"Why do you work for her?" he asked in disgust as he stared at the now-closed door.

"Because it's part of my lease agreement."

"That's ridiculous."

"I'm not adding to my indentured servitude by standing out here talking about the fairness of it. I want you to be straight with me. Why did you really come over?"

"To tell you about Emily."

"And . . . ?"

"I was worried about you."

"That much is obvious. Why? I know this isn't just because you worried how I'd take the news."

His eyes held mine. I could feel the weight of the unspoken words between us.

Brady broke first. "You said you would check in with me, and you didn't. And then you didn't answer your phone. I knew you were supposed to be working for Ava, so I came to see if you were here, and when I didn't see your car, I panicked."

I bristled at being watched so closely. "I parked my car behind Momma's catering business. Now tell me why you're worried."

"A lot of people around you have died within a very short period of time."

"And you think I'm next? Why?" A light bulb flickered on in my head. Did Emily have the same mark on her leg? Brady wasn't a stupid man. He would have noticed a detail like that. But he had no idea how I'd gotten that scar, let alone that I had a stalker.

"I care about you," he said in frustration. "I'm not sure how to make that any clearer."

I tried to picture Emily in her apartment, facing the same man I'd encountered ten years ago, and nausea roiled in my gut. I closed my eyes and took several breaths through my nose, praying it would pass. Oh, the terror she must have faced . . .

Had he told her that he'd chosen her because of me?

Then another wave of guilt and horror hit me. How would my mother react to this news?

"Maggie." I felt Brady reach for me, but I jerked out of his grasp as I opened my eyes again.

"Sorry," I said, brushing the back of my hand across my clammy forehead. "I just need a moment alone."

"You should take off the rest of the day and go home."

Home. Where was home? The apartment behind this house? My mother's? New York City? It sure didn't feel like Brady's apartment, even though I'd sought refuge there.

And now I needed refuge more than ever.

Part of me wanted to ask Brady about the mark. I was desperate to tell someone, especially someone who could possibly help, but Brady was holding something back. Was it really official police business, or was it something else? I wasn't willing to take a risk, so until I knew more, I needed to distance myself from Brady to protect the people I loved.

I put a hand on my hip and gave him a bit of attitude. "We both know Max Goodwin's murder had nothing to do with me. It was a case of being in the wrong place at the wrong time. And sure, I was supposed to meet Walter Frey the night of his death, but Dr. Lopez killed him to keep him from talking to me—and Dr. Lopez is no longer a threat. I have no idea who killed Emily, but why would it have something to do with me?"

Some sick part of me was proud for carrying off my speech when all I wanted to do was burst into tears, but I had a façade to maintain. Too bad I'd never get the theatrical recognition this performance deserved.

"Maggie," he pleaded. "Please."

I narrowed my eyes. "What do you know that you're not telling me?"

We had a staring match that lasted for several seconds before I flung out my hands in frustration. "I need to get back to work." I opened the door and started to walk back inside, but Brady grabbed my arm and gently tugged me back.

"I don't want us parting like this," he said. He reached for my necklace, softly brushing the pendant before dropping his hand.

My irritation softened. Brady's reasons for holding back information might be more legitimate than mine. "I really do have to go back to work," I said, resting my hands on his chest.

"I'll say," Ava said in a short tone from just inside the open front door. "You've broken your bad news, Detective Bennett, and now my house needs to be cleaned. While you're worried for Magnolia's safety for some unknown reason, I can assure you that she is safe while under my roof. No miscreant will get over my threshold."

Her promise seemed unlikely given the fact that she had to have barely weighed one hundred twenty pounds soaking wet, but she looked fierce enough to win a round of hand-to-hand combat with anyone stupid enough to try to take her on.

"See?" I said with a forced smile. "Safe as can be. I promise to call you when I leave."

"Okay," he said reluctantly.

"Good day, Detective Bennett," Ava said as she marched over and shoved him out the front door, which she then locked behind him. She turned her scrutinizing gaze on me. "Why was he really here?"

I was barely holding myself together. I wasn't sure I could endure an interrogation from Ava Milton. "He's worried about me."

"Why?" she asked in a tone that suggested she didn't think worrying about me was worth anyone's time.

"Because nearly every person who's been murdered in Franklin in the past four weeks had some connection to me."

"He thinks you're the murderer?"

"No. The opposite. He's worried I'll be murdered next."

Her eyes narrowed into slits. "And do *you* think you'll be targeted next?"

"No," I said, holding her gaze. No, my stalker seemed content to continue toying with me.

"Then why are we wasting our time standing here talking about it? Have you finished mopping the floor?"

My face flushed with irritation over being treated like a five-year-old, but it was better than the shock and guilt I felt over Emily's death. I'd take any distraction I could. "No, ma'am."

"Then get busy. I still have another job for you to do."

I spent the next half hour mopping her floors, making sure I didn't leave any streaks, but all that alone time with my thoughts had made me an emotional mess. I kept swiping at tears as I worked, and Ava's looks of irritation told me that she probably thought I was weak. Some poor frightened woman scared for her life. While she was partially right, I was more worried about the people around me. What was the best way to protect them?

When I declared my job completed, Ava examined my work, acting like someone had stuck a bumblebee up her butt. She crossed her arms and tilted her head. "I think I see a streak by the settee next to the fireplace."

"I'll take care of it." I didn't see it, nor was I convinced it existed, but I also didn't feel like arguing with her.

She pursed her lips. "No. Come upstairs. Your next job is in the attic."

I followed her up the main staircase, then up another narrow staircase to her musty attic. Flimsy boxes had been spread out everywhere, a few with their lids removed, revealing stacks of papers and newspaper clippings.

She waved her arm around the room. "This has become a fire hazard, but the task is overwhelming. You're going to help me sort through it all."

There had to be over a hundred boxes stacked around the attic. The sight of them instilled me with a powerful urge to spin around and run, but for some reason my stubbornness kicked in. I would do this, if for no other reason than to prove to Ava Milton that she couldn't scare me away. "So where do we start?"

"We?" she asked in a condescending tone. "Do you have a mouse in your pocket? I will not be helping. This will be *your* project."

"Okay . . ." I tried to keep my voice cheerful, refusing to give her more evidence that I was weak. "Just tell me what you'd like me to do. Throw them out?"

"Good heavens, no. I need you to sort through them and figure out what needs to be kept and what needs to be disposed of."

My mouth dropped open. "Miss Ava, how will I know what you want to keep and destroy?"

"Use the sense in your head that God gave you, Magnolia Steele," she said as she picked out a box that didn't look as old as some of the ones in the back of the attic. When she saw the look of worry on my face, she sighed. "Sort them into piles, and I'll check on you in an hour to find out how you're doing."

"Okay."

She set the box down in the single empty patch on the rickety wood floor. "You can work there." With that, she was gone.

I took the box and moved to the edge of the space, thankful I'd worn yoga pants. There had to be twenty years' worth of dust caked over everything. I was going to have to change before I met Momma for lunch, but I couldn't do it in my apartment. Maybe Ava would let me change in her powder room. I could use my broken front door as an excuse—I sure wasn't telling her about the cameras hidden all around the apartment.

And I still hadn't told Ava I was leaving early.

But I also realized I needed to warn Belinda that she might be next on the killer's list. I couldn't stop thinking about that photograph of Belinda he'd sent me. Glancing over my shoulder to make sure Ava was really gone, I called Belinda instead of texting.

"Magnolia," she said in a warm voice. "I was just thinking about you."

"You were?" I asked in surprise.

"I really enjoyed our breakfast this morning. We should try to get together more frequently."

We'd shared at least three meals a week since my move back to Franklin. If circumstances had been different, I might have thought she was clingy, but I suspected something else was up. "That would be great," I said.

"Mr. James," Belinda said, her voice muffled. "Could you give me a moment to talk to my sister-in-law?"

His voice was faint in the background. "Of course. Tell her I'm waiting for her call."

"Will do," Belinda said. Several seconds passed before she spoke into the receiver again, and when she did, her voice was much quieter. "Magnolia, are you okay?"

"I'm fine. In fact, I was calling to check on you."

"Me?" she asked in surprise. "Whatever for?"

"Belinda, I don't know how to tell you this, but Emily Johnson is dead."

"I know," she said softly.

"What? How?"

"It doesn't matter. Your safety is what matters."

"Why would you think I'm unsafe?"

She hesitated. "Because Emily was your attorney, and people around you are dying," she gushed out. "It makes me nervous for you."

Why did she sound so flustered?

"I'm fine. I'm at Ava Milton's house, which is probably safer than being locked up at the South Pole. I'm more worried about *you*." I decided to borrow her own reasoning. "If people around me are dying, then you're at risk."

"Me? I'm fine. Please don't worry about me."

Why did she sound so certain? Now I was being totally paranoid. Most people never thought they'd become a killer's target. After all, a regular person had a greater chance of getting struck by lightning or getting killed falling out of bed.

"I'm sorry, Magnolia, but I have to get back to this meeting. Can we talk later?"

"Yeah, sure."

"Be careful," she said. Then she hung up.

When had Belinda started taking meetings with Bill James?

But if Brady had warned me to stay away from Bill James, should I be worried about my sister-in-law? Or was she safe because she was married to Roy?

I needed to get back on task.

Releasing a massive sigh, I lifted the lid off the box and took out the first piece of paper, a newspaper article about the opening of a strip mall on Highway 96. The article was dated twenty years before. Why in heaven's name would she need to keep a newspaper clipping about a strip mall? I set it to the side, my new discard pile.

I shuffled through multiple clippings about society events before dropping them all into the discard pile. A photo caught my eye, and I retrieved the page and took a closer look. While it was a picture of a Franklin doctor and his wife at a heart disease fundraiser, the photographer had captured a clear image of my father behind them, talking to a man I didn't recognize. I set the paper down next to me, the lone keep item so far.

I continued sorting through the clippings, scanning the photos more carefully. There were several other photos with my father in the background. But I'd started looking for other familiar faces too—and found them. There were several shots of Walter Frey and Steve Morrissey. I even found a photo of Steve and his first wife, the woman he'd left to marry Shannon. I was halfway through the box when I realized I was piecing together my father's life twenty years ago—when he had been part of the Jackson Project. There wasn't any mention of the land scheme. Instead, with the exception of the occasional article about a store opening, most of the clippings covered the social scene in Franklin and Nashville. But I could see a pattern. My father had attended every major fundraiser the year I turned eight.

And so had Bill James.

chapter eight

I started making a mental list of things to ask my mother, and Daddy's year as a social butterfly was definitely on there. I vaguely remembered him being gone a lot for a short time when I was in grade school, which was an oddity, especially since I remembered him being home most nights until the months leading up to his death.

I got up and found a notebook and a pencil on a table made of sawhorses and plywood. I took both over to my floor space and spread out the articles, making a list of the events and dates, coming up with a rough calendar covering seven months in the social season of 1996. Next, I pulled out my cell phone and looked up the dates of the Jackson Project. Sure enough, the land project had been announced two months after my father started attending the social events in earnest.

Daddy and Bill James had been trolling for investors.

Had he thought the project was on the up and up? Or had he known it was shady to begin with? I liked to think he hadn't known, but after everything else I'd found out about him—not to mention the massive stash of gold Colt and I had found in that dog—I was reserving judgment and trying to stay neutral.

"Have you made any progress?" Ava asked, catching me deep in thought.

I jumped and spun around to face her. "Miss Ava."

"I haven't forgotten my own name," she grumped, then let out a loud whoosh of air as she reached the top step. "Tell me about your progress."

I gave her a blank look. "I've made it about halfway through the box. And I'm still not certain how you want me to sort them."

"Only halfway?" she asked in dismay. "I have another box you need to go through tomorrow."

I stared up at her, unsure of how to respond. On the one hand, I was scheduled to work as a hostess at her weekly Thursday morning Bible study tomorrow, after which I had to put in a shift at Rebellious Rose until six, which didn't leave me much time to work on Ava's attic. But in just one box, I'd discovered answers to questions I hadn't even known to ask. Sure, I could come back in a day or two, but I'd waited fourteen years, and I was finally getting somewhere. I didn't want to wait any longer.

"I can take this box home tonight and work on it in my apartment. Alvin has me scheduled to work tomorrow from one to six, but I'll see if I can get someone to cover for my shift."

She shook her head. "Take the box home, but come over at seven tomorrow. You can work on the second box before you start your hostessing duties."

I nearly protested the time—shoot, eight thirty was early enough—but it occurred to me that maybe the real purpose of this exercise was for me to find clues about my father's past. I'd asked her what she knew about his supposed affair with Shannon Morrissey; maybe this was her roundabout way of helping me. "Yes, ma'am. I'll be here. I can work for a couple of hours, then change before I serve at your meeting. I would hate to look disheveled for your guests."

She glanced down at the clippings and my list, then held my gaze. "The moment I met you, I knew you were smarter than most people perceive you to be. Don't disappointment me, Magnolia." She lifted her chin. "At my age, my image is everything. That you recognize this is proof enough that I was right about you."

Her praise meant more than it should have because I was fairly certain she wasn't just talking about looking good. To hide my shock, I glanced down at my phone, surprised to see it was almost one fifteen. "Miss Ava," I said, resisting the urge to cringe in expectation of her wrath. "I'm supposed to have lunch with my mother at two. Would you mind if I take off early?"

She frowned. "Why would I mind? Rumor has it your mother isn't feeling well. You should look after her."

How had Ava found out about my mother's illness? She wouldn't have been able to cut it out of a newspaper, but then I suspected the written word was only one source of Ava Milton's information. Eavesdropping on her Bible study last week had proved to me that she was aware of all the goings-on in town. How else would she have known about Emily's murder before it showed up on any news program?

I decided to neither confirm nor deny my mother's illness. "Thank you. I'll show up for work bright and early." My clothes were filthy and I really needed a shower. After I grabbed the catering uniform from my apartment, I'd need a place to change. "Speaking of which . . . would you mind if I change in your powder room? I don't feel comfortable changing in my apartment with no lock on the front door."

"Your door's been taken care of," she said as she started down the stairs again. "Your new keys are on the table in the kitchen. Please try to refrain from destroying the new one."

I started to protest that I hadn't been the one to destroy the door, but there was no denying I was the cause. Besides, Ava was already gone—she'd descended the staircase quicker than I would have thought possible for a woman her age. Instead, I scooped up the papers and put them back into the box. For once I didn't mind having homework.

Ava wasn't downstairs when I walked into the kitchen, but I found the keys on the table just as she'd said I would. They weren't the only things I found. When I walked out the back door, Colt was sitting on the bottom steps of the stairs to my apartment.

How could I have forgotten that he'd had his own homework assignment? But more importantly, why hadn't he answered my text?

His legs were extended and crossed at the ankles. His elbows rested on the step behind him. He sat up the moment he saw me.

"Can't you fulfill a simple request?" I asked in a short tone as I walked toward him.

His brow lifted and he held out his hands. "*What?*"

"I asked you to let me know that you got my text!"

He lifted his shoulder into a lazy shrug. "I'm fine, Maggie Mae. Stop worrying so much."

Part of me wanted to snap at him, but I knew Colt wasn't used to answering to anyone. He probably thought I was turning into a nagging woman. While the thought pissed me off, I decided to let it go this time. The important thing was that he was safe. "I'm surprised you didn't come in."

"Your new front door is locked."

"I meant to Ava's."

He climbed to his feet. "I'm not her favorite person right now."

That piqued my interest. "Who is? But I thought you could sweet-talk any woman. What did you do to tick her off?"

He scowled. "Nothing for you to worry your pretty little head about. What's with the box?"

I wanted to press him, but I knew him well enough to know it wouldn't work. I'd find out some other way. "Homework from Ava. Now I have to go upstairs and get a change of clothes before I meet Momma for lunch at Puckett's."

He didn't move from the base of the stairs. "Homework?"

I shrugged, deciding he didn't need to know, and started to walk past him, but he grabbed my arm and stopped me, seriousness washing over his face. "Mags, there's something I need to tell you."

"Emily?" I asked in a whisper.

"You know?"

I nodded and blinked when my eyes started burning again. "Brady came by to tell me."

He leaned his face close to mine, close enough that I could smell his shampoo. "I think you should let me handle the whole gold issue by myself."

"What?" I jerked my head up.

"It's too dangerous. I think you should lay low and not draw any attention to yourself."

I shook my head in confusion, then narrowed my eyes. "Wait. Are you trying to pull one over on me?"

"No. I'm trying to protect you."

"Don't do that," I snapped. "Don't pretend you're trying to be a hero."

"Maybe I want to find whoever took it too, Mags. Maybe I don't like that they're messing with your life."

I narrowed my eyes. "Doubtful."

He grinned, but it didn't reach his eyes. "You know me too well. Okay, here's the deal. I'll find the gold for you and take sixty percent. My percentage plus a finder's fee."

"No way."

"Okay, Fifty-five, forty-five."

I needed Colt—there were too many things going on for me to pour all my concentration into the gold, and there was no doubt Colt had resources I didn't. But if I left this to him, I'd have to trust him not to cheat me.

Then again, it had never been about the gold for me. It was more about the story behind it. "Fifty-fifty," I insisted nonetheless.

His eyes widened slightly; then he grinned. Obviously he'd expected me to push back more. "Okay, so the next part of Operation Gold is flushing out whoever set up those cameras in your apartment. I take it you didn't get any reaction from Bennett?"

I shot him a glare. "How did you come to *that* conclusion?"

His eyebrows rose. "The fact you're still speaking of him so fondly." His response was a little sharp.

I started to protest that I'd only mentioned him in passing, but I didn't see the point. "He spoke to Owen on the phone last night, but if Owen has seen the footage, he didn't let on."

"Do you think he would tell him?"

"Maybe not on the phone. He'd probably handle it more sensitively."

"So we can't rule Frasier out."

"No." I frowned. "But we need to get the cameras out of there ASAP."

"I'm ready for Stage One, but I need a little more time."

"What? Why?"

"Just stay with Brady for a few more days. We don't want to screw this up."

"What are you waiting on?"

He hesitated. "I'm getting a friend to help me."

"Help you do what?" When he didn't answer, I shot him a glare. "This was supposed to be between you and me."

"He doesn't know any details."

"Then what are you doing?"

He groaned. "I'll have a plan in place by tomorrow. I'll tell you more when I have it nailed down."

"I want to know before you do anything."

He smirked and gave me a salute. "Yes, ma'am."

I scowled. "The sooner this gets done, the better. I need to go in there now to find a change of clothes before I meet Momma for lunch. Those cameras creep me out. I want them gone."

His brow furrowed and he studied me for several seconds. "I know, Mags. I hate it too. But we only get one shot at this, right?"

"Yeah," I said with a sigh. "You're right."

"Then trust me. I need to set this up, so follow my lead."

"Your lead? Just tell me what you plan to do. I'm an actress, Colt, and I'm pretty damn good at it."

"I know, but go with it anyway." Then he grabbed the keys out of my hand and bounded up the stairs. By the time I reached the landing, he had already stomped inside.

"I don't like it, Magnolia," he said in a stern voice. "Just let me handle it."

This was his way of getting me to play along? Vague dialogue cues? "Yeah," I muttered, walking into the kitchen. I set the box on the island, then opened the fridge and grabbed a bottle of water, pretty much one of the only things in there. "Why am I not surprised a good old

114

Southern Georgia boy would say something so misogynistic?"

"You know it's not that," he said, his face pleading. "I'm protecting you. I promise I've hidden it somewhere no one will find it. The less people who know where it is, the better. And that includes you." He was either wasting his time trying to break into the country music world instead of acting in LA, or he was being sincere. For some reason, I believed the latter.

I took a long drink and my stomach rumbled, reminding me that I hadn't eaten since breakfast. I waved the open bottle in a wide sweep toward him. "Fine, but I'm only giving you until the weekend, and then I want to see it for myself."

"Fair enough." He snatched the water bottle from my hand and took a swig. "You still meeting Lila for lunch?"

"Yeah." I needed to change, but it would look suspicious if I took clothes with me and didn't change here. "I have to get ready. You can leave if you want."

"Nah," he said, handing back the water bottle. "I noticed your car's not out front. I'll wait and take you to meet her."

I headed for the bedroom, telling myself this was no big deal. I was wearing a bra and panties, which provided the same amount of coverage as a bikini. Besides, I was used to quick costume changes backstage, and anyone with access to YouTube could see a whole lot more of me. But this was different. This was a violation of my privacy.

But I sucked it up and pulled a white, button-up shirt from a hanger and grabbed a pair of khaki pants. If I had been wait staff, I would have worn black pants, but

Momma and Tilly had long since learned it was best to keep me in the kitchen at catering events. I tugged down my yoga pants, taking comfort in the fact that my T-shirt was long enough to cover most of my backside.

"It's set," I heard Colt say in a low voice in the living room.

After pulling on my khakis, I edged closer to the cracked door.

"She doesn't suspect a thing."

My first reaction was horror. Colt was a fucking traitor.

"Tonight behind Stringer's in the industrial park in Franklin."

I tugged my T-shirt over my head and slipped my arms into the shirt, quickly securing the buttons as I continued to listen.

"I'm not bringing all of it. Just one bar to prove I have it. But we can't be seen together. Send me the amount we agreed upon for the one bar, and I'll leave it behind the barrel in front of Space #145. You can pick it up after eleven o'clock. Then contact me later and we'll negotiate the terms for the rest."

I peeked out through the crack. Colt's back was to me and his phone was pressed to his ear.

He started to turn around and I backed up, trying to control my anger. But the anger faded as quickly as it had sprung up. This was probably part of his master plan. Make a phone call while I was in the other room so the people behind the cameras would believe I didn't know anything. But he also said he was setting up a plan for tonight, and I suspected that was because he was trying to keep me out of harm's way. I was going to confront him later.

Since I didn't know when I'd be moving back in, I grabbed a couple of days' worth of clothes and stuffed them into my last bag. Then I left the room and found Colt opening a cabinet door. "You really need to have more food options."

"I've been busy."

Colt glanced over with a grin, but something shifted in his eyes when he saw the deep V of my shirt. "I'm almost ready," I said. "I need to grab a hair tie out of the bathroom."

I grabbed one out of the bathroom drawer and slid it over my wrist. Before leaving, I did up another button on my shirt. Colt was standing in the middle of the living room when I walked back out, and he snagged my arm.

"You still sleepin' at Detective Bennett's place tonight?"

I wasn't sure staying with Brady was the best idea after Emily's murder, but I had nowhere else to go. "Yeah."

"Why the hesitation? Having second thoughts?"

What was he doing? "I'm not discussing my love life with you."

"Come on, Magnolia," he said playfully. "You love it when I talk dirty to you in bed."

His mouth lowered to my neck again, sending shivers down my back. The haughty comeback died on my lips.

I pressed my palms to his chest, meaning to push him away. Some distant part of my brain screamed at me to step away, but the rest of me needed this, needed Colt. I'd always figured there would be explosive chemistry between us, but this was a terrible idea. Yet, I stayed in place, tilting back my head to give him better access while releasing a low moan.

"So tell me yes," he murmured, moving to my ear and sucking my earlobe between his lips. "Tell me you'll go with me."

"Colt . . ." I had no idea what he was talking about. What was the right response?

"It's just a masquerade ball," he said a little louder this time. "Borrow a dress from Belinda. Plus, she'll be there too, so you'll have someone to talk to while I'm networking it up."

I leaned back to search his face. "You want me to go to the Middle Tennessee Children's Charity Masquerade Ball on Saturday night?"

A sexy grin spread across his face. "Do you know of any other masquerade balls?"

"No, but it doesn't seem like your kind of thing."

"Because I don't have money?" he asked dryly. "We both know that's about to change. I need to socialize. Network."

I froze. That was exactly what my father had done years ago. What if . . .

"Belinda says this is big. Everyone will be there. Momma's gonna want us to work."

"I already have the night off, and you know she doesn't really need you." His lips skimmed my cheek, inching closer to my lips. "It's time for you to plan your future, Magnolia, and we both know Southern Belles Catering is *not* it."

"Then what *is* my future?" I asked, momentarily forgetting we were being watched. "A recording contract with you?"

"You're not thinking big enough, Maggie Mae," he said with a chuckle. "One million in gold will get us a hell of a lot more than that."

I looked away. "Yeah."

"So you'll come?"

If most of Franklin society would be there, I could ask questions disguised as small talk. "Yeah," I said, looking up into his crystal blue eyes. "I'll go."

Why did I feel like I'd just made a deal with the devil?

chapter nine

As soon as we got into Colt's truck, he shot me an apologetic look. "Sorry to play dirty in there—literally—but we need whoever's watching to think we're lovers, and that you're playing Brady."

"Why? You already pulled that stunt yesterday," I said. "And trust me, Brady didn't act like he was suspicious of anything." Should I pretend like I didn't hear him on the phone or confront him? Who was I kidding? "So what was that phone call about?"

He paused and turned to face me. His expression was carefully guarded. "How much did you hear?"

"Enough to know you're supposedly meeting someone."

"It's a false lead. I had to make whoever put the cameras in your apartment think it was real."

"I thought you said you were planning something tomorrow."

"It came to me on the fly...so we can get those cameras out sooner."

His call seemed premeditated, so I wasn't sure that was true. "And how do you plan to catch them?"

"I have my ways." He gave me a long look. "You changed clothes in your bedroom. Even though you know the cameras are in there."

I shrugged, not wanting to admit how violated I felt. "I flashed my boobs to millions of people on the internet. What's a bra and panties to some pervert? He's probably pissed that he couldn't watch us *do it*."

Colt didn't say anything, but after he steered out of the driveway, he reached out and took my hand. He drove a block before he finally said, "This is probably going to get harder, Mags. I still think you should change your mind about digging deeper."

"Here's a little thing you don't seem to know about me, Colt Austin," I said, jerking my hand free. "I'm pretty damn stubborn."

He broke out into a genuine laugh. "You think I haven't figured that out? I'm not *that* stupid." Something in his tone jolted me.

"I never said you were stupid, Colt."

He didn't respond.

I turned in my seat. "Why are you doing this?" I asked.

He kept his eyes on the road, but his hand was squeezing the steering wheel with more force than necessary. "We've already had this conversation. More than once. It's becoming tedious."

"But you didn't answer me. Not really."

He pulled to the side of the road, across the street from the restaurant where I was supposed to meet my mother. His grip tightened and he stared out the windshield. "You really haven't figured it out?"

"I wouldn't be asking if I had."

He shook his head and turned to face me. "I told you. I'm a greedy son of a bitch, and I want half the gold."

Four weeks ago, I would have bought that answer, but not now. I'd just have to accept that he was helping and figure out the why of it later. Colt Austin—the man who wrote country songs about pickup trucks and beer—wasn't used to feelings.

"Colt."

"Your mother's waiting, and there's something I need to do before I show up at the Belles."

"What?"

He tilted his head to look at me. "Now, I didn't go asking what you did with Detective Hot Stuff last night, did I?"

I flushed.

His eyebrows rose slightly. "On the other hand, based on the way you're blushing, maybe I should reconsider. You know I like a sordid tale." His clenched jaw was at odds with his glib tone.

I opened my mouth, about to apologize, but for what? Sleeping with Brady? That was ridiculous. Sure, Colt and I flirted, but he flirted with everyone—men included. He'd never once given me any indication that he wanted something more. In fact, he'd done exactly the opposite.

His jaw loosened and defeat filled his eyes. "Seriously, Mags. What did you hear on the call?"

The sudden change in his demeanor worried me. Did this mean he really planned to double-cross me but was now having regrets? "Only that you're meeting someone," I said, playing dumb. "No other details, which is why I'm asking now. Tell me what's going on."

"I already did."

I wanted to press him on it, but I needed to get inside. "I'll let this go. *For now.*"

"Oh ye of little faith. I'll tell you when I know something."

But that wasn't true. Was he protecting me or playing me? "I'll see you later."

He turned back to look out the windshield, acting slightly troubled. "Yeah."

I got out of the truck, my heart feeling heavy. I'd been unhappy and lonely in New York, but I'd experienced more emotional turmoil in the last four weeks here than in the entire ten years I'd lived there.

When I walked into the restaurant, I didn't see my mother anywhere. My heart slammed into my chest and my head grew fuzzy. Had my stalker done something to her? But then I realized I was several minutes early—a rarity for me. The hostess led me to a table, and I followed her on rubbery legs, unsure how many more frights I could take. The waitress came over and took my drink order, then walked away.

The door to the restaurant opened, and a small, frail woman walked in, scanning the restaurant before her gaze stopped on me.

It was Momma.

How could she have changed so much in only a few days?

I stood as she headed my direction, willing my eyes to dry up. Momma abhorred pity even more than she abhorred weakness.

"Hi, Momma," I said before I leaned in to hug her. She felt like she would break.

"You act like you haven't seen me in ten years."

I stiffened at the dig, but she chuckled and mischief lit up her eyes. "Bad joke."

I grimaced and my heart felt even heavier than it had after walking away from Colt. "I'm sorry, Momma. So sorry for wasting so much time."

She shook her head and wagged her finger at me. "Nope. Let's have none of that. We've made our peace, haven't we?"

She'd apologized for treating me so coldly after my father left, and I'd apologized for running away, but we'd both left a lot unsaid. Still, sometimes a person just needed to know when to let something go. "Yeah. Fresh start."

She gave me a curt nod. "Good. Now tell me more about this police detective."

I laughed. "You mean Brady?"

"Have you been shacking up with any other Franklin police detectives?"

"No." But her mention of Brady reminded me of Emily. Somehow I'd forgotten about her over the last hour. I'd wanted to forget. Momma and Emily had gotten close enough for Momma to have her on speed dial. I was pretty sure she didn't know about the murder. How did I tell her?

"Momma, have you seen the news today?" But even as I asked, I wondered if that was the right approach. I hadn't seen—or read—the news since arriving at Miss Ava's house this morning, so I wasn't sure anything had been made public.

"No." She paused. "Was there anything about you in it?"

"No. Not me this time. Emily."

"Emily?" she asked in wonder. "Did she have some big case that made the news?"

I was going about this all wrong, but I didn't know how to do better. Folding my hands in my lap, I forced out past the lump in my throat, "No."

"She was on vacation last week. Her first in years. She was supposed to come home yesterday. What could she have made the news about?"

"Momma," I whispered. "Emily's dead."

Her eyes grew wide. "No. That's not right. How could she be dead? She has her whole life ahead of her."

I reached across the table for her hand—a gamble. "She was murdered."

She didn't pull her hand away as I'd expected. Instead, her face paled and she slumped forward a few inches, looking even smaller, even sicker. "How?"

"I don't know all the details, and I don't even know if it made the news yet. Brady came to tell me at Miss Ava's. He knew that Emily had been my attorney, so he wanted to tell me in person." No need for her to know that he also thought I was in danger.

"What happened?" she choked out.

"I don't know."

Her gaze jerked up to mine. "He told you at Ava Milton's house? Surely she knew some details, and lorded them over you."

"You don't want to know."

Her eyes blazed with anger. "I'm a grown woman, Magnolia Mae Steele. You do not tell me what I do or don't want."

Her words were harsh, and I was relieved she'd regained some of her strength. "Emily's neighbor found her dog in the hallway in the middle of the night. When she went to return the dog, she found the door unlocked and Emily in the kitchen. She was already dead."

My mother's trembling hand rested on the table. "How was she murdered?"

"I don't know. And that's the truth. Brady refused to tell me anything, and Miss Ava didn't know." I paused, feeling nauseous. "But she said there was a lot of blood."

Momma's face took on a greenish-white cast, making me worried. The waitress showed up with my water, and I grabbed it from her and thrust it toward my mother. "Drink this."

Momma took the glass, but immediately set it on the table. "A glass of water isn't gonna solve anything, Magnolia." A soft smile lifted her lips. "But I love you for trying to make me feel better."

The waitress took a step away from the table. "I can come back and check on you in a minute."

"I know what I want," Momma said, not looking at the waitress. She ordered a burger and fries, then shot me a look. "What? I'm already dying. Might as well eat whatever I want."

The waitress now looked horrified.

"I'll take the strawberry salad," I said, shoving the menus at her. "And another glass of water."

She nodded, turned on her heels, and left.

My mother looked better, but not by much.

"I'm so sorry about Emily," I said again.

"You didn't kill her," she said dismissively. Then her eyes jerked up to mine. "Oh, Lord. Do you have an alibi?"

I couldn't hide my small smile. "Yeah. I have a very strong alibi. I was with Brady from around six last night until he was called in on the case at four this morning."

"Every minute accounted for?"

I lifted an eyebrow. "You think I'm a likely suspect?"

"Well, you *did* have a motive."

"I forgave Emily a long time ago for all her backstabbing in high school." Okay, so "long ago" was only four weeks ago. I'd done a lot of growing in a month. "And it sure wasn't worth killing over."

"I know you didn't do it," Momma said with an aggravated wave of dismissal, but it was barely a movement, as though she couldn't find the energy to complete the physical task. "But that doesn't mean the police will believe it."

"I was with Brady. I'm pretty sure I'm safe."

Momma was silent for a moment and then shook her head. "I can't believe someone hurt her."

"Me either." I paused before adding, "I know you were close to her."

"After you left . . ." Momma said. "She helped fill the void."

"I know." I hesitated, worried that she might pass out. "Maybe you should go home. This is quite a shock."

Fire blazed in her eyes. "I'm made of sterner stuff than that, Magnolia."

"Of course you are. But you haven't been feeling well . . ."

Her back straightened. "I'm feeling just fine. Well enough to have lunch with my daughter." She rested a hand on the table again, disguising the fact that she was doing it to hold herself up. "Part of the reason I wanted to have lunch with you was to discuss . . . practical matters."

I tried not to stiffen. "What does that mean?" I asked, even though I knew.

"What happens when I die and after."

I breathed in slowly, filling my lungs, trying to inflate myself with the courage to deal with this. I didn't want to have this discussion, but I was practical enough to know it needed to be done. She'd told me some of her plans, but I knew there was a lot more for us to discuss. I straightened my back and lifted my chin, preparing myself. "Okay."

Surprise flashed in her eyes. "I expected more of a fight."

"Then how about we bargain for my cooperation?"

"What do you want?" she asked, and I was happy to see some of her color return. Momma had always thrived on confrontation.

"I want to hear stories about when I was a kid."

She sat back in her seat. "Magnolia, you don't have to barter for that."

"Then you win," I said with a small smile. "So tell me what you want to say."

She spent the next ten minutes telling me all the details of what she'd planned out.

"There's a DNR in my medical records," she said, holding my gaze. "That means no machines. No feeding tubes. If I go into a coma, you have to make sure they follow my orders."

"You're asking me to just let you die?"

"I'm dyin' anyway, Magnolia Mae. At least let me have some say in the matter."

I forced myself to nod. She was right, however much it hurt.

She told me where to find her will and how to contact her attorney. "You know I'm leaving you the house, but it will be easier with probate if I put you on the deed before I die. I have the papers with me, so I want you to come to the bank when we're done so you can sign and get it notarized."

"Roy's gonna have a fit."

"You told me that last week. Let him. I let him get away with far too much. I should have had a stronger hand with him, and a softer one with you."

"Water under the bridge, Momma."

She paused, then said in a soft voice I wasn't used to hearing, "But it's still in view, Magnolia. Still in my memories, haunting me."

Tears stung my eyes and I swiped at my left one. "Let it go. Neither one of us is perfect."

She grinned. "Tilly thinks you and I are too much alike for our own good."

I laughed. "I always knew Tilly was smart."

"I've already made arrangements with the funeral home and picked out my casket, along with all the other macabre details," she said.

The only way I knew how to handle this was to pretend it was happening twenty years in the future, because Momma would get ticked off if I started crying.

"Oh, come on," I teased. "You're not going to let me pick any of that out? I bet they have one that's sparkly."

Her mouth pressed tight, but then she continued, ignoring my statement. "Roy and Belinda would insist on the top-of-the-line model, wanting to keep up appearances and all that." She waved her hand. "What do I care if I'm buried in a pine box or a fancy, gold-plated one?"

The waitress showed up with our food just then. She gave my mother a frightened look, as if worried Momma might fast-forward her sickness a few weeks and pass away at the table, and then set our plates in front of us and scurried away.

I leaned forward and lowered my voice. "I'm not letting you be buried in a pine box, Momma."

"I didn't pick out a pine box, but I didn't get the top of the line either." She grabbed a french fry. "And I want to be buried in my catering uniform. Don't you let Roy convince anyone otherwise."

I grinned. "And Grandma's secret wedding cake cookie recipe?"

"No. I'm giving that to you, not that you'll know what to do with it."

"I can bake cookies without burning them. Sometimes." I picked up my fork and began to mix the dressing around my salad.

"Pick any old uniform, nothing special," she said, focusing on assembling her burger, then looked up and pointed a finger at me. "But make sure it's clean. I swear I'll come back and haunt you if you bury me in dirty clothes."

Looking at her now, I had to wonder how much time I had left with her. I'd held it together for our whole discussion, but now my chin started to quiver.

Momma's eyes softened. "Everyone has to die sometime, Maggie Mae. I wouldn't have planned on leaving yet, but I've made my peace with it."

I picked at my salad, but I couldn't summon much of an appetite even though my stomach was empty. "But I haven't."

She patted my hand. "I know. I know."

"Can we go to Emily's funeral together?" I asked.

She gave me a look of surprise. "Yeah." She took a bite of her food, then said, "I think you two could have been good friends."

"We definitely weren't enemies anymore," I said. "And I was torn up hearing about her death."

"She knew how much your leaving hurt me. She asked all your friends if they knew why you'd left."

My fork froze midair.

"Magnolia?"

Was that why she'd been chosen? Had the murderer found out about her investigation? Was it possible she'd finally dug something up?

"I'm sorry," I said, putting my fork down and picking up my water glass. "It just makes me so sad."

131

"Then let's talk about something else for a little while. My side of the bargain was to tell you stories from your childhood. Let me tell you the story of when you were born."

I smiled. "You've already told me, not that I mind hearing it again."

"But I didn't tell you how I almost killed you."

My mouth dropped open. "*What?*"

She took a deep breath before launching into her tale. "I was two weeks late. I'd dragged your father to the hospital twice with false labor and vowed I wouldn't look like a fool again. The night you were born I'd had contractions all day, and by that evening they were one minute apart. Your father was ticked that I still didn't want to go to the hospital, so he finally picked me up and carried me to the car, not an easy task when I was as huge as a whale. But he was scared to death my stubbornness would risk my safety and yours."

I smiled. "That sounds like Daddy."

"I was fit to be tied, but I let him take me to the hospital. He wanted to carry me inside, but I told him that bein' in labor didn't make me an invalid. They wheeled me back, and by the time they got me to the labor room, I was already feeling the urge to push. But when they hooked me up to the monitor, your heartbeat started crashing with the contraction, so they rushed me off to the OR for an emergency C-section. I'll never forget the look of pure terror on your father's face when he thought he might lose us both." She paused, her voice turning soft. "When I woke up, he was sitting next to my bed, his face pale as a sheet, and I was sure my stupidity had gotten you killed. I started to cry, but he leaned over and kissed me. He said, 'I was sure I was going to lose you, Lila. Don't you ever scare me like that again.'

"'The baby?' I asked.

"'She's fine,' he said. 'Perfectly healthy and a set of lungs that will rival yours. But we almost lost her too.' Then tears filled his eyes and he said, 'She's a precious gift, Lila. We can't take our responsibility lightly again. We have to do everything in our power to protect her.'" Momma looked up at me. "I don't think I did a very good job of protecting you, Magnolia."

A lump formed in my throat, but I pushed past it. "Don't be silly. You raised me just fine."

"Something happened that night," she said, her words barely audible. "The night you disappeared."

"It's more of that water under the bridge."

"I found the blood."

We stared at each other for several long seconds without speaking. I finally scrunched my mouth to the side, a dismissive gesture, and said, "I'm not sure what you're talking about."

"Roy tried to hide it, but I found the towel. And your dress. It was dark by the time you came home that night, so I told myself it was mud on your skirt—and it *was* muddy, but once I picked it up the next day, I realized there was a lot of blood on it too."

I wasn't sure what to address first. The fact that Roy had hidden my bloody garbage or that Momma knew something bad had happened. "I thought we agreed to leave the past in the past."

Her troubled eyes held mine. "Were you raped, Magnolia?"

Her hand was shaking on the table, so I reached over and covered it with my own, holding her gaze. "No," I said in a firm tone. "I was *not* raped."

She looked relieved, although not unburdened. "But something bad happened."

"What does it matter if it did?" I removed my hand and shrugged. "It's done." How could I ask her about Roy's odd behavior without giving anything else away?

"I can—" Momma started to say, but my ringing cell phone interrupted her.

I grabbed it out of my purse, realizing I hadn't checked in with Brady after leaving Ava's. Sure enough, his name was on the screen. "Sorry, Momma. I have to take this." I answered the phone and said, "I know, I was supposed to let you know when I left, but I'm fine. I'm eating lunch at Puckett's with my mother right now."

"I know," he said. "I can see you."

"What?" I glanced around the room, and sure enough, he was standing in the doorway.

He flashed me a grin, then started toward our table.

I stood to greet him. "What are you doing here?"

"I'm picking up a takeout order for me and my partner."

"Late lunch?" I asked. "You must be really busy today."

"Yeah." He didn't elaborate.

"Momma," I said, turning toward her. "You remember Brady."

"I believe I met you as Detective Bennett," Momma said with a disapproving frown.

Brady gave my mother his full attention. "Our introduction wasn't under ideal circumstances, but I hope you don't hold that against me. I really like your daughter and hope to spend a lot more time with her."

"You were doing your job," she said, holding his gaze. "And I was doing mine."

Brady had questioned her about the night of my father's disappearance—and she'd told him next to nothing. I had no doubt her *job*, as she saw it, was to keep quiet to protect me.

"Would you like to join us?" Momma asked. I shot her a look of surprise. "What?" she said defensively. "I want to meet at least one of your adult boyfriends."

Brady looked to me for direction.

I shrugged. "If you have a few minutes, I'd love for you to sit with us."

His face lit up. "I'd like that." He sat in a chair and I flagged down our waitress. After he told her his name, she headed back to the kitchen to check on his order.

"So," Momma said, her back stiff as a board. "Your name is Brady Bennett, and you're a Franklin police detective."

"Yes, ma'am," he said with a friendly smile. "I've lived here my entire life, so I'm fascinated by Maggie's life in New York."

"Because of her video?" Momma asked.

His smile fell. "No. I've never seen her video."

That earned him a look of grudging approval.

"How long have you had your catering business?" Brady asked.

"Long enough," Momma said. "Why did you decide to become a cop?"

Brady blinked, obviously caught off guard by her doggedness, though I wasn't sure why—she'd ripped into him the day he interrogated her. "I planned to be an attorney, but realized I thoroughly enjoyed investigating."

"Is your father a cop?"

"No. He's an insurance salesman."

She nodded again. "What did you find out from your investigation into my husband's disappearance?"

He was surprised by this too. "Not much. Everything seemed to lead to a dead end."

"Do you think it was a coincidence that that dentist crawled out of the woodwork after my daughter came home?"

Brady shot me a look before turning back to her. He must have thought this conversation would go very differently.

"No," Brady said. "I think Magnolia's questions drew him out."

"Do you think it's over?" she asked.

Brady stared at her for several seconds. "Yes, Mrs. Steele, I think it is."

His answer surprised me, but not my mother. If he thought everything was settled, why was he so worried about my safety?

"You care about my daughter?"

"Yes. I do."

136

"Then leave this in the past where it belongs. Just let it be, and it will all go away."

Brady nodded as he grabbed my hand. "I'm glad to hear we're on the same page."

They might be on the same page, but I was in a different book.

chapter ten

Brady stayed a few more minutes, chatting with my mother about his parents and his brother and sister. Then the waitress brought over his order, and he leaned over and kissed me on the cheek. "When will you be done tonight?"

"I don't know yet," I said, hoping my mother didn't volunteer the information.

"Let me know when you do know." Then he glanced at Momma. "Mrs. Steele, it was a pleasure getting to know you better."

Her answer was a frown.

As he walked out the front door, her frown deepened. "I don't like him."

"What?" I asked, in shock. "Why?"

"I don't trust him."

I rolled my eyes. "You name one boyfriend of mine you ever trusted."

She remained silent. Her assessment of Brady bothered me more than I wanted to let on, especially since she was generally a good judge of character.

"You didn't even like Tanner. And *everyone* liked Tanner."

"Tanner McKee was a weasel."

Well, she wasn't wrong there. "What about Colt?" I asked, choosing someone I knew she trusted—despite how most people felt about him. "Would you trust him?"

"With my business and my life, but I wouldn't trust him for a minute with you."

"I rest my case," I said, though we both knew I hadn't proven anything.

Momma pursed her lips and pulled out her wallet.

"No," I said, pushing her hand away from the black folder. "Let me get it."

"You don't have a pot to piss in."

"Maybe not," I said with a laugh. "But I have twenty-five dollars to pay for lunch." I tossed the cash on the table, satisfied there was enough for a generous tip. "Let's head to the kitchen together."

Momma got up and faltered, grabbing the back of her chair to steady herself. "We need to go by the bank first."

I'd forgotten about that part. "Okay." I reached out to grab her arm, but she shot me a glare. "I'm perfectly capable of walking on my own."

Her steps seemed to loosen as we walked toward the bank, but her chest was rising and falling at an alarming rate given that we'd only walked a block and a half at a slow pace.

I had so many questions about so many things, but I figured out a way to possibly get my mother to answer one of them.

"I know I'm getting the house," I said cautiously, "but what about all the stuff Roy has in the garage? If I sell the house, what should I do with it?"

"Let Roy get rid of it. I've been telling him for the last year to move it out, but he always tells me he'll get around to it and never does, which is completely unlike him. I've even asked Belinda to do it a few times, because she's one of the most organized people I know, but she always has an excuse."

"Who does it belong to?"

"One of Roy's friends."

"That's what Belinda told me—she said it all belongs to Roy's friend who moved to Hong Kong. Tim or Todd . . . I'm pretty sure it was Todd."

Momma stopped. "Did you say Todd? His friend Todd is married with two kids. He lives right here in Franklin."

My breath caught and I stopped next to her. "Maybe Belinda was confused."

She shook her head. "That woman never forgets a name or a face."

"Why would she give me false information?" I knew my mother wanted me to stop digging, but I decided to take a chance. "I found something of Daddy's in there with the rest of that stuff."

She frowned and shook her head. "No. You're mistaken. That's not possible."

I tugged her next to the windows of a clothing store and lowered my voice. "It is. Remember that plaster dog I gave Daddy for his birthday when I was a kid? I found it in the garage."

"There must be a million of those dogs out in the world," Momma said. Her tone was dismissive, but I thought I heard her voice quaver a little. "You found it at the surplus store, and they had ten or more of them."

How far was I willing to go? How much did she want to know? I decided to be honest with her. "Colt saw me eyeing it, so he carted it to my new apartment."

"Why in the world would he do that?" she asked, shifting her weight impatiently. She started to walk around me, but I blocked her path.

"Because it reminded me so much of Daddy. But when he got it upstairs, the bottom of it broke, and we realized there was something in it."

Her eyes darted to the street before settling back on me. "Magnolia. You need to let sleepin' dogs lie."

"Pun intended?" I asked, which drew an exasperated sigh out of her. I pressed on. "I found a note, Momma. Addressed to me. From Daddy."

Her face paled. "Let it go. Do you hear me?"

My back stiffened. "Why are you so dead set against me finding out the truth?"

Her fists clenched at her sides. "You know your father was involved in something illegal, so why in the Sam Hill would you want to unearth more of his crimes? We're disgraced enough . . . why would you want to attract more?"

I took a step back, feeling like she'd slapped me across the face. "You mean *me*? My performance on opening night?"

"No," she said, her tone softening. "I'm talking about your father. Tongues are wagging, and they'll wag even more."

"So?" I asked. "What do I care what people think? You sure as hell never have."

"All the gossip is hurting the catering business, Magnolia. We've lost several jobs because of it." She pushed out a breath and leaned her shoulder against the building. "I may be dying, and you may not want the business, but Tilly does. And those people we hire need their paychecks."

"I had no idea."

"I figured you didn't."

"But I still want to know, Momma." I grabbed her upper arms. "I *need* to know. You always told me to never hide from the truth, even when it's hard."

She shifted her eyes to the street, then back to me. "When the hell did I ever tell you such a thing?"

"All the time when I was a kid. Pretty convenient of you to forget."

"The stakes are a lot higher now," she said, sounding weary. "There's a big difference between being grounded and getting killed."

"You also taught me to be strong in the face of adversity," I countered.

"You're supposed to outlive me, Magnolia," she said with tears in her eyes. "I can't let you get yourself killed over something stupid that your father did."

"But I'm not doing it alone." I didn't have Colt's permission to tell anyone about his involvement, and something told me he'd particularly object to Momma knowing, so I lied and said, "Brady will help me."

"He said he was leaving it in the past."

"I'll convince him. But even if I don't, I have a right to know what Daddy got mixed up in. At least tell me what you remember and let me decide whether to pursue it or not." Tears clogged my throat. "I'm not nearly as foolish as you think I am."

Her jaw tightened. "I know you're not foolish, Magnolia, and you have more self-preservation than I've given you credit for. Don't look at me like that," she said in disgust. "I might not know what happened to you the night of your graduation, but I've figured out that you left to protect yourself."

My eyes flew open. "Momma . . ."

"Let's make a deal. You quit lyin' to me, and I'll start tellin' you what I know."

I was sure I must have heard her wrong, but she stared at me with a look of determination. "Okay."

She dug her cell phone out of her pocket and started typing.

"What are you doing?" I asked.

"Telling Tilly we're gonna be late. Let's go." She started walking toward the catering office.

"Where are you going?"

"We can't talk about it out here on the street, now can we?"

"No, I guess not . . ." I said as she took off without me.

She crossed to the parking lot and headed toward her car.

"Where are we going?" I asked as she unlocked her door.

"Somewhere private to talk."

I suspected she meant her house, but when we were both seated and situated, she surprised me by pulling out in the opposite direction.

"Where are we actually going?"

"So impatient," she said, but it lacked her usual bite. "You'll find out when we get there."

She headed south before turning west, out to the countryside to Leiper's Fork. She turned again, this time down a country road, and then again, onto a private drive. I was sure she'd lost her mind, but I didn't dare question her. Had her illness affected her mind?

Finally, she stopped on the side of the road, in front of what looked like a small century-old house that had obviously been restored but was looking a little run-down. She turned off the engine and shifted in her seat to study it. "This is where it all began."

"Where what began?"

"The end."

I shook my head, even more concerned about her. "What does that mean?"

She sat back in her seat and closed her eyes. "This is where your daddy met Bill James."

"Bill James lived in this little house?" I asked in disbelief.

A grin cracked her face—and I had to admit, Bill James was about the last person I could imagine living in a homey place like this. "No. Your father and I used to live in this small house."

"What? I thought you'd always lived in *our* house."

"Sure, after we got married." She gave me a wicked grin. "But we lived in sin first, and this is where we lived."

The house didn't look like much. It was pretty tiny on the outside, and the landscape was overgrown. "How did Daddy meet him?"

"Believe it or not, it was at a barbeque we hosted. We invited a lot of friends, and Bill was a friend of a friend. They both worked for financial planning firms, and they became instant friends. Bill convinced your father to leave his firm and start a firm with him."

"I had no idea. But why are you showing this to me instead of just telling me?"

She reached for the door handle and got out of the car.

I got out too and walked to the front of the car to meet her. "Momma, what are you doing?" I found myself whispering even though no one else was around. "Somebody owns this place."

"Yeah," she said in disgust. "Bill James."

I blinked, sure I'd heard her wrong. "What? Is it a rental property?"

"No." She started walking toward the house.

I trailed behind her, completely confused. He obviously didn't live in what was probably a two-bedroom home. "Why would he buy this place?"

"Now that's a good question," she said as she walked up to the front porch and inserted a key into the doorknob.

The door swung open, and she walked into the empty living room.

"How do you have a key?" I asked, still standing on the front porch.

"I used to live here."

"Why wouldn't he change the locks?"

She stood in the middle of the small room and turned around to face me. "Because he's an arrogant asshole. He thinks he's untouchable, and up until now he has been."

What was she talking about? A buzz of excitement tickled my spine, but I couldn't ignore that we were about to enter a house we had no business being in. "This is trespassing."

"No one's here to see us." She headed toward the kitchen.

I turned around and looked toward the empty road, then groaned and followed my mother inside, shutting the door behind me. No need to make us look any more suspicious than we already did. "Why are we here?"

When she didn't answer, I followed her into the kitchen. Empty. There was an open door next to the refrigerator, so I edged over to it. "Momma?"

"In the basement," her muffled voice replied from the dark staircase.

The basement.

My head grew fuzzy and my knees turned weak. I stumbled and my butt hit the counter. I lifted my hand to my chest in an attempt to ground myself.

"Magnolia," she said impatiently.

My breath came in rapid pants, and memories of the night I was held hostage in a basement ten years ago swamped my head. My stomach churned and I swallowed, frustrated and angry that I could still be paralyzed by the mere thought of descending the staircase. I was perfectly safe, for God's sake. My dying mother was down there getting more irritated by the second that I was dragging my feet.

I could do this. I was tired of giving that man any more power over me than he already had.

I took a deep breath, steeled my back, and headed down the stairs.

chapter eleven

Halfway down the dark staircase, a mildew odor filled my nose. I stopped, holding the wood handrail in a death grip.

"Did you get lost?" Momma asked from around the corner.

"Sorry," I said, trying not to sound breathless as I reached the concrete floor. The space was dimly lit and confining. There were a few towers of boxes in front of me, and an ancient-looking washer and dryer hulked against the wall to my left. "Why are we down here? It stinks."

"You said you wanted answers."

I rounded the corner and found my mother standing beside a filing cabinet and an old kitchen table with metal legs. There was a stained map spread out on the tabletop.

I moved closer to the map, seeing that it was a plot survey. My mouth dropped open. "Is that a map of the Jackson Project?"

"So you've figured that part out, have you?" I heard the pride in her voice.

"Yeah. But only bits and pieces. Daddy sold shares to the Jackson Project, but the people in charge of it had gotten permission to tear down historic homes through bribery. Once that was made public, the whole project fell through because of legal fees, and a lot of investors lost money."

"And you know who his partners were?"

"Bill James."

"Obviously."

"Walter Frey was the CFO, and Neil Fulton was Winterhaven's defense counsel."

"Very good. And who else?"

I didn't know for certain, but decided to take a stab at the answer. "Steve Morrissey, Christopher Merritt, Geraldo Lopez . . ." I hesitated, scared to have my fears confirmed. "And Max Goodwin."

"Yes, but not the Christopher Merritt who disappeared three years ago. His father, Christopher Merritt, Sr. And yes, that snake was part of it too."

I shook my head as I studied the map. "How did the police not put them together in any of their investigations?"

"Some of them were silent partners."

"There was one more," I said, turning to face her. "Someone with a name ending in *–ogers.*"

She nodded. "Rowena Rogers."

I tried to hide the shock that my mother had known all along. "Did Geraldo Lopez kill her too?"

"No. She disappeared, out of sight, although it never made the news. She used to be one of Ava Milton's cronies," she said. "And I had no idea how people were vanishing, although I did suspect Steve Morrissey was behind your father's disappearance."

"Why didn't you tell the police?" I asked incredulously. "He would have literally gotten away with murder."

"We all have our reasons, Magnolia," she said, lowering herself slowly into a folding chair. "Why didn't you go to the police ten years ago?"

I stared at her as the blood rushed to my feet. "You're not going to ask me why I didn't tell you?"

"I know why you didn't tell me. But you could have reported it without telling me. Was it because the officers didn't believe your story about your father arranging to meet with Walter Frey the night of his disappearance?"

"No. You want to know the truth?" I asked, feeling the weight of my past pressing on my chest, making it difficult to breathe. I tugged at the neckline of my shirt. "I blocked it out."

Her eyes narrowed. I could tell she suspected I was trying to get out of answering.

"I remembered running into the woods, but at some point, everything blacked out. I woke up hours later, lying on the ground at the edge of the woods, soaked to the skin from the rain. I had a massive headache and a lump on the side of my head, and I was so dizzy I could hardly walk up the hill to the house. I stopped to vomit, but all I could think about was getting in the house so I'd be safe."

"And I berated you," she said quietly.

"I couldn't remember anything other than that something really bad had happened. I knew I was in danger, and that me being at home somehow put you and Roy in danger. So I left the next day."

"You left to protect us?"

"And myself," I said. "It wasn't a completely selfless move."

"And the blood on your dress?"

"I had a cut on my leg."

She was quiet for several seconds. "And do you remember now?"

"Yes," I said slowly. "It came back in bits and pieces, but I remember it all now."

"What happened?"

How much should I tell her? The bare minimum. "I stumbled upon someone torturing a woman, and he said if I told anyone, he'd kill you and Roy." I held her gaze. "His head was covered with a hood, so I never saw his face, but he knew my name."

She sat back in her chair, looking like she was about to tip over from exhaustion and grief. "Was it Bill James?"

I wasn't surprised she'd mentioned his name. I had my own suspicions of my father's former boss, especially in light of Brady's insistence that I not meet with him. "I don't know. Why do you think it might have been him?"

She stood, which took such obvious effort I almost offered to help. "That's why we're here. Why would Bill have bought the house your father and I used to own?

Even stranger, why would he have tried to hide that fact? He bought it through a subsidiary of a company he owns, but I found out nonetheless. I think he's hiding something here and he wants to make sure no one finds it."

"What?"

She picked up a paper off the work table. "Not what. *Who*. His wife."

Panic wrapped me up like a dirty, unwelcome blanket, and the edges of my vision turned black. I knew I was about to pass out, but I couldn't pass out in this basement. I stumbled to the chair my mother had just vacated and sat down, leaning forward to get the blood back into my head.

I felt my mother's hand on my back, moving in slow, soothing circles.

"What makes you think that?" I finally asked.

"She disappeared before your father and I were married. Brian and Bill had just started their business. Since they didn't have a lot of money, they worked from their own home offices and sometimes worked together. Your dad and I had gone to Seattle for my college friend's wedding. Bill needed a client file, so Brian told him to come by our house and pick it up."

"What does that have to do with his wife?"

"When we got back, the house was a mess. I could tell that Bill and some of his friends had partied here, and I was pissed as all get out, but that was the extent of it . . . until I heard she'd gone missing. She'd been at the party, but no one remembered seeing her afterward."

"You think Bill James killed her. Why?"

"Rumor had it that she was sleeping around. Bill didn't like it."

"So he killed her? That wouldn't be a smart move. Still, I don't understand what it has to do with him buying your house."

"There was a leak in the basement," she said, moving to a far corner and pointing to the floor. "We had to have some of the concrete ripped out and replaced. We had it done while we were on our trip, so we wouldn't have to deal with the noise and the chaos."

I swallowed bile as I realized what she was saying. "You think his wife might be buried under that concrete? Did you tell the police?"

"Your father worked with the man, so I didn't want to falsely accuse him. Besides, it seemed so unbelievable . . . But I wasn't sure, so I called in an anonymous tip and told the police about the party, and how the floor had been replaced that same weekend. They never came to check it out. Her credit card was used in Las Vegas several days after she disappeared, so they decided she must have run off."

"And you don't believe it?"

"Bill was on a business trip when the card was used. His flight was to San Diego and he paid for a hotel there, but . . . he could have booked a hotel in her name and driven there to check in."

"Did the desk people remember seeing her check in?"

"It never got that far. Her family corroborated his story. I bought the whole thing until a couple of years ago, after Roy started working for Bill. We all met for dinner, and something he said about his first wife made me think he really did it."

"What did he say?"

"He looked me in the eye with his sneaky smile and said, 'If you're smart enough, you can pull one over on anyone and everyone.'"

I shook my head. "As eager as I am to pin this on him, that's pretty generic."

"The way he looked at me . . . I would bet everything I own that he knows I'm the one who called in the tip."

"How?"

"I don't know. Just a gut feeling."

"So how'd you find out he owns the house?"

"When I need to think, I drive around, and sometimes I would find myself driving past this house. I saw it was for sale; then a few days after that dinner, I discovered it had been sold. I don't know why—maybe it was intuition—but I had a dying need to know who had bought it, especially since months passed without anyone moving in. That's how I found out."

"And you barged in and checked it out?"

"No. I only checked it out after you came back and everything was all boiling to the surface. Now I'm certain Bill James killed his wife and he bought this house to help cover his secret."

My mother truly believed Bill James had killed his wife, and she was not prone to fanciful ideas.

"So he bought the house to ensure his secret," I said. "What about all this other stuff?" I made a sweeping gesture that encompassed the filing cabinet, table, and boxes.

"The Jackson Project. Photos of big-name clients. Files on everyone in his group." She paused and looked into my eyes. "It's his trophy room, Magnolia."

Oh, God.

Panic shot through my body. This time sitting down wouldn't be enough to stanch it. I was going to throw up on the floor.

"I can't stay down here." I bolted up the stairs and found the bathroom just in time. I vomited into the toilet full of mold and water stains, then threw up again from the stench of the toilet. When I was sure I wouldn't barf a third time, I turned on the water in the sink. It sputtered, but nothing came out of the faucet.

"The water's turned off," Momma said from the hall. "But the electricity's on."

Great. I was leaving evidence of our trespassing behind. "So he can see when he goes down into the basement," I said, wiping my mouth with the back of my hand. "Can we leave now?"

"We need to get back anyway. Tilly's probably in a tizzy running the kitchen by herself."

I made a beeline for the front door. "How can you calmly tell me that Daddy's old partner is a monster, then talk about the catering kitchen in the next breath?"

"I've known about this a helluva lot longer than you. The shock's worn off."

We went out the front door and Momma locked it behind us. As we walked toward the car, I noticed she was moving slower than before. Our visit to the house had taken something out of her too, only she had a lot less energy than I did right now. I held out my hand. "Let me drive. I miss driving out here in the country."

She handed me her keys with a look that told me she didn't buy my excuse for a minute.

"Aren't you worried about Roy working for Bill?" I asked after we were both in the car.

"Of course. I've tried to warn him that Bill is dangerous, but he always tells me not to worry."

"As in he's not worried because he doesn't perceive a threat, or he thinks he can handle it?"

"I'm not sure," she said as she rested her head on the seat back. "But I have to trust he'll be okay. I don't know what else to do."

Roy didn't think Bill was a threat to him because he was probably part of whatever his boss was currently mixed up in. Now I was even more worried about Belinda getting ensnared in something deadly.

"I remember going for drives when I was a kid," I said as I started the car, "but I don't remember ever driving by this house."

"I didn't start driving by here until . . . after your father died."

Died. That was the first time she'd conceded that he'd been killed instead of running off with Steve Morrissey's wife. I briefly considered telling her about the serial numbers of the three gold bars, but quickly decided against it. I needed to wait until I had something concrete. "Did you *ever* think Daddy ran off with Shannon Morrissey?"

"No."

I turned to look at her. "Yet you didn't press it."

"When the police made up their minds so quickly, I decided not to try dissuading them. I knew your father was part of something he was ashamed of, but he refused to talk about it much. I decided dead or run off, it was all the same—he was gone. My job was to protect you and Roy."

She pointed out the windshield. "Why are we still sitting here? Did you forget how to drive?"

I hid a grin as I pulled away from the curb and made a U-turn in the road. "You said Bill James worked with famous people."

"Their connection with Max Goodwin garnered them a country music client or two."

"Any I would know?"

She rattled off a few names I vaguely recognized from the radio, then several I didn't. "Bill took the higher-profile clients," she said. "Your father preferred the new up-and-comers like Clint Duncan and Rusty Blankenship."

"And Tripp Tucker," I said. "He sued over the Jackson Project."

"Oh, yes. Tripp Tucker. You probably don't remember, but he came over to the house a few times for dinner. The poor kid's father ran off when he was a toddler, and he really looked up to your daddy. Brian tried to keep him on the straight and narrow, but Tripp ultimately flamed out."

"He died?" I asked in surprise.

"No. He had one media disgrace too many." She leaned her head back on her seat. "His label cut him, and he was bitter and angry."

"Which is why he sued Daddy and plenty of other people."

"Yeah. He lost the last of his money with that land deal. Last I heard, he's here in Franklin, living off the residuals from the songs he wrote, but he's not living high on the hog. Just gettin' by. He wasn't the only one your father took under his wing. So many young kids come to

Nashville to try to make it, and when they finally get some success after scraping by for years, they want to blow it. Your father tried to teach them how to budget and how to invest."

"I didn't know."

"That was the way he wanted it. He didn't want you kids near those boys. Tripp was the exception. Your daddy took it hard when he turned on him." She looked out the window. "Some of those boys were one-hit wonders, waiting for their call back into the spotlight. A few of them were at Luke Powell's party."

That got my attention. "Were any of them Max Goodwin's clients?"

"Most of your father's country music clients came from Max."

I cringed. "I can't believe Daddy worked with a snake like him."

"He hated that man."

"Then why did he work with him?"

"I asked him that question a million times, and the answer was always the same—the money. But I knew he was lying. I suspected Max had something on your father and kept him on a line."

"What could he possibly have had on him?"

"I don't know, but the reins began to chafe at the end, and I know your daddy had had just about enough. Maybe Max figured it out and that's what happened to him."

A month ago, I would have denied the possibility that my father could have done something horrible enough to be blackmailed. Now I wasn't so sure. But if Max had known my father well, Max must've known who I was before he invited me to dinner in New York a couple of years ago. Which meant he'd known full well he was hitting on Brian Steele's daughter.

Disgusting.

But that also meant Momma knew exactly who he was when she saw him at Luke Powell's party, and she'd said nothing. Nothing then and nothing after he was murdered.

Why?

I parked in the lot behind the catering kitchen and handed Momma the keys after I turned off the engine.

She took them and held on to my hand. "There's something else we need to discuss."

"What?"

"The business. What role do you want to play?" Her eyes held mine, showing no emotion.

"I'd like to be part of it," I said. "I know I can't cook worth crap, but I think there's still a role for me."

She nodded and a small grin lifted her lips. "I agree. You'll take on that role tonight, and I'll train you."

"Okay . . ."

She seemed to have more energy as she opened the car door and strutted across the parking lot to the back door, but before she opened it, she turned back to me. "No one else knows about that house I brought you to."

"I'm not going to tell anyone."

"I know. But I still needed to say that. No one. No. One."

I grinned despite myself. "I'm well aware that anyone and no one are synonymous in this instance. But don't you think you *should* tell someone?"

"Who am I going to tell? Buying a house and storing paperwork in the basement isn't exactly illegal."

"But it's mighty suspicious."

She frowned. "We've got work to do." Then she pushed open the door and walked into the kitchen, although it was obvious she wasn't up to her usual energy level. Two of the kitchen help was already there—a young woman who was saving up money to go to culinary school and a middle-aged woman who had confessed to me the first week I started helping that she didn't need the money. She was just bored. They were helping Tilly prepare tonight's menu—some kind of chicken, accompanied by several vegetable options and, judging by the smell filling the room, Tilly's homemade dinner rolls.

"Listen up," Momma said in a booming voice. "Magnolia's takin' charge tonight."

"What?" I gasped.

The kitchen staff grumbled, but the grin on Tilly's face told me she was pleased. At least someone was happy.

Momma pulled a clipboard off its nail on the wall and handed it to me. "This is tonight's menu. I'll tell you how long each item takes to prepare, and you can write it down next to it. Tilly knows how to make sure everything's done on time, but she much prefers the cooking while I like the managing."

"You mean bossing people around," Tilly said.

Momma shrugged with a glint in her eyes. "That too."

I leaned close to Momma and whispered, "I can't boss these people around."

"Why the hell not?" Momma asked in a not-so-quiet voice.

"Because I don't know what the heck I'm doing."

"Well, you're about to get a crash course."

She wasn't lying about the crash part. I spent the next half hour taking charge of the kitchen, preparing for tonight's event—a church banquet in Brentwood. She told me what to do half the time but let me fumble through the rest. Colt walked in through the back door at five. He stopped and did a double take when he heard me telling one of the staff how to order the pans.

He stopped in his tracks. "Is it bring-your-daughter-to-work day and somebody let Magnolia pretend to be Lila?"

Tilly laughed. "Something like that."

I shot him a glare, but couldn't hold it for long. If he was teasing me, he must have gotten over his sullen mood.

Colt started loading the van, and once it was ready, we left the two women to clean up the kitchen. He and I rode together while Momma and Tilly took Tilly's car. When we arrived at the church, the waitstaff had already begun setting up, but Momma had me take charge for the rest of the night. Part of it was that she wanted to train me, but I couldn't help wondering if she was also too tired to do it herself. She spent a good portion of the night sitting in a chair against a wall, and I caught her dozing more often than not.

I made quite a few mistakes and pissed off the staff—not that I could blame them—but I'd started feeling more confident by the time we finished. As we started to load up the vans to go back to the catering office, Momma's face beamed with pride. "You did well, Magnolia. Better than I expected."

"Thanks, Momma." Her approval meant a lot.

"Do you like doing it? I don't want you doin' this because you think it's what I want. I want *you* to want it."

"I liked it more than I expected," I said honestly. "And while part of me hated you for tossing me into the deep end, I also know why you did it."

She smiled, but she still looked so exhausted . . .

"Momma, Colt and I have the cleanup covered. Why don't you and Tilly head home?"

She started to protest, but then she conceded. "Okay."

Colt didn't look very pleased with my suggestion, but he kept his mouth shut.

"Leave the dishes for tomorrow," Tilly said. "We'll wash them in the morning." Then Momma and Tilly walked out the back door and into the parking lot.

Colt stepped up behind me and put his hand on my shoulder. "She's not looking good, Maggie Mae."

"I know," I said as I gnawed on my bottom lip. She'd gotten worse so quickly. How much longer did we have left?

Colt dropped his hand and grabbed a pan off the counter. "I can't believe you volunteered us to finish cleaning up." He pulled his phone out of his pocket and checked the screen.

I put a hand on my hip. "You got a hot date?"

He glanced up. "What?" Then he gave me a sly grin. "I'm going to listen to a friend play in Nashville. I would have asked you, but you're sleeping with Hot Stuff."

I didn't believe him for a minute. He'd set up that meeting with his contact, and the guy was supposed to pick up the bar of gold at eleven. Had Colt already dropped it off? Would he have risked leaving the remaining bar of gold behind a metal drum all this time? Doubtful. Otherwise, the person behind the cameras could have picked it up hours ago. Colt probably planned on lying in wait to see who showed up. "Who's the friend?"

"You don't know him."

"Obviously. I don't know any of your friends." And I hardly knew anything about them either.

"Let's hurry or I'm gonna be late." He grabbed a pan and headed out the back door. The two remaining waitstaff helped pack up the rest of the linens and dinnerware.

Ten minutes later, we were both in the van and headed back to the catering kitchen. Colt bounced his leg most of the way, checking the time every thirty seconds or so. When he pulled into the parking lot, he turned off the engine and shoved the keys into his pocket.

"Why don't you go unlock the back door and turn on the lights," he said as he opened the driver's door. "I'll help unload the pans and then take off."

"Why are you so antsy?" I asked. "You don't usually get so excited over women."

"I told you I'm going to listen to a friend, and he starts playing at eleven."

He didn't fool me for a minute. He'd set his trap, and now he was intent on watching it. I'd struggled most of the evening, wondering whether to confront him with what I knew, but in the end, I had decided to keep playing dumb and follow him. If Owen was behind the cameras, Colt was walking into danger. If he wouldn't let me walk in there with him, side by side, then at least I'd have his back. So to speak. I didn't have a weapon, but surely there was something I could do to help. I couldn't let him go alone.

"You head home," Colt said. "We can just come in early to clean out the rest tomorrow morning."

"I can't. I have to work at Ava's Bible study."

Colt opened the back doors of the van as I unlocked the kitchen door. After I went inside and turned on a few lights, I came back out to help Colt carry in the pans. Once we got them all inside, I opened the back door and said, "Why don't you go? I'd hate for you to miss hearing your friend."

"Thanks," Colt said, running for his truck. "I owe you."

He was going to owe me all right.

I grabbed a pan and put it into the commercial sink, then hurried over to the still-open back door and watched out of the crack as Colt steered out of the parking lot.

He wasn't going to pull one over on me.

I locked up the kitchen and ran over to my car, but when I turned the key . . . nothing. The engine didn't turn over, and the interior lights didn't come on. The battery was dead.

Dammit.

This had the stink of Colt all over it. I knew I hadn't left the lights on to drain the battery, which meant he must've messed with my engine. I climbed out of the car and popped the hood, grateful the overhead lights in the parking lot were bright enough to illuminate the engine.

My phone rang in my pocket. I expected to see Colt's name on the screen, and even had a few choice curses prepared for him, but I saw Brady's name instead.

"Hey," I said as I lifted the hood of my car. "Sorry I haven't checked in yet."

"I was calling to see when you thought you might be home."

Home. Brady's apartment wasn't home. Still, I liked the idea of having a home with someone. A peaceful, settled life. Brady could give me that, couldn't he?

My mind shifted to Colt, but I immediately threw the idea out. Guys like Colt were dead end—I *knew* that.

But at the moment, I had bigger issues to deal with, like the fact that Colt had disconnected my battery cables. At least it was an easy fix. "I'm not sure."

"Surely you're not still at the church. I know the dinner was finished over an hour ago."

I froze with my hand on the first battery cable. "How did you know that?"

"I'm not keeping tabs on you," he added quickly. "It just so happens that I have a friend who goes to the church you catered. I'd mentioned that your mother owns the catering business, and he called a few minutes ago to tell me how impressed he was."

"Huh." That was a huge coincidence, and I wasn't sure I liked it. I'd always been independent—even before my move to New York—and it felt suffocating to have someone monitoring my every move. Even if his intentions were good.

"So where are you?"

How was I going to explain that I would be another hour or more? I was tired of coming up with lies. I made a snap decision. "I'm not coming over tonight," I said, grabbing one of the battery clamps and hoping I put it on the right screw. "I'm going to stay with my mom."

"Maggie, if I pushed too hard—"

"It's not you," I said. "It's just . . . you saw my mother today. It's like she aged ten years in only a few days. I feel like I need to stay close to her right now."

"Okay. I understand. Will you let me know when you're safely locked inside your mother's house?"

"Yeah." I clamped the next cable to the battery. "But I have to clean up the catering kitchen first, so it might be a while."

"Okay. Just be safe."

"I will." I hung up and let the hood slam shut before climbing behind the wheel. Closing my eyes and crossing my fingers, I turned the key, hoping Colt hadn't messed with anything else. The engine turned over and purred.

I smacked the dashboard. "Take that, Colt Austin."

chapter twelve

I headed toward the industrial park. While I knew where it was, I wasn't familiar with the area, and I needed to park my car far enough away that Colt wouldn't see me.

When I got to Cool Springs Boulevard, I turned off and parked in the Starbucks parking lot to make a plan. I found a map of the industrial park on my phone. It consisted of four buildings—three were in a row, and the fourth was perpendicular to them. There was a street on the east side of the complex, and there was an apartment building to the south. A strip mall lay to the north and a residential neighborhood to the west—the back side. I'd seen bigger, but I had no idea where space #145 was located, and most industrial parks were wide open with few places to hide.

Dammit.

First things first—I had to figure out where to park. After studying the map, I decided to leave my car in the lot of the apartment building next to the industrial park. Then I'd walk over and slink into the shadows.

Finding a parking spot was harder than I'd expected, but I finally parked on the side of the building, away from the main street, and looked at the time. 10:45. I was cutting it close.

I got out, leaving my purse on the floorboard of the car, and shoved my keys into my pants pocket. According to the satellite map on my phone, the buildings were accessible through a thin line of trees that bordered the apartment parking lot. Thankfully, it was late enough on a weeknight that there'd be no one around to question why I was slinking off through the woods. Unfortunately, it also meant that there was no way of seeing the spiderwebs until I stepped into them. The slow drizzle that began to fall from the sky didn't help matters.

When I broke through the other side, I was at the south end of the industrial park, facing the corner of the first of the three buildings in a row. A semitruck was parked next to the first building and a Dumpster was against the wall of the second. There were no vehicles or anything flush to the side of the third building. The industrial park was wide open, so at least that direction provided places to hide. Torn over which way to go, I decided to walk the length of the building before deciding.

I stayed in the shadows and began to inch my way down the length of the building, trying not to slip on the damp grass as I searched for Colt's truck, not finding it. If he was here, he was in the back. I could march in bold as I pleased, but that seemed like a bad idea. Better to hang back in the shadows and slink my way in.

Since time was getting away from me, I took off running along the tree line, moving back the way I'd come—toward the south end of the park. I bolted for the semitruck, slipping between it and the building, and then inched along until I could peer into the alley between the first and second buildings. Nothing.

Colt had said he was putting the gold behind a barrel at space #145. I needed to get my bearings. The building next to me had multiple garage doors along the building—like a storage unit—with numbers in the three hundreds, starting with #331. The building across from me had a mixture of the garage doors as well as metal, regular entry doors. The first space was marked #230. A quick calculation told me I needed to go to the back alley.

Glancing in all directions, I made sure no one else was in view before I ran across the alley to the second building. There was no room to slide between the Dumpster and the building, so I skirted it, ducking into the shadows on the other side as the rain began to fall in earnest. The alley sloped down, making the back side of the building a good three feet taller than the front.

I took a deep breath and peeked around the corner. There was another semitruck parked in front of a loading dock, its back end to the industrial garage door. A wrought iron fence ran along the edge of the alley, which was wider than the other alleys I'd seen. The sound of an approaching car on the other side of the industrial park kicked up my adrenaline. If it came my way, I'd be discovered, but if it went the other direction, it would be completely out of my field of vision. Which meant I'd miss seeing the cameraman if it was him. Or her.

I ran for the semi.

When I reached the truck, I got down on my hands and knees and crawled under the trailer, then hid behind the side-by-side set of giant tires on the back end, molding myself around the axle. At least I was out of the rain, but enough rain had seeped into my shirt to plaster it to my arms and shoulders. My ponytail dripped a line of water down my neck.

Light showered down from a street light at the end of the building, illuminating the figure of a man who was glancing in my direction. It was Colt.

As the roar of the approaching car grew louder, I realized my mistake. If each building had thirty spaces on every side, #145 would be right around the middle—where I was currently hiding.

Torn between locating the metal drum where Colt had supposedly hidden the gold, and hiding from the headlights of the approaching car, I chose self-preservation.

I plastered my back to the wheels closest to the building, hoping the wheel and the shadows would hide me from view. I dug my phone from my pocket and read the time—10:55. Five minutes before Colt had told the (almost certainly fake) person on the other line to pick up the gold.

A dark sedan slowed to a crawl as it reached the semi, then inched around the cab of the truck at a snail's pace. When it reached the other side, it stopped with the engine idling. The slow thump of its windshield wipers set me on edge.

My heart beat against my chest and fear crawled up my spine as I heard the dull clunk of footsteps on the concrete.

Where was Colt? Had he snuck around the corner and out of sight?

As the footsteps moved closer, I realized that if the person looked under the truck, I'd be in plain sight. I scrambled toward the wheels directly in front of me. Pain pulsed through my left hand, and I looked down to see I'd rested my palm on a piece of jagged wire jammed beneath the wheel. I bit my lip to keep from crying out. After a beat, I held my breath, listening for the sound of footsteps over my heartbeat pounding in my ears, but the rain was falling hard enough to drown out the sound.

After several seconds, curiosity got the better of me, and I peered between the two sets of tires to see what was going on, hoping the shadows would hide me since the sedan's headlights were pointed in the opposite direction. A man in dark pants and a dark, hooded jacket was bent over what I'd bet a dog full of gold was space #145. After several seconds, he emerged with a packet in his hand. His back ramrod stiff, he stared at the end of the alley before turning to face the truck. The shadows covered his face.

I held my breath again, but he got back into his sedan and drove to the end of the block. I had a minor freak-out, worried he might see Colt, but he turned right, and the sound of the car's engine grew softer as it drove away.

I waited a good thirty seconds after the sound of the car disappeared before I started to crawl out from under the truck. "Colt!" I shouted over the rain. "Where are you?"

A solid metal door ten feet from the barrel opened and Colt stepped out of it. "Magnolia? *What the fuck?* What are you doing here?"

"I knew you were coming. I heard your phone call in the apartment." My hands hit the wet pavement, and I was halfway out when I was jerked to a halt. My pant leg had snagged on the piece of wire.

"You could have gotten yourself killed!" he said, sounding pissed. "Get out from under there *now.*"

"I'm trying," I grunted as I reached behind me and tugged on my pant leg.

The sound of a revving engine—a car, moving fast—filtered to us from the front of the industrial park.

"I'm not shitting, Magnolia." His voice rose in pitch. "Come on!"

"I'm not either!" I said in a panic. "My pants leg is caught on a wire."

"*Dammit!*" Colt disappeared, the door shutting.

"You're leaving me?" I cried out in disbelief, my pants no closer to being free. I was about to start crawling back under the truck to hide when Colt burst through the door, running for the semi with something in his hand.

He dove under the truck with me as headlight beams lit up the alley from the opposite end.

"Fuck!" Colt spat out as he held up a pocket knife. "He figured out the gold wasn't there."

The sight of Colt brandishing a knife and pointing it in my direction caught me off guard. I shrank back into the wheel well.

He gave me a look of disbelief, but didn't comment as he sliced through the fabric and cut me free.

Now was not the time to fall apart.

The sound of screeching tires filled the air, and suddenly the headlights were illuminating the area under the trailer. The car was headed toward us.

I pulled myself together as Colt practically threw himself on top of me, shoving me into the wheel well. "Did they see us?" I asked in panic.

"We're about to find out," was his tight reply.

The car came to a skidding halt, and seconds later a male voice shouted, "Come on out, Austin!"

"He knows who you are?" I whispered.

"Of course he knows who I am," Colt said in disgust, then his voice softened. "I don't think he knows you're here. Stay hidden and let me deal with this."

"No!" I whispered-shouted. "He'll kill you."

"No. He wants the gold, and he doesn't think you know where it is."

"I *don't* know where it is."

"Exactly. That makes you expendable. He thinks I'm the only one who *does* know, and he'll never get it if I'm dead. So trust me on this."

I grabbed his sleeve in a tight grip and twisted to look up into his face. "No! Colt, *please* don't do this."

"I'm tired of waiting, Austin," the voice shouted over the rain. "And I know you're under the trailer, so come out before I start shooting!"

I strained to hear the voice better, trying to figure out if I recognized it, but there was so much noise interference—the rain, the windshield wipers, my frantic heartbeat—it was hard to tell. Besides, if it was Owen, I'd never heard him shout like this before.

"Maggie," Colt said, sounding frantic as he tugged at my hand. "Let go. He's going to kill you."

"He's going to kill you too," I said in a tearful voice.

"No. He won't," he whispered. "Just trust me, okay? Now listen. If I say go, run for the door I just came out of. Got it?"

"What about you?"

"Don't worry about me. I'll follow." Then he broke free of my grip and shouted, "I'm coming. Don't shoot!"

I started to cry. I couldn't let him get killed because of me. "Don't do it."

Colt cupped my cheek and searched my face. His own face was shrouded in shadows. "Mags. I've got this. Promise me you'll stay hidden unless I yell go."

I wasn't sure I had another choice. I nodded. "Okay."

Still holding the side of my head in his palm, he leaned in and placed a quick kiss on my forehead. "Good girl. Be ready to run as fast as you can if I give the word."

Then he handed me the pocket knife and shouted, "I'm coming out, and I'm unarmed."

"Then do it!" the man shouted.

Colt crawled on hands and knees. "Don't shoot."

"Keep your hands where I can see them!" the man shouted.

It maddened me, but I still couldn't tell if I recognized his voice.

Colt got to his feet and took a step.

I realized the phone was still in my left hand and the knife was in my right. I put the knife down, swiped at the screen, and opened the camera app with fumbling fingers, turning on the video. I held it out enough to pick up a glimpse of Colt.

"Stop right there!" the man shouted in a raspy voice. "Where's the gold? The package was empty."

"I don't know," Colt said. "But I know it wasn't meant for *you*."

"Don't be a smart ass, or I'll shoot you where you stand! I want that gold bar *now*!"

Shit. This guy wanted to know the location of the gold, and Colt was clueless. I wasn't so sure Colt would escape this unscathed.

"I left it there," Colt said. "My contact must have taken it."

"I want it!" the man shouted. "And the rest of the gold too."

"And I want a brand-new Lexus, but we don't always get what we want."

A gunshot rang out, and I nearly dropped the phone and screamed. There was the sound of metal hitting metal—the bullet must have ricocheted off the metal floor of the trailer several feet from me. Clapping a hand over my mouth, I turned and tried to peek around the tire to make sure Colt was okay. He was still standing.

"I don't have the gold," Colt shouted, sounding panicked. "Stop shooting at the ground!"

The man didn't answer and there was silence for several moments, long enough to worry me. I peeked through the tires, poking my phone out to capture the guy on video. I wanted confirmation that it was Owen Frasier—and so far I didn't have it.

The figure stood in front of his car, the headlights on behind him, casting his face in shadows, not that I could see much of his features anyway. He was still wearing that hooded jacket, and the hood was up and over his head. It was impossible to tell who he was. I moved quickly behind the tire, out of sight, but continued to hold up the phone.

"Where's the gold?" the man shouted.

"It's hidden."

"I want it by Saturday night. Or I'll kill Magnolia. I swear."

"I'll get it!" Colt insisted.

"I know you'll be at the fundraiser Saturday night. Bring it there. I'll be in touch with instructions."

"To a masquerade ball?" Colt asked in disbelief. "Am I supposed to show up as King Midas?"

"How you transport it is your problem!" the guy shouted.

It seemed like the bad guy's problem too—he was going to have to cart it off after Colt delivered it . . . but what was I thinking? Colt couldn't deliver something he didn't have.

"Don't try some bullshit move on Saturday," the man said. "I won't be so forgiving next time. In fact, I know Magnolia is hiding underneath that trailer, and I just might take her with me as collateral to prove I'm serious."

Oh shit. I tried not to panic as I picked up Colt's knife. Everyone knew better than to bring a knife to a gunfight, but it made me feel better to have some sort of weapon.

"What the hell are you talking about?" Colt asked.

"I saw someone else under there when I pulled up, and I know you two are working together."

For the first time since I'd known him, Colt didn't have a smart-ass answer.

"Not to worry," the man shouted. "It's in my best interest to leave her alone for now. Remember—Saturday night. I'll let you know the time later. And don't tell anyone about this, or I'll kill her anyway. Now turn around and place your hands on the truck and stay that way until I leave."

Colt didn't answer, but I heard a slight banging sound on the metal to my side. Seconds later, the car began backing up, then got to the end of the alley and took off.

I turned off the camera, which most likely captured nothing more useful than a bunch of images of the bottom of the trailer, and waited what seemed like forever. It was most likely about ten seconds, but Colt finally said, "It's safe to come out."

I peered around the side and then glanced up at Colt, who now stood several feet away from the truck, scrubbing his hands over his head.

"Was it Owen?" I asked as I crawled out, still holding the knife. I cringed when the rain started pelting me again.

"I don't know." He sounded frustrated. "But I don't think so. The headlights made it impossible to get a good look. But it really didn't sound like him."

I debated asking whether he'd had enough previous contact with Owen to recognize his voice—and if so, why—but decided to let it go. Priorities. "What are you going to do? We don't have the gold."

He paced a couple of steps. "I don't have the answer for that either." Then he turned and reached for me. "I think he's gone, but we need to get the hell out of here."

A new wave of fear hit me, anchoring my feet to the concrete. There was no way for Colt to comply with the guy's demand. "What are we going to do?"

"*I'm* going to find the gold. Now come on." He marched over, took the knife from me and closed it in a single, fluid movement, and then grabbed my upper arm.

I came to my senses and shuffled my feet to keep up as he dragged me through the door and into the dark space beyond it.

"I know you didn't put the gold bar in the package," I said, "but do you still have it?"

"Yeah. I have it," he said. "Obviously handing it over wasn't in our best interest, but I had to give him something. And I had a feeling he might come back after the note I left." A thin beam of light clicked on, and I realized it was from Colt's phone. It lit up the space enough for me to see it was a small office area, but Colt was already opening another door and pulling me with him.

The flashlight beam didn't cast much light, but I could tell we were in a small warehouse space and Colt's truck was in front of us.

"What did it say?"

He chuckled. "Let's just say I insulted him in almost every way a person could, from his masculinity to his intelligence."

I glanced around the room. "How did you get in here?" I asked.

"A friend of a friend." Still gripping my arm, he pulled me around the back of the truck and to the passenger door. After he shoved me inside, he shut the door and disappeared, but a garage door was already opening into the alley on the opposite side.

Now I knew where Colt had disappeared to after the sedan pulled up. He must have run around the building and come into this space, but I still wasn't sure how he could have watched the guy pull up and check behind the barrel.

He got into the truck as the garage door continued to open.

"What was your big plan?" I asked. "Were you going to confront him?"

"Does it look like I intended to?" he asked in a short tone.

"Then how were you going to find out who it was?"

He turned to me with anger-filled eyes. "I had a plan, Magnolia, and you just fucked it up."

My stomach tightened as he started the truck, maneuvered it into the alley, and then parked and got out, leaving his door hanging open. He punched a code into the key pad on the side of the building, and the door began to close.

He got back and shifted into drive. "Where's your car?"

"In the apartment parking lot, next to this property."

Colt drove down the alley, then turned toward the back of the industrial park instead of the entrance.

"Why are we going back this way?" I asked. Did he plan to go back and look for evidence by the barrel?

"I'm trying to save your life." He shot me an exasperated glare. "Do you trust me, Maggie? From here on out, I need you to trust me. Because you're either all in or you're not. What do you pick?"

I had several reasons not to trust Colt—I was sure he had his own agenda—but I was also sure he'd keep trying to protect me. He'd proved that several times. I made my decision—stupid or not, only time would tell.

"I'm in."

chapter thirteen

y nerves were so strung out, I didn't even realize where Colt was going until he pulled up to a metal box on top of a pole. There was another gate at the back of the property. He rolled down his window and punched several numbers into the pad.

"How do you know the code?" I asked as the gate began to slide open.

He frowned as his hands held the steering wheel in a death grip. "I told you. I have a friend of a friend." When the door was open wide enough, he drove through the gate into the neighborhood I'd seen on the satellite map.

"Why are you going out this way? My car's in the parking lot behind us."

"Because he might be watching the front." He kept darting glances at the rearview mirror intently as the gate closed behind us. Probably making sure the guy didn't follow us.

"He knew I was there."

He sighed as he drove away from the park. "Not a surprise, I guess. If he made out a woman, it wouldn't be a leap for him to assume it was you. I need to figure out what to do with you."

His phrasing caught me off guard. I involuntarily sucked in a breath and slid toward the passenger door— and was instantly filled with shame. I *knew* he wouldn't hurt me, yet my instincts had taken over. I was in survival mode.

He shot me a glance with narrowed eyes. "That's the second time tonight you've acted like you're afraid of me. Why?"

"It's not you," I said. "Just all those years in the big city. Instinct."

He didn't look convinced, but he let it go as he continued to drive, checking his mirrors. Several blocks later, the street ended at the junction of another street. After taking another sweeping glance at our surroundings, he turned right, even further away from my car.

I almost asked him what he was doing, but I'd already told him that I trusted him. And while that didn't mean I was going to let him call all the shots, I decided to keep my mouth shut for now.

Colt turned right and drove for nearly a half mile until we came to a church on the right side of the road. He pulled into the lot and parked in the back, out of sight from the road.

"Why are we back here?" I asked, turning in my seat to face him.

He was quiet for several seconds. "I'm trying to figure out what to do to make sure you're safe."

I started to shake, both from fright and the cold—my clothes and hair were soaked. Colt slid off his jacket and draped it over my shoulders, then turned on the heater.

"He didn't threaten to hurt me until Saturday night, right?" I paused, preparing myself for an argument. "Maybe we should tell Brady." Sure, if the guy turned out to be Owen, Brady and Owen were friends, but I had to believe he would protect me, and Colt in turn.

Colt smacked his open palm on the steering wheel. "I *knew* you would want to tell him. I warned you not to get close to him."

"Colt," I said, turning sideways in my seat and leaning toward him. "He can help us."

Rage filled Colt's eyes. "I swear to God, Maggie, if you tell him, we are done as friends."

I gasped, feeling like he'd just stabbed me with his pocket knife. I'd expected him to fight me on it, but I'd never expected his reaction to be this strong. "Colt!"

"End of discussion."

"Is this because you have a record? You think he won't treat you fairly?"

He shot me a look.

"I know about your past, Colt. Or at least that you have one. It stands to reason you'd have a record."

"It's more complicated than that. I'll tell you what I can, but for now, please trust me that we need to keep all of this as far away from the police force as possible. And that includes Bennett."

I didn't protest, mostly because I had no idea if Brady would believe Owen might be out to hurt me. "Okay. But I want to know about your original plan."

183

"I told you."

I waited for him to continue, and when he didn't, I prodded. "Yeah, you have a friend of a friend who owns the place. Got it. But that doesn't explain your plan."

"I put the envelope behind the barrel around ten forty-five. Then I waited for him to show up."

"Your phone call this afternoon was a fake, right?"

He grinned. "Not entirely. I called my cell phone carrier and ignored the prompts."

"Sure, he showed up, but we're no closer to figuring this out. It was hard to make out his voice, but it sounded raspier than Owen's. So if it wasn't Owen, was it someone working with him or someone else entirely? And if it was someone else entirely, he has to be someone familiar with my father's friends, or one of yours."

He shot me a scowl. "I'm not ruling anyone out right now, but my guy is a vault. I trust him. I still think it's Owen or one of his cronies. But maybe the footage will help tell us."

"How did you know I took a video?" I asked.

His eyes widened. "*You* took a video?"

"Yeah, but I don't know what we'll see. I didn't think of it until he came back the second time, but I was trying to keep out of sight, so it was at the wrong angle. Probably blurry, too, because of the rain." I narrowed my eyes.

"Let's see it."

I pulled out my phone and played the footage. Between the rain, the bad camera angles, and the blinding headlights, it quickly became apparent I hadn't gotten anything useful.

Shutting the app once the video was finished, I snuck a glance to Colt. "If you weren't talking about my video, what *were* you talking about?"

"The reason I chose that location in the first place. I have access to the security cameras on the loading dock." He dug his phone out of his pocket, swiped the screen, and pulled up an app. After logging in, he held out the phone so I could see it, showing me the current view of the loading dock area—dark and raining. Then he touched the screen and the image started rewinding at a rapid pace. He clicked on it again, slowing the recording down, and then pressed play. I watched as Camera Colt appeared with a folded-over manila envelope. He disappeared when he got within a couple of feet of the building.

"Why'd you disappear?" I asked.

"The barrel was out of the camera's range," he said. "Denny—my friend of a friend—had some trouble with vandalism, and he installed the surveillance system to see who was responsible. There's a camera on the other side too. But the barrel is just out of view."

"And he just gave you the password to look at the footage?" I asked in an accusatory tone.

"Hell, I set it up for him."

"*What?*"

"I have several skill sets," he said with a smirk. "How do you think I found those cameras in your apartment so quickly?"

Good point.

"I would have angled the ones at the loading dock differently for this," he continued, "but I didn't have time, and it would have been difficult to explain why I was messing around on the roof." He started the footage again, and Camera Colt stepped back—presumably from the barrel—and walked offscreen to the right.

"Denny typically doesn't have deliveries on Wednesdays," Colt said as he fast-forwarded the video. "That truck wasn't supposed to be there. I was counting on being able to use both cameras." He slowed the feed down to normal time again when the sedan came into view. The man got out of the car, advanced toward the barrel, disappeared, and then returned to his car. He glanced around before getting into the sedan and driving away.

"Anything useful?" I asked. I hadn't seen anything that looked helpful, but Colt was obviously more experienced with this sort of thing.

"Not from this angle. Let's watch the rest of the footage, although I'm pretty damn sure he stayed out of range when he came back."

He let the tape continue to play. I could see my head peeking out from under the trailer, then Colt diving underneath. Headlights shone on the wet pavement; then—several long moments later—Colt crawled out with his hands up. Neither the guy nor the car were visible.

"Shit," Colt cursed. "Let's try the other camera. I was hoping to at least get a license plate number."

"If you got one, you could find out who it belonged to?"

He shot me a look that suggested my question had insulted him to the core.

"Sorry."

He tapped the screen, and sure enough, a new angle showed up—the semi from the other side. There was some distortion, probably from the raindrops, but the view was clear enough. A car whizzed backward across the screen, but Colt kept rewinding.

"What are you looking for?" I asked.

"You. I want to see when you showed up." As if on cue, I appeared on the screen, scooting backward out from underneath the trailer. He stopped the video, then let it play normal time. "What gave you the idea to hide under there?" he asked.

"I heard the car and knew I had to take cover."

"He could have killed you, Magnolia." Colt sounded pissed again.

"We've already established that, but from here on out, you can't exclude me from your sting operations."

"Why would I include you?" he asked in disbelief. "There was absolutely no reason for you to be there tonight. Hell, the only reason I came was to verify that he showed up and capture him on video."

"You're telling me you wouldn't have gone out when he came back?"

"Hell, no. I'm not an idiot. I would have let him spout off and hopefully incriminate himself—or at least give me something I could use."

"So I risked your life," I said as horror washed through me. "It's my fault he made that ultimatum."

He sighed and slumped back into the seat. "I understand why you did it. Hell, I would have done the same thing in your shoes, but I didn't tell you what I was doing for this very reason. I didn't want you to put yourself at risk. But from now on out, I'll tell you what I can."

"What you *can*?" I asked in disbelief, jerking my hand from his. "Why not everything?" Then it hit me. "You're not just doing this for me. I don't think you're even doing it for the gold, but it's sure a nice bonus. What are you up to? *Really?*"

He remained silent.

All my insecurities came to roost. Men had always used me and then tossed me aside. I couldn't ignore that most of them had been like Colt—womanizers. But I'd considered Colt a friend, my first real male friend, and I hadn't expected this from him. Then it occurred to me, once again, that Colt didn't have friendships with women. Shoot, even Belinda had pointed that out. The truth was hitting me square in the face, and I was hurt and embarrassed. "You're using me."

He remained silent, confirming my fears. I reached for the door handle, but he leaned over and gently grabbed my hand. "Maggie, stop."

I did as he said, mostly because I couldn't believe he wasn't really my friend. Right or wrong, I'd grown to count on him. I wasn't sure I could endure losing him right now. "I want the truth. Are you using me?"

"I know it looks that way."

No admission of guilt, but no denial either. My wounded pride turned to anger. "For how long?"

He looked out the windshield.

Colt was the person whom I had trusted and confided in the most in all of this. I couldn't do this alone, and I sure couldn't handle his betrayal. "Was any of it real?" I asked through tears that clogged my throat.

"Maggie." He choked on my name.

"You're not even going to tell me how you're using me or how long you've been doing it?" I shook my head. "Scrap that. I know how long. I'm not stupid. You started using me the night we met at Luke Powell's."

"I'm your friend. I swear."

"But you won't deny you're using me?"

"I promise you that it's not like it sounds."

"It sounds pretty bad, Colt."

He turned to me. "I know."

"You just begged me to trust you, only to admit you're using me. Why the hell should I trust you?"

Something shifted in him—the expression on his face shuttered, and when he spoke, he sounded unlike himself. "I got caught up in something years ago, and I'm still paying for it."

"Your record?"

He didn't answer, but I could read between the lines.

"You're not even going to lie and come up with some bullshit answer to smooth this over?"

Exhaustion covered his face. "I'm tired of lying to you, Maggie. I don't want to lie anymore."

"You don't have to lie anymore. We are no longer friends." I reached for the door handle, but he pulled me back, more forceful this time. He grabbed my shoulders, turning me to face him. "You're not safe, Magnolia, and not just from Frasier. You've stirred up a hell of a lot of shit that has been lying dormant for years. They've been waiting for you. You're the trigger that started it all over again."

I lost all my fight. "What are you talking about?"

"You know what I'm talking about. Your father."

My anger resurfaced. "So your job is to spy on me? Find the gold and share it with your buddies?"

"It's not that simple, Maggie."

I pointed my finger in his face. "Don't! Don't you dare call me Maggie. Only my friends call me Maggie."

"I am your friend," he said, but he sounded tired. "I may be the only real friend you have in this whole mess." He reached for my arm, but I jerked out of his reach.

"Don't touch me."

"Look," he said as he ran his hand through his hair. "I know you're pissed, and I understand, but I really do care about you. Think about it—why would I have saved you back there otherwise? I'm doing everything in my power to make sure you're safe. I can't say the same about everyone else in your life."

The sad part was I suspected he was right. "Who are you?" I asked, my voice shaking.

"I'm exactly who I said I was. Colt Austin. Aspiring country music singer and song writer. Part-time employee for Southern Belles Catering."

I shook my head. "No, you're more than that. You're leaving out a piece."

"Your friend," he said quietly, inching closer. "And more." Before I could react, he lowered his mouth to mine, hauling me to his chest in a tight embrace. Maybe he expected me to resist—part of my brain screamed to resist—but my body disobeyed. I kissed him back with a desperation so deep I couldn't find the bottom.

Desperation because I knew the truth, and I hated myself for it: I wanted Colt. I'd always wanted Colt. Brady was a kind and decent man who offered the promise of a good and normal life—the kind of life I'd once imagined with Tanner—but some screwed-up part of me didn't want that. Instead, I wanted what I knew would ultimately end up hurting me, because I knew deep in my gut that Colt Austin would hurt me, yet some stupid part of me didn't care.

What the hell was wrong with me?

Still, I kept right on kissing him, my lips begging him to be the man I needed. My heart told me that he cared about me—he'd risked his life for me—but my head insisted his actions might be driven by some ulterior motive he refused to share.

My head won out. I put my hands on his chest and shoved him away.

"Don't." I choked on the word as a sob bubbled up. "You used me. You betrayed me. But I guess I'm the fool, huh? Because I kissed you back, just like one of those stupid twits who follows you around."

"No," he said, anger in his eyes. "You're not like them. You mean more."

"Then prove it! Tell me what you're doing."

"I can't."

I wiped a tear from my cheek, some stupid part of me refusing to believe he was the bad guy here. Surely there was some explanation. Why would he be so invested in this investigation? My gut told me it was more than the gold. "Are you with the police? Undercover?"

"No, Maggie. I'm not an undercover cop."

"Then what are you?"

"A man in shit so deep he can't see any way out of it."

And I was in there too, mucking around with him.

"What do you really plan to do with the gold?" I asked, sounding as weary as I felt.

"Honest to God, I want to take the gold and leave the country. With you, Maggie. I'm not leaving without you." He paused and searched my face. "If you believe nothing else, believe this—I will never hurt you. And I won't let anyone else hurt you either. I should have known Lopez would come looking for the gold, even though I have no idea how he tracked it to you. Rico was careful when he started digging."

Holy shit. Colt knew details about my father. "Me," I said in a whisper. "I asked him if the missing money could have been hidden in small packages. He said it was bigger than drugs. What was my father involved in?"

He shook his head.

"What do you want?" I asked, knowing I sounded desperate. "I'll give you anything you want for what you know. You want all the gold? You can have it. Just tell me what you know."

"Oh, Maggie. I can't."

"Can't or won't?"

"Both."

I turned away from him. "Take me to my mother's."

"I know you're pissed."

I swiveled back around. "*Pissed?* You treat me like I'm some stupid idiot, unworthy of the truth or unable to deal with it, and you think I might be *pissed?*"

"No. I'm not treating you like an idiot. I'm trying to protect you."

"Why does everyone think I need protecting?" I shouted. "Sure, I may not be a cop, but I can handle bad things. After everything I've been through, I think I've proven that."

"What have you been through, Maggie?" he asked quietly. "Why did you slink away from me twice tonight? There was pure terror in your eyes when you saw the pocket knife in my hand."

Oh, shit. I had said too much.

"What happened the night you disappeared?"

It was the second time I'd been asked that question today, but unlike my mother, Colt didn't deserve answers. Not when he was keeping them from me. "None of your fucking business."

He sighed and turned back to the steering wheel, grabbing hold of the lever to shift gears, but he paused. "I know it may not seem like it, but I *am* on your side. I'm stuck in the middle of something I don't want you involved in, but I'm doing everything in my power to keep you safe." Then he put the truck in drive and drove around the side of the building.

We were quiet on the ten-minute drive, and the closer we got to Momma's house, the more my anger subsided, replaced by uncertainty.

Colt pulled into my mother's driveway. He grabbed the steering wheel, his jaw tightening. "I think you should go to Bennett's tonight."

"You could kiss me like that and still send me back to Brady?" I asked in disbelief.

He didn't answer for several seconds. "I care about you enough to do whatever it takes to keep you safe."

I'd never been more confused in my life, but I had to believe Colt wanted me to be safe. Otherwise, he would have left me behind earlier, after the sedan came back. Had he cared more about his safety than mine, he would have slipped into that building alone. Instead, he'd stared down the barrel of a gun in the hopes it might keep me safe. A gun he wouldn't have faced if I hadn't shown up. And I had to agree with Colt's reasoning about going to Brady's, even if I felt lower than scum for going back to him after I'd so willingly kissed Colt.

I shrugged off his jacket, letting it fall to the seat, then opened the truck door. Colt grabbed my arm. "Maggie. Text me when you're in his apartment, okay?"

"Yeah." I hurried out before he could say anything else and ran up to Momma's front door. I unlocked the door as quietly as I could and let myself in, hesitating for a moment as I watched Colt pull out of the driveway. I went into the kitchen to find a piece of paper and a pen to write her a note saying my car had broken down so I'd borrowed hers, but I'd drop it off at the catering business early in the morning and walk to Ava's. Maybe she could call Tilly to pick her up. Then I grabbed the keys out of the bowl on the entry table and left.

I was paranoid enough to continually check my rearview mirror, but the drive was uneventful. Then again, I was probably safe—at least from this threat—until Saturday night. I'd worry about how to handle this newest threat tomorrow.

Once I was in the parking garage, I parked in a space in front of Brady's car, relieved to have gotten there safely. After I got out, I walked toward the elevator but tripped on a crack in the sidewalk and put my hand on the hood of his car to keep from falling on my face.

It was warm and water droplets still covered the roof and hood. Brady had driven it recently.

I took a second look at it. Brady drove a dark sedan like the one that had been at the industrial park tonight.

I gasped and stumbled backward. There had to be an explanation. I almost didn't go up but decided I was being overly paranoid. Brady had checked in with me throughout the day to make sure I was safe, and like Colt, he had shown that he was concerned with my well-being.

Still, my nerves were frayed, and I spent the whole elevator ride up to his apartment second-guessing my decision. By the time the elevator doors opened, I'd decided to go back to Momma's. Tomorrow I'd find some time to buy another gun to replace the one that had been stolen from my purse with the gold—I'd feel better if I could protect myself rather than relying on someone else. But just as I was about to push the call button to close the doors, I saw the door to Brady's apartment open. Owen stepped out. He glanced at me and did a double take.

My body froze, and I started to panic, but I told myself to calm down. I had no proof that Owen was the man in the parking lot. In fact, I suspected he wasn't. But I didn't have time to speculate about what he did or didn't do or know. I had to assume the role of a good girlfriend, and I had to assume it fast.

Brady noticed his odd behavior and stepped over the threshold, carrying a large mailing envelope in his hand. "Maggie. You said you were staying with your mother."

"I changed my mind," I said, still in the elevator as I kept my gaze on Owen. The doors started to close, and I snapped out of my daze, telling myself that I had to sell this. I reached out an arm to keep the doors open. "Sorry. I'm just a little surprised to see Owen here so late."

"I'm here on police business," Owen said. He was sniffling, and I noticed his nose was red like he had a cold.

"Oh! I'm interrupting. I can go."

Brady shook his head. "No. Owen was on his way out."

"Yeah," Owen said. "I'm not feeling so great. I plan to go home to bed." His voice sounded mostly normal, but it had that tight, strained sound that often comes with a cold. I suspected he would be incapable of yelling without his voice distorting.

No. My imagination was kicking into overdrive. Wouldn't he look at me differently if he'd just threatened to shoot me less than half an hour ago?

I stepped out of the elevator, and Owen's gaze scanned my body up and down. "Did you get sprayed by a dirty puddle?"

I knew I was drenched, but I glanced down, and sure enough, I had dirt and grease stains on the knees and on the outer edge of my right thigh. *Think of something!* "My car broke down," I said. "And I was trying to figure out what was wrong."

Concern filled Brady's eyes. "Why didn't you call me? I would have helped you."

I smiled, trying to push all my negative thoughts away and play the girlfriend role. "I'm a grown woman in the twenty-first century, Brady Bennett," I teased. "I don't need a man to save me."

"I know you don't *need* one," Brady said softly. "But there's nothing wrong with asking for help."

"Well, Momma and I sorted it out, so no worries."

"What was wrong with it?"

"I'm not sure, but we checked all the usual issues, then called Momma's AAA and had it towed."

"How did you get here?"

"I borrowed Momma's car." I glanced up at Owen. "Are you here about Emily Johnson's murder?"

He looked startled. "Yeah, in a way." The words ended in a cough.

"I hope you get the monster who did this," I said in all sincerity.

He seemed caught off guard by that too. "We're working on it."

I reached up on my tiptoes and kissed Brady on the cheek. "I'll let you two get back to your police business. I'll just go inside and get ready for bed."

Brady offered me a smile. "I'll only be a few minutes."

"Take your time."

I walked past Owen, feeling his gaze on me as I went inside.

"Why are you acting so weird?" Brady asked in a hushed voice.

"Are you really sure about this?" Owen asked.

I'd walked into the hallway that led to the bedrooms, moving slowly, acting unhurried, but as soon as I was out of sight, I texted Colt that I was at Brady's. I considered telling him about Owen but decided I'd tell him tomorrow.

I hustled into Brady's bathroom and turned on the shower before hurrying back out into the hallway. No way was I going to miss this conversation, but I wanted them to feel they didn't have to hold back. That there was no way I could hear them.

"Do you have any idea how hard it was to get all the information in there?" Owen asked.

"Thanks," Brady said. "I'll never tell anyone I got it from you."

"You won't have to because it will be too damn obvious. How'd you know, anyway?"

"An old case of mine," Brady said. "I'll talk to you in the morning."

"Hey, before you go," Owen said. "About Magnolia..."

"No. I'm not having this conversation again. Good night."

I hurried back into the bathroom, now facing a new dilemma—I was in desperate need of a shower, but there was no way I could sleep with Brady after that kiss with Colt. Not that I was about to let Colt know how I felt about him.

Also, there'd been something weird about Owen's visit tonight, something that made me feel like Brady wasn't totally being on the up and up either. Part of me wanted to leave, but how would I explain my sudden departure to Brady without looking suspicious? Where would I even go?

I would spend the night in the apartment, no matter how slimy I felt, but nothing more.

What on Earth was I going to tell him, though?

I locked the bathroom door, then quickly unbuttoned my shirt and dropped my pants. I had just gotten into the shower when I heard him banging on the bathroom door.

"Maggie?"

"I'll be right out!"

I expected him to put up a protest, but I didn't hear anything else as I quickly washed my hair and body. I realized my fatal mistake as I grabbed the towel and got out. I hadn't brought any pajamas in with me.

But when I opened the bathroom door, Brady wasn't in the bedroom, even though the covers were rumpled like he'd been in bed.

I quickly grabbed my most modest pair of pajamas—a pair of shorts and a loose shirt—put them on in the bathroom, then wandered out to the living room to find Brady.

He was standing in the kitchen with the envelope in his hand, looking at something printed on stiff, shiny paper. A photograph? When he noticed me, he quickly stuffed it back into the envelope. "Feel better?"

"Yeah. Sorry I locked the door. Habit."

"But you live alone."

"For one week. After ten years of roommates, it's going to take longer than that."

He walked over to me and leaned down to give me a kiss, but I turned my head, letting his lips brush my cheek.

"I have a terrible headache," I lied. "I can see you're engrossed in whatever Owen brought you, so why don't I go to bed and let you keep working on it?"

"Are you sure?" he asked, not sounding convinced.

I glanced up at him, overwhelmed with guilt. "Yeah," I said, glancing away. "Especially if it helps you find whoever killed Emily."

He pulled me close, resting his chin on top of my head, and I resisted the urge to cry. I didn't deserve someone like him. I didn't deserve a normal, happy life, and thanks to my own fool heart, I was never, ever going to have it.

I pulled away and headed down the hall, too ashamed to speak, but I could feel his eyes on me. I stopped in the doorway and glanced back at his worried face.

"Do you want to take something?" he asked.

I gave a tiny shake of my head. "I already did. Good night, Brady."

"Good night."

As soon as I lay down in bed, my head started racing over the entire day, but I'd been up since the early hours of the morning, and exhaustion soon won over. Yet as I drifted off, I realized Brady had been up just as long.

What was in that envelope?

chapter fourteen

I woke up in a cold sweat and tangled in the sheets, traces of my nightmare lurking in my subconscious. Brady wasn't in bed, and the digital clock on his nightstand read 3:44. Had he gotten another phone call in the night?

I got up and went into the bathroom, then wandered into the kitchen.

Brady sat at his kitchen table with a bunch of papers and photos spread out before him. His head jerked up when he saw me. "Maggie. What are you doing up?"

"I woke up and you weren't there. I thought maybe you got called in on a case. Did you ever come to bed?"

"I did, but I woke up and couldn't go back to sleep." He stood and walked around the table toward me. "I would have told you if I had to leave."

I tried to look around him, tensing when I saw a photo that looked like a naked woman in an awkward pose. Had Brady gotten out of bed with me to look at porn? But a second later, I registered that it was a photo of a dead woman. I wasn't sure that was much better. "What are you doing?"

"Just going over some paperwork," he said, putting an arm around my back and ushering me back to the bedroom.

"How long have you been up?"

"Long enough that I'm ready to go back to bed." He guided me to the edge of the mattress and lifted the covers. "Hop in. I'll be back after I get a glass of water."

I did as he asked while he headed back into the kitchen. After a minute or so, I heard the water running, and Brady appeared a few moments later. He set the glass on the nightstand and then slid in beside me, pulling my back to his front. His hand reached under my shirt, skimming my stomach. I resisted the urge to pull away.

"Say, are you working for your mother Saturday night?"

After the last fundraiser I'd worked ended in murder, Momma and Tilly forced me to take the night off. Still, I wasn't about to tell Brady I'd agreed to go with Colt. "I'm not sure," I hedged. "Why?"

"My mother wants me to go with her to a fundraiser. My father will be out of town on a business trip, and she doesn't want to go alone."

"The Middle Tennessee Children's Charity event?"

"That's it. Is your mother catering it?"

"Yeah. But you know it's a masquerade ball, right?"

He groaned. "My mother failed to mention that part."

"You'll be fine," I said. "Most people don't wear their masks for long."

"I don't suppose I can convince you to come with me?" When I didn't say anything, he continued, "I don't want to pressure you. I realized you'd need to ask your mother for the night off if you work."

Crap. Colt had asked me to the same event, and I'd said yes. If I went with him, I was sure to run into Brady. Part of me wanted to avoid the fundraiser all together, but if Colt actually found the gold and followed through with the handover, it didn't feel right to skip out. I owed it to him to accept the risk too. Nevertheless, I took the chicken way out. "I'll think about it."

"Good." He pulled me closer and buried his face into the back of my neck.

I closed my eyes, but all I could see was the photo of the dead woman. "What were you looking at?" I asked.

He stiffened, then pulled me closer. "I told you. Paperwork."

"For a case?"

He rolled me over to face him and caressed my face. "This kills me, Maggie, especially when I know trust is a huge issue with you, but most of my job is confidential."

"So it was for your job?"

"Yes."

"I saw a photo of a dead woman. How can you stand it?"

"What I see is hard sometimes."

"Like with Emily?"

"Yes. But I'm her advocate now, if that makes sense. She can't help herself now, so I need to step up and seek justice for her." He paused. "That sounds corny."

"No," I said softly. "That sounds noble." It only drove home my heart's stupidity.

"My mother hates what I do—in fact, I got an earful this afternoon when she called about the fundraiser. She wants me to go into insurance with my father."

"I can't see you as an insurance salesman," I said.

"I'd hate it. I like what I do . . . but I hope it doesn't get in the way of starting something with you."

He fell asleep soon after, but I couldn't stop thinking about those files and the fact that he'd gotten up to look at them after he came to bed—if he'd even come to bed. I lay in the dark for what seemed like forever until I finally decided to get up. I slid out from underneath Brady's arm and carefully got out of bed, trying not to disturb him. When I was standing next to the bed, I hesitated. What if Brady found me doing what I planned to do?

I crept into the hall and turned back to look in the room. Brady was still asleep.

I'd do this quickly.

Tiptoeing into the kitchen, I turned on the light over the stove—enough light to see what I was doing but hopefully not enough to wake Brady. I spun around, looking for the envelope, and found nothing. Where had he stashed it? He hadn't been out here for more than a couple of minutes max, which included gathering up all the photos and papers. That would have left him with precious little time to hide it. If I found it, though, and he caught me looking at it, I wouldn't be able to claim I'd stumbled upon it.

I had to be really sure this was what I wanted to do.

And I was . . . because something about the woman whom I'd glimpsed in that photo looked familiar, and it would eat at me until I figured out why.

I opened drawers and cabinets, searched under the sofa and behind the drapes. I was about to give up when I decided to check the coat closet, and that's where I found it—hidden in a basket of gloves and scarves. Which meant Brady really hadn't wanted me to find it.

What was he hiding from me? Why?

I took the envelope into the guest bathroom and locked the door behind me. Sitting on the tile, I dumped the contents onto the floor. There were multiple photos of dead women, all naked and all covered in blood. I closed my eyes and took a deep breath. I was going to see this through.

I opened my eyes and picked up one of the papers. It was a police report of a woman's murder, which had occurred twenty years earlier. Her body had been found in the woods up in Hendersonville. Her cause of death had been blood loss due to a cut through her carotid arteries, but her body had sustained multiple cuts, mostly angled lines, but also one oddly shaped cut.

My heart slammed into my throat. An oddly shaped cut.

There were few clues and no leads. The murderer was never found.

I knew I should look at the photos of her body, but I couldn't bring myself to do it.

I picked up the next report. Another female victim, this one murdered seventeen years ago. It was a similar case—her body had been naked, covered in cuts, one of them distinctly unusual, and she'd bled to death. She had been found one hundred miles west. No leads. No resolution.

There were two more reports, a murder fourteen years ago, and then one ten years ago. Ten years . . . Her body had been found the first week of June, near Clarksville. Same cause of death as the others.

Without reading anything else, I knew. She was the woman who had been tortured in the basement of the house I'd stumbled upon in the woods. No wonder I hadn't found anything about her murder in the news. He'd taken her body over an hour north. Her name had been Melanie Seaborn, and her murderer had never been found.

But I knew he was out there. Waiting. Stalking me. Still killing women.

I had witnessed this poor woman's torture. I owed it to her to see her photo. But I had to flip through several other crime scene photos before I found hers. I tried to look away, but the vacant look in the women's eyes caught my attention. The same monster had ended all of their lives.

Was it Bill James?

But I let that thought go as I found Melanie Seaborn's photo. She lay in a ditch, completely naked. Her body was very pale, and there was a slit across her throat. I recognized her face from that night ten years ago. Her photo was the one I'd seen on the table. My brain just hadn't connected the dots—maybe it had been making a last-ditch attempt to protect me from what I'd seen, from what I knew. But now that I had the photo in front of me, there was no denying it. I remembered her frightened face now, her terrified eyes. She'd probably hoped I could help her, but I'd been tied up and injured myself, too weak to help either one of us. I saw the knife slashes on her body. The cuts I'd seen him slash onto her flesh that night in the basement.

Then I saw the mark on her thigh. The C with a slash through it. The same mark I bore on my own thigh.

I picked up the other photos and found the same mark on every single woman.

Brady knew that my scar hadn't been caused by any cookie cutter. He had chased me down yesterday morning after Emily's murder, fearing for my life. I'd suspected why—and this seemed to verify it. My stalker had murdered Emily, and he must have carved that horrible mark into her leg. And now Brady had a packet of photos of murder victims, all bearing the same mark.

Why hadn't he confronted me about it? Did he think I was selfish for not telling him the truth? *Was* I selfish for keeping the information to myself?

There was a loud rap at the door, and I let out a half-scream as Brady called out, "Maggie? Are you okay?"

I gathered up all the photos and papers, desperately trying to stuff them into the envelope. What was I going to do?

I did the least productive thing I could come up with. I started to cry.

*Dammi*t.

I didn't have time for this. I needed to figure out a plan.

But there wasn't any time for that. The door burst open and Brady stood in the opening, worry filling his eyes.

Then his gaze fell to the envelope in my hands and the papers still on the floor, and he squatted in front of me.

"Maggie."

I looked up into his face, unsure of how to handle this.

He took the envelope from me and then rose, pulling me to my feet. He wrapped his arms around me, tugging me flush against his chest, and I sobbed against his shirt.

We stood in the bathroom for several minutes, and when I started to settle down, he led me out to his living room. Once we were seated on the sofa, side by side, he took me in his arms.

I felt equally terrified and protected. I told myself that it was a good thing that Brady knew. The weight of the truth had begun to crush me. Now I could share it with him, and he could help protect Momma and Belinda.

"Maggie," he finally said, breaking the silence. "When did you really get that scar?"

"Ten years ago," I said. "The night of my high school graduation." Then I told him everything. How I'd caught my best friend's boyfriend cheating on her in the woods behind my house. The hooded man who had dragged me down to the basement of the house where I'd found refuge. How I slipped in and out of consciousness after he'd slammed my head into the metal pole. The woman's screams—Melanie's screams—had almost deafened me. How he'd carved that symbol on my leg as a warning to keep my mouth shut. Then I'd come to outside in the rain, lying on the ground in the woods, remembering only my fear and the certainty that I needed to leave and stay away. Then how it had started coming back in bits and pieces as soon as I returned to Franklin.

"I was sure I'd imagined it," I said in a shaking voice. "I *hoped* I'd imagined it, so I went out into the woods to look for the house. I don't know why . . . to prove it didn't happen? To prove it *did?* But I found it, still abandoned, and that's when everything came flooding back. I knew I had to tell someone, so I went to the police station, ready to tell my story, but then I had second thoughts. I was already under suspicion for Max Goodwin's murder. I realized what a stupid idea it was to come forward now, especially since I didn't have any solid information. Besides, it happened ten years ago."

"That was the night you were at the police station. The clerk at the desk said you had information you wanted to share."

"I chickened out, and then I saw you, and I was so shocked you were a cop, well, there was no way I was going to tell you anything."

"I'm glad you told me now," Brady said quietly.

I looked up at him. "Emily had the mark, didn't she?"

His fingers lightly stroked my arm. "Yes. She did."

Fresh tears welled in my eyes. "It's my fault she's dead. I knew it as soon as you told me."

"No, Maggie. It's not. It's the fault of the person who killed her."

"If I'd told you . . . but I was scared he'd hurt Momma or Belinda."

"Why would you think that?"

"He's been texting me."

"*What?*" He jerked upright. "Jesus. The night Walter Frey was murdered . . ." His eyes widened. "The text you were going to show me was from him."

I nodded.

"Magnolia. Why didn't you tell me?"

"Because he sent me a text warning me to keep my mouth shut. There was a photo of Belinda attached to it." Tears clogged my throat. "He hates that I'm here with you. He killed Emily to remind me not to tell you. Her death is my fault."

"No. It's definitely not."

He was kind to try to reassure me, but I had information he didn't. "There might have been another reason he picked her," I said. "After I left, she asked a lot of questions about why I took off. My return to town seemed to renew her interest. I never told her anything, but maybe the murderer knew."

"That's just speculation," he said calmly.

"Maybe. But it was definitely a warning. He told me so." I grabbed his arm, frantic. "You have to protect Momma and Belinda. Can you put them under police protection?"

"It doesn't work like that," he said softly.

"You're not even going *to try*?"

"There are other ways we can fight him. Can you show me the texts? If there's a number attached, we'll have a way to track him."

"They came from a blocked number. Can your people still track it down?"

"Maybe." His face remained calm and reassuring despite the fact I was becoming more and more agitated. "Who else knows about this?"

"About what? My attack?"

"Yes. That. The reason you ran off. The texts." He gestured to my leg. "Even the scar. Who else knows?"

"No one," I said slowly. Momma knew some now, but I wasn't going to admit that yet. "Why?"

"Because we can keep this to ourselves. We can pretend like you didn't tell me."

That was not the reaction I'd expected. Then again, he'd gone to great lengths to hide that file from me, and he hadn't said one word to me about the connection between my mark and this . . . this serial killer's calling card. Something wasn't right here.

"Can I see the texts?" he asked. "Did you really delete the one you received the night of Walter Frey's murder?"

"Yes. I've deleted all of them, but I took screenshots first."

He was silent for a moment. "Colt's text . . . that night at the restaurant. He sent it to cover for you."

I avoided his gaze. "I guess you really are a good detective," I said with a forced grin.

"So are you two . . . more than friends?"

Before last night, this would have been an easy answer; now it was ten times more complicated. Still, I spoke the truth. "We're friends."

He took my hand and caressed the back of it with his thumb. "Can I look at the screenshots?"

"Yeah," I said, standing and tugging my hand free. "My phone's next to the bed."

"I can get it," he said, but he sounded . . . eager. I suddenly had reservations about showing him. But why? Common sense told me that I should tell him everything now that I'd shared the hardest bits. That I should tell him about my suspicions of Bill James, but common sense also told me something was off. His implication that he'd keep this between us, that he wouldn't take it to any greater authority, just didn't sit right.

"No," I said, already heading to his room. "I'll get it."

I hurried to the nightstand and picked up my phone, relieved I'd insisted on it when I saw two texts from Colt and one from Belinda. Colt's texts had both come soon after midnight, the first acknowledging my text that I was safe. The second was something I definitely didn't want Brady to see.

Got a good lead on a possible location for Au. Let you know more tomorrow.

Au? What was Au? Then my high school chemistry class came rushing back. Au was the symbol for gold. *Good thinking, Colt.* But how had he come across a lead so late last night?

The text from Belinda was even more mysterious and had been sent at 5:12.

We need to talk. Text me when you can.

Was she okay?

"Maggie," Brady called from the other room. "Are you okay?"

"Uh . . . yeah . . ." I considered texting Belinda back, but Brady would probably get suspicious if I took too long. Plus, I didn't want her reply to come while he was looking at my phone. As I headed back down the hall, I pulled up my photos app and found the hidden folder.

Brady had gotten up while I was gone and stood in front of the coffee maker, pouring water into the machine.

"I figured neither one of us was likely to go back to sleep after this."

"True."

He put the pot on the burner and turned it on. "Did you find the photos?"

"You're not going to file a police report?"

He walked over to me and rested his hands on my shoulders. "Do you want me to file a police report?"

I shook my head slightly. "Uh . . . no, but isn't that beside the point?"

"No. It's exactly the point." He bent at the knees so our eyes were level. "You were scared to tell me because you were afraid of what I'd do once I found out—create a report, bring lots of other cops into the investigation. Sure, I could do that, but what purpose would it serve?"

"What I know might help catch him."

A soft smile lit up his face. "Maggie, I'm working Emily's case. If you tell me what you know, I'll use that information to help find the killer. Then no one else needs to know about your involvement, and you're safe. But even better—you'll know you can trust me."

Except his reaction was having the opposite effect. Alarms were ringing in my head. First he'd concealed the real reason I was at the bar the night Walter Frey was murdered, and now this. I needed time to think.

"The photos?" he gently nudged.

I almost didn't show him, but at this point, why continue to hide them? What kind of person would I be if I withheld information that could help find the killer?

I scrolled up to the first message and handed my phone to him. He sat at the kitchen table, and I lowered myself into the chair beside him. "I received the first one the night I came back. After Max's murder."

Welcome home, Magnolia. I've been waiting.

Brady looked up at me. "That's creepy as shit, Maggie. Why didn't you go to the police?"

"I didn't remember anything at that point. I had no idea what he was talking about. I thought it could be a crazy stalker after the whole YouTube incident."

"Let me see the next one."

I took the phone and swiped the screen, showing him one after another, reliving each horrifying threat as I did so. In addition to the screenshots of the texts, I'd also taken pictures of the magnolia blossom left for me on Momma's porch and the poor dead cat that had been left for us too.

Brady studied the screen for several seconds longer than necessary to read the messages. "You've communicated with him," he finally said.

I realized I hadn't told him that part. "Yes."

His eyes lifted to mine. "Would you be willing to talk to him again?"

I froze and stared at Brady in horror. He might as well have asked me to light myself on fire.

"Just bear with me," he said in a pleading tone. "He thinks you haven't told anyone. We could set a trap for him."

My mouth dropped open.

"Okay," Brady said patiently. "I can tell you're unnerved. We'll revisit the idea later." He grimaced. "Sorry. It must have been overwhelming for you to finally unburden a decade-old secret."

I forced a tiny smile. "Yeah."

He reached over and covered my hand on the table. "Look, I can see that me not taking an official report is bothering you. I can do it if you'd like. I'm just trying to make this easier for you. You've been through one traumatic experience after another. I'm just trying to protect you."

I resisted the urge to stiffen my back. Everyone kept telling me they were doing things to protect me, but I was having trouble believing it. Besides, something told me I had to rely, first and foremost, on myself.

"Come here." He set my phone on the table, then stood and tugged me up into his arms. I closed my eyes as I leaned my head on his shoulder, not sure whether to believe him or not. When he said it like that, it sounded perfectly reasonable. But it still *felt* wrong.

"What do you want to do?" he asked while I was still in his embrace. "How about we go over the benefits of either option?"

"Okay," I said, suppressing a yawn. "But I need some coffee first." And the opportunity to stall and think things through.

A slight grin tugged at his lips. "Good idea." He dropped his hold on me and returned to the coffee maker.

I needed to go to the bathroom, but my phone was still sitting on the table, unlocked. I hesitated to leave it there, allowing Brady full access while I was out of the room, but it would look suspicious if I took it with me. "I'll get the creamer."

"Sit," he insisted. "You must be emotionally exhausted."

"Thank you." How could I doubt Brady when he'd always been so insistent about protecting me? But then again, was it normal for him to be this protective? I understood he was a cop, so it was probably an instinct, but his attention had always seemed so personal. Colt, I understood to some degree. We'd been friends for four weeks, and while he'd offered help in the beginning, it was only in the last week or so that his intentions had begun to seem more genuine and from the heart. I'd grown to trust him, which now seemed foolish after he'd revealed he was caught up in something dirty.

My mind was whirling with half-formed thoughts, suspicions, and theories, though, and there was no way I was going to figure this out now. I sat down, and before I knew it, Brady was handing me a steaming cup of coffee. He took his seat and watched me.

I resisted the urge to squirm under his scrutiny. It was becoming more and more clear to me that I'd been drawn to Brady because I'd thought he could protect me. Not only that, deep down I'd been sure I would reach a point where I could entrust him with this terrible secret and that he'd make me feel safe when I did. Only, I wasn't feeling that way at all.

"So let's consider your options," he said.

My stomach tightened into a ball.

"If you don't file a report," he said, "the killer will have no idea you've told anyone. And since we can't provide protection . . ."

"But *why* can't you protect them?"

Sympathy filled his eyes. "Budget constraints, the fact that there haven't been any substantive threats other than

216

a text . . . And even if we did, it wouldn't last very long. This guy's been at this for years. I suspect he'd be patient and wait for the protection to go away."

I cradled my hands around the mug to hide their shaking. "So you're saying that this is a way to protect them. He'll leave Momma and Belinda and everyone else I care about alone."

"So far no one else has picked up on the strange marks on the victims. They go back twenty years, but the bodies were spread all over Middle Tennessee and separated by several years. Then ten years ago, as far as I can tell, they stopped." His gaze held mine. "Until you showed up. A few days later, his first victim in a decade appeared, and for the first time, the body was found in Franklin. Before Amy Danvers, they were all scattered around."

My peripheral vision began to darken and tunnel. "He killed Amy."

How could I be so stupid? Of course, Amy. The police had asked Belinda if Amy had been a cutter. While I'd started to suspect someone else had murdered Max Goodwin and Neil Fulton, it hadn't occurred to me until today that the man who'd tortured me could be responsible for Amy's death. And if she had been killed to conceal the identity of Max and Neil's real murderer, didn't that mean the serial killer was connected to whatever conspiracy my father had been involved in? But I wasn't ready to make that connection, at least not with Brady.

I lowered my head between my legs to keep from passing out. I'd personally known two of this serial killer's victims, and a third had been murdered in front of me. It was too much.

Brady's hand rested on my upper back and began to rub up and down in a soothing motion. "I'm sorry. I thought you saw her file in the packet."

"Her photos were in there?" I asked in a shaky voice.

"No. Just her report."

I took several deep breaths, then lifted my head. I refused to look weaker than I already had. "You told me it was a suicide."

"The report ruled it a suicide," he said softly, "but it always felt a little off. Yes, her wrists were sliced and there was a note, but she had that strange mark on her leg. The one you have. It was a little too neat for me." His expression turned earnest. "But I'm worried for your safety, which is another reason I want to keep your involvement quiet. I told you I suspect there's corruption in the police department . . . Let's just say I think it would be better if your name stayed out of any reports."

I sat back in my chair, my heart kicking into a gallop. "Am I in danger from the police too?"

"No. But I would feel better keeping any attention off you, which means I need to tell Owen. I need help."

Should I tell him about the little chat I'd had with Owen two days ago? Or the possibility that he'd either installed those cameras in my apartment or knew who had? But it didn't seem like the right move to ask Brady to pick between me and his best friend. "No. No Owen."

"Maggie . . ." he said in frustration.

"No. His uncle was involved in all of this years ago. I don't trust him."

"He likes you, Maggie. He's concerned about you."

I stilled. "How do you know that?"

"He's asked about you. Everyone in the department knows Emily was your attorney, and he's worried how you're handling it."

"What did you tell him?"

"I haven't told him anything. There wasn't anything to tell, but now there is, and I need his help. I can't do this alone."

My alarms were going off again. "What do you mean you can't do it alone? Isn't there a whole team of police working on Emily's murder?"

"Of course." He sat back in his chair and groaned in frustration. "But at this moment, I'm the only one who's tied all of these cases together, and I don't trust everyone in the department. I *need* Owen to help me investigate."

He didn't trust his department to handle a serial murder? How corrupt *were* they? That sounded . . . wrong. "What about the FBI?"

"I'll call them in, but I need Owen's help too. I need to tell him *everything*."

There was no way in hell I was going to agree to that. "Didn't he pull all those case files for you?"

"I need to tell him what happened to *you*."

I looked away. This conversation would not end well.

"Maggie, I think you're letting his uncle's involvement in your father's case cloud your judgment. Owen's a great guy. Sure, I think he's gotten sidetracked by his own mission to clear his uncle's name, but the whole thing ripped his family apart. The guy I know would have never lied on a report about a victim's cell phone being stolen."

"You knew all along?" I asked in disbelief.

"Of course I knew, but I also had no idea why Owen was lying about Frey's phone, so I went along with it, hoping there was a method to his madness."

That meant Brady had lied to me. "Why hide the reason I was at the bar from Owen?"

"The less he knew about your involvement, the better." He shifted on the sofa toward me. "He blamed your family for what happened to his uncle's reputation on the force. And in turn, I suspect he blamed you. But now that he knows you, he's realized you have nothing to do with it. You were a kid when it happened. You're an innocent caught up in the madness. You're not responsible for your father's actions."

"But he didn't trust me, which means he was watching me. That's why he showed up at my apartment so quickly after I called and told you that Geraldo Lopez was trying to kill me."

"And that's how I know that Owen is still inherently good. He protected you."

I almost told him I was sure he was wrong. Owen had shot Dr. Lopez to keep him from telling me something. Besides, Owen had made it pretty clear he didn't think of me as an innocent.

I looked into Brady's warm and concerned face. Would he believe his best friend was more crooked than he thought? All I knew was that, uneasy as I was, I still needed Brady's protection, and the surest way to alienate him would be to tell him his best friend might be trying to kill me.

chapter fifteen

Part of me wanted to run far away until the entire mess was resolved, but I wasn't going anywhere now that I was finally getting answers. I had to go back out into the world. Hopefully I could do it armed with more information.

"What is Bill James's involvement?" I asked bluntly. I wasn't ready to share anything Momma had told me, especially since she'd asked me not to tell anyone. "Why did you warn me to stay away from him?"

"I think he's dangerous."

"Obviously. Why?"

"I'm sure James was much more involved in a land project your father was running than he claims."

I held up my hands. "Whoa. Wait. You think my father was running the Jackson Project?"

"You know about the Jackson Project?"

Crap. He had no idea what I'd learned over the last few days. "Ava Milton mentioned it yesterday."

That piqued his interest. "After I told you about Emily's murder?"

"No. I was cleaning a bunch of newspaper articles out of her attic. She's hoarded boxes and boxes of them. I'm surprised the fire marshal hasn't fined her."

"So what do you know about the Jackson Project?" he asked.

How much should I confess? "I know that he suggested some of his clients invest in the project, but it got sued and his clients lost a lot of money."

"Magnolia," he said in a patient voice. "Your father knowingly bilked millions of dollars from investors in the Jackson Project."

"Okay . . ."

"He brainstormed it. It was his pet project."

"*What?*" Feeling like I was about to jump out of my skin, I got to my feet and walked over to the window.

Brady stood too, though he had the sense to stay several feet away. "I'm sorry."

I kept my back to him as I watched the horizon turn pink through blurry eyes, which pissed me off. I'd kept my shit together for ten years, fourteen if you counted my father's disappearance, and I did. I'd been called delusional and a liar in my insistence that my father had been innocent of any wrongdoing. But the deeper I dug, the less I recognized the man I'd loved. Nevertheless, I was done with crying. Crying didn't solve shit . . . unless you were trying to weaken a man's resolve. In this case, my tears weren't going to do a single thing to change the facts.

"No," I said as I clutched the neckline of my pajama shirt, twisting it around my fingers in an effort to ground myself. "I knew he was involved, but not that he was in charge."

"He did a good job of hiding his involvement by using Winterhaven, a dummy corporation, but Owen figured it out. Even if your father created it, I'm sure Bill James is dirty, and I wouldn't be surprised to find out he played a role in all those kidnappings and disappearances."

"And murders," I added. "There were recent outright murders, but let's also call the disappearances what they were. Murders."

"But recently they got sloppy," Brady said. "They never left dead bodies behind before Goodwin's murder. And now Amy's murder . . . I have to wonder if the serial killer is tied to the other disappearances and murders. It all changed with Max Goodwin's death."

The day I came back. It couldn't be a coincidence that the serial killer had started killing again, and Daddy's old business partners had started dying within days of my return.

"How many women?" I asked.

He looked startled. "What?"

I spun around to face him. "How many women have been murdered by the serial killer?"

He rubbed his forehead with the back of his hand. "I don't know, Maggie. Eight. Maybe more. That's if we count Emily Johnson and Amy Danvers. Amy's case was curious, but then I saw the mark on Emily . . ."

"How did you know the details of Amy's body before you got that packet? I thought her case was handled by the Brentwood police."

"It was, but I'd become invested in the case because of your involvement. And like I said, the suicide seemed fishy to me, so I asked to see the report. It was the photos that stuck with me. No one thought much of the cuts on her legs, but I knew I'd seen that mark before."

"So you knew about the other women before Amy?"

"Yes and no. I knew about the murder in Clarksville. I remembered seeing the mark on her leg."

"That case was ten years ago," I said. "You didn't graduate from the police academy until eight years ago. How could you have seen it?"

"It was a cold case kind of thing. Groups that try to solve unsolved mysteries."

"You joined it as a cop?" I asked in disbelief.

The first hint of irritation filled his eyes. "I wasn't a detective when I joined the force, and I told you that I like investigating. So yeah, I joined a few online groups. They had no idea I was a cop. It was with that group that I heard about another murder, the one from fourteen years ago. So I started looking into other cases and realized there must have been a serial killer."

"Why haven't you already contacted the FBI?"

"I *did*. A guy contacted me; he looked over the cases, then said it was nothing. But it doesn't seem like nothing to me. So I contacted them yesterday, and they're coming in to take a look." His eyes searched mine. "Maggie, now that you're involved, I'm more determined than ever to find the bastard." He hesitated. "In all honesty, you shouldn't have even looked at the files, and I definitely shouldn't have shared what I did, but I thought you had a right to know."

I remained silent, still seeing those dead women in my head. Even if I hadn't seen her photo, Emily was one of them now. And even though I knew Brady was right—that the murderer had killed her, not me—I felt responsible.

Who would be next?

Brady moved in front of me and rested his hands on my shoulders. "You can't tell anyone that you know about the cases. I put my job on the line by telling you what I did. If it got out that I shared confidential information, I would lose my job."

"Okay," I said, quieter than I'd intended, but the shock of the whole situation was hitting me hard. "It's not like I've told anyone else about that night anyway."

But that wasn't true. I'd told my mother less than twenty-four hours ago. A decade-old secret treated like yesterday's gossip. I couldn't help wondering if I'd pay a price for that.

I noticed the clock on the stove read 6:45. "I have to get ready for work."

"Right now?"

"I have to be at Ava's early today."

"Why?"

I narrowed my eyes. "Because she's one of my bosses, and she told me to come in early."

"She can't make you work overtime to pay off the damage to the apartment. You were *attacked*, Maggie. If that's what this is about, let me know, and I'll see if I can do something before you have to resort to hiring an attorney."

I shook my head. I wasn't sure whether to feel grateful or annoyed. The last thing I needed was Brady butting in any more at Ava's. I was a grown woman who didn't need the guy she'd been staying with to stand up for her. "No. That's not it. She knows I'm looking for some extra money, so she's given me extra chores to do this morning," I lied. "It was actually very sweet of her."

"Ava Milton sweet?" he asked in disbelief. "That's a first."

"So you *do* know about her?"

"By reputation. Everyone in town knows she's a busybody and a bully."

I nearly protested the bully label, but I could see how she'd earned it. "I'll admit that she's difficult to work for, but I've worked with plenty of difficult people before. She's more bark than bite."

"Then you haven't gotten to know the real Ava Milton yet." He lifted his hand to my cheek. "Thank you for sharing your experience with me, but I need to ask something of you. Something that will be really hard."

"I already told you I wouldn't say anything about the other women."

"That's not it." He paused. "I need you to take me to the house. The one you found before you came to the police station."

I took a step back, bumping into the window. "The house where I was held hostage?"

"Yes."

I wasn't surprised by the request, but I started shaking anyway.

"I'll be with you the entire time," Brady said, resting both hands on my upper arms. He bent a little at his knees, making our eyes level. "And it will be just you and me. No one else, so you won't feel intimidated or concerned that anyone is watching you."

"Don't you need to bring the other police?" I asked. "The guys who collect evidence and take photos? Shouldn't we tell them?"

"No. I'll see it with you first, and then I'll bring them in later."

"How will you explain finding it? Won't you need to tell them about me?"

He rose to his full height and kissed my forehead, his lips lingering for several seconds. "Not if I do this right. I'll have someone call in an anonymous tip or something. I'm going to protect you, Maggie. I promise."

"But—"

His phone rang in the bedroom, and he gave me a pleading smile. "You trusted me enough to tell me your story. Trust me to protect you in this too."

Something about it didn't feel right, but Brady had already admitted that he suspected cops on the force were dirty. I decided to ignore the niggling feeling that suggested he wasn't on the up and up. "Okay."

His phone continued to ring, but he asked, "Can you get away this afternoon?"

"Don't you need to answer your phone?" If someone was calling him this early, it had to be important.

"It can wait. This is important. What do you have going on this afternoon?"

My heart raced at the thought of going back to that house, but it made sense that he would need to see it. I'd told myself there wasn't any evidence there after all these years, but that had partially been to assuage my guilt because I was too worried about what my stalker would do if I told anyone the truth. "I have the Bible study until twelve thirty. Then I work at Alvin's until six. He wants me to help him with inventory after we close at five."

"What about after?"

A shiver ran down my spine. "It gets dark soon after six."

"I'll have a flashlight." His eyes hardened. "And my gun."

Common sense told me that the killer wouldn't be there, but I was still terrified.

"I hate to ask you to do this, Maggie, and I wouldn't if it weren't important."

My mouth was dry, but I managed to say, "I know."

"I'll be with you every step of the way. I won't let anything happen to you." He searched my face. "Do you believe me?"

I nodded, then whispered, "Yes."

He took my hand and pressed it to his chest. "Thank you for that."

I nodded again, unsure of what to say.

"I can pick you up from Alvin's shop if you'd like."

"Okay. We'll drive out to Momma's and hike through the woods behind the house. I'll need to bring a change of clothes."

"Is that going to be a problem?" he asked.

"No. I can change at Momma's." His phone started to ring again. "I heard her and Tilly say they were going to see a movie. Now go answer your phone."

"Thank you, Maggie. I know this is hard." He kissed my forehead again, then headed down the hall to his bedroom, leaving me standing in the living room.

I could think of ten million things I'd rather do than go back to that house, but I'd do it if it helped Brady find the killer. I owed Emily, and so many other people, much more than that.

chapter
sixteen

"There's the box?" Ava asked when I walked in through the back door, slightly sweaty after my five-block walk from the parking lot outside of the Belles, made more strenuous by the fact I'd packed up all my belongings at Brady's and brought them with me. There was a huge pot on the stove and several baking sheets were spread across the counter.

I closed my eyes, then blinked them open. "I'm sorry. I forgot it." How could I have been so stupid? I'd been so anxious about going to that house later, I'd spaced out about everything else.

"Did you get it done?"

"No, ma'am." But I wasn't so sure it mattered, at least from my perspective. I'd been searching the box for clues about my father's involvement in the Jackson Project. I'd gotten plenty of information from other sources.

"Why do you look so bedraggled?" she asked, narrowing her eyes. "You look like you've been awake for two days."

She wasn't far off. "I haven't been sleeping well."

"Well, be sure to put plenty of concealer on to cover those bags under your eyes before you play hostess in a couple of hours. I can't have you looking bad in front of my guests."

I nodded slightly, too tired to get angry. "Yes, ma'am."

I started to head out the swinging door toward the dining room, but she called after me in a harsh tone. "Where do you think you're going?"

"Back upstairs to work on the other box of papers."

"That can wait," she said briskly. "I need your help in the kitchen."

I turned around but stayed in the threshold between rooms. "Like I told you, I'm not much help in the kitchen."

"Poppycock," she said, grabbing an apron out of a drawer. She started to hand it to me, but after she got a good long look at my jeans and well-worn, blue, scoop-neck T-shirt, she stuffed it back in the drawer. "There's plenty you can do." Then she reached for a coffee mug, filled it with coffee, cream, and sugar, and handed it to me as I approached her. "Here. You look like you could use this."

I took it from her, trying to cover my shock. "Thank you."

"Don't be thinking I've gone soft," she snapped as she grabbed a spoon and started to stir something in a bowl. "I need you to perk up, or we'll never get everything done."

I hid a small smile as I took a sip. Maybe there was something to my mostly bark and little bite theory after all.

"I need you to remove those croissants from the baking sheet and put them on that blue and white plate," she said, her side still to me. "Are you capable of such a simple task?"

"I hope so. I'll do my best."

The corners of her mouth twitched. "At least you're honest."

I started working on my assigned job, and to my surprise, she broke the silence.

"Are you still searching for information about your father?"

I stopped mid-scoop, then resumed my task. "Yes, ma'am. There was helpful information in that box you gave me."

"Is that so?"

I nearly laughed at her smug tone. I decided to be honest with her. "I found out he was part of the Jackson Project. A big land deal gone wrong."

She tsked and shook her head. "Quite a few people lost money on that venture."

"I also had no idea my father had helped manage some country music artists' money."

"He was known for it for a while, which was why I was so surprised to hear he'd run off with Shannon Morrissey."

"He didn't run off with Shannon Morrissey," I said with a frown. "Geraldo Lopez killed him." Or at least that's what a lot of people believed now. It didn't explain the serial numbers on the gold.

"Are you sure about that?"

I froze. What did Ava Milton know? And more importantly, why hadn't she told anyone? "What do you know about my father?"

"More than we have time to discuss before my meeting."

I shook my head and pointed my spatula at her. "Do you really think you can drop a statement like that and expect me to stand around with my tail between my legs, waiting for you to decide when to give me another nugget of information?"

She dropped her utensil into her bowl and slowly turned to face me, her face expressionless.

Ava was going to fire me, and I probably deserved it. Even so, I sure as hell wasn't going to apologize. I held her gaze, accepting her challenge.

Our stare-off lasted several more seconds before her head dipped slightly, a gleam of approval filling her eyes. "She has a spine."

"I have a hell of a lot more than that. What do you know about my father?"

Her head tilted to the side, and she studied me as though seeing me for the first time. "Contrary to what you might think, Magnolia, I do have a career. Do you know what it is?"

My gaze landed to the multiple baked goods in various stages of completion on the counters, but as well-known as she was for her culinary endeavors, I suspected that wasn't what she meant. "No, Miss Ava. I have no idea."

"Come now, Magnolia. I pegged you as being brighter than that. What do I have in my attic?"

She had boxes and boxes of information. Ava Milton wasn't a mere gossip. She used the information she collected. "Are you a blackmailer?"

To my surprise, she burst out laughing. When she finally settled down, she was still smiling. "On occasion, if I'm being entirely honest, but only when it was for the greater good."

"So what do you do with the information you gather?"

"I save it. I dole it out when needed. I correct wrongs and reward rights."

"That's not really a career, is it?" I asked. "You don't get paid for that kind of thing."

"It depends on your definition of being paid." She waved her hand toward my baking sheet, which still held several croissants. "Get back to work. Are you incapable of working and talking at the same time?"

"No, ma'am."

She picked up her spoon and continued to stir. "Many people were upset with your father after that land deal went south, but two country music artists lost everything. One sued your father and various others and won. The second remained angry but silent. He held quite a grudge."

"Tripp Tucker sued Daddy. I found that in the box. Who was the other?"

A smug grin lit up her face. "Someone didn't do her homework."

"Most of the people who were involved in Daddy's business deals are dead. Walter Frey, Steve Morrissey, Max Goodwin, and Neil Fulton. Christopher Merritt disappeared like Shannon Morrissey and Daddy."

"And Geraldo Lopez," Miss Ava added. "He's dead."

"Owen Frasier killed him."

"And that's an interesting coincidence, don't you think?" she asked.

"Because his uncle was the detective who investigated my father's disappearance?"

"Very good, Magnolia." She sounded pleased. "But before we move to Gordon Frasier, you're missing two people from your father's group."

"Bill James and Rowena Rogers."

She glanced over her shoulder at me, her eyebrows raised.

"But I hear Rowena Rogers disappeared."

"Did she?"

I stopped scooping the croissants. "You know everything about everyone. How could you not know?"

She turned at the waist to look at me. "I don't know everything, Magnolia Steele. I don't know why you left town a decade ago."

My face flushed and I glanced down at the baking tray. "I'm not sure that's entirely true, Miss Ava. I suspect you have your suspicions."

She chuckled. "I've heard the usual. You ran away after a fight with your mother. You were pregnant and ran off to have the baby."

My head jerked up. I hadn't heard that one.

"You were deluded into thinking starring as Maria in *West Side Story* onstage at Franklin High School qualified you to act on Broadway."

My mouth twitched. "I made it to Broadway."

"My personal favorite was that you ran off with an older rich man and he dumped you in New York, and you were too embarrassed to come home."

If only. "And which one do you believe?"

"None of them." She had a knowing look in her eyes that chilled my blood.

She couldn't know, but my heart kicked into a gallop all the same.

"Something bad happened to you that night, Magnolia Steele. You ran away to save your life."

chapter seventeen

I forced a laugh. "That's pretty fanciful for you, Miss Ava. You strike me as being much more grounded."

"Nothing about me is fanciful, Magnolia Steele."

Cold sweat broke on my forehead. Ava Milton might think she knew something, but if she expected me to verify it, she had another think coming.

To my surprise, she simply let out a loud sigh and set down the bowl of icing she was working on. "Rowena Rogers may not be in the public view," she said, returning to the pot on the stove, "but she's still around."

"Do you know where she is?"

"Sometimes the things we search for are hidden in plain sight."

"Does that mean you're Rowena Rogers?"

She laughed. "No. I have far more class and tact than that tart . . . but mention her to our guests before the Bible study and find out for yourself."

"You want me to have a conversation with your guests?"

"If you so choose. I'm considering nominating you to be a trial member."

I wasn't sure which was more shocking—that she was considering making me a member or that I might take her up on it.

Ava got back to work, but she refused to discuss anything related to my father. Instead, she had me make a batch of scones, which made me more nervous than I cared to admit. Under her watchful eye, they turned out perfectly. Part of me wanted to tell my mother about my baking victory, but I suspected she wouldn't appreciate that I'd achieved it under her nemesis's tutelage.

Forty-five minutes before the guests were due to arrive, Ava sent me to my apartment to shower and change. I almost told her about the cameras in my apartment and begged to shower in her house instead, but decided not to press my luck. Now that Colt was certain he'd figured out who'd hidden the cameras—Owen—there was no point in leaving them there. I'd find the camera in the bathroom and rip it out myself.

But when I walked out the back door, Colt was waiting on the steps to my apartment again, and I released a surprised squeak.

"What are you doing here so early?" I asked, rushing up to him. He was still wearing the shirt he'd had on last night, and his hair was smooshed on one side. "You look like shit." That was probably the only time I'd be able to honestly tell him that, so I decided to not waste the opportunity. Even so, the memory of our kiss flooded my head, making me warm in places that had no business being warm on a cool April morning.

Colt seemed oblivious. He made a face and groaned. "Rub it in, Maggie." He'd used my nickname, so I decided he couldn't be as pissed as he sounded.

I really needed to get ahold of myself, but my reaction to him only drove home the fact that I was right to pack up my things and leave Brady's. It wasn't fair to him when I was lusting after somebody else. And Colt Austin to boot. That pissed me off since I'd vowed from the moment I first laid eyes on Colt to not fall for him. "What are you doing here?" I asked in a clipped tone.

Surprise filled his eyes. "Checking on you. And bringing you this." He pulled my purse out from behind his back.

That knocked my irritation down several pegs. "You stopped by my car?"

"I wanted to make sure it was still there, undisturbed. And it was."

"Then how did you get my purse? I'm pretty sure I locked the car."

"I have my ways. Do you want me to take you to get your car when you're done here?"

"Yeah. Thanks." One problem solved. Three hundred and thirty-six more or so to go.

He climbed to his feet, although it looked like it took more effort than it should have.

"Owen was there when I showed up at Brady's doorstep last night."

Colt did a double take. "What? How did that go?"

"Surprisingly okay, although he mentioned my wet, dirty clothes. Since I couldn't confess I'd been hiding under a semi, I told him it was because my car had broken down. Thanks to your minor sabotage, it wasn't a total lie."

He had the good grace to grimace with guilt. "Good thinking. Do you know why he was there?"

I hesitated, realizing I'd compartmentalized what the people around me knew. While Colt knew the most about my father, he knew nothing about the night I'd been held captive. Brady only knew some things about my father, but he knew everything about that night. I wanted to tell Colt the whole story—I'd wanted to for a while—but he was keeping important information from me. "You still have your secrets, and I still have mine, remember?"

Anger flashed in his eyes.

"He wasn't there about the industrial park incident," I said, feeling slightly guilty. "He was dropping off a packet of information that Brady had requested."

That piqued his interest. "Do you know what was in it?"

"How would I know?" I hedged. "It was police business."

He shot me a look that let me know he didn't buy it. "I'm surprised you haven't asked about my text from last night. Don't you want to know about the lead I found?"

I hadn't forgotten, but he'd caught me by surprise. He hadn't given me a chance to ask. But his prompting reminded me that I'd texted Belinda back—twice—and still had no response. I was starting to get worried. I was also tired and cranky, so I snapped out a response, "Are you going to hold your information hostage? You don't tell me unless I tell you?"

He studied me for a moment as though trying to decide whether to answer before he said, "Get into a lover's spat with your *boyfriend?*"

My guilt for kissing Colt—and enjoying it far too much—had ruined everything with Brady, but I wasn't about to admit it to him. "Shut up, Colt. Tell me or don't, it's up to you."

"Jesus," he spat out. "What is your *problem* today? You want to hear the information about the gold or not?"

God. I really was a giant bitch. "Yeah. Sorry. I didn't get much sleep last night."

"Yeah, me either." He rubbed the back of his neck. "I got some information on the history of when the pieces were made and who they were sold to."

"They can track that?"

"Not all of it, but some. Most of them were minted in the U.S., but some came from Switzerland. I'm trying to find out who your father took it from."

Out of habit, I nearly protested his accusation against my father. Accepting that Daddy was a criminal would take some time. "But I thought we'd proven that he'd taken it from Steve Morrissey."

"Sure looks that way, but I think we should find things out for ourselves instead of taking a lying murderer's word for it."

He had a point.

"I've also discovered that Lopez often stayed at a friend's house down in Chattanooga. I'm going to check it out. There's a chance he could have left the gold there."

"You think he had time to go down there and back?"

"He stole it from you on Friday afternoon. It's a two-and-a-half-hour drive, and since few people knew he made a habit of staying there, it would have been a safe place to hole up."

"Why wouldn't he have just kept it in his car?"

"Would you carry around one million in gold in your car?" Colt asked.

"You're asking the wrong person," I said. "I had it stuffed around my apartment." I pursed my lips. "Keeping it in a safety deposit box would have been smarter."

"In your case, yes. But in Lopez's situation, the police thought he'd been kidnapped and possibly murdered." He put an arm around my shoulder and squeezed. "We'll get it back."

"I hope so. Our lives depend on it."

"So you didn't tell Bennett?"

"I said I wouldn't," I said in a snotty tone. Besides, since other issues had seemed bigger, I'd put it farther down on the priority list. It was a sad day when all your other problems were bigger than an ultimatum to deliver a million dollars' worth of gold or die. "We're on our own with this. If we manage to actually find the gold, we have to hand it over."

"Hell no, we're not giving that asshole our gold. We're keeping it. And if you don't want your share, I'll keep all of it. But at the moment, I want food. Is your apartment still as bare as a grocery store two years into a zombie apocalypse?"

I shot him a glare. "When would I have gotten food? Never mind, don't answer that. Look, I can get your food

242

if you promise to come up and rip out all of those cameras."

His forehead furrowed. "I don't know, Mags . . . We're still not sure who it was since we're pretty certain it wasn't Frasier."

"Then I guess we'll get our big reveal on Saturday night when we hand it over."

"So does that mean you're still going to the masquerade ball with me?" he asked.

There was no way Colt was going to do this drop-off without me, even if he didn't have anything to turn over. "Yeah."

He grinned. "We'll be the sexiest couple there. People won't be able to keep their eyes off us."

That was what I was afraid of. "I'm going to ask Belinda for a dress. Do you have a tux?"

"Do I have a tux?" he asked, sounding incredulous.

"Do you or don't you? If not, I'll see if we can get one from Belinda."

He snorted. "She'll never give me a tux."

"What happened between you two?" I asked. "Why don't you get along?"

Surprise washed over his face. "Who said we don't get along?"

I realized I'd never witnessed anything overtly hostile between them, but little things—more so on Belinda's end than on Colt's—had implied they shared a mutual disregard. "My mistake."

"Well, in any case, I have a tux. A black one."

I didn't like the way my mind wandered to what Colt would look like dressed to the nines. It made me breathless.

"Back to the cameras," I said, trying to stay on task. "They are coming out. *Today.*" When he didn't answer, I said, "You wouldn't believe the spread Ava made for her Bible study. There are some little mini quiches in the warming drawer, and she also has lemon poppy seed muffins and blueberry scones. And those are just the starters."

"Ava's pissed at me. She'll never let me have anything."

I was still curious about that, but there was no time to ask. In a matter of minutes, I had to be in Ava's dining room looking like I was attending a debutante tea. I'd pry it out of him later. "I know for a fact that she's upstairs getting ready, but I suspect she won't take long. I'll even let you take a plate of food on the honor system."

He licked his bottom lip. "Deal."

"Follow me." I led him through Ava's back door and into the kitchen. His eyes lit up at the literal smorgasbord of brunch pastries.

"You're sure Ava's upstairs?" he asked, glancing around with a guilty look.

"Yep." I opened the pantry and pulled out a container of freshly ground coffee. "Quick. Grab something and bring it with you. I'll make coffee in my apartment."

He picked up a blueberry scone and held it in front of his face, taking a big whiff. A smile that suggested he'd discovered the secret to life spread across his face. I couldn't help inflating with pride since they had been my first successful baking endeavor.

Grabbing a plate, he took the scone, two mini quiches, and a couple of muffins. After he poured himself a glass of orange juice, I opened the back door. "Come on. You've taken half the food and I'm going to have to rearrange it all, but I'll gladly do it as long as you earn it. Time to debug my apartment."

Once we got inside, Colt quickly dispatched two cameras from the bookcase and one from the kitchen while I started a pot of coffee.

"The bathroom next," I said. "I need a quick shower."

I followed him in as he pulled out a small disc and wire from behind the light fixture over the sink. A dark look crossed his face as he stuffed it into his jeans pocket. "The fucker could see into your shower."

I shuddered involuntarily. I was pretty sure the creepy feeling of being watched would last long after the cameras were gone.

He circled the room, taking a framed print of a seascape off the wall and looking it over before he hung it back up.

"I thought you said there was only one in here."

"Can't be too thorough," he muttered as he stood on the side of the tub looking around the shower head.

"Well . . . thanks."

"No prob." He headed for the door. "You're good."

I shut the door behind him and turned on the water, worried he hadn't gotten them all. The shower was probably the shortest of my life, and I quickly wrapped a towel around myself and cracked open the door.

"All clear?" I asked.

Colt was sitting at the island with a cup of coffee and half his food gone. His gaze strayed to my legs, and I became instantly aware of the fact that I was wrapped up in a towel that only barely covered my butt. "Your bedroom is clear," he finally said, returning his attention to his plate.

"Where did you put the cameras?" I asked. "Can they still hear us?"

"They're down in my car."

"Not the trash? Why didn't you flush them?"

He shook his head. "So wasteful, Magnolia Steele. I can sell them or use them myself."

"What would you use them for?"

He looked up at me, his eyes serious. "I think we both know I have several side jobs to pay the bills."

He'd admitted to installing the cameras outside the loading dock, but the way he'd said it suggested the deal had been brokered under the table. What exactly did he do when he wasn't working for the Belles and singing in bars? Belinda had mentioned his arrest, and he'd been open enough about his seedy past, but I hadn't thought he was still involved in anything devious. Then again, after last night, I wasn't sure about anything. I needed more answers, and I needed them soon.

"For God's sakes, Magnolia," he groaned. "Put some fucking clothes on."

I cringed, having somehow forgotten I was still standing in the skimpy towel. "Sorry."

Darting into my bedroom, I found my last clean dress and quickly put it on, then went into the bathroom to put on a little makeup, making sure I used plenty of concealer to cover the dark circles under my eyes and some still-fading bruises. After I rolled my hair up into a French twist, I returned to the living area and found Colt lying on my sofa with his eyes closed.

"You're already done?" he asked, squinting one eye open.

"Yeah, what of it?"

"I just expected you to be more high maintenance."

"Does that statement apply to my appearance or to me in general?"

"Both." His eyes sank closed again. "I'm going to hang out here and take a nap while you're doing the Bible study thing."

I walked into the kitchen and poured a cup of coffee. "Why is Ava mad at you?"

"That's none of your—"

"Come on. You know ten times more information about me than I know about you." On second thought, that was probably a *low* estimation.

He lifted his head and glanced back at me. "Here's the thing you need to know about Ava—what happens between you two needs to stay between you two. So if you want to know why she's ticked at me, ask her."

"She's told me all kinds of things this morning," I said. "She just might tell me."

"No skin off my back," he said, settling down on the sofa again. "But be wary: her information always comes at a price."

Something I'd already suspected.

I glanced at the clock and saw I had ten minutes before I had to head back over. I started to grab my phone to search for the latest information on Emily's murder when the box from Ava's attic caught my attention. Ava had chided me for not finishing my *homework*. Was there something else in the box she wanted me to see?

I took off the lid, sat on one of the barstools, and began to flip through the articles, searching for any information I might have missed. Five minutes later, I was only halfway through the clippings when a name listed in a write-up about a literacy fundraiser grabbed my attention.

"Charles Rogers, president of Grobbel and Rogers Financial, was in attendance with his wife Rowena. The Rogerses, who have been long-time supporters of literacy, generously gave the charity a ten-thousand-dollar donation."

The clipping had photos, but I didn't recognize anyone in them, and there wasn't a picture of the Rogerses. Grobbel and Rogers Financial? Had Daddy convinced another financial planning firm to join his project?

I set the clipping aside and kept looking through the pile. Several items later, I found a program for a ladies' garden luncheon that listed Rowena Rogers as the treasurer of the garden club.

I glanced at the clock—I only had five more minutes, but I was determined to find out more before I left, especially if Ava was going to let me ask questions. I picked through several more clippings and was about to wake up Colt and assign him the task when I picked up a clipping and froze. There was a photo of a woman I'd seen before.

Once with Walter Frey at Mellow Mushroom, and the second time at his funeral.

Her chin was lifted and her mouth held the barest hint of a smile. She looked like she didn't take shit from anyone and was more than happy to hand out lots of it in return. She was younger than the woman I'd seen in person—her hair was darker and she had fewer wrinkles—but there was no doubt it was her.

The title read, "Franklin Woman Honored for Her Work in Children's Literacy," and underneath the photo, the caption read, "Rowena Rogers."

chapter eighteen

My mouth dropped open. Ava had said she was hiding in plain sight. Then why did my mother think she'd disappeared? Then again, Momma had said that Rowena's disappearance never made the news. Obviously she'd gone into hiding.

My phone started to vibrate on the counter, and I was relieved to see Belinda's name on the screen. A quick glance toward Colt confirmed he was out like a light, so I took my keys and walked out to the landing, shutting the door behind me as I answered the call.

"Belinda, are you okay?" I asked in a rush as I locked the door. Colt was inside, but he didn't need some bad guy walking in on him.

"I'm fine. Just checking on you."

She sounded worried, and I had to wonder what had incited her anxiety. The timing with last night's adventure seemed suspect, but then I realized she was probably paranoid about my safety after Emily's murder.

"I'm okay," I said, doing my best to sound breezy. "Say, before I forget, remember that masquerade ball you mentioned? It just so happens I got invited to go too."

"With Brady?" she asked, and I was surprised she didn't sound more excited.

"Actually, no . . ." This wasn't going to go well. "With Colt."

"How did *Colt* get tickets?" She sounded incredulous.

"I don't know. He asked me to go because he didn't want to go alone."

"Which means he has two. Magnolia, those tickets start at $250 and go up to $10,000 per table. What kind of tickets did he get?"

"I don't know," I murmured as I glanced back up at my apartment door. Where had Colt gotten that much money, and why would he spend it on masquerade ball tickets? I wasn't entirely buying the networking story. But I wasn't going to say any of that to Belinda, who'd already tried to steer me away from a friendship with him. Maybe it was stupid and naïve of me, but I needed Colt right now. I also definitely needed to go to that stupid ball, which meant I had to ignore the warning signs waving in my face. "But I do know I need a dress and a mask, which means I have to ask a pretty huge favor."

"You want me to help you find something to wear?"

I'd left a few gorgeous dresses at my ex-boyfriend's apartment in New York. With only two suitcases to pack my clothes, I'd brought only the essentials. But now I needed a dress, and the ones I'd previously owned were probably hanging in the Salvation Army on 46th Street.

"I don't have a lot of money," I said, feeling embarrassed that I was reduced to groveling. "I was wondering if I could borrow one."

She was silent for a moment. "On one condition."

"What?" I cringed, bracing myself.

"I get to pick it out. You can veto it, but I get to choose."

Last week, we'd played a game—she'd guessed which of her new wedding dresses would fit my personality, and she'd been shockingly correct, even down to the fact that I was keeping a deep, dark secret. But I reasoned a formal dress would be safe, and Belinda had excellent taste. "I thought you were going to ask for something hard. Sure."

"How about you come by my shop after you get off work at Alvin's? I'll show you what I've picked out. I was going to see if you could have dinner with me anyway, so two birds with one stone."

I hesitated. "Brady has something he wants me to do."

"Surely you could stop by on your way," she cajoled. "We can reschedule the dinner."

"He's picking me up from Alvin's when I get off at six."

She was silent for a long moment. Then she said, "I have an ulterior motive for wanting you to come by the shop. I really need to talk to you, and I know you're working Ava Milton's Bible study before you go to Alvin's."

If this had been a dinner date, I would have canceled in a heartbeat. But I'd promised to take Brady to that house, and while I wanted to see Belinda, I wasn't sure that was a good enough excuse to cancel.

When I didn't answer, she said, "It's about Roy. It's important."

I gasped. Was she finally going to share what was going on with him? "I'll try, but I don't have a date with him," I said. "It's official business."

"About Emily's murder? Are you a suspect?"

I forced humor into my voice. "One of the benefits of sleeping with a cop is you have an ironclad alibi when a murder's been committed in the middle of the night." Then I realized how bad that sounded. "I didn't mean to sound glib."

"No, I understand. It's like the Grim Reaper is following you around. If you had no outlet to ease the stress, you'd go mad."

"Yeah," I said, shuddering at the thought of a guy with a hood and a sickle following me around. A hooded serial killer with a hunting knife was enough.

"Magnolia?" Belinda asked, and I realized I'd missed something she'd said.

"I'm sorry. I think I had a bad connection there for a moment."

"I said I hope you can get out of your plans tonight." The desperation in her voice caught my breath.

"I'll talk to Brady . . ." I said, feeling anxious at the thought of canceling, but truth be told, I wasn't eager to go back to that house, and for some reason, I was unnerved at the thought of going back with Brady. "Belinda, I have to go, or Ava's gonna kill me. I'll text you when I find out if I can come by tonight. But be careful, okay?" I pleaded. "There's obviously some homicidal maniac out there."

"You too," she said quietly. "Promise me you won't take any chances today."

Something had her spooked, and I suspected it had more to do with Roy than the killer. All the more reason to try to see her. "I promise," I said as I started to open Ava's back door. "You too."

The clock on Ava's wall read 9:14, one minute before the time she'd told me to return, which I figured would win me some brownie points, but she wasn't in the kitchen, or anywhere downstairs for that matter. I decided to send Brady a text after the Bible study to see if we could postpone our hike into the woods. I needed to figure out where I was going to stay tonight, not to mention what excuse I was going to come up with for leaving.

I shook my head. Time to stop obsessing about my love life and get to work.

I'd only helped set up one of her Bible studies before, but I remembered how we'd prepared for the last one. I started carting the dining room chairs out to the living room, then covered the table with one of the tablecloths and used the other to create tiers for the food. It helped that I'd worked in the kitchen and knew what we were serving. At nine twenty-five—five minutes or so before the guests would start arriving—Ava finally descended the staircase. After her gaze swept over the living room, she made her way into the dining room and surveyed the food table.

"We never discussed how you wanted the food arranged today," I said, feeling more nervous than I'd expected. Ava may have been more amicable this morning while we were preparing the food, but she had a reputation to maintain, and I knew she'd micromanage every last detail.

I pointed toward the tiers. "I spread the baked goods around the quiches, and I used your blue set of china to switch things up from last week. The coffee's almost finished brewing, and I squeezed fresh orange juice for the *special drinks*." Special drinks were what Ava and her guests called the alcoholic beverages that quite a few women had requested last time. I'd been shocked to discover that guests at a Bible study imbibed at nine thirty on a Thursday morning, but who was I to judge a few old women for wanting to feel good while they gossiped under the guise of studying scripture?

Her face looked pinched. She opened her mouth to say something and then folded her hands neatly in front of her. "This is acceptable."

From anyone else, I would have considered this an insult. I suspected that was high praise from Ava Milton.

Her gaze dropped to my neckline, and for a moment, I thought she was going to chastise me for my lower—yet still decent—neckline. "I see you removed the necklace."

I reached for it, and panic rushed through me when I realized it was gone. I didn't remember taking it off. Where was it?

I didn't have time to go over my past day's activities to figure out where I'd lost it because the doorbell rang—an old-fashioned tone that lasted several moments.

Ava turned to me looking irritated. "Are you planning to just stand there gawking?"

I hadn't answered the door last time. She'd instructed me to stay behind the table and remain silent unless I was helping her guests.

"Did I stutter?" she asked after I still hadn't moved.

"No, ma'am. I'm going," I said as I hurried for the front door. I plastered on a warm smile. *Magnolia Steele will be filling the role of the "good hostess" for this morning's performance.* I opened the front door, already in character. "Good morning!"

I recognized the older woman in an ivory silk blouse and ivory linen pants from the previous week. Her eyes widened when she saw me. "*Magnolia.* Does Ava know you're answering the door?"

So I wasn't the only one who found the arrangement unusual. Was Ava setting me up? "Yes, Miss Blanche," I said. "Miss Ava sent me over to greet you. Please, come in."

She brushed past me, then gave me a questioning look before heading straight to Ava, probably trying to figure out what was going on. Eavesdropping on that conversation seemed like a good idea, but the doorbell rang again.

I spent the next five minutes greeting the women, but it occurred to me that I'd never get answers managing the door. Bombarding the guests as they walked in with "What can you tell me about Rowena Rogers?" obviously wasn't the way to go. Better to butter them up with Ava's delicious food and maybe go a little heavier on the *special* drinks.

I approached Ava and discreetly suggested that perhaps I should be attending to the guests at the refreshment table. The gleam in her eyes told me she knew exactly what I was up to. She gave me a curt nod.

I took over my serving duties, much more comfortable behind the scenes than in Ava Milton's spotlight. I suspected there'd be a price to pay for the attention she was giving me, but I couldn't bring myself to care. This was my chance to glean more information, although I had yet to figure out how to broach the subject of Rowena Rogers.

The opportunity came ten minutes later when two of the women were loading their plates with quiches. They were alternating between convincing themselves the quiches were practically calorie-free since they were so small and discussing an upcoming bond election for the library. Though I could have settled their argument about the quiches by telling them Ava had used heavy cream, that didn't seem like a good ice breaker. The library, on the other hand, was an ideal lead-in to questions about Rowena.

"Williamson County has one of the best library systems in the state, don't you think?" I asked in a super-sweet voice.

One of the women turned up her nose. "*One* of the best? It *is* the best. This bond will ensure its first-place ranking."

Crap. I'd already offended her. "We don't want to lord it over the more unfortunate library systems now, do we?" I said in an affable tone.

Her companion—Janine—grinned. "She does have a point, Marie."

Marie didn't look as convinced, but I only needed one of them to talk to me.

"Now that I'm back in town," I said, pouring Janine a cup of coffee, "I would *love* to participate in some volunteer organizations. I heard there was a literacy charity. Do either of you know about it?"

The two women exchanged questioning glances before turning back to me.

"Yes," Janine said as she took the cup I handed her. "Ava knows all about it. You should get it from her after the Bible study."

"I'll be sure to do that," I said. "Are any of the women who attend Ava's Bible study part of the charity?"

"No," Marie said in a stern voice. "Not anymore."

"Oh?" I asked, feigning ignorance. "Someone used to be a member?"

"Rowena Rogers," Janine said in nearly a whisper. "But she quit the charity *and* the group."

"And everything else," a woman who had walked up to the table said as she grabbed a plate.

"Did she move away?" I asked.

"No. She was involved in a *scandal*," Janine volunteered with a look of glee in her eyes. But that glee instantly turned to panic, and her eyes searched the room. It was no surprise when her gaze landed on Ava, who was in the middle of a conversation close to the front door.

"Janine," Marie admonished.

Janine looked guilty, but she lowered her voice and leaned in closer to the other woman. "*Please*. It's not like you weren't discussing it at a meeting two months ago."

"We don't discuss members with non-members," Marie said with a frown.

Janine's back stiffened. "Well, Rowena's not a member anymore, now is she?"

Marie snatched a scone off the table. "And you won't be for long if you keep talking like that." She walked away, but Janine lingered.

"Would you like me to fix you a special drink?" I asked her. She seemed like a good target since her lips were already loose without any help from alcohol.

She wavered.

"I have a new drink," I said, offering her a warm smile. "It's made with raspberry lemonade and is very refreshing. I hear it's supposed to warm up today."

"You wouldn't mind?" she asked.

"Of course not! It's my job. I'll be right back."

I hurried through the door to the kitchen and mixed up her drink, adding a few fresh raspberries to the glass as a garnish.

Her eyes lit up as I walked back into the dining room. Yes, she was the perfect person for me to question. She was softer than the other woman, more open, and she was also one of the younger members, probably in her late forties or early fifties. The way her eyes kept darting around the room screamed outsider, as though she worried she'd do or say something wrong and be shown the door.

She reached for the glass, but I didn't let go. I'd added enough vodka to get her pretty tipsy. If she was insecure about her place in the group, I'd hate to be responsible for her embarrassing herself.

"I'm sorry, Miss Janine," I said in a syrupy sweet voice just this side of sounding fake. "I just realized I was a little heavy on the *special* ingredient. Perhaps I should make you a new one."

She gave me a conspiratorial grin. "We both know the special ingredient is alcohol."

"Vodka," I whispered. "But I'm pretty sure it's stronger than it tastes, and I wouldn't want to be responsible for landing you in Ava's bad graces."

Janine chuckled. "I'm already there." She grabbed the glass out of my hand and took a long drink. "You're like a breath of fresh air. What's Ava up to hiring you?"

I remained silent, unsure of how to answer, especially since she'd spoken my own question out loud.

She glanced back at the refreshment table and grabbed a half-empty plate of spinach and bacon quiches. "Doesn't this need to be refilled?"

I started to get ticked off, then realized what she was up to. I took the plate, headed through the swinging door to the kitchen, and grabbed the pan from the warming oven. Janine came through the door several seconds later.

"Ava's up to something," she said without preamble, her voice practically an octave lower than the sweet simper she'd used in the other room. I was pretty sure this was the real Janine. "She prefers her help to keep quiet unless spoken to, and she never has them answer the door. Why is she treating you so differently?"

"I'm guessing you know who I am," I said, dropping the pretense of refilling the plate.

"Magnolia Steele, which is even more curious. She can't stand your mother."

"Then maybe this is her way of trying to get under my mother's skin," I said. "It's quite a trump card for her to get the daughter of the best caterer in town to work at her event." I suspected it had more to do with my father, but I wasn't sharing that information.

"That's likely part of it, but there's more," she said, staring out the back window at the garage. "You're living in the apartment out back, aren't you?"

"Yes."

"So she's keeping you close."

I hadn't looked at it that way. Could there be some truth to what she suggested? "I was led to believe she's had her previous help stay there," I said.

"Who told you that?"

I slowly turned to face her. "I don't remember." Which was true. Had Colt insinuated it? "Why?"

"In the four years I've attended these meetings, she's never once had someone living in that apartment. You're the first."

The blood rushed to my feet. "What?"

"You didn't know?"

"No." Reflecting on my conversations with Colt and Ava, I realized neither had mentioned previous tenants, but neither had told me it was a new venture either. I'd just presumed.

Why would Ava want me in her backyard? It hardly seemed like chance that a woman with boxes of articles about the Jackson Project in her attic had decided to rent her garage apartment for the first time in years to me, the daughter of the founder.

I would worry about that later. I needed to focus on Rowena. "You said you joined the Bible study group four years ago? Did you know Rowena Rogers well?"

"No one knew Rowena well. She kept to herself."

"You said she left because of a scandal."

Her eyes lit up. "Oh, yes. And it was quite the scandal indeed. Rumor had it she was having an affair with Karen Merritt's husband."

"*Christopher* Merritt?"

"Yes." Her mouth puckered with disapproval.

"How long ago?"

"Three years. Word got out after he took off."

"After? How did it come out?"

"Karen realized that all his late-night meetings were with Rowena."

"But isn't she older than him?"

"By nearly twenty years. Her husband was a friend of his father's. But she received a lot of money from her husband in the settlement, and Chris was struggling to provide for his kids and a wife who wanted to look like she was more well-off than she actually was." She shook her head. "Not that it did her much good since she ended up leaving the Bible study too. The members have standards to maintain."

"I'm sure they do," I said absently. "How long ago were Rowena and her husband divorced?"

"Oh," her eyes lit up. "Rowena and Charles weren't divorced. Charles was killed in a car accident fourteen years ago. Rowena sued and won a lot of money."

Fourteen years ago? That couldn't be a coincidence. "I heard Rowena disappeared, but Ava says she's still around, and I've actually seen her. Do you know where she lives now?"

"Up in one of those big fancy houses in Brentwood facing Highway 65, but she's going by her middle name and her maiden name now—Nicole Baker. Frankly, I'm surprised you saw her. I hear she rarely leaves her house."

"Maybe I just thought I saw her," I said. "At Walter Frey's funeral."

Her eyes widened before she grinned. "That seems unlikely. She and Walter hated each other."

"Why?"

Her mouth twisted to the side before she shook her head. "I don't know. But I *do* know Walter was in a mess of his own last year. Something to do with an illegal property sale. Whatever it was, Ruby Frey left the group. Ava told her she didn't have to, but she left anyway."

Did that have anything to do with his partnership with Daddy and the others? There were so many leads to follow that it was hard to know where to start. But the whole apartment issue had crawled under my skin. "Do you know about Colt Austin?"

A knowing smile lit up her face. "How do *you* know Colton?"

"He's the one who introduced me to Ava. He asked her to rent the apartment to me." When Janine started to laugh, my stomach sank. "What's so funny?"

"You think Colton talked her into it?" she asked in disbelief. "Magnolia, no one talks Ava into anything. Everything is always her idea, even if the people around her don't realize it."

This was exactly what I'd feared. "Do you know how Colt started working for Ava or what he did?"

For the first time, she looked hesitant to talk. "There was a situation that needed help outside our usual sphere. I'm not sure how Ava found Colton, but he quickly had it dispatched."

"Situation. What situation?"

"I . . ."

The door burst open and Ava shot me a glare. "Magnolia, what are you doing back here? You've been absent from your post for nearly ten minutes."

"It hasn't been that long, Miss Ava." I wasn't even sure it had been five.

"Are you sassing me?" she asked with a raised eyebrow.

"No, ma'am. Just making an observation."

Her attention shifted to Janine. "And what are *you* doing? Have you volunteered to become part of the kitchen staff?"

"No, ma'am," Janine stuttered, her face flushing. "I came in to see what was taking Marjorie so long."

"Her name is Magnolia," Ava said, her voice dragging as though discussing this exhausted her. "And she is *my* staff, not yours. I will see to her." Ava kept her hard stare on me while she stepped to the side, making it obvious that Janine was dismissed. The woman shuffled past her, nearly spilling her drink. When the door shut, Ava asked, "Did you get what you needed out of her?"

My mouth dropped open. "What?"

She rolled her eyes. "You're a resourceful girl. I was counting on it. So did you get your information?"

"Enough for now, I think."

"Good. The meeting will start in ten minutes. I'd like you to sit in the back and take minutes. A stenographer notebook and pen are on the breakfast table."

"What—"

"Is there a problem, Magnolia?"

I swallowed. "No, ma'am. I'm just surprised."

"Well, pull your jaw off the floor and resume your buffet attendant job until I say it's time."

I'd have to stay late to clean if I sat in on the meeting, which would leave me with a very short window of time to get my car, but Colt and I could work that out later.

"Yes, ma'am. I wouldn't miss it."

"Good. Don't disappoint me, Magnolia Steele."

I wasn't sure how she thought I might disappoint her, let alone why I even cared about pleasing her, but I did. Maybe that was how she kept all her cronies in line. Score another one for her powers of manipulation.

I resumed my task of refilling the quiche plate, then hurried back out to the dining room. Several guests had noticed my lengthy absence and shot me looks of pity— which was likely because they expected me to be fired.

I ignored their stares, and my churning gut, for another ten minutes before Ava called the meeting to order.

While everyone made their way out to the living room, I carried a few plates into the kitchen and grabbed the stenographer notebook and pen. By the time I returned, all the women had taken their seats.

Ava stood at the front of the room, her back stiff and her hands laced in front of her. She glanced up at me and then tilted her head toward an empty chair in the back. "Magnolia will be joining us today and taking the minutes."

A murmur went through the room, and several women glanced over their shoulders at me.

I took my seat and pinned my gaze on the notebook. Ava was definitely up to no good, but who was her intended victim? I was terrified I was going to end up like Carrie on prom night. Except Ava Milton wouldn't use pig's blood. No, I suspected her weapon of choice would be far worse.

"What on earth is this girl doing here?" Georgine asked. I remembered her from the last meeting. She had given Ava plenty of trouble then, and her tone implied she planned on a repeat offense.

Ava looked unruffled. "She's here because I want her here. Do you have a problem with that, Georgine?"

Georgine jumped to her feet, shooting me a look that suggested I was lower than pond's scum. "She's Brian Steele's daughter. It's bad enough that she's serving us food."

The room became so quiet the ticktock of Ava's grandfather clock was deafening.

Ava's eyes became small pinpricks, the only sign that Georgine had gotten under her skin. "I will repeat myself," she said in an icy tone. "And, for the record, I *loathe* repeating myself. Magnolia Steele is here because I asked her to sit in the back and take notes. If you have a problem with this, Georgine, feel free to find the door."

Georgine stood in place, her face turning red as she clenched her hands at her sides and engaged in a staring match with Ava. Obviously Georgine was a fool—and despite her desire to make her wishes known, she didn't have what it took to best my landlord. Sure enough, five seconds later Georgine sat down in her chair with a grunt, her back ramrod stiff.

I wrote down: *Miss Ava used her badass skills to shut down Georgine.*

"Now, does anyone else have any objections?" Ava asked, surveying the room.

No one dared to answer.

"Very good," she said with a tiny smile, pleased that she had won her battle. "We shall begin with old business. We raised $5,000 to donate to the Boys and Girls Club in the name of Walter Frey." She gave a small nod.

I wrote down: *$5,000 to B&G Club in Walter Frey's name.*

"Thank you for your generous giving. Edie, how are we doing with the meals we are providing to the Frey family?"

Edie talked about who had signed up and criticized one of the women for delivering a subpar meal of leathery pork chops with an overly tart lemon basil cream sauce and slightly wilted kale. The woman who'd dared to serve such a disaster hung her head in shame while the other women shot her mixed looks of pity and disgust. Edie reminded several women of their upcoming deliveries and the standards they had to maintain. The last thing I wanted to do was log each and every casserole, so I put down: *Two weeks of meals to Ruby Frey.*

Then Ava launched into a discussion of various odds and ends I found extremely boring. Though I doubted anyone needed a detailed record about the garden club or

Sophia Regis's bout of pneumonia, I took diligent notes while trying to stay awake. Too many late nights and early mornings at Brady's had caught up with me, and my eyelids were heavy with exhaustion.

I began to wonder if it was safe to move back to my apartment. Colt had removed all the cameras, and the person who'd planted them wasn't likely to bother us before Saturday night. While I was hesitant to move back there alone, especially in light of everything I'd learned about the serial killer, I wasn't sure where else to stay.

"Continuing new business," Ava said in her stick-up-her-butt tone. "I move that we remove Janine Cumberland from the group."

I gasped and nearly dropped my pen on the floor.

"What?" Janine asked, barely above a whisper. "Why?" But she shot a guilty look back at me.

"You know full well, Janine," Ava said in an icy tone. "Would you like me to spell it out in front of everyone?"

My skin turned cold and my hair stood on end. Ava was getting rid of her because I'd gotten her to talk—the very thing Ava had encouraged me to do. I was the reason this woman was being kicked out.

Janine's face paled and she shook her head. "No."

"Feel free to leave," Ava said. "We'll wait."

The woman leaned over and reached for her purse under her chair, but dropped it. The contents spilled out, and she dropped to the floor, her hands shaking as she scooped up her lipstick and car keys.

When Ava's eyes met mine, she had the satisfied look of a cat full of cream.

chapter nineteen

Fifteen minutes later, Blanche read a Bible verse—the most cursory part of this Bible study—and Ava declared the meeting adjourned. The reverend had showed up the week before, but there was no sign of him this time. The guests grabbed their purses and vacated the premises within two minutes. But I didn't sit around and wait to watch them leave. Instead, I headed for the refreshment table and grabbed two plates to carry into the kitchen.

The table was cleared off, and I'd already begun putting food away when Ava walked through the door. I ignored her and continued putting the leftover poppy seed muffins into a Ziploc bag.

"Go ahead and get it off your chest," she said.

Telling her how I felt would be a huge waste of my breath and my time. People like her thrived off reactions. The best way to tick her off would be to show no reaction at all.

"Really, Magnolia. Nothing to say?"

I turned toward her with the bag in my hand. "Actually, there is something."

A smug look washed over her face. "Go on."

"Have you considered taking the leftovers to a homeless shelter?" I asked, keeping my tone light and breezy. "It seems so selfish to not share them."

The gleam left her eyes. "I'll take it under consideration."

"Okay," I said. "Then I'll just leave them on the counter. Or if you like, I can put them in a bag and drop them off myself."

"Now you're babbling," she said in a harsh tone.

"Am I?" I asked. "I'm sorry. I'll just quietly do my job." I started storing the quiche in a plastic storage container.

"I know you want to talk about Janine."

"What you do in your meetings is your concern."

She remained behind me, staying silent as she watched me work.

I snapped the lid on the container and put it on the counter next to the refrigerator.

"For God's sake, Magnolia Steele," she groaned. "I thought you had more backbone than this."

"What do you want from me?" I asked, letting my anger bleed through and instantly regretting it when I saw the triumph in her eyes. *Well, shit.* I'd already failed, but I could still turn this on her. "Why am I really living in your apartment?"

Her confusion made my slip worth it. "You needed an apartment."

"You never rented it to anyone before. Why me?"

"Why *not* you?"

I could see she was regaining control of herself, but I wasn't ready to let this go. If she wanted a reaction out of me, she was going to get it—and then some. "You rented it to me because of my father."

"Really, Magnolia. Given his reputation, your connection to him would more likely be a deterrent."

"You want me to find out about him. You asked me to look at that box in the attic on purpose."

"So dramatic," she said, clucking her tongue. "I gave you that box because I want my attic cleaned out. Have you sorted through it as I asked?"

"No."

"You really are an insolent girl, aren't you?"

"Why did Colt start working for you two years ago?"

"That's none of your business."

"It is my business if he's my friend."

She lifted her eyebrows with a smug smile. "Is he?"

I tried to hide how much her question bothered me. "What does *that* mean?"

"If you were as smart as I thought you were, you'd know."

She was trying to get me to turn on Colt, but I wouldn't let her twist me into knots and sidetrack me. I decided to try a different angle. "Why do you care so much that I find out the truth about my father?"

She looked me up and down, as though deciding whether I deserved an answer. Finally, she said, "I have my reasons."

"Your reasons." I picked up the empty plates and took them to the sink. "When you told me that your business is information, I knew I'd have to pay for what I learned."

"And what is it that you think you're paying?" she asked in an indignant tone.

That was the scary part. I'd gotten piece after piece of information, and aside from my role in poor Janine's dismissal, I had yet to pay any price. Which meant I was now beholden to Ava Milton, even if I'd never agreed to any terms.

I opened her dishwasher and began to load it with plates as I rinsed them off.

She stood behind me for several seconds. "Don't you think of leaving before all of this is cleaned up. Remember that whatever personal plans you may have for later are not my concern."

I didn't answer, continuing my task. The angry part of me demanded I walk out, pack up the few belongings I had in my apartment, and never speak to Ava Milton again. But another part of me said to swallow my pride and not rush into a hasty decision. My apartment represented freedom and Ava dangled answers. Was I willing to forsake either?

She turned and left the room, leaving me in uneasy silence.

A half hour later, I unlocked my apartment door and found Colt still asleep on my sofa.

"Do you have any idea what time it is?" I asked as I shoved his leg.

His body jerked and he lifted his head. "What?"

"It's twelve fifteen." I crossed my arms and gave him a disapproving look. "I hope you got enough beauty sleep."

He sat up and rubbed his eyes. "What are you doing back already? I thought you said you wouldn't be back until after twelve thirty."

"The Bible study ended abruptly, which worked in my favor since I couldn't clean up the kitchen during their meeting like I did last week. This time I had to wait until after."

"Why did the meeting end abruptly?"

"I could tell you," I said, plopping into the overstuffed chair. "But then I'd have to kill you."

"Ha. Ha. Very funny."

To hell with all her secrecy. "She fired someone."

He grinned. "You? That would explain why you're back early."

"No, I still have my job, which flies in the face of all reason." I shook my head. "She dismissed one of the women in the Bible study." I narrowed my eyes. "Did you know that their Bible study consists of reading one Bible verse and the rest of the time is spent gossiping?"

He yawned and stretched his arms over his head. His T-shirt clung to his chest and arm muscles, and his hem lifted enough to show a sliver of skin above his waistline, making my stomach flutter. *Dammit.* I needed to get control of myself. Thank God I looked away before he noticed.

His grin fell. "You're not supposed to be talking about what goes on during those meetings, Maggie."

"Why? What's the big secret? I have a notebook full of minutes I took, which include such scintillating discussion points as the group's plan to deliver meals to

Ruby Frey for the rest of the week and who had the most beautiful tulip display. Oh!" I exclaimed, as though just remembering it. "And that Janine Cumberland was dismissed in the most humiliating way after offering me information that Ava encouraged me to get."

"Slow down there," Colt said, then scrubbed his hand over his face. "What are you talking about?"

"I should have known she was up to no good. She was all sweet and helpful."

"Janine Cumberland?"

"No! Ava. Keep up."

"When the hell has Ava Milton ever been sweet and cordial?"

"Exactly!" I exclaimed, pointing my finger at him. "That should have clued me in that she was up to no good."

"What does that have to do with her getting rid of Janine?"

"I asked Ava for information about someone my father worked with, and she encouraged me to ask her guests about her."

"Stop and think about this," he said, leaning over his legs and resting his elbows on his thighs. When I didn't answer, Colt gave me a wry grin. "She's a tricky one."

"Don't look so smug about it. Why don't you tell me how I got this apartment?"

He sat up. "What?"

"I found out that I'm the first tenant to live here. It's quite a coincidence, considering that Ava's taken an interest in feeding me information about my father."

"What the hell are you implying?" he asked, getting pissed. "You signed the lease and moved in. End of story."

"And what happened before that?" I asked. "More specifically, I want to hear about the conversation you and Ava had about offering me the apartment."

"I don't know," he said defensively. "That was so long ago."

"Bullshit. I moved in *a week* ago. Your idea or hers?"

He didn't answer—and from the set of his jaw, he didn't plan to.

"That's okay," I said as I got to my feet. "That's answer enough. Are you my friend or not?"

He grinned, but it looked forced. "Ava must have really unsettled you for you to ask me that."

"Answer the question."

He stood and his eyes narrowed. "I risked my life for you last night. If that doesn't make us friends, I don't know what does."

"One would think so, right?" I asked, taking a step toward him. "But you're hiding things, and that alone is reason enough for me to call you into question."

"It's not like you're not hiding things from me either," he shot back. "I suspect you've got more secrets than I do."

"Fine! You want to know all my secrets? I'll tell you every single last one of them. But you have to share yours too."

His shoulders dropped in defeat. "Maggie. You know I can't."

I stormed over to the door and reached for the doorknob. "Then get the fuck out."

Colt didn't move. "Don't be stupid. You need me."

He was right. I did, and that pissed me off even more.

I slammed the door shut and fastened the deadbolt.

"Oh, you locked us in. Maybe you're interested in other kinds of secrets." Colt grinned, but it didn't look genuine. I was quite certain this was the same look he gave women to get them to leap into bed with him.

"Stop it," I said in disgust. "I know what you're doing. It's not going to work."

He pushed out a heavy sigh and flopped back down onto the sofa. "Let's play a game."

"What kind of game?" I asked suspiciously.

"It's like strip poker."

"Are you *kidding* me?"

"Calm your ass down," he said as he reclined and stretched his arm along the back of the sofa. "I said *like* strip poker. Take a seat. You're going to like it."

I groaned. "Spoken like a man."

"Come on. I'll even start."

"Just so we're clear, I'm not stripping, and I don't want to see your bare chest." That was a blatant lie, and I hated myself for it.

"More's the pity. I'm not starting until you sit down."

I sighed as I settled back into the chair I'd vacated a few minutes ago. "I'm sitting, but make this quick. I have to get to work at Alvin's."

His grin faded. "Ava was the one who told me to offer you the apartment."

My stomach fell to my feet. I'd suspected, but it felt different to hear it confirmed. "How long ago?"

"A week after you came back. When she realized you were staying."

"Why?"

"I don't know, and that's the God's honest truth, Maggie."

"And you just went along with it?"

"Ava has ulterior motives for almost everything she does, but in your case I figured it was just to get a dig at your mother. Harmless enough, and it would help you out by giving you a place to stay. Now I'm not so sure." He sat back. "Okay, it's my turn to ask you a question."

"I didn't know this was a question game. Maybe I would have asked you something different."

He shrugged. "You asked me a few minutes ago, and I answered."

Was I up to playing this game? I could tell him as much or as little as I wanted, and he *had* answered my earlier question.

But how much should I say? My gut told me to trust Colt, but it had steered me wrong before, and besides, I knew he had his own agenda.

Colt's gazed pinned on me. "What have you learned about your father since you've been back?"

"Daddy wasn't the perfect man I thought he was," I said, resting my forearm on the arm of the chair. I kept my gaze on the *Southern Living* magazine on the coffee table. "I think he might have scammed a bunch of people with some kind of land project in north Nashville. It went belly-up, and a lot of people lost their money."

Colt was quiet and I lifted my gaze to his face. Our eyes locked. I tried to read him and failed.

"It had to hurt like hell to find that out," he said. "He fell quite a ways off his pedestal."

"You're making fun of me."

"No, but I know you idolized the man. I'm surprised you believe it."

"Why wouldn't I believe it?" I asked, shifting in my chair. I was starting to get pissed. "I'm looking for the truth, no matter how difficult it is to hear."

He pushed out a heavy sigh. "No, your goal was to clear his name. It's not turning out the way you wanted, but you're still looking anyway." His eyes locked on mine. "You're a better person than I am."

His statement shocked me, not only because he'd acknowledged my pain, but also because he seemed so genuine. So serious. There was no sign of his usual protective coating of humor and charm.

"He was involved with a lot of people . . . most of whom are now dead or have disappeared. The ones we knew about—Walter Frey, Geraldo Lopez, Christopher Merritt, and Steve Morrissey—but also some we didn't, like Max Goodwin and Neil Fulton. And I finally tracked down the final name on that list Walter Frey had intended to give me. Rowena Rogers."

Colt's face didn't change. "Never heard of her. Who is she?"

"She was married to a financial planner with another firm."

"He wasn't named?"

"Her husband was killed in an accident fourteen years ago."

His eyes widened. "Interesting timing."

"I know, right? She was part of a scandal around the time Christopher Merritt disappeared. People thought they were having an affair. She disappeared after that, although not like the others. She changed her name to Nicole Baker and keeps to herself."

"And you're certain she's still alive?" he asked.

"That's what Janine said. But I know for a fact that she was alive and well, and here in Franklin last week."

He narrowed his eyes. "How?"

"I saw her. Twice." I told him about her connection with Walter Frey, then paused and said, "She told me it was my fault he was killed. That I'd stirred everything up again by asking about my father."

"That's a crock of bullshit," Colt scoffed. "Did you force Walter Frey to be part of that land deal? Did you force him to be in cahoots with your dad and that dentist?"

"No, but I forced him to meet me at the bar."

"So? He was up to shady shit long before you left town."

"I could have gone to the police."

"And you did. You called Bennett."

And look where that got me. "But that wasn't really like going to the police."

"Because Bennett hid your involvement?"

I nodded. "Because of Owen."

"Probably."

"No," I said. "For certain. Brady told me last night."

He looked suspicious. "Why would he tell you that?" He leaned forward. "What did you tell him?"

"Nothing about last night. It was just . . ." How would Colt take this? "When I got to Brady's apartment, Owen was at the front door, handing off an envelope to Brady." I hadn't intended to tell him this much, but as soon as the words started tumbling out of my mouth, I knew I wanted him to know.

"What was in the envelope?"

I wrapped my arms around myself and shook my head in a jerky motion. "Nothing to do with Daddy."

"How can you be sure?" he demanded.

"Because I saw it," I said, trying not to cry. "I saw the photos and the reports. Emily was murdered by a serial killer."

"*What?*" He sat back in his seat, his eyes wide in shock. "That's not what the news reports are saying."

"Yet it's true."

"Why haven't they made this public?"

"I don't know," I said, but that wasn't entirely true. Brady seemed to be the only one who had connected the dots, and he hadn't told anyone else on the police force. Despite his insistence that he was protecting me from the shady characters on the force, I couldn't help asking myself that same question: Why?

chapter twenty

W hy did he target Emily?" Colt asked, obviously still in shock.

I'd told him there was a serial killer, and while I wasn't ready to confess everything, I needed to tell him something. I held on to myself tighter. "Because of me."

"You? Why?"

I shrugged. "Maybe because she was my attorney, and I'm a bit 'notorious.'" I used air quotes to emphasize my point.

"That seems like a stretch."

"Nevertheless, Brady confirmed there's a link."

That got his attention. "What link?"

"He was vague about the details," I lied, surprised that I really *did* want to tell him. Who would have thought that once I uncorked my decade-old secret by spilling the beans to my mother, I'd end up wanting to word-vomit my story to everyone. But that wasn't entirely true. I wanted to tell Colt because, despite his admission that he had an ulterior motive for working with me, I knew deep in my soul that he was my friend.

"That's bullshit, Magnolia!" he said. "You have a right to know!"

I didn't answer.

He pushed out a frustrated sigh. "Does he think you'll be a target next?"

"He doesn't know."

He sat up, looking agitated. "Then what the hell are you doing working at Ava's Bible study? Why aren't you under police protection?"

I gave him a tiny grin. "Can you imagine if Ava tangled with a serial killer? The serial killer wouldn't stand a chance."

"I'm serious, Magnolia."

"And so am I. Honestly, I think her death stare would be enough to do him in."

He grinned in spite of himself, but it quickly fell away. "I planned to go to Chattanooga tomorrow morning, but now I think I should stick around."

"Don't be ridiculous. You have to look for the gold."

"The gold's not much good if you're dead."

"Why, Colt Austin," I teased, "if you're not careful, I might start to think you actually have feelings for me."

He didn't smile, but he didn't look away either. And that scared the crap out of me.

I broke eye contact first. "I need to get to Alvin's. I'm going to be late."

"We didn't get your car."

I shook my head as I stood. "I'll get it later."

"I'd help you after you get off," he said, remaining on the sofa, "but I have something else going on tonight."

"Something that has to do with the gold?"

"No."

I waited a beat before saying, "You're not going to tell me what it is?"

"It doesn't have anything to do with you."

And we were back to this. "Fine. Whatever. I have to start a load of laundry before I go, so feel free to leave whenever you like." I headed into the bedroom and sorted the dirty laundry on my bed into piles. But when I grabbed a pair of jeans, my breath caught in my throat. I'd forgotten to text Brady. If he insisted on keeping our appointment, I'd need to bring something to wear for our hike into the woods. I didn't have anything better to bring than dirty jeans and a T-shirt, but there didn't seem much point in wearing clean clothes for a hike. The rain last night was bound to make it a muddy mess.

Just like the night it had happened ten years ago.

Panic buzzed at the edges of my awareness, threatening to bloom into a full-blown panic attack. After a half-minute of me picturing myself on a beach and the sun warming my skin—one of the relaxation methods I'd picked up over the past ten years—I calmed down enough to send Brady a text.

Can we reschedule tonight? Belinda needs me.

I picked up an armload of whites to put into the small washing machine tucked into the linen closet. I stopped as soon as I walked out of the bedroom, shocked to see Colt still on the sofa.

"I thought you were leaving."

He snorted. "*You* said I was leaving. I never said any such thing. If you think I'm leaving you alone with a serial killer who might be targeting you, then you've got another think coming."

I gave him a look of disbelief.

He stretched his arm along the back of the sofa. "I thought you were going to be late for work? Let me drop you off."

I watched him for a couple of seconds, trying to figure out if he was up to something, but he seemed to be on the up and up. "Okay . . ."

After I started the load, I grabbed the jeans, T-shirt, and a pair of athletic shoes in case I couldn't back out of my hike with Brady. As an afterthought, I grabbed a light jacket in case it cooled off. Unfortunately, I'd already gone through my limited stash of tote bags to take things to Brady's. I'd have to store the loose clothes in the back room at the shop. Alvin would grill me all afternoon until I gave him a decent excuse.

Turned out Colt beat Alvin to it. He eyed the stack of clothes in my arms as I grabbed my purse.

"What?" I asked with a hint of attitude.

"What plans do you have with Detective Hot Stuff that requires jeans and tennis shoes?"

"Who says my plans are with him?"

"So they're not?"

I shook my head. "You have your mysterious plans, and I have mine."

He followed me out the door and grabbed the keys out of my hand to lock it behind us. "Do you think it was a good idea to start a load of wash?" he asked as he followed me down the stairs. "It will start to stink before you get back to put it in the dryer."

"Imagine that," I said sarcastically. "A man who's a laundry expert."

"Have you ever seen me in dirty clothes?" he asked as he walked around to the passenger side of his truck and opened the door for me. "I know my way around a washer and dryer."

I narrowed my eyes and stared up at him. "Like you know your way around a truck?"

"What?" he asked. "You've got your arms full, and I'm capable of being a gentleman."

He gave me a big toothy grin as he shut the door behind me. Seconds later, he slid behind the wheel.

"Thanks for your help, Colt."

He shot me a tight smile. "I'm your laundry hotline should you need the help. When do you plan on coming back?"

We both knew that wasn't what I had meant. "Tonight." I hadn't been entirely sure until the word left my lips.

His eyebrows rose. "Bennett's staying with *you* tonight?"

"No," I said slowly. "I'm coming home alone."

He was quiet for a few seconds. "I was joking this morning about the lover's spat, Mags."

"I know . . . It's complicated."

"So is this a *you're not ready to live with him yet* complicated, or a *we're taking a break*?"

I wasn't ready to tell him I was ending things with Brady, worried he'd read too much into the timing with his kiss.

"You're not staying alone, are you?" he asked.

I almost gave him an answer, or something approaching one, when I realized why he was pressing me. "I'll be fine."

We rode in silence until he pulled into the parking lot behind Rebellious Rose a few minutes later. I started to open the door, but he stopped me.

"Maggie, wait."

I let go of the handle and looked back at him. This was serious Colt again.

"You need to be careful, and you need to be able to protect yourself. Have you replaced the gun that got stolen?"

"No."

Leaning over me, he opened the glove box and pulled out a towel-wrapped object. He placed the mystery thing in my open palm, and its weight and shape immediately erased the mystery.

"Keep this with you," he said. "It's loaded with a full clip, which means you have twelve bullets, so make them count if you need to use it. But you have no business getting into any gun battles, so it should be enough." He grabbed my arm. "If you're in danger, shoot to kill. Do you hear me? Don't try to be a hero because that always bites you in the ass," he said bitterly. "You kill the bastard and save yourself."

I nodded absently as I stuffed the still-wrapped gun into my purse. He sounded like he was speaking from experience, which made me all the more curious about his past.

"You need to get a gun in your name as soon as possible. Today. See if Alvin will let you take a break to get one."

"I don't have my car, Colt. It's still at the apartment."

He groaned. "Shit. That's right."

I offered him a smile. "It's okay. I'll see if Belinda will take me to get it. She might ask questions, but she'll drop it when I refuse to give her answers. I'll go first thing in the morning."

"Call me if you need me, but I'll be busy tonight. I won't be able to get away." He paused. "Mags, I think you should stay at Bennett's tonight. It will be safer if he's with you."

"I'll be fine, but thanks for being concerned. I mean it."

He gave a quick nod, his lips pressed into a tight line. I looked back a couple of times, even after I went through the back door of the shop, and he was still there, watching me with a blank face.

Turned out my purse was big enough to accommodate my clothes. I explained the athletic shoes by telling Alvin about my plan to walk to Belinda's store when I got off. Just like last week, he tried to pry information about Ava's Bible study out of me, but I just grinned and told him tall tales that were obvious lies, like that Martians had crashed the party and spat their tea in Miss Ava's face.

We were busy again—which was great for job security—but I didn't have much time to check my phone. By the time we closed, Brady still hadn't responded to my initial text, or the one I'd sent during a quick break a couple of hours earlier. In fact, I was beginning to worry about him. I still hadn't told Belinda whether or not I was coming by her shop. When Alvin locked the door at five, I texted Belinda and told her that I still hadn't heard from Brady, but I'd let her know as soon as I did.

I got started with my inventory count in the back of the store, quickly becoming so absorbed I'd lost track of time. So I was shocked when I heard Alvin say, "Magnolia, I thought you were going to Belinda's shop."

My head jerked up from my count of antique crystal drawer pulls. "I am."

"She's outside the front door."

I climbed to my feet as Alvin let my sister-in-law in. She was wearing a pair of light-blue linen pants and a white button-down, short-sleeve blouse with light-blue buttons to match her pants.

I brushed off my hands as I walked toward her. "Belinda, I wasn't expecting you."

She offered me a sweet smile. "I finished up early, so I thought I'd drop by. This way I get to see Alvin too."

Alvin beamed. "It's always a pleasure to see you, Belinda."

"I know you're working on inventory," she said. "You can put me to work if you'd like. Free labor."

He waved his hand and laughed. "Don't be silly, but if you want to go back and keep Magnolia company, feel free. She's still got fifteen minutes left." He grinned. "And I can't thank you enough for recommending Magnolia. She's a wonderful addition to the staff."

"She *is* wonderful, isn't she?" Belinda asked. "I'm so grateful she's part of our lives."

A blush rose to my cheeks, catching me by surprise. Belinda was one of the best parts of being here in Franklin. It was humbling to hear her tell Alvin she felt the same way.

Belinda followed me to the back of the store. "I still haven't heard from Brady," I said in an undertone. I checked my phone again, and sure enough, still nothing. My stomach twisted with worry. I knew his job was dangerous, and despite my need to back off from our relationship, I still cared about him.

"That's okay. I'll help you count until he gets here."

Belinda was one of the nicest people I knew, but her offer struck me as odd. So did the fact that she'd shown up without any warning. Nevertheless, I handed her a basket full of napkin rings made from vintage silverware. "Well, thanks. You can work on these. They all have different patterns. You just have to count how many forks and how many spoons."

"Okay," she said with a sweet smile.

I'd lost track of my crystal drawer pull count, so I started over, not a huge deal since the final count was twenty-six.

"I found you the most beautiful dress," Belinda said as she wrote her counts down on the clipboard Alvin had given me. "I can't wait to see it on you."

I wanted to ask her about Roy and also about her meeting with Bill James, but this wasn't the place to get into that discussion. Especially with my gossipy boss listening.

After I'd counted a stack of napkins and recorded the quantity, I tugged my phone out of my pocket and checked it again. Still nothing from Brady and it was 5:58. Now I was really worried. I was about to confess as much to Belinda when Alvin said, "You're quite popular tonight, Magnolia. Now Brady's here."

My eyes widened in surprise. Why hadn't he answered my texts?

Belinda dropped the aprons she'd been counting and stood. "Hello, Detective Bennett," she said in a very business-like voice.

Brady looked surprised to see her. "Belinda."

I felt a strange vibe coming from both of them. Did they know each other? Then I remembered Belinda had dropped some clothes off at Brady's apartment over the weekend. She'd made a comment about how Brady wouldn't let her in to see me. Was she holding a grudge? It seemed unlike her.

"You didn't answer my texts," I said in an accusatory tone even though I was grateful he was okay.

"I was busy," he said, walking over to me and pulling me into a hug. His lips brushed my temple, and he kept his arm around my back as he turned to face Belinda. "I'm surprised to see you here."

"I'm sure Magnolia told you that something came up, and I need to steal her away for the evening."

Brady stiffened. "We had plans."

Belinda offered him a sweet smile, but there was a glint of determination in her eyes. "I know, but seeing how you've had her since Saturday, I'm sure you can let me have her for one night."

I glanced between the both of them, trying to figure out what was going on. Alvin had picked up on the weirdness too, and he was openly staring, his mouth gaping. This would probably give him gossip fodder for a week.

Finally, Brady glanced down at me. "Maggie?"

"Do you have any leads on Emily's case?" I asked.

His eyebrows rose. "No."

Now I was really torn. Taking Brady to the house could help him find the killer, but if it was really important, why hadn't he made this official? Not even Miss Ava could have held it against me if I'd left her Bible study to help out a murder investigation. Tromping through the muddy woods at night seemed like a bad idea. And I couldn't ignore the little voice inside me that told me not to go. I'd relied on my instincts a lot since I'd come home four weeks ago, and so far they hadn't steered me wrong. "I'm going to ask for a rain check. Belinda really needs me tonight."

Brady looked incredulous. "This is important, Magnolia."

I turned my attention to Belinda. "Can you give us a minute?"

She looked torn, probably worried Brady would convince me to change my mind—maybe that was why she'd dropped by in person. But when I gave her a reassuring smile, she turned and gave Brady the best glare she was probably capable of giving. "I'll go have a chat with Alvin."

I waited until she moved to the front of the shop, then walked toward the back door and waited for Brady to join me.

"Maggie," he said in a pleading tone. "You can hang out with your sister-in-law anytime. Hell, you just had breakfast with her yesterday morning. But there's a serial killer on the loose, and what I find in that house could help me break this case."

I had to admit he was convincing, but then something unsettling occurred to me. "How did you know I had breakfast with Belinda yesterday?"

He gave me a sheepish grin. "I told you that you're famous. One of the detectives I work with saw you there."

I put my hands on my hips and squinted up at him. "And he just happened to mention it to you? Why would he tell *you*?"

"*She* knows you're staying at my apartment. Gossip travels fast."

The indignation bled out of me, and I dropped my hands to my sides. His explanation made sense, but it still made me uneasy, especially since he'd also known about my presence at the church dinner the other night. All the more reason to take a few steps back from our relationship.

"Brady . . ." I paused, realizing this was terrible timing, but then again, there probably *wasn't* a right time. "I packed up my things this morning. I'm going to stay somewhere else tonight."

His body went still. "Why?"

I took a breath and lifted a shaky hand to the base of my throat. "A million reasons. My life's an utter mess, and I need to get it under control before I start a relationship. Also, there's the fact that a killer might be after me."

"All the more reason to stay with me!" he whisper-shouted.

"No," I said, gaining more courage with every word. "It's a terrible reason. I'm mistaking my need for protection for romantic feelings."

"Are you saying you don't have romantic feelings for me?"

I did, but not like I had for Colt. However, I was sure he wouldn't appreciate the comparison. "You know I do, but I think it's best if I rely on you less right now."

Anger filled his eyes. "I knew we were moving too fast."

"Maybe so, and I'm sorry if I hurt you," I said, even though I couldn't really regret sleeping together. He'd found my scar, and I'd discovered the serial killer connection. It had (hopefully) brought us one step closer to finding the murderer. But Brady was a good guy, and I *did* regret causing him pain. "Please try to understand."

He was quiet for a moment, then gave me a soft smile. "I want what you want, Maggie. If you need to take a break, I understand."

"Really? Brady . . . thank you."

"I've told you before that I'm a patient man." His face hardened a bit, as though preparing for a fight, then he pushed out a breath. "But I still need you to take me to that house tonight."

"I'm sorry, but I still can't go," I insisted. "Belinda needs me."

"*Needs you?* What does she need you for?"

While I understood why he was being short, I didn't like his abrasive tone. "Why didn't you answer my texts today?"

"I told you—I was busy."

"You couldn't have told me you were busy?"

He clenched his jaw, then turned to the side and looked out the back window into the parking lot. "You're right. I'm sorry."

I'd expected him to come up with another excuse, so his apology caught me off guard. "I'm still not going tonight. Besides Belinda needing me, I don't think it's a good idea to be hiking in the woods after the rain last night, let alone in the dark." I lifted my chin. "I can't handle going out there at night. We have to do it during the day."

His jaw tightened and irritation flashed in his eyes, but he said, "Okay. What's your schedule like tomorrow?"

The tension in my shoulders eased slightly. "I work for the Belles tomorrow night, but I'm also supposed to work for Miss Ava," I fibbed. I wanted to track down Rowena Rogers—or at least try—and I had no idea how long that would take. "But I'm going in later. Close to noon."

Brady frowned. "That woman can't make you pay off the debt for those damages, Magnolia. If that's what's going on, tell me right now and I'll deal with it."

"I told you. It's for extra money. And if that were the case, *I'd* deal with it."

After several moments of somewhat uncomfortable silence, he said, "I'm not sure I can get away tomorrow, but I'll let you know."

"Okay."

"What are you and Belinda doing, anyway?" Brady asked. "I realize you're not staying with me, but I'm still worried about you."

Oh crap. This was about to get a whole lot harder. I didn't want him to know about the dress, the ball, any of it. Not yet.

To my surprise, Belinda walked up to us and looped her arm through mine. She beamed up at him. "Roy's out of town, so we're having a good old-fashioned slumber party."

The look on his face suggested he didn't buy it for a minute, but she'd just given me a safe place to stay tonight. I resisted the urge to throw my arms around her neck and give her a hug.

But Brady wasn't fazed for long. He lifted an eyebrow in a teasing manner, even though the look in his eyes wasn't playful. "On a school night?"

Belinda squeezed my arm and leaned her head against mine. "I know. That's what makes it more fun."

"Where are you girls staying?"

"My house," Belinda said with a smile. "Magnolia's going to help me with a special project for the wedding I'm putting on tomorrow night." A mischievous grin lit up her face, and she leaned closer and lowered her voice. "Only, she doesn't know it yet."

The Brady I'd gotten to know would have laughed at that, but the man in front of us only stared at her. Of course, he had plenty of reason to be stressed, between Emily's murder and its possible connection to so many others, not to mention I'd just broken up with him. I felt terrible for hurting him, but I wouldn't be doing either one of us any favors if I stayed.

"I'll be fine, Brady."

The fear in his eyes felt genuine, which made me feel guilty for not entirely trusting him. Still, I didn't want to go out to that house tonight, and now more than before, I didn't want to stay at his apartment.

"There's still a murderer out there, Maggie," Brady said. "I'm worried about you."

"I have a top-notch security system, Detective Bennett," Belinda assured him. "And I have a marble rolling pin I can use in self-defense should it come to it."

"Magnolia's life isn't something to joke about," he said in a harsh tone.

"Is there something new I should know about?" I asked as fear wormed its way through my gut.

"No. But I'm still very concerned."

"I'm concerned too," Belinda said. "I'm sorry I made light of a serious situation, but I assure you, my home is like a fortress. My husband tends to lean on the side of paranoia. We have cameras outside, double deadbolts, and even a panic room."

I shot her a look of disbelief, sure she was joking, but she was dead serious.

She and Brady began stare-off number two, and finally Brady caved. "Please check in with me tonight. And keep your phone with you so I can check on you."

"I will."

I knew I should feel guilty for ending things with him, but all I could feel was relief, not just that I'd broken up with him, but that he wasn't watching over my shoulder. He was a police detective and I knew I should trust him, but my gut told me to be wary.

I wasn't sure what to make of that.

chapter
twenty-one

Brady insisted on walking us to Belinda's car, which she'd moved to the back parking lot. Why hadn't she knocked on the back door?

She stopped next to her car and turned to look up at him, her key fob dangling from her hand. "As sweet as your concern for Magnolia is, it seems overzealous. Is she in any danger?"

Brady held her gaze. "She has ties to several people who have been murdered since she came back to town. I think my concerns are justified even if there is no clear connection."

The setting sun had made the sky a pallet of pinks and oranges and reds, casting Belinda in an unearthly glow. She looked more like an avenging angel than a wedding planner. "She'll be perfectly safe with me."

Standing in the parking lot like a sentinel, which now seemed more suffocating than protective, he watched us drive away.

"I know this is none of my business," Belinda said, her eyes firmly on the road. "But how serious are you and Brady?"

I resisted the urge to squirm. "We just got involved last week."

"That doesn't necessarily mean anything," she said in an even tone. "I have plenty of brides show up who have only known the grooms a few months."

My mouth dropped. "I'm not getting married."

"I never said you were," she said, unruffled by my protest. "But you can still get serious."

"Let's just say he wants a relationship, and after a brief attempt, I've decided it's a bad idea."

"You broke up with him?" When I didn't respond, she said, "It's obvious he's not ready to let it go."

"I suppose." I sure wasn't about to admit how unsettled I was by the way he was handling my experience with the serial killer.

She grinned at me. "I'm your sister-in-law. I think it's my job to quiz you on your love life."

Like you answer questions about your love life with Roy? But I was smart enough to keep that to myself. Instead, I got the point across by asking, "Is Roy really out of town?"

"Yes." She glanced my direction again. "I would never bring you to my house if he was there. I would never willingly subject you to that." She hesitated. "But if you're really in danger, maybe we should just head to my house. It really is safe. You can come with me to the shop in the morning and try the dress on then."

"Yeah," I said. "I don't really feel like trying dresses on anyway."

We were quiet the rest of the drive to the neighborhood she had brought me to the night of the Bunco party nearly a month ago. She pulled into the driveway of a brick two-story house with a full front porch. Even in the fading sunlight, I could see the yard was lush and green, and the landscaping was impeccable. While I knew Belinda had excellent taste, part of me wondered if it was also my brother keeping up appearances.

She pressed the garage door opener and the door rolled up, revealing a nearly empty garage except for the shelves lining the back wall, stacked with an assortment of coolers, paint cans, and tools. All very neat and tidy.

As soon as she pulled into the garage, she pushed the button to close the door and stayed inside the car until it was completely closed. She turned to me with a small smile. "You can't be too careful."

Her behavior led me to believe this was a habit.

Belinda unlocked the door to the garage, and led me into her kitchen. She turned off the alarm at a keypad next to the door, then quickly turned it back on.

"Do you really have a panic room?" I asked.

Her serious eyes met mine. "Yes." Then, as if she'd said nothing more startling than that it might rain later, she walked into the kitchen and set her Kate Spade purse on the breakfast room table.

"Belinda, your house is beautiful," I gushed as I took it in. The kitchen was decorated in warm creams and reds, with granite counters. It was open to a living room with overstuffed furniture, vintage light wood tables, and heavy drapes. Both rooms looked like they could have been in a decorating magazine featuring French Country design.

I'd expected her home to be as well put-together as she was, but this house looked like a builder's showcase. The closer I looked, the more I realized there were no hints of the things that made a house a home—an open book, put down mid-read, a grocery list on the fridge, a stack of unopened mail. No shoes in the corner or even dirty dishes on the counter or sink. While the house had touches of Belinda all over it, it didn't have the warmth I'd come to love about her.

"Would you like a glass of wine?" she asked as she stopped in front of a small wine refrigerator.

"Yeah . . . Do you really want to cook dinner?"

She laughed. "We have to eat, don't we?" She selected a bottle of wine from the fridge and quickly removed the cork. After retrieving two white wine glasses from the hanging display over the wine refrigerator, she gave us each a healthy pour.

"I'll help, but it might be safer if I'm a bystander rather than a contributor."

"Nonsense." She waved one hand in dismissal as she handed me a glass of white wine with the other. "I know it's customary to serve red with salmon, but I think the lime and cilantro warrant the Pinot Gris."

"Belinda."

Her eyes lifted to mine.

"You don't have to put on an act with me."

Her eyes widened, and the horrified look on her face made me think I'd said the wrong thing, but then tears filled her eyes. "I know. That's one of the reasons I love you."

I thought she might elaborate, but she just took a more-than-healthy gulp of her wine. When she set the glass down and opened the fridge, it was akin to saying we'd put the subject to bed. For now. "I know Lila insists you're hopeless in the kitchen, but I refuse to believe it."

"I made scones with Ava for Bible study this morning," I said. "She directed me, but I made them. Even Colt thought they were good."

She grinned. "Colt would eat shoe leather and think it was good as long as it was free, but the fact Ava Milton served them at her infamous Bible study is the sure sign they were a success. All the more reason for you to help."

"Why are you and Colt at odds?" The question gushed out.

She stood in front of her open fridge and glanced over her shoulder at me. "What makes you think we're at odds?"

"Little things you've said here and there. And the fact you think it's a bad idea for me to be his friend."

"It's more like I worry about you. I know Colt's reputation."

"I'm a big girl. I know he's incapable of a relationship. I'm not interested in him that way."

She didn't respond. I nearly protested more but realized I'd only incriminate myself, especially since I knew I really did have feelings for him. I was pretty near to babbling as it was.

"So tell me what to do."

We made the dish together, Belinda leading me the whole time, and by the time the salmon was finished baking, we'd prepared the jasmine rice and finished our bottle of wine.

Belinda opened a new bottle and refilled both of our glasses, then set the table, complete with cloth napkins and perfect place settings.

I watched open-mouthed as she carefully plated the food on a platter, but then I realized something—this perfection was so ingrained in her, she couldn't help herself. I took the spatula she was using to scoop out the salmon and pushed her to the side. "I'm taking over. Go sit down."

She gasped, but picked up her wine and the newly opened bottle and sat down.

Knowing full well she was watching, I scooped a piece of salmon and dumped it on top of the piece that was already on the plate before setting the dish on the table.

Belinda looked horrified when I set it down in front her. She started to reach for the serving spoon, but I lightly slapped her hand. "Don't you dare touch that."

Then I set the pot of rice on the table, using a dishtowel as a trivet.

"Magnolia!"

For the pièce de résistance, I ripped two paper towels off the roll and stole the cloth napkin out of her lap, replacing it with the paper.

"Is this some kind of protest?" she asked, her words slightly slurred.

I sat in the chair across from her, suddenly feeling sad. "No, Belinda. This is how normal people eat."

Tears filled her eyes again, but this time she gave in to them. "Damn you, Magnolia," she said, but it lacked the venom to hurt.

"You said you wanted to talk to me about Roy, but we just made this delicious dinner and I don't want any talk of him to ruin it. So I say we eat and then we can talk."

She nodded and wiped the tears from her cheeks.

"If you were serving this," I said in a teasing tone as I picked up the salmon serving spoon, "I suspect you'd plate this with the salmon on a bed of rice. Am I right?"

She laughed. "Of course."

"That's what I thought." I dumped the salmon on her plate, making sure it broke into a few pieces instead of keeping its shape as a perfect fillet. Then I placed a heap of rice on top, still using the salmon spoon. "There. That's better." I served my own food the same way.

"You're a terrible influence," she said as she picked up her fork.

"Just one of the many reasons you love me," I teased, but I had to wonder if there was some truth to that. I was definitely a rule flaunter, and my brother hated it. To be friends with me was a mini act of rebellion.

I took a bite of the food I'd served upside down and moaned. "Damn. I really *can* cook."

She laughed, despite the fact that we both knew she'd cooked most of the dinner. My jobs had been relegated to stirring the rice and chopping up the cilantro. "Thanks for letting me assist you."

We managed to steer the conversation around the topics we'd agreed were undesirable, and Belinda told me about the most recent wedding she'd put on.

By the time we finished, we'd polished off the second bottle, but Belinda had drunk most of it. Her unhappiness became more apparent with each glass, so palpable I nearly choked on it, but I was at a loss as to what to do other than just be with her and let her know I loved her even if she was capable of being imperfect.

When we finished, she started to get up with her plate.

She was wobbling like a top at the end of its twirl, so I pushed her back down and took her plate from her hand. "I'm cleaning up, something I'm quite good at, apparently. So you sit there and keep me company."

She didn't protest like I'd half expected her to. I wondered if now was a good time to bring up my brother, but worried she was too melancholy.

I didn't need to think on it too hard, because she brought him up first. "Roy's at a convention in Las Vegas."

"Do you really want me to spend the night?"

"There's no way I'd let you spend the night alone in your apartment."

"I could always stay with Brady." Not that I had any intention of doing so.

She took a sip of wine. "Don't make a deal with the devil, Magnolia. You may think it's worth it, but it will kill you in the end."

"Is that what you think I'm doing?" I asked.

Her eyebrows rose. "Isn't it?"

"No. I ended it." I supposed I'd made a deal, but I didn't think of Brady as a devil. However, she was obviously speaking from personal experience. "What kind of deal did you make with Roy?"

She laughed, which sounded a touch hysterical. Then she shook her head. "That's not why you're here."

"Then why *am* I here?"

"I lied to you, Magnolia. I can't tell you about Roy. Not yet."

"Okay . . ."

"You're not angry?"

I walked over to her and knelt in front of her. "This may be hard for you to accept, but I like you, Belinda. Not because you're my sister-in-law, but because you are an amazing person, which has nothing to do with how well you dress, how beautifully you decorate your house, or whether you use cloth napkins. All you had to do was ask me to come over, no explanation required, and I would have come in a heartbeat."

She started to cry in heavy sobs.

Oh, Belinda. What has my brother done to you?

Unsure what would comfort her the most, I kept kneeling in front of her, holding her hand in mine. In a minute, she settled down, but her chest heaved as she tried to catch her breath.

I got up and got her a glass of ice water. "Feel better?" I asked after she took a long gulp.

She shook her head. "I don't deserve you."

I released a bitter laugh. "I know plenty of people who'd say the same thing but mean the opposite."

She continued to shake her head. "I know things."

That caught my attention. "What kind of things?"

Her eyes lifted to mine. "I think Bill James might have killed Emily."

I nearly lost my balance as the room swayed. "What makes you say that?"

"I found a file with her name on it in his office. I saw it on his desk yesterday morning."

I blinked. "Why would he have a file on Emily?"

"Exactly. Why?" She paused. "But that's not all. He had a file on you too."

Another wave of panic washed over me, and I sat down before it could pull me under. Belinda was confirming my suspicions. Momma's suspicions. "You think he's going to kill me?"

"It sounds preposterous, doesn't it?" she asked with a tiny giggle.

"I didn't ask if it was preposterous. I asked if you thought he was going to kill me."

"Honestly," she said, her eyes full of tears. "I don't know."

"Why would he want to kill me?"

"I don't know that either." She took another sip of wine. "But I can't go to the police. Those files aren't exactly hard evidence that he may have murdered anyone, and Roy would kill me. But I know I have to protect you."

"So your plan is to keep me in your fortress until Roy comes home?"

"No." Her eyes met mine. "We're going to snoop in Bill James's office."

chapter
twenty-two

I doubt I would have been more excited if I'd just gotten the role of Glinda in *Wicked* on Broadway. "Are you kidding?"

"You don't have to come . . ."

"Oh, I'm coming." Realizing I sounded too eager, I said, "If for no other reason than to be your designated driver. You're sauced."

She laughed. "I had to get drunk to get up the nerve to suggest it to you."

"You really thought I'd say no?"

"I knew you'd say yes."

I chuckled even though my stomach was flipping in anticipation. I planned to look for a whole lot more than a couple of files. "If we're snooping, there's another place I want to search afterward."

"Where?"

Crap. I'd promised Momma I wouldn't tell anyone about it, but she hadn't said anything about not bringing anyone there. "It's a surprise. We can go there after we finish up in Nashville." When I saw her hesitation, I said, "Trust me. This will be worth it."

In fact, every time I thought about that basement, I got more and more ticked that I hadn't pulled myself together enough to do a proper search. There could be real evidence in that filing cabinet, not to mention . . .

No, I didn't want my thoughts to go there just yet.

Belinda got up and insisted on helping me clean, but when she said she needed to change clothes, I sent her upstairs. After I started the dishwasher and wiped down the table and counters, I left the kitchen for the living room. While I was curious about Roy's home, I was more interested in anything personal belonging to Belinda.

Bookcases flanked the fireplace. Most of the shelves were filled with books, and the few tasteful knickknacks on display looked generic. But one caught my eye, a tiny blue bird. I picked it up and instantly regretted it when I realized how delicate it was. It was obviously old, and there were cracks in the paint underneath the shiny surface.

Belinda came down the stairs wearing jeans and a T-shirt.

"This is yours," I said, holding up the bird. "I know it's not Roy's."

"It was my grandmother's," she said, looking nervous. "She used to call me her little blue bird because she said I sang like a songbird. I got it when she died."

I realized I was making her anxious, so I set the bird back down on the shelf. "You never talk about your family."

"The past is in the past."

I realized I knew very little about her past. All I knew was that she'd come to Nashville five or six years ago after growing up in Mississippi, she was an only child, and both of her parents were dead. She didn't much like to talk about her loss, and whenever the topic came up, she'd quickly brush it aside, telling me she was stronger than her past.

I wished I were stronger than mine.

I moved in front of her. "I used to think so too, but now I know better. If we don't acknowledge the bad things in our past, they become festering wounds, Belinda. Mine have come back tenfold, and I'm dealing with them now."

"Your father?"

"And other things."

Tears welled in her eyes again. "I'm still too drunk to have this conversation," she said as she walked past me and picked up her purse off the breakfast table. She handed me the car keys. "Let's go. You'll have to drive."

"I'd already figured *that* out."

I intended to ask her more about her family on the drive up to Nashville, but all the wine and the motion of the car put her to sleep. I parked in the garage Daddy had always used when I was a kid and turned off the engine.

Belinda was still asleep in the passenger seat, and I briefly considered going up to the office without her. There was probably a key on her key fob, and I was worried she'd still be too drunk, but I needed her. If someone saw me snooping around, they were likely to call the police. But if Belinda was with me, we could say she was getting something from Roy's office.

"Belinda," I said as I gently shook her arm. "We're here."

"The Duncans are okay with the gardenias instead of peonies . . ." she mumbled with her eyes closed.

"Belinda," I said louder. "Wake up. We're here."

Her eyes opened and she struggled to focus on my face. "Magnolia. What are you doing here?"

Great. "We're at Roy's office. We were going to look through Bill's office, remember?"

She squinted her eyes. "Oh. Yeah."

"Are the keys to the office on the car fob?"

"No." She sat up, and it took her three attempts to pick her purse up off the floor. After she got it into her lap, she dug around until she pulled out a plastic name tag with a magnetic strip on the back. "This. We need this."

I took it from her and turned it over in my hand. JS Investments and Roy Steele were printed on the front.

Belinda reached for the door handle, missing it the first time and nearly falling out of the car.

No matter how much I wanted this to work, there was no chance it would. Not tonight. "Belinda, I think we need to try this another night."

"No. No." She righted herself and waved her hand at me. "Tonight's the only night. I have a wedding tomorrow night, and the ball is Saturday." She spun around to face me. "Wait until you see your dress. It's beautiful. You're going to love it."

I put my hand on her shoulder. "Forget about the dress. I'm sure the one you picked out is perfect." But that didn't help us right now.

"It has to be tonight, Magnolia," she said, staring into my eyes. "If he killed Emily, I'm scared he's going to target you next."

I was scared of that too. Part of me considered calling Brady, but I was pretty sure there wasn't anything he could do. He was a Franklin detective who had no jurisdiction in Nashville. Besides, Belinda was right—the files she'd seen weren't grounds for a search warrant. I knew Brady suspected Bill James of something, though he hadn't exactly been loose-lipped about it.

Maybe we were we overreacting. Those files could have some innocuous purpose, although I wasn't sure what. But I couldn't forget the look in Momma's eyes when she'd told me about her suspicions about Bill James's wife. Nor the fact that the serial killer had recognized me that long-ago night. He'd known my name.

Even if Bill hadn't killed Emily and Amy and all those other women, I could still look for a connection to the shady business deals he'd brokered with my father, although I suspected those records were at the house in Leiper's Fork.

I was definitely going there next . . . with or without Belinda. I was having serious doubts about taking her upstairs right now.

Belinda took a deep breath and pushed it out, then gave me a serious look. "I can do this. Now let's go."

I frowned. It still seemed like a terrible idea, but I wanted her to come along. "Okay. Let's give it a go."

She got out and I met her at the back of the car. When she wobbled, I reached out for her, but she pushed my hand away.

"I can do it."

Belinda seemed to gain more coordination by the time we got to the entrance to the building. I swiped the name tag and the door popped open. "Okay," I said. "We're in."

We rode the elevator up to the floor for JS Investments. I glanced through the glass door to see if we had any witnesses, but it was after eight on a Thursday night. No one was around the reception area, and all the lights were dimmed, a good thing since Belinda had to slouch against the wall while I swiped the card on the pad beside the door.

Once we were inside, I turned on my phone's flashlight and led Belinda past the reception area and into the hallway behind it. "I noticed Roy was using Daddy's office," I said, pointing the beam of my flashlight that direction. "Is Bill still in his old one?"

For some reason, Bill had always had the big corner office, even from the beginning. Daddy had never seemed to care, but it had bugged Momma plenty. I couldn't see Bill giving it up.

"Yeah. In the back. But we need a key." Thank God she seemed to be becoming more alert.

"Do you *have* a key?" I asked.

"Roy has a key. He's not supposed to, but he keeps one in his desk."

"Do you have the key to Roy's office?"

She dangled a small key chain and single key in the beam from my phone flashlight, casting giant shadows on the wall. I had to wonder if we were playing this right. If we were caught, we'd look far more suspicious wandering around in the dark than we would if we turned on a few lights. But I preferred no one knowing we were here at all, and the overhead lights would be a dead giveaway.

No lights.

Roy's office was halfway down the hall. Without a word, Belinda moved toward it, and I shined my flashlight on the knob while she unlocked the door.

I followed her in and glanced around the shadow-cast room, surprised how much it still looked like Daddy's office. I'd visited this office a few weeks ago, of course, but I'd been too busy dealing with Roy's $50,000 offer to leave town at the time to pay much attention.

"Belinda," I said as she wobbled over to Roy's desk in the tinny light from my phone. "Why was Roy so desperate for me to leave town?"

She stopped and glanced up at me. "Magnolia, that's water under the bridge."

"Maybe for you it is, but it's still pretty fresh for me."

"I'm not sure what happened between you two, but he still holds a deep-seated grudge."

Understatement of the century.

She sat in Roy's chair and I stood behind her while she opened one of his desk drawers. Everything was arranged in a neat and orderly fashion. Just what I'd expected from my tight-ass brother. The keys were in the back corner. She quickly snagged them, then got up and walked toward the door more quickly than I could follow her, leaving me to shine the light behind her, casting long, creepy shadows onto the hallway wall. She seemed determined now, and that determination seemed to have sobered her up. There was barely a wobble in her step as she headed straight for

Bill's office, me trailing behind her with my little light. I held my breath as she stuck the key in the lock.

The knob turned and she stood up straighter, looking me in the eye. "Whatever we find, Magnolia, I am here for you."

I tried to hide my surprise over her statement, not because I was shocked she'd offered her support, but because it almost sounded like a warning.

Without giving me time to respond, she opened the door and marched right over to Bill's desk. "Shine the light over here," she said as she started thumbing through papers. "I remember seeing them on a stack of files. There were more of them this morning."

"If they're not there, maybe they're in a filing cabinet," I suggested.

Rather than answer, she sat in his chair, opened his desk drawers, and started digging around. I was sure it was a wasted effort, but she exclaimed, "Got it!"

Excited, I hurried behind her and shined the light on the manila folder in her hand. She set it on the desk, and sure enough, my name was handwritten on the tab in block letters—Magnolia Steele.

I felt like I was going to throw up, but I had to keep it together this time. "What's in it?"

She opened the folder and I gasped at what she found.

Nothing. It was empty.

Belinda glanced over her shoulder at me, her eyes wide.

"Did you see anything in it this morning?" I asked.

She shook her head. "But I saw Emily's first, and there were papers in hers—a mix of handwritten and printed documents. Bill was looking at the handwritten one on top when I walked in. Sometimes I bring the office staff pastries, and I walked in to bring one to Bill. He wasn't expecting me, so he only tried to hide it after I slipped into his office. His hands slipped, and it fell on the floor, scattering the papers everywhere. I stooped to pick them up, and I saw the kind of information you'd get from a private detective report. Places she'd lived, where she'd gone to school, even her credit report." She looked in the drawer again, then back up at me. "Emily's is gone."

"Why is mine empty?"

"I don't know," she said. "But he became agitated when I started to help him, and told me to leave them alone. In fact, he looked agitated before he even noticed me."

"Does he know you made the connection to Emily?" I asked.

"Honestly, I don't know. I tried to play it off, but I'm no actress," she said. "I'm positive he saw my shock."

"Belinda," I said sharply, suddenly wanting to take her far, far away, anywhere but here. "You're in danger. If Bill's the killer, and he knows you saw Emily's file, he might kill you to keep you quiet."

She straightened up and looked into my eyes. "This is crazy. I know I brought you here, but now it seems like a big conspiracy theory scenario. Bill wouldn't do this," she said, but it sounded like she was trying—and failing—to convince herself.

I heard a banging noise in the front reception area and someone coughing. My heart slamming into my rib cage, I grabbed the empty file with my name on it and stuck it back into the drawer. "Come on," I whispered as I snagged her arm and pulled her into a closet I'd noticed by the office door.

I managed to shove her inside and push in after her before the office door burst open. Someone shuffled into the room, leaving a smoky odor in their wake. It smelled like he or she had been to a bonfire. More coughing followed.

The intruder was silent for several seconds. Then I heard a man mumble, "Shit. Shit. Shit."

The sound of running water filtered through the side wall of the closet, and I remembered that Bill had his own private powder room off his office.

There were splashing sounds and more mumbling, along with more coughing. I considered using this opportunity to make our escape, but it would be dangerous, and maybe we'd find out more by staying. I tried to glance at Belinda, but she held her finger to her lips.

We stayed put.

The water turned off, but the noise was replaced by the sound of cursing. Then he was abruptly cut off, and I heard the man gasping for breath as another round of violent coughing overtook him. "Is it *here*?" he asked.

Who was out there? It made sense that it was Bill James, but the voice was too shaky and raspy from coughing for me to be sure.

"I have to find it." He sounded desperate.

Oh, God. Don't look in the closet.

I heard drawers opening and closing, file cabinet drawers slamming, and even more cursing and coughing, which seemed to be getting worse.

Did he have a cold?

The sound of a ringing cell phone broke the silence, and Belinda jumped behind me, making a small thump against the wall.

I nearly panicked, but at the same time the ringing stopped and the man said in a distorted voice, "Hello?"

I held my breath and willed my heart to slow down so I could hear his conversation over the whooshing pulse in my ears.

I strained to hear what he said, but between his coughing and his hoarse voice, I couldn't make out what he said. Was this the voice I'd heard last night in the industrial park?

"I still can't find the gold," the man said, sounding closer. "But I have a lead, and I think I'll have it soon."

Silence fell, and I held my breath. Who was on the other line?

"Saturday night. At the fundraiser. We'll meet there."

The coughing became more violent and sounded closer.

We were going to get caught.

But the man walked past the closet door and exited the office. We waited until we heard the faint sounds in the reception area disappear and then waited a good ten seconds more before opening the closet door and exiting into the office.

"Was that Bill?" I asked, spinning around to face Belinda.

"I don't know. It didn't sound like him, but . . ."

I decided to keep my suspicions about who it might be to myself. "I know where we have to go next," I said, opening the office door.

"Don't you want to search the office more? We still haven't found Emily's file."

If Bill James had a trophy room like Momma had suggested, I had a sinking suspicion I knew exactly where to find the file.

I didn't talk much on the thirty-minute drive to Leiper's Fork. There were too many thoughts tumbling through my head. It made sense that Bill James would want the gold if he'd been a part of the Jackson Project, and whatever other schemes he and the others had pulled. But why kill all those people? Why murder so many women?

I needed to turn this over to the police, but I didn't trust them. I wondered if I should tell Brady about the files in the basement, but I didn't entirely trust him either. Besides, if I did, I'd never get to look at them. The police would take over. And while I knew that's exactly what *should* happen, I had to see the files for myself, even though I had no idea why.

I also needed to tell Colt the latest about the gold, but I couldn't do that with Belinda in the car. It would have to wait.

Belinda was quiet the entire ride too, other than a few short exchanges between us. Even though she'd suspected Bill was a murderer, it had shaken her to overhear that phone call. The person we'd heard had basically confessed to murder. I was far ahead of her on the scary crap train. I needed to let her catch up.

She didn't ask where we were going, proof of how much she trusted me. Or that she was still too tipsy to put much thought into it. Maybe both.

But as I approached the country road I needed to turn onto to get to the house, I knew something was wrong. Smoke billowed thick and heavy into the night sky, and flashing lights bounced off the road and the trees.

"Oh, my," Belinda said, sitting upright in her seat. "That looks like a terrible house fire."

My heart heavy, I drove past the turn and continued on down the road.

"Why do I have a feeling that's where we were going?" Belinda asked.

"Because you're smart."

"Well, it sure explains the smoky smell. What was it?"

Now that I thought about it, there might be one bright spot out of all of it. Perhaps burning the place down would bring one aspect of the past to light. "The place where Bill James's first wife might be buried."

"*What?*"

I told her about Momma's suspicions, about how Bill James had bought the house years after Momma and Daddy had moved out of it.

"Why would he have bought it?" she asked, her forehead furrowed.

"If you'd buried a dead body under a concrete slab in a basement prone to leaks," I said, "wouldn't you want to make sure it stayed buried? What better way than to buy the house? And it's vacant. No one lives there."

"That's . . . not normal."

"Exactly."

"That still doesn't explain why you thought we needed to come here."

I hadn't told her about the files I'd hoped to find, and I decided it didn't matter now—anything flammable in that house had been destroyed—and besides, I'd already told her plenty she'd have to keep from Roy, whose motivations I didn't begin to understand.

"Just a hunch."

We drove the rest of the way to her house in silence. As soon as we went inside, she turned to me with dull eyes. "I'm going to go to bed. You'll sleep in the guest room tonight. I'll show you where."

I followed her upstairs, and she stopped at the first door on the left. "Here's your room. There are towels and toiletries in the attached bathroom. I'll bring you a nightgown and clothes for tomorrow." She paused. "I have to be in the office at nine."

I could read between the lines. "So what time do we need to leave? Eight forty-five?"

"I'll be downstairs making breakfast at eight."

"You don't need to make breakfast for me," I protested.

"I do it every day for Roy," she said with a tight smile. "It's good to develop and maintain habits."

And my Stepford sister-in-law was back.

"Belinda. You don't have to stay with him. Come live with me. My apartment's small, but we can make it work." I gave her a goofy grin to lighten the mood. "I'll even let you have the bed."

She pulled me into a hug so tight I could barely breathe. Then she let go, looking more defeated than ever. "You can't tell Roy what we did tonight."

"I won't."

"Thank you." She turned and walked out of the room. "If you want to start your shower, I'll just put the clothes on your bed."

"Belinda," I called after her, and she came back to fill the doorway. "Thank you for everything. For trying to protect me. For being my friend."

Tears filled her eyes again. "I think you and I are more alike than you realize," she said. Then she turned and left the room.

What could she have meant by that?

But I was exhausted and about to drop. I took a quick shower and found a pile of clothes on the bed, just like Belinda had promised. After I put on the nightgown and brushed my teeth with one of the packaged spare toothbrushes in the drawer, I grabbed my phone out of my purse to call Brady about what I'd found.

But I dropped the phone on the bed when I saw the message on the screen.

It was a photo of my magnolia necklace on top of a topographical map—just like the map of the Jackson Project I'd seen in the basement of Bill James's house.

The text that came with it sent icy fear through my veins.

Missing something?

chapter
twenty-three

Despite my exhaustion, sleep was elusive. After fifteen minutes, I got up and took one of the melatonin pills I'd seen in the bathroom. If I couldn't sleep safely in Belinda's fortress of security, I couldn't sleep anywhere.

I passed out soon after I went to bed, and slept dreamlessly until my alarm went off at seven thirty. I felt like I'd been run over by a truck, and I was slow to move until the memories of the previous night hit me full force. I sat up in bed and covered my eyes.

I was still living in a nightmare.

If the killer had found my necklace in the basement, it made sense that he'd immediately destroyed the evidence there. Which made it all the more likely Bill James was the killer. And he probably assumed I knew a boatload more than I did.

Shit.

I needed to tell the police about what Belinda had found, and it made sense to tell Brady, even if I didn't quite trust him. He was the only one who had realized we were dealing with a serial killer. The only one who had made the connection to my father's mess. It felt like I had no other choice but to tell him.

As soon as I had a plan, I dialed his number. He answered on the first ring. "Maggie? Is everything okay?"

"Yeah," I said, running my hand through my hair. "Actually no. It's not."

"Tell me where you are; then hang up and call 911," he said in a panic.

"No." I shook my head, realizing I was handling this all wrong. "I'm fine. I just found out something shocking that I thought I should share with you."

"Okay," he said, sounding calmer. "I'm listening."

I couldn't tell him I'd found this out last night, or he'd justifiably wonder why I hadn't told him sooner. "Belinda told me something concerning this morning at breakfast."

"What's your hesitation, Maggie?"

"What?" I asked in surprise.

"I can tell you're hesitant to tell me. Is it Belinda? Are you still worried about her safety?"

The fact that he knew I was holding back spooked me. "Uh . . . yeah."

"If you tell me, we can protect her, Maggie. And you too."

But he'd told me he *couldn't* protect her.

"Bill James," I said, still not sure what to confess to him. "Belinda told me she saw files on his desk yesterday."

"What kind of files?" he asked.

I stopped. "You can't tell anyone this came from her. If my brother finds out, he might kill her. Literally, Brady. I know he's hurt her before."

He was quiet for a moment. "Maggie, you have to realize you're hamstringing me. It's not even my jurisdiction, and I have to have legitimate cause to get the Nashville police involved. What if she makes an anonymous tip like you did with Lopez's disappearance?"

"Only a handful of people work in the office. It will be obvious it was one of them."

"See?" he said, sounding more hopeful. "Then James won't even suspect her. He'll think it was one of his office staff."

I wasn't sure that was any better. If Bill had killed all those women, what was to stop him from killing one of the people in his office to keep them quiet? But I doubted that would happen. Bill knew Belinda had seen those files. He'd know it was her. Still, I'd initiated this call, and I had to tell Brady something.

"There were two files. One with Emily's name. It was full of information about her, like her previous addresses and work and school history."

"Like a background check?"

"Yeah."

"Anything else?"

"I don't know if there was anything else in that file, but there was another file."

"Who was that one on?"

"Me," I whispered. "And it was empty."

"Where are you now?" he asked, his voice calm and direct like it had been when I'd called him the night of Lopez's attack. This was Brady in his prime.

"I'm in Belinda's fortress."

He paused. "Can you stay there today? When is your brother coming back into town?"

"Uh . . ." I ran a hand over my head. "I don't know."

"You need to stay out of sight today. Somewhere James wouldn't think to look for you. And if he knows about your brother's animosity toward you, he'd never look for you there."

He had a point. "I'll talk to Belinda."

"Let me know what she says. I'll do more digging into Bill James."

"Thank you, Brady."

"Maggie, thanks for calling me. Even if we aren't dating, I'm here for you."

"Thanks."

Since I'd showered the night before, I got dressed and went down to the kitchen, tracking the coffee smell like a bloodhound.

Belinda was sitting at the breakfast room table and glanced up from her planner. "Good morning, Magnolia. There's coffee."

I picked up the cup she'd left next to the coffee maker and used the creamer she'd left out too. After I poured my cup, I sat down across from her. "How are you feeling today?"

She grimaced. "Embarrassed."

"Embarrassed? Why?"

She kept her gaze on her coffee cup. "I made a fool of myself last night."

"Please," I said, waving my hand. "That was nothing. Hell, I embarrassed myself in front of the entire world. I was the only one who saw you last night."

Her eyes lifted to mine. "And that's what makes it worse. Do you honestly care what all those strangers think of you? Or do you care more about what your momma thinks? Or me or Colt?"

She had a point. Still . . . "Belinda, everyone has to let loose sometimes. And you've kept everything bottled up inside for so long, you had to let some of it out. Otherwise, you'd burst. Do you know how honored I am that you felt safe enough to let loose with me? You trusted me to make sure you were safe." I pressed my hand to my chest. "That's a huge gift to me, Belinda. Especially after everything in my past."

"But I didn't drink to let loose," she said, rising from her chair with her coffee cup. "I got drunk to find the courage to do what I needed to do. And I didn't even do it."

That got my attention. "You took me to the office and showed me the files."

She refilled her coffee and kept her back to me.

"Belinda," I said in a sterner voice than I'd intended. "What did you plan to do?"

She turned to face me. "I love you, Magnolia, and I will protect you. You can't come to my shop today."

I stood next to my chair. "Why not?"

She ignored my question. "See if Colt will come get you. You can stay until noon, when I expect Roy to come home. If he finds you here . . ."

"He won't." I was torn between being hurt that she still wouldn't confide in me and grateful she was trying to protect me.

"Roy . . . He can't know that I took you to the office. No one can."

Oh, crap. I had to warn her. "Belinda." My stomach cramped and I placed a hand on my abdomen to keep from hunching over. "I told Brady."

The color drained from her face. "Told him what?"

I took several steps toward her, but she cringed away from me. "I told him about the files. But I didn't tell him we went there last night. He thinks you told me about the files this morning. I told him what we found in Emily's . . . and mine."

"How could you?"

"Belinda, if Bill killed those women . . ."

"Do you have any idea what you've done?" she asked in the most hateful tone I'd ever heard from her.

If she'd slapped me in the face, it wouldn't have surprised me more. "I tried to keep a man from killing more innocent people."

"I trusted you," she said bitterly. "I shouldn't have told you, and now you've ruined everything."

"What did I ruin?" I asked in a teary voice. Had she told me to keep it a secret? I'd shared so many secrets and half-truths I was struggling to keep up.

Belinda turned her back and headed for the stairs. "I'm going to get ready to leave. I trust that you'll have someone pick you up within the hour."

"Belinda!" I called after her. A huge weight pressed into my chest, and I gasped to catch my breath.

I picked up my phone and called the first person who came to mind.

"Momma?" I said when she answered. "I'm at Belinda's. Can you come get me?"

"Magnolia? Are you crying?"

"What?" I wiped a tear from my cheek. "No. I'm fine. But I'm at Belinda's, and I need someone to pick me up."

"I can't, Magnolia," she said, sounding weak. "I'm not feeling well."

Fear knifed into me. "I should come check on you."

"You'll do no such thing," Momma said. "I'm at Tilly's and she's taking good care of me." She paused. "I can probably send her."

"No, she needs to stay with you. I'll take care of it. Don't worry."

I could call either Brady or Colt, but I was tired of relying on other people, particularly men. And while I knew I was in danger, Brady had said I should be safe if I stayed away from my usual places. That I could do.

I used my Uber app to call for a car. When it showed up ten minutes later, Belinda still hadn't come down, but I'd found a piece of paper and left her a note next to the coffee maker.

Belinda,

I hate that I hurt you. You're the sister I always wanted and I love you. I don't want to lose you. Please tell me what to do to make this better.

Love,

Magnolia

I had the Uber take me to my car, which was still in the apartment complex parking lot. The driver gave me a sideways glance that suggested he considered this a drive of shame, but I didn't care, even if the guy recognized me.

I needed to get a legal gun, but I had no idea where to get one. A quick search brought up several gun stores, but none of them opened until ten. It wasn't even nine o'clock.

Unsure of what to do, I called the next person who came to mind.

"Maggie?" Colt asked, sounding groggy with sleep. "Are you okay?"

Someday people would stop answering the phone asking if I was okay. "No, not really, but before you freak out, it's not what you think. It's Belinda. She's so angry with me."

Colt groaned. "Maggie, I love you, but I'm not getting dragged into a girl fight."

I tried to ignore the shock his words sent through me. He hadn't meant it like that anyway; it was just something people said. So why had it sent a bolt of warmth through my chest?

Focus.

"It's more than that, Colt. I have to talk to you. It's important."

"Give me half an hour. I'm not home."

"That means nothing to me," I said. "I don't even know where you live."

"Never you mind about that," he said, sounding more alert. "Let's meet for breakfast. How about—"

"Not in Franklin. Let's meet up in Nashville."

"Okay." That caught him by surprise. "Uh . . . How about the Frothy Monkey? I'll meet you there in thirty minutes." Then he hung up.

I considered calling Brady to tell him where I was going, but I knew he'd never approve of my outing. I considered asking him to not use the information I'd given him. But there was no way he could ignore it, and I didn't even want him to. If he could stop Bill James from killing more people, it was worth losing Belinda, even if it ripped my heart to shreds.

I figured there was little chance I'd been followed. I'd stayed at Belinda's, something totally out of character for me, and then taken an Uber to a place I would normally never leave my car. But I found myself glancing in the rearview mirror every few seconds for any suspicious cars.

Colt was waiting for me when I walked into the crowded restaurant. He was already at a table, his hand cradling a cup of coffee.

His eyes lit up when he saw me. "Maggie, it looks like you got some sleep last night. The bags under your eyes aren't as big as they were yesterday."

I gasped in horror and reached for the small mirror in my purse.

He laughed. "I'm teasing. Believe it or not, it's good to know there's still a little vanity left in there."

I shoved the mirror back in my purse. "What's that supposed to mean?"

"Nothing," he said, his voice smooth as silk and honey. "I'm just trying to take your mind off your troubles."

"I think I'd need to be in a coma for that to happen." I took the coffee mug from his hand and took a sip.

He laughed. "Yes, Magnolia, you can have a drink of my coffee."

The waiter came over and Colt flagged him down. "We're ready to order."

"I haven't looked at the menu yet," I protested.

"Trust me," Colt said, then ordered another cup of coffee and a water, a Farm Breakfast with bacon, and an omelet with ham, swiss cheese, avocado, and spinach.

When the waiter walked away, I asked, "Which one is for me?"

"The omelet, of course," he said, snatching back his coffee. He turned sideways to look out the window. "But when it gets here, if you want mine, we can switch."

"How did you know I'd order an omelet that way?"

He turned back to face me. "It's what you always get. I probably know you better than you think."

We locked gazes for several seconds, long enough for me to feel something shift between us.

It startled me when a cup of coffee entered my field of vision, breaking our stare. "Here you go," the waiter said in a cheery voice as he set the cup and a coffee carafe on the table. "Your breakfast will be right out."

Whatever magic had been going on between Colt and me was gone, yet I knew it was still simmering beneath the surface. I wasn't sure what was developing between us, but my instinct told me to trust Colt. And not just with the gold.

Oh, crap. How could I have forgotten?

"I thought you were going to Chattanooga this morning," I said.

He lifted his shoulder into a half-shrug. "Some things came up."

What could be more important than the gold? Especially to Colt who wanted the gold before it became a matter of life or death for me. "Are you still going?"

"As soon as we finish breakfast."

I leaned back in my seat, prepared for a fight. "I'm coming with you."

His brow lifted. "I thought you were working at Alvin's this afternoon."

"I'm going to call in sick."

His eyes narrowed. "You don't trust me?"

"It has absolutely nothing to do with trusting you and everything to do with evading a serial killer."

He bolted upright and leaned his forearm on the table. "What happened last night?"

"Nothing as exciting as you seem to be thinking."

"What happened, Magnolia?"

I leaned closer and said in a quiet voice, "I think I know who the . . . is." I grimaced, not wanting to use the word killer again in such a public place.

"Who?"

Should I just blurt it out? But it wasn't like Bill was famous. No one would connect any dots. Still, I kept my voice low enough for only Colt to hear. "Bill James. Daddy's partner."

His face remained expressionless. "Did you hear this from Bennett?"

"No. I was the one who told *him* about my suspicions."

"How did you come by this information?" Then his eyes widened with understanding. "Ah . . . now I get why Belinda's pissed at you."

I looked down. "Yeah."

Colt grabbed my hand and squeezed. "It will be okay. She'll get over it."

"You really think so?"

Indecision wavered in his eyes.

"She's the only friend I have here," I said, sounding like a pathetic high school girl.

He squeezed my hand again. "That's not true. You have me, Mags," he said softly, then shifted his hand around until his fingers laced with mine. "I'm here."

I searched his eyes for a hint of teasing, preparing myself for him to say, "Ha! Fooled you!" but I only saw a man who looked like he was really seeing me for the first time. Or maybe felt comfortable showing me for the first time.

"I stayed with Belinda last night," I said.

Relief filled his eyes, but he quickly covered it. "You said you were staying at your place, so I stopped by around ten last night to check on you. When you weren't there..."

"You thought I stayed at Brady's."

He nodded.

"No. I'm not staying with Brady anymore. I broke up with him last night." What would Colt think of that? I started to pull my hand away.

His grip tightened. "So? I'm sure he'll still let you stay with him. Guys like Bennett have an inherent need to protect people. He'll still protect you."

"I can't stay with him now." I looked down at our still-joined hands. "It feels like leading him on. Before . . . I wasn't sure what I wanted." My gaze lifted to his face. "Now I am."

Recognition flickered in his eyes, even though I hadn't intended to give him the message I'd just conveyed. I suddenly felt exposed and vulnerable, more vulnerable than I could ever remember being with anyone, but equally exhilarating and horrifying was the realization that I'd opened myself up to Colt Austin.

He quickly shuttered his emotions and his eyes darkened. "This is about keeping you safe."

If he was talking about my heart, he wasn't telling me anything I didn't already know, yet here I was, holding on to his hand for dear life, ready to jump headlong into danger.

"I've spent the last ten years trying to be safe, and all it ever brought me was loneliness." It was true. Not only had I run away to save my life, I'd walled up my heart to avoid getting hurt. Only, I'd still been hurting all along. "Maybe it's time to stop trying to be so safe."

He shook his head, an internal war waging in his eyes. "Don't be stupid, Maggie. The whole reason I'm going after the gold is to keep you safe."

"Not the *whole* reason . . ." I said in a teasing tone.

When he didn't answer, I knew I was making the right decision. He was fighting this just as much as I had been.

I clasped his hand with both of mine. "For the first time in a long time, I'm ready to live my life, Colt. We're so much alike, you and I, and I think you're ready to live your life too."

His face was blank, but his eyes gave his indecision away. "You'll regret it."

"Like the woman who hurt you before?" I asked. "Maybe, but I'm willing to take the chance."

"Maggie, you don't—"

I leaned forward and kissed him, my lips soft and gentle. He'd been on the verge of saying something, so his mouth was still forming the word, but it only took him a second to shift gears.

His free hand lifted to my face and he took over, deepening the kiss in a show of PDA I wouldn't usually embrace.

But I didn't care. I forgot where I was. I forgot that a killer had put me in his sights. I forgot that Belinda was mad at me and that Momma was dying and that my acting career was in the toilet. Right here, right now, there was only Colt. And this felt so, so right.

A throat cleared next to us, and our waiter laughed. "Here's your breakfast."

I sat back, slightly embarrassed, but more worried that I'd caught Colt by surprise and he would put his guard back up.

The waiter set our plates on the table as Colt watched me in wonderment, as though he couldn't believe what had just happened.

A warm smile spread across my face, and he smiled back with twinkling eyes.

He looked . . . happy.

Even though my life was tangled up in horror and confusion, I felt good—elated even. It didn't matter that it didn't make any sense. I was tired of ignoring my emotions or forcing them to make sense. For the first time, I was going to just *feel*.

Colt picked up his fork, his gaze still on me, but it turned more serious. "Okay, so you know this means you're coming with me to Chattanooga, right? I'm not leaving you by yourself with a serial killer on the loose."

No matter what was happening between Colt and I, the outside world still needed to be dealt with, but staring at him now, I didn't feel so *alone*. "Yeah. Is there a plan?"

"Not really. I found out the place belongs to Lopez's secret boyfriend, and his boyfriend died a couple of months ago. The house is currently unoccupied and in probate, but rumor has it that Lopez still went there often."

"Do you think Lopez killed him?"

"He had a heart attack playing tennis. But a logical leap."

"We're just dropping by the house in broad daylight?"

"Anthony—Lopez's boyfriend—had a wife and kids before he came out as gay. There's a dispute between Anthony's kids over who gets the house. If someone sees us, we can play it a number of ways—but my favorite is that we're appraisers from the bank. But I doubt anyone will care."

"I say go with appraisers."

He grinned. "Appraisers it is."

We decided to take my car to Chattanooga since it got better gas mileage. We finished breakfast; then Colt followed me in his truck to the Embassy Suites parking lot in Franklin. After he parked, he slid into the passenger seat, carrying a small package in his hand. He tucked it under the seat, then caught me by surprise when he leaned over and kissed me.

"That's going to take some getting used to," I said as I started to drive.

He grinned. "I'll give you plenty of chances."

While I had gotten a good night's sleep the night before, Colt looked utterly exhausted. After he gave me the address of Anthony's house to plug into my phone, I encouraged him to take a nap. When I pulled into the neighborhood two hours later, I shook Colt's arm.

"Colt, we're here."

He came awake instantly and bolted upright, a much different reaction than I'd gotten from Belinda the night before. He glanced at the clock on my dashboard. 12:12.

"That's still Central time, right?"

"Yeah," I said absently, remembering Chattanooga was in the Eastern zone.

He frowned. "We should have gotten an earlier start, but there's no helping that now."

"I'm sorry."

"Mags." He grabbed my hand and squeezed it. "It's good. I had a late night, so I decided to catch up on some sleep. But I need to be back by eight for a gig in Nashville. Depending on how sneaky Lopez was, we may find ourselves wishing we had more time. But I wanted to be done before it got dark anyway. No need to have neighbors wondering why lights are on."

"True."

The map told me to turn, and I pulled into the driveway of a small house that looked like it had seen better days.

"Small is good," Colt said. "Less surface area for us to search."

I stared at the house, gripping the steering wheel.

Colt's hand lifted to the back of my neck, and he massaged my tense muscles. "Mags. This will go faster if I do it myself. Drop me off and I'll look for it."

"That's a lie, and we both know it. I can't let you do this by yourself. Part of the reason you're here is for me."

"Not entirely, and you know it," he said, his hand still working its magic. "I've never made any secret about the fact that I want part of the gold. I need you to know that hasn't changed."

I turned to face him. "And if you suddenly said it wasn't your goal, I wouldn't trust you at all. The fact you've made no secret of wanting a stake makes everything you say more real. You know?"

He grinned. "So you're saying that you trust me more because I'm a greedy bastard?"

I laughed in spite of my nervousness. "Exactly."

He leaned forward and kissed me slow and lazy. His hand rested on the base of my neck while his thumb lightly caressed my skin, sending shivers of pleasure down my spine.

"If you're trying to seduce me," I said against his lips, "it's working."

He pulled back and smiled. "And to think—I'm only just getting started." He reached for the door handle. "Go to the mall or even a movie and wait for me to call. This will probably take a few hours."

I stared at the house, ashamed to admit that part of me wanted to let him deal with this on his own. Not only did I dread spending hours looking for a needle in a haystack, but I was also scared to death of getting arrested for breaking and entering. But how could I live with myself if Colt got busted without me? He had a record, so his fate would be much worse. "How sure are we the gold's in that house?"

"Ninety percent."

"Not one hundred?"

"Nothing's a sure bet, Mags. Especially not me."

I turned to study his face. "Believe it or not, I'm not stupid."

His body stiffened in defensiveness. "I never said—"

"Relax," I said reaching for the door handle. "I'm a big girl. Let's go find the gold."

Taking the lead, I walked up to the porch, bold as I pleased, leaving Colt to trail behind me. When we got to the front door, I noticed Colt had slipped on a pair of leather gloves. He handed me the small package he'd brought with him from his truck and then quickly opened it, revealing several small, slender tools.

"I have to pick the lock," he said. "This should be quick."

He was right. He had the doorknob and deadbolt unlatched in twenty seconds. Taking the tools from my hands, he pushed open the door with his hip. "Don't touch anything when we get inside."

Crap. How had I not considered that? Leaving fingerprints was a very bad idea. "How will I help if I can't touch anything?"

He didn't answer, just gestured for me to go in, then closed the door behind us.

When I turned to ask him what he wanted me to do, he grabbed my arm and tugged me to his chest. I gasped as his mouth lowered to mine, and his tongue took advantage of my parted lips.

My body melted into his as I wrapped my hands around his neck.

His arm wrapped around my back, holding me in place, while his still-gloved hand tilted my head back to deepen our kiss.

He lifted his head and grinned, an infectious smile that warmed my heart to match the rest of my body. "You have no idea how long I've wanted to kiss you like that."

"You kissed me just this morning. And out in the car."

"Not like this. I want more, but it will have to wait. Right now we need to find that gold."

He kissed me again, softer this time, his teeth and tongue teasing my bottom lip, but he left me breathless all the same. He placed both hands on my hips and stepped back, watching me with a grin.

"I still don't know what I can do," I said. "I don't have a pair of gloves."

"You can still leave, Maggie. Come back when I'm done."

"No way." I looked around the living room, filled with streamlined contemporary furniture, and spotted a small closet. "Open that door."

He laughed. "Just because I kissed you doesn't mean you get to boss me around."

"Shut up and open the closet door."

Grinning, he opened the closet door and rummaged around in a basket on the top shelf. When he turned around, he had a pair of knit gloves in his hand. "Try these. They look like they'll be too large for you."

I grabbed them from him and tugged them on. Sure enough, there was a half-inch at the end of each finger, but it would be better than doing nothing.

"Okay," Colt said. "The goal is to find the gold but leave no signs that we've been here. We'll start in the kitchen and work our way through the house."

By the time we'd made it through the entire house, I could see why Lopez had ripped my apartment apart during *his* search.

Colt glanced at the clock in the master bedroom and grimaced. "We're running out of time. We need to check the basement next."

Fear skated along my skin, but I told myself there was always a chance it could be a finished basement with bright overhead lights.

No such luck.

Colt opened the basement door in the hallway, and my breath caught at the sight of the dark, gaping hole.

No. No. *No.*

Colt was halfway down before he realized I was still up at the top of the stairs. "Maggie?" His eyes narrowed and he climbed up a step. "Maggie. What's wrong?"

I closed my eyes and took a deep breath. Someday I'd be able to jog down a dark staircase into a basement. But today was not that day.

I couldn't catch my breath, and I felt hot all over. I jerked the gloves off my sweaty hands, stumbling backward until my back hit the wall.

"Maggie?" Colt's eyes were wide with worry as he raced back up the steps, tugging off his own gloves as he went. He grabbed my elbow as he helped me sit on the floor.

I started to cry—heavy, heaving sobs that stole breath I couldn't afford to give up.

Colt sat next to me and wrapped an arm around my back, letting me nestle my head against his shoulder. I cried until my face tingled from hyperventilating. I covered my mouth and nose with my hands and tried to take slow deep breaths.

Colt's hand lifted to the back of my head, and he stroked my hair. I sank further into him, somewhat surprised he was being so tender and supportive, but that part of him had been there all along.

When my face stopped tingling, I lowered my hands and looked up at him. "I'm sorry."

"Sorry for what?" he asked. "Jesus, Mags, the shit you've been through the last week . . . you were due a breakdown."

"I've wasted time we don't have."

"I'll cancel my gig tonight."

"You can't do that."

He gave me a mischievous smile. "I can do pretty much whatever I want."

"Let's go find the gold in the basement."

"Deal." He stood and reached his hand down to me, then pulled me up and into a hug. "Everything's going to be okay, Mags. I promise. I won't let anything happen to you."

"You can't promise that, Colt."

He held my gaze and grinned. "Didn't we just establish that I can do whatever I want? Well, I decided I won't let anything happen to you."

I searched his eyes. "Can you cure claustrophobia?"

"Oh, shit. I forgot." My mouth dropped open and he said, "I remember your freak-out while working in the basement the day after you came back."

"But . . ."

"I'll be with you every step of the way." He took my hand. "Magnolia Steele, you can do anything you set your mind to. You can do this. One step at a time."

I knew he was referring to the stairs, but I related it to discovering the truth . . . one step at a time. And while I knew we were making progress, it was too little, too slow.

We were ultimately going to pay the price.

chapter
twenty-four

It only took us ten minutes to find the gold in the basement.

"Maggie," Colt called out in excitement. "I think I found it."

I'd been searching through a stack of boxes in the corner while Colt had been combing through shelves covered in tools and paint cans.

"All of it?" I asked.

He lifted a paint can with his fingers. "No. But judging by the weight, a good portion of it."

Dr. Lopez had hidden it in Ziploc bags, stuffed into three separate paint cans. Colt washed the bags off in a utility sink, while I went upstairs and found clean Ziploc bags as well as a canvas tote bag.

As soon as we finished the transfer, Colt put the cans back where he found them, and I made sure the sink was clean.

I was eager to get out of the Chattanooga house, but the thought of returning to Franklin lodged a great big boulder in the pit of my stomach. There was a killer waiting for me there, and I still didn't know where I was staying tonight. If I confessed the danger I was in to Colt, he would probably let me come with him to his gig, but was that a good idea?

A terrible feeling stole over me as Colt pulled onto the highway. I was sure something was wrong, beyond the normal dose of crazy, but when I checked my phone, the only message I'd gotten was a check-in note from Brady, telling me he didn't have any news yet.

I'd hoped to get a text from Belinda, but so far there was nothing. I told myself she'd forgive me in time. I had to believe it was true.

Even though I'd had plenty of sleep the night before, my breakdown earlier had worn me out. We weren't on the road more than ten minutes before I fell asleep.

A couple of hours later, I woke up to my cell phone ringing.

"Maggie," Colt said, his voice tight. "You need to answer that."

"What?" I asked, sitting up in the passenger seat.

"It's Tilly. You need to get it."

I pulled my phone out of my purse, wondering if Colt had suddenly become psychic because, sure enough, it was Tilly.

"Hey, Tilly," I said, casting Colt a weird look. "What's up?"

"Maggie. It's your momma."

I gasped. Bill James had killed her. "What happened?"

"Your momma is at Vanderbilt Medical Center. Her doctor admitted her." She paused. "Maggie, sweetheart. You need to get here as soon as you can."

"Oh, God," I breathed out. "Is she dying?"

"She's *been* dying, sweet girl," Tilly said in a broken voice. "But the end is coming faster than we'd hoped."

Pure panic flooded every cell of my being. I wasn't ready to lose my mother yet. We were still fixing us. There was still so much I wanted to say to her. So much I didn't know.

I looked out the windshield, searching for a road sign or mile marker to see how far away we were. "Colt. How far are we away from Vanderbilt Medical Center?"

Colt covered my hand with his own. "Twenty minutes, Mags."

"Twenty minutes, Tilly," I breathed into the receiver. "I'm twenty minutes away."

"She's in room 433."

"Okay." I hung up the call and clutched my phone in my hand. "I need to call Belinda . . . and Roy."

"Tilly's already called them."

I blinked and shook my head. "How do you know that?"

"Tilly texted me first."

"Why would she do that?"

"She knows how difficult it's going to be for you with Roy there. She wanted to know you'd have someone to have your back."

"But she'll be there, right?"

"Maggie, Tilly's barely holding it together herself."

"And Tilly texted you to come with me?"

He squeezed his hand. "Yeah."

I didn't have the presence of mind to ponder that as much as I probably should have.

Twenty minutes later, I was hurrying toward the hospital entrance, dangerously close to losing it. I reminded myself that I had to hold it together for Tilly and Momma.

Colt slipped his hand in mine and held tight. He was right by my side, step for step. "I've got your back, Mags. You can do this."

I wasn't so sure, but I didn't have a choice.

He continued to hold my hand in the elevator and down the hall on the fourth floor, but as we approached room 433, he dropped my hand and slid his arm around my back.

Tilly stood outside Momma's room, along with Roy and Belinda. Tilly's face was pale, but she seemed to be holding her own. Roy looked like he was angling to pick a fight, and Belinda seemed so small and sad and fragile next to my brother. I wanted nothing more than to rush forward and pluck her away from him.

"Magnolia," Roy said in a harsh tone. "I was hoping you wouldn't make it, and look at the garbage you brought with you."

"Roy," Tilly admonished. Belinda seemed to shrink into herself even more.

"You have no say in any of this, Tilly," my brother barked. "You have no business being here at all. This is a family matter."

I was about to rip my brother to shreds, but Colt's hand dug into my hip. He leaned into my ear and whispered, "Wait for it."

I barely had to wait before Tilly launched into him.

She pointed her finger into his chest. "Don't you dare start with me, Roy Michael Steele. I have more of a right to be here than you do. I knew your mother before you were even thought of. I changed more of your diapers than I can count and got an eyeful of the itty-bitty dick you were born with, the one you've been trying to compensate for your entire life." She looked over at Belinda. "Darlin', I've got a catalog full of dildos I'd be happy to loan you to make up for his under-endowment. I've wanted to offer it before, but refrained since I considered you and your husband *family.*"

"Tilly!" Belinda said as her face turned red.

"Enough," Roy snapped.

Tilly wasn't done yet. If anything, she seemed to have gained strength from her first round. "Your mother coddled you, and for the most part, I kept my mouth shut. I knew why she did it. It was no secret that Brian doted on your sister, but you turned sullen and entitled and just downright mean. Your poor mother didn't realize the damage she'd done until it was too damn late. I love your mother more than anyone God's seen fit to put on this earth, but she's far from perfect. After she lost your sister, she was so desperate to keep you in her life that she gave you anything and everything you wanted—worse, she looked the other way when you showed your ugly side." She took a breath, her hands shaking at her sides. "I may not be your mother, Roy Steele, but I'm pretty damn close, and I'm not putting up with this bullshit anymore."

My mouth dropped in disbelief, but Colt was prepared for what came next. He'd already dropped his hand from my back in anticipation, and he lunged for my brother just as Roy lifted his arm to strike Tilly.

Colt shoved him three feet backward into the wall— one hand pressed to his chest, the other clutching the hand Roy had raised to hit Tilly. Roy struck the drywall with a loud thud, and the back of his hand smashed a piece of glass artwork on the wall. Blood started dripping from his cut fingers. Colt leaned his face close to Roy's and said, "You dare to touch her, and you're a dead man, Steele."

Roy looked murderous. "I'll press charges, Austin." He writhed against the wall and tried unsuccessfully to break free of Colt's hold.

"You go ahead and try, but Tilly and Magnolia will be here to testify that you were about to strike Tilly."

"Belinda will take my side."

"Still two against one," Colt said, his arm muscles bulging as he maintained his hold. "Three if you count the nurse in the hall behind you who saw the whole thing and is about to call security."

"All right!" Roy shouted, his whole face turning red. "You win."

"And just so we're clear, you touch a hair on Tilly or Magnolia's heads, and you will spend the rest of your life regretting it. Got it?" Roy didn't answer and Colt gave him a shake. "Do. You. Understand? Feel free to nod if you can't choke out the words."

Roy glared at him for another two seconds before giving a sharp nod.

Colt dropped his hold and took a step back. "I think you and Belinda should wait in the visitor's area until your mother is ready to see you."

"Who the hell do you think you are?" Roy demanded, his eyes wild with anger. He cradled his bloody right hand to his chest. "Who gave you the authority to tell me what to do?"

"From this point forward, consider me Tilly and Magnolia's bodyguard, and I'm issuing a restraining order. If you don't stay at least twenty feet away from the two of them, I'll kick your ass whether you touch them or not. Got it?"

Roy gave him a look of violent hatred, but he didn't respond in any way. Instead, he spun around and headed down the hall.

It was then that I noticed all the people standing in the patients' doorways, gawking our direction. But as Roy headed toward them, they scattered out of sight.

"*Come on, Belinda,*" Roy hollered.

Belinda shot Tilly a horrified look before turning around and trailing after my brother. She didn't look at me at all.

I watched her walk away, and Tilly put her hand on my shoulder. "She made her choice, Maggie."

I wasn't so sure she had.

"I'm sorry about this ugly incident," Colt said in an apologetic tone to the nurse, who'd approached us now that Roy was gone. "I'd be happy to pay for the damage."

"Like hell you will," the nurse said with a grin. "He deserved that and more. Never could stomach a bully." She walked past him and patted his arm. "I'll get housekeeping to clean up the broken glass." She winked. "And not to worry—security *is* on its way . . . to the visitor's waiting room."

"Thank you, Colt," Tilly said, wrapping her arms around Colt's back and hugging him. "I do believe he would have hit me."

"He won't dare touch you now," Colt said, glancing down the hall toward the waiting room. "I'll make sure of it." He pointed to the closed door with the number 433 on the plaque. "Can Maggie go see her momma now?"

Tilly shook her head. "Not yet. Her doctor is performing a procedure. That's what originally riled Roy up. He didn't like that he had to wait. The nurse who witnessed the incident caught an earful earlier."

They continued to discuss Roy's escalating behavior, but I tuned them out as I stared at Momma's door, wondering what waited for me on the other side. Would she look much worse than she had at lunch two days ago?

The guilt was overwhelming. I should have stayed with her last night. I should have never moved out. I'd wasted precious time with her. What had I been thinking? I'd wanted to protect her, yes, but I should have found a way to stay with her anyway.

The door opened and a woman wearing pink scrubs walked out, letting the door close behind her. "Are you Magnolia?" She stood directly opposite me, only a couple of feet between us.

"Yes."

Colt stood on one side of me, his arm wrapped around my back, and Tilly stood on the other, grabbing my hand and clutching it tightly enough to cut off my circulation.

"I'm not going to sugarcoat it, Magnolia. Your mother is very sick. She has a low white cell count from her last round of chemo, which made it easier for her to pick up an infection. If she'd come to see me a few days ago, I could have treated it with oral antibiotics, but now it's spread throughout her body. She needs an IV antibiotic, but she's refusing treatment." She hesitated. "I'm sure she's told you about her DNR, and her request for no heroic attempts."

I nodded, surprised I was listening to this dry-eyed. It was taking everything in me to follow what she was saying. "And she'll die if she doesn't take the antibiotics?"

"There's a chance she'll fight it off, but it's very, very small."

"That damn stubborn woman," Tilly muttered in a broken voice.

I felt myself on the verge of cracking, but I couldn't let that happen. Not now. "Can I go in and talk to her now?"

"We just put in a port to make it easier to draw her blood and administer the medication if she changes her mind. The nurse is cleaning her up, but she'll be finished in a minute."

"Thank you."

As I watched the doctor's retreating back, I turned her words over and over in my head, struggling to understand my mother's decision. I understood her request to withhold machines to prolong her life, but I'd never considered penicillin to be a heroic effort.

Colt's hand tightened on my waist. "Maggie? How are you doing?"

"Fine."

"Do you need to sit down? This is a lot to process on top of everything else."

"I'm fine."

A nurse emerged from the room and held the door open. "You can come in now."

I looked past her and saw my mother on the hospital bed. She was a ghost of the woman who had raised me. Suddenly, I understood my mother's choice. Her entire life, she'd balked against doing things any way but her own. It made sense that she'd want to leave this earth on her own terms.

Colt gave me a slight nudge, and I crossed the threshold, wondering how much time she had left. I needed to play a role, or I'd fall to pieces. But what role should I play? The answer was so obvious that I couldn't believe it had taken me more than an instant to figure it out.

I would play my mother.

I steeled my back as I walked into the room. "Momma. I never knew you to be so dramatic. You're supposed to leave the drama to me."

She turned to face me and smiled. "You've had a monopoly on drama for years, Magnolia. Maybe it's my turn." Her smile fell. "Did you get the help you needed this morning?"

"Yeah," I said. "It was all taken care of."

Tilly moved to a chair in the corner and hung her head.

Colt put one hand on my shoulder and the other on the handrail on Momma's bed. "I'm here for her, Lila."

Momma lifted her eyes to Colt. "I lost her once . . ."

He held her gaze. "It won't happen this time."

"You two realize I'm right here, don't you?" I asked, trying to sound annoyed, though I was secretly curious that they seemed to have had this conversation before.

Tilly laughed. "Don't waste your breath, darlin'."

Colt scooped up Momma's hand. "Lila, don't you worry. I won't forget my promise."

Tears filled her eyes and she mouthed, "Thank you. You're a good man, Colt Austin. You're finding your way. Don't listen to the naysayers."

He choked up and laughed. "Don't be getting soft on me, Lila. I need you riding my ass."

"Someone else is gonna have to take over that job."

Colt leaned over and kissed my mother's forehead. "Then I guess the job's gonna have to stay vacant." He turned around and gave me a hug, and I was surprised he seemed to need strength from me and not the other way around.

I held him close, closing my eyes as I pressed my cheek into his chest, his steady heartbeat in my ear reassuring me.

"I'll be in the waiting room," he said. "Keeping an eye on your brother."

"Thanks," I whispered.

As soon as he walked out, I immediately returned to Momma's bedrail, resting both hands on it this time. "I don't believe you. You raised me to never be a quitter."

She sighed, tilting her head back to stare at the ceiling. "I'm not quitting, Magnolia. I've fought."

"Do you remember when I had strep throat when I was in second grade?" I asked.

She chuckled, but it was weak. "You and Roy missed the Easter egg hunt at church. You were beside yourself. Your father hid a bunch of eggs at home for you two. He could never stand to see his Magnolia's blossoms fade, he used to say."

"I'd forgotten that," I murmured. "But I was thinking about the antibiotics. The doctor gave me pills instead of the liquid, and I refused to take them. Do you remember what you said?"

She shot me a grin. "Take the damn pills, or I'm going to whip you?"

"Oh, Momma . . ." I rolled my eyes. "You said our life lessons often come with a bitter medicine, but we have to take it to be better people."

She reached for my hand and rested it on her stomach. "I was too hard on you, Magnolia. I'm so sorry for that."

"That isn't the point of this story, Momma. You said I had to take the medicine." I paused. "I need you to take the medicine."

A weak smile lifted her lips. "Oh, Magnolia. You never could understand a metaphor."

"Lila!" Tilly gasped.

"She took the damn thing literally, Tilly."

"Well, of course she did! You were talking to an eight-year-old!"

"I've taken my medicine, Momma," I said softly, tears gathering in my eyes. "I think I'm becoming a better person."

Her smile fell. "Magnolia, you are a beautiful girl, inside and out. I'm so proud of the woman you've become, but you were always in there. I'm sorry if I've made you believe differently. Your father would be disappointed in me." She looked defeated, and I couldn't help wondering if that was part of why she was giving up. "I wasted our precious gift."

"It's not too late," I said through teary eyes. "Take the antibiotics."

She gave me a sad smile. "I'm not going to get to tell you all those stories, Maggie. I'm sorry."

I choked on a sob. "You could if you wanted. You're giving up on me again."

"No, Magnolia. No." Tears slid down her face. "I'm tired. I'm so tired." She sighed and closed her eyes. "I'm sorry I'm letting you down again, but I just want to stop hurting."

She'd been hurting for years—I'd been the source of a good portion of her pain. I needed to perform one selfless act and give her what she wanted. Even if it was the hardest thing I'd ever done. "Okay, Momma," I said in a whisper, my heart ripping to pieces in my chest. "Okay."

"Roy's going to fight it. I need you to stand strong."

She was putting me in an impossible situation, yet I found myself nodding. "Okay. Anything, Momma."

"Lila!" Tilly protested, getting out of her chair and rushing up to the side of the bed. "You stupid, stubborn woman. The world's not done with you yet."

"Maybe I'm done with the world, Tilly." Momma turned her hopeful gaze to me. "Is Roy here?"

356

I tried to keep the sting of her request from showing. Of course she wanted him. "He and Belinda are in the waiting room. I'll go get them, but I'd like to come back when they leave. I want to stay with you."

She nodded but didn't say anything.

I walked out of her room on autopilot, not stopping until I found Colt sitting in a chair in the waiting area. He sat slumped in his chair until he saw me; then he got to his feet. I saw Roy and Belinda out of the corner of my eye, sitting in the opposite corner of the room.

"Roy," I said without looking at him. "Momma is asking for you."

He stood and arrogance rolled off him in waves. "Of course she is. I'm the one who was there for her after you ran off."

I knew he was searching for hurtful things to say. After Momma died and Roy found out the details of her will, things would get worse, but he didn't scare me. I'd handled a whole lot worse than my brother.

I glanced up at Colt. "I'm hungry. Would you like to get something to eat before your gig?"

He smiled down at me. "Absolutely."

We started down the hall, and he glanced over his shoulder at my brother and Belinda as they headed toward my mother's room.

"I can stay, Mags. I can cancel."

I shook my head. "No. Roy can't touch me. He's scared of you now. Go to your gig and don't worry about me. I'm planning to stay with Momma tonight."

"Okay," he said reluctantly.

"Where are you going to hide the . . . ?" I knew he'd understand my unfinished sentence. We'd left the gold hidden in my car.

He turned serious. "I'm not sure. But I swear I'll keep it safe."

I grinned. "I know. You've got big plans for it."

He stopped and looked uncertain before he said, "Tomorrow we'll talk more about . . . everything."

Everything felt like a heavy topic I wasn't sure I was ready for.

My phone vibrated in my pocket, signaling an incoming text from Brady.

Sorry I couldn't get away for our trip in the woods, but I wanted to fill you in on Bill James.

While I wasn't disappointed about the field trip—I hadn't exactly been in a position to go either—I was eager for what he had on Bill. Had my brother's boss been arrested?

Colt stopped walking. "Is everything okay?"

I came to a halt beside him. "I'm not sure."

He glanced down at my phone, his back stiffening slightly. "What were you and Bennett going to do in the woods?"

How was I supposed to answer that? I opted for my go-to reaction when backed into a corner. "*Wow*. A few kisses and you think eavesdropping on my conversations is acceptable now?" I asked in a snotty tone.

My phone vibrated again.

Bill James has a solid alibi for the night of Emily's murder.

"Shit," Colt said, rubbing the back of his neck. "So James isn't the serial killer?"

"You're eavesdropping again." I tried to muster a sharp tone, but I was too nervous to pull it off. I tapped out a response.

Did you talk to Bill? What about the files?

He responded within seconds.

Bill James left town yesterday afternoon. He won't be back until tomorrow.

Then who had been in Bill James's office? And more importantly, who was the killer?

chapter twenty-five

The next morning, I woke up in the recliner in Momma's hospital room with a stiff neck, a sore back, and an overwhelming sense of grief.

My mother wanted to die. She was leaving me.

She'd slept most of the night despite the fact that the nursing staff had come in to check on her every hour or two, but my own sleep had been sporadic.

I grabbed my phone to check the time and saw a text from Brady.

How's your mother?

I texted back: Sleeping.

His reply came back seconds later.

Want to meet me for coffee in the lobby? Fifteen minutes?

He'd been worried about where I was staying last night, so I'd told him I would be at the hospital with my mother all night.

Sounds good.

I got out of the chair and stretched, then walked over to Momma's bed to check on her. While they had turned off the constant beeping of her monitors, I found it reassuring to watch the steady beat of her heart on the screen. Proof that she was still alive.

After I went to the bathroom and washed my face, I headed downstairs. I'd just walked out of the elevator into the sunny lobby when I saw Brady walking through the front doors carrying two cups of coffee.

I met him in the middle of the lobby with a grateful smile. "When you mentioned getting coffee, I thought you meant here. There's a coffee cart by the cafeteria."

His face lit up when he saw me. "I decided the two of us have enough risks in our lives at the moment. No sense playing Russian roulette with coffee."

My smile felt somewhat convincing. "Good point." I gestured to the leather chairs spread around the lobby. "Would you like to sit and talk for a bit?"

"Yeah," he said softly. "I would."

The lobby was nearly empty at seven in the morning, giving us plenty of seating options.

"So has your mother's condition changed?" he asked as we settled into two chairs next to each other.

I took a sip of my coffee. "No, but it's about to get worse. She's been fighting cancer for several years, and her doctor thinks this is it."

His eyes widened. "Really? I can't believe it. I just saw her a few days ago."

"She has an infection. It's taking over her whole body."

"Maggie, I'm so sorry."

I didn't say anything. There was nothing to say about my mother. She'd made her choice. But there were plenty of other things to talk about.

"Are you certain about Bill James?" I asked.

He set his cup on the table between us and leaned forward, lowering his voice. "Yeah. He was in Las Vegas. Your brother provided his alibi for the trip."

"And you're sure about his alibi for the night Emily was killed?"

"Yeah, there was a woman at his house when the Nashville police dropped by. She says she's his girlfriend. Swears he was with her that night."

"So you're no closer to finding the killer than you were before?"

"We'll catch him, Maggie."

I nodded absently. Something about this didn't feel right.

"We haven't seen each other since Thursday evening," Brady said as he squirmed in his seat. "I wanted to talk about that." His warm brown eyes lifted to mine.

I lowered my gaze to the cup in my hands. "Brady . . ."

"Maggie, you don't have to explain. I know things were moving too fast for you. I wanted to let you know I understand, and I wanted to apologize for being difficult when you told me."

"Brady . . ." I let my voice trail off, unsure what to say.

"It's okay. But I want you to know that I'm still here if you need me. I'd like to think we were becoming friends before we slept together. I'd still like to be friends."

I offered him a grateful smile. "Me too."

"We're still working together to catch a serial killer, so we need to be able to talk openly to each other." He gave me an earnest look that made him look more like a Boy Scout than a cop. "If you need anything, don't hesitate to call me, okay? I still plan to keep checking on you."

I stood and gave him a hug. "Thank you, Brady."

He released me and grinned. "We may be apart at the moment, Magnolia Steele, but that doesn't mean we're completely finished."

I had to tell him. I couldn't lead him on. "Brady." I paused and took a breath. "Colt . . . he's . . ."

He shook his head, his grin wavering. "I know you're scared of the idea of us. You do what you need to do to be ready."

Then he turned around and headed for the front doors.

"Brady," I called after him.

But he was already out the door.

My brother came back midmorning, and I got the impression he was performing a perfunctory visit until I heard him at the nurse's desk.

I'd insisted on staying in Momma's room while he was there, but I'd quietly followed him out after his five-minute stay. He'd stopped at the nurse's desk, demanding to see the head nurse. I stayed in the hall, hiding behind a volunteer cart loaded with magazines and books, not wanting to be connected to his brewing tirade.

She arrived seconds later, although I could only see a snippet of her blue scrubs peeking around the corner. "Can I help you, Mr. Steele?"

"I want to know who I need to talk to, to override this idiotic decision my sister has made."

"Mr. Steele," she said in a softer tone. "Your sister had nothing to do with your mother's decision. The staff heard her and your mother's friend trying to get her to change her mind. Your mother's mind was made up before she even came into the hospital."

"Then tell me what I need to do to overrule it. Get an attorney?"

The nurse's voice was full of compassion. "Mr. Steele, you'd be wasting the precious time you have with her if you resort to that. Do you really want to be at odds with her at the end?"

"I can't lose her." My brother's voice broke. "She's all I have. I can't . . ."

"Losing a parent is hard," she said. "I can arrange for you to speak to one of the chaplains."

"I'm not religious," my brother snapped.

"You don't have to be. You can—"

"No." My brother's asshole attitude was back. "If you can't help me with this, I'll find someone who can."

As he stomped off, it occurred to me that I didn't know my brother at all.

Colt came by to see us around noon. He poked his head in the door and glanced at my mother, then at me in the recliner.

I pushed off my blanket and got to my feet.

"How's she doing?" he asked as he approached me.

"The same," I whispered. "She's been sleeping since last night. She rouses when the nurses poke her too much, but other than that she sleeps."

"She's a fighter."

Even when she said she wasn't.

"Want to get some lunch?"

"I'm not really hungry, but I could use some fresh air."

We headed to the ground floor and took a walk outside. When I wrapped my arms around my body to hold off the slight chill, Colt wrapped an arm around my back and pulled me closer.

"Do you want to skip tonight?" he asked quietly. "I can handle . . . things."

I looked up at him. "Do you have a plan to get out of handing over the gold?"

Something shifted in his eyes. "Whatever it takes to keep you safe."

For the first time since yesterday, I had reservations about trusting Colt. I stopped walking. "So you *are* handing over the gold?"

He didn't answer.

"I need to know what you're planning."

"It's not set in stone, Maggie. It's a fluid plan."

"Which is bullshit speak for either you don't know or you're not going to tell me."

"There are a lot of factors to consider."

How could I be so stupid? "You're giving it to *them*." I stated it as fact.

"*Who?*"

"Whoever you answer to." When he didn't say anything, I took a step backward. "You are so full of shit. You're not coming up with a plan. You're following orders." God, how could I have been so stupid? "*I'm* your orders. Get Magnolia to trust you so she'll go along with anything you say. Good job, Colt. The harder-to-get the girl, the bigger the feather in your cap."

He stared at me in disbelief. "You think my intentions toward you are disingenuous? *After yesterday?*"

I wrapped my arms around myself. "I think you like me, sure, but I think you like yourself more than everyone put together."

Pain flashed in his eyes before a sneer chased it away. "You said you liked that about us, Magnolia. That we were so *alike.*"

"I was like that when I came back to Franklin, but I'm changing. I thought you were changing too. My mistake."

He put his hands on his hips and gave me a look of disgust. "Just like a woman to want to change a man."

I dropped my arms. "I didn't try to change you, Colt, and you know it. You were changing all on your own."

"I've been getting soft," he said, losing his anger. "And soft is dangerous."

I was handling this so badly, letting my stupid feelings and pride get in the way. Someone from Colt's past had a hold on him, and instead of helping him, I was ripping him apart. I moved closer and put my hands on his chest. "We can do this together."

"We *have* been doing it together."

"No, not really. We've been working side by side, but not *together*. You're hiding things from me."

"You're hiding things from me!" It was our same old tune—a sad song we'd written together.

He tried to pull away, but I held tight and refused to let him go. "Then let's stop hiding things."

The hard lines around his eyes faded, and he lifted his hand to my face. "Maybe you took it as a joke, Maggie, but I meant what I said. We should take that gold and run. We can leave right now."

My mouth dropped open. "You can't be serious."

"I'm deadly serious." Excitement filled his eyes as he grabbed my upper arms. "We're good together. We could be happy."

I could imagine it now. The two of us on a beach somewhere, sucking down tropical drinks and holding hands. Life happy and undemanding and simple. The old me would have jumped on the chance to run away, and that's how I knew I'd changed. "Not this way, Colt. I can't leave Momma."

"She's already left you."

His words were like a slap in the face.

He pulled me into a hug and cupped my head, holding me close. "I didn't mean it like that. I'm sorry."

But it was true, and it hurt like hell.

I still clung to him, refusing to cry. "I can't leave."

"I know, Mags. I know." He lifted my face and kissed me with a tenderness that caught me off guard. When he lifted his head, he searched my eyes. "I have to go."

"Can I trust you, Colt?"

He didn't respond. Then he grinned, but it looked forced. "There's only one person you can truly trust, Magnolia, and that's you."

"That doesn't answer my question." Then again, maybe it did.

He kissed me again before he took a step back and dug in his pocket. "Your car's in the parking garage. I got a friend to help me." He pulled out my keys and handed them to me. "If you decide to come tonight, let me know as soon as possible."

"So you can factor it into your plans?" I asked quietly.

"Yeah." He watched me for a moment and then shoved his hand back into his pocket. "I got you something else."

He handed me a folded slip of paper. When I opened it, I saw Rowena Rogers's name along with a Brentwood address and a phone number.

I glanced up at him. "How?"

"One of the perks of who I know."

Why did I have a feeling that these mystery contacts of his would be more of a threat than I'd expected?

chapter twenty-six

I looked at the paper in my hand, mulling it over. Momma had been asleep since last night, and the nurses had said she was holding her own. I could spare an hour, couldn't I?

As I headed to the parking garage, I made a quick call to Tilly.

"How's your momma doin', sweet girl?" she asked when she answered.

"The same. She's been asleep since last night."

"She could pull out of this."

"Yeah," I said, even though we both knew it wasn't true. "I was calling to check on you. I wasn't scheduled to work at the big fundraiser, but since Momma's not there . . . Well, I was just calling to see if you need me."

"Your momma got that culinary school to help, and at this point there's too many cooks in the kitchen, pun intended." She chuckled, but it sounded forced. "Colt said you were going as his guest."

"He invited me," I conceded.

"And Belinda said she picked out a dress for you."

I wasn't so sure about that now. Another thing to worry about if I decided to go. "Sounds like you're getting all kinds of second-hand information about me."

"Maybe if you told me yourself . . ." Her voice trailed off, but it sounded good-natured and not pouty. "Maggie, when your mother . . . when she's gone, I don't want to lose you again. I'm not sure I can handle losing her, let alone you."

"You won't, Tilly. I'm sticking around for a while." Just one of many reasons I couldn't run off with Colt, as tempting as it was to flee our problems. Tilly needed me and Belinda needed me too, whether she accepted it or not. Besides, I was tired of running. I was tired of hiding.

I knew what I needed to do.

"Tilly, I have to run an errand. I'm headed into the parking garage, so I'm going to lose you. If I don't talk to you before tonight, good luck."

"I'll see you at the party, sweet girl."

Time would tell.

I worried about finding my car, but it was in the same place we'd parked the night before. I unlocked the trunk and lifted the floor cover to reveal the spare tire, the hiding place Colt had used for the gold. Sure enough, it was gone.

If I was going to confront this woman, I couldn't do it wearing my dirty jeans and the T-shirt I'd planned to wear to hike in the woods, now smelling like a musty house and hospital antiseptic. Unfortunately, I was officially out of clean clothes.

I'd reached yet another low point in my life.

A quick stop by a trendy store at the mall yielded two nice outfits that put a significant dent in what little money I had left in my bank account. I went to my apartment next, intending to move my laundry from the washer to the dryer, but was shocked to discover it had already been moved. Two shirts and a dress, all shrinkable, had been hung to dry in my closet.

Colt.

A lump formed in my throat. As stupid as it sounded, this was better than flowers or an expensive dinner . . . if I overlooked the fact he'd probably picked the lock to get into my apartment. And I did because I suspected he had only broken in to make sure I was safe.

What was I going to do about Colt?

After a quick shower, I changed into an understated pale-pink blouse with a cream-colored suit and cream heels. If I wanted to meet Rowena Rogers on a level playing field, I had to look the part. I grabbed my cream Coach purse and stuffed it full of makeup along with my wallet. If I was going to the fundraiser, I needed to be able to get ready . . . Though there was the small matter of a dress.

My makeup was understated to match my outfit, and I dried and lightly curled my long, dark hair. Pleased that I looked the part, I locked up my apartment and headed toward Brentwood. I'd half-expected my domineering landlord to intercept me, so at least something was going my way.

By the time I got to Rowena Rogers's house, I still hadn't figured out what to say or even what to ask. Part of me wasn't sure what I was looking for. What was the point? My father had been a criminal. My mother was dying. My brother hated me. My sister-in-law thought I'd betrayed her.

What did it matter who'd done what fourteen years ago?

I looked at my reflection in the rearview mirror, surprised to see how much I'd changed in the last month. This wasn't just about me anymore. This was about discovering the truth and possibly the identity of a serial killer.

After parking the car in Rowena's driveway, I reached under the passenger seat and pulled out the gun Colt had given me. I hadn't allowed myself to bring it into the hospital, so I'd stowed it there for safety. I unwrapped it, making sure the clip was loaded, and shoved it into my purse. While I doubted I would need a gun to face a woman whom I suspected to be in her seventies, I wasn't giving anyone the benefit of the doubt.

Clutching my purse to my side, I walked up the driveway to the imposing, ten-foot-tall wood door of the opulent two-story brick home. Every click of my heels filled me with confidence as I assumed a role—a young woman determined to find the truth, no matter what the cost.

I rang the doorbell and waited for a good thirty seconds before Rowena Rogers opened the door.

"Magnolia. So you found me," she said as though she'd been waiting.

"Yes."

She lifted her head and literally looked down her nose at me. "I suppose you're here for some answers."

So much for me taking charge. I gave her my own snooty look. "Some things have come to light, and I'd like to ask you about them."

She folded her hands neatly in front of her waist. "*Some things have come to light,*" she mocked. "So mysterious."

I held my temper. "I guess you would know since you're full of mystery yourself."

She grinned. "Touché, Magnolia Steele. Score one for you."

I needed more than a zinger. I needed her to talk.

"I don't have much time," she said. "But I can spare you a few minutes." She stepped back, moving out of the way. "Come in."

I followed her into the marble entryway, shutting the heavy wood door behind me. She led me into a sunny room with a white marble fireplace, dark hardwood floors, and furniture in tasteful but cold shades of sage green and pale yellow.

"Have a seat," she said, gesturing to a sofa. "Would you like some tea?"

"No, thank you. Just the chat."

"Well, I want some tea. I'll be back."

She disappeared through a door on the wall with the fireplace, leaving me to stew over what I wanted to ask her.

Bill. No matter what alibi he had, it all seemed to connect back to Bill.

Rowena returned five minutes later with a tray heaped with a teapot, two teacups, and a plate of cookies and scones.

I watched as she set the tray down on the coffee table in front of me, then perched on an armchair across from me and poured tea into two cups.

I gestured to the tray. "I'm amazed you put this together so quickly. It's almost as if you were expecting me." Even as I said the words in jest, I wondered if they were true. Had she known Colt was giving me her contact information?

She released a polite laugh. "One has to love a good electric kettle." She glanced up. "How do you prefer your tea? The English way?"

So we were ignoring the fact that I'd already declined her offer? Was this a test to see how compliant I would be? Or was it a polite offer?

"Yes, please," I said, hedging my bets. Might as well be polite. For now.

Rowena placed a sugar cube in each cup and then topped each one off with milk. Handing me a cup and saucer with a spoon on the side, she gave me a patronizing smile. "I believe good manners are the basis of a moral society. Don't you, Magnolia?"

"And do you believe that Bill James has good manners?" I asked as I delicately stirred my tea, then rested the spoon on the saucer and gave her a polite smile.

Her eyes lit up, and she picked up her cup and took a sip. "I suppose you know him better than I do."

"What makes you say that?"

"He was your father's partner. You spent a significant amount of time with him."

Except we hadn't, not really, and now I could see that Momma had kept us from him. "I was a child," I said, setting my cup and saucer on the table in front of me.

"Exactly," she said, her eyes narrowing. "And you were a child when your father left. Children's memories are not to be trusted. They are viewed through a skewed lens, Magnolia. You need to let this witch hunt go. You caused damage fourteen years ago, and you are blazing a path of destruction now."

"With all due respect, Mrs. Rogers, there is a killer on the loose."

"A killer who lay dormant until you returned."

"If that's true, then what happened to Christopher Merritt three years ago? I know you two were meeting, and unlike the gossips here in town, I don't believe for a minute that you were having an affair."

She narrowed her eyes to pinpricks. "You think he wouldn't have me as a lover?"

I crossed my legs, trying to look as demure as possible. "No, I think you wouldn't have *him*."

Rowena laughed and set down her cup. "I'm happy to see you have just as much spunk as you did when you were a child."

"We've met before?" I asked, then amended, "Before last week?"

"Of course. I was very close to your father," she said with an air of naughtiness.

I wasn't going to take the bait. I needed to get this back on track. "When did you meet my father?"

"A very long time ago. You were a toddler, and your mother was huge with your brother in her belly. Your father was quite proud of you. Talked about you ad nauseam." She grimaced, as though she found the memory distasteful.

Ignoring her dig, I continued, "Was it a professional meeting?"

"If you call a fundraiser where investors kiss rich people's asses a professional meeting, then yes, it was a professional meeting."

"So you met at a fundraiser?"

"You really want to go down this path?" she asked. Her question held an ominous tone.

Did I? Was it really worth the bloodied price? But I'd come this far. There was no turning back now. "Yes."

Rowena sat back in her chair and rested her hands on the wooden arms. "Then proceed at your own risk, but a word of warning—I have plans this afternoon, so I will likely cut you off when I'm out of time."

I suspected she'd cut it off as soon as she'd told me everything she wanted me to know. I knew I was being played, yet I had no choice but to follow her rules. "Who was in charge of Winterhaven?"

Her eyes lit up. "Oh, someone has been doing her homework." She rested her hands on her lap. "Your father, believe it or not." She waved a hand. "Well, he wasn't in charge publicly, but he was calling the shots. The Jackson Project was his idea, and he brought many of us on board to invest in it as well. But I'm sure you heard it all fell apart." She made a face. "Nasty business. Max and Neil vowed to get revenge, but Bill protected your father. He made sure they never touched him . . . until Brian turned on *him*, that is."

I tried to hide my shock. "My father turned on Bill? When? Fourteen years ago when he disappeared?"

She laughed and shook her head. "You poor girl. You always believed he was dead. Brian was counting on that. He was so certain the testimony of his precocious daughter would convince the police he'd come to foul play. But his plan didn't exactly work out, of course. Max and Neil changed things."

My heart raced, but I forced myself to maintain my cool exterior. Rowena was counting on me falling apart, and I wasn't going to give it to her. I was a coldhearted woman no one could touch. If I repeated it enough, I'd believe it. "What does that mean? How did they change things?"

"They knew Brian was planning to take off, so they planned to catch him in the act and punish him. They had Shannon abducted and killed, then planted her car at the airport along with your father's. Max knew a woman who worked at an airline, and in exchange for a hefty bribe, he got her to claim they'd boarded a plane to the Caribbean. Max had paid for the tickets several days in advance with Shannon's credit card so there would be a paper trail."

"It couldn't have been that easy."

"It was easier than you might think, particularly if that's what the police wanted to believe."

"And my father?"

"He escaped, unscathed, of course, and boarded a plane, but not with Shannon. And under an alias. Rumor has it he went to Tahiti. Or Bora Bora. He took the knowledge of the location of the money with him."

"Walter Frey, Geraldo Lopez, and Christopher Merritt's father knew about this? They condoned it?"

"Not at first, but Bill kept them in line. Everyone has their secrets, Magnolia. Things they never want shared in the light of day. Geraldo hid that he was gay. Walter hid that he'd committed incest with his niece. Christopher went on binges with prostitutes and cocaine."

I felt like I was going to be sick. "And Steve Morrissey?"

"Steve Morrissey was tired of his trashy wife and found out his prenup wasn't as ironclad as he'd hoped. He gave Max and Neil permission to use her in their scheme."

"But Shannon's sister said she had proof that her husband had been laundering money."

She chuckled. "Poor naïve Magnolia. You're just as gullible as poor Shannon. It was all planted. So were the rumors that she and your father might have been working together to take information to the police."

"Bill was involved?"

"He was the mastermind, my dear. Your father double-crossed him and took his money. Much more than a measly million."

"He took Bill's *money*? Everyone thinks Shannon stole money from her husband's account."

She waved her hand again. "Smoke and mirrors. Your father stole from the business. He'd been planning it for years."

He'd planned to leave my mother, Roy, and me?

"This must be quite hard to hear, Magnolia."

I fought to keep control, but then I realized this woman might be feeding me a pack of lies. "I want the truth," I said in a firm voice. "Where's my father now?"

"That's anyone's guess, although rumor has it he pops back into town every few years to get a peek at the people he loved."

Shock washed through me. Could the man in the ball cap have been my father? I'd assumed he was paying attention to me because he was the killer, but . . .

Rowena stood. "This stroll down memory lane has been amusing, but our time is up."

"Two quick things," I said as I stood, hanging my purse on my arm. "What happened to your husband?"

For the first time, she looked affected by her evil tale. "Unlike the others, he didn't have a vice to keep him in line. When he threatened to tell . . . he met his untimely demise."

"They tampered with his car?"

She didn't answer.

"And your vice?" I asked, holding her gaze.

A wicked smile crossed her face. "Your father. Our affair was brief but fiery. If word got out that the esteemed Rowena Rogers had slept with a family man . . ." She tsked. "I used to care about things like that back then."

The blood rushed from my head. Of all the things I'd heard about him, for some reason this was by far the hardest to accept.

My whole childhood had been a lie.

But I was a grown woman now, and I needed to pull myself together. "Was Gordon Frasier dirty?" I asked.

"Did he help cover up Shannon's murder and my father's disappearance?"

A sad smile surfaced on her face. "No, poor Gordon was simply caught in the middle of something out of his control, but I hear his nephew is set on clearing his name."

But was he doing it by devious means? "How do you know about Owen?"

"I have friends in many places. Now you need to go, Magnolia, and get ready for your date tonight. A beautiful man always deserves a beautiful woman, and your man is as stunning as your father was back in the day."

My mouth dropped open. Who was she talking about? But it made sense that she'd know about my entanglement with Brady if she had friends who kept tabs on Owen. Still, why had she shared so much with me if she believed I was involved with a detective?

She followed me to the door. When she opened it, I walked onto the front step and turned to face her. "Why did you tell me this? You know I could tell the police, and they could arrest you as an accomplice."

"You're not going to go to the police, Magnolia. You have too much to lose. One million dollars' worth. Be a good girl and do the right thing. Don't end up like poor Shannon."

With that, she slammed the door in my face.

chapter
twenty-seven

As soon as I pulled out of her driveway, I called Colt.

"Maggie?" he answered, sounding on edge. Probably because I only called when I was in trouble. The rest of the time I texted. "Is everything okay?"

He'd given me Rowena's information. Had he set me up? Was he the handsome date Rowena had mentioned? I couldn't help but think about how she'd had that tea tray ready to go. "How did you get Rowena's information?"

"Maggie . . ."

"You're not going to tell me?"

When he answered, his voice was guarded. "I can't."

"Why not?"

"I promised."

"Since when do you keep promises?" I asked.

"Since when did I break a promise to you?" he demanded angrily. We were silent for a moment, and when he spoke again, his voice had lost its edge. "You called her?"

"No, I went and saw her."

"Who's with your mother?" He sounded agitated.

"The hospital staff."

"Why didn't you ask me to go with you? What if that woman was dangerous?"

"She *is* dangerous." I pushed out a breath of frustration and pulled into the parking lot of an insurance company so I could look up an address on my phone. "I'll tell you the rest later, but she knows about the gold, Colt."

"She came right out and said that?"

"She never mentioned the word 'gold,' but when I asked her why she'd given me so much implicating information, she said I wouldn't turn her in because I have too much to lose—one million dollars' worth. Then she told me to do the right thing or end up like Shannon Morrissey."

"Fuck."

"Exactly."

"What did she confess to?"

"Who's controlling your puppet strings?" I countered.

"Dammit, Magnolia! Did she say anything about tonight specifically, or was it just a general threat?"

I replayed the last few minutes of our conversation. "Just in general."

"Then she doesn't necessarily know anything. If she knew Walter Frey—or hell, even heard the damn news— then she knew about the money. She was fishing and used it as bait. Did you give her anything?"

I replayed the conversation again. "No. I only asked questions." But I realized I needed to tell Colt everything; otherwise, he was going into a dangerous situation not completely armed. Still, I didn't want to tell him on the phone. I needed to do it in person.

"Good." He sounded relieved.

"I'm coming tonight," I said. "Although I still don't have a dress. I'll come up with something."

"Then I'll meet you out front of the Savannah House at eight thirty," he said. "Don't bring your car. Take a taxi or an Uber."

"Okay," I said. "See you then."

"Maggie!"

"What?" I asked quietly.

"Watch your back. Do you have the gun? It's under the seat."

"I have it."

"Good. Bring it tonight."

I hung up and looked up the address I'd decided to visit. When I found it, I plugged it into the GPS on my phone and tried to talk myself out of this rash decision. I suspected it wouldn't end well.

Like that had stopped me before.

I headed out of the parking lot, and thirty minutes later, I pulled up in front of a house I barely remembered. Shivers cascaded down my spine. This was utterly stupid, yet I was determined to see it through. I picked up my phone, opened an app to record conversations, and then tucked it into my purse. Hopefully it wouldn't be too muffled. My gun was in there too if I needed it.

Before I walked up to the door, I sent Colt a text with the address of where I was and told him to come looking for me if he hadn't heard from me in twenty minutes. Then

I stuffed my phone back into my purse before he could talk me out of it.

I rang the doorbell, and it was only a few seconds before a young woman who looked to be in her early twenties opened the door. "Oh," she said, sounding surprised. "Magnolia."

My eyebrows rose. "Do I know you?"

She giggled. "No. But I know *you*. Come in. He'll be excited that you're here."

"He's home?"

"Yeah." She gestured to the living room full of black leather furniture. "Have a seat. I'll go get him."

I was too nervous to sit, so I moved around the room, pretending to look at the artwork and the view out the window. But I saw him in my peripheral vision as soon as he entered the room. Steeling my back, I turned to face him.

Bill James filled the doorway, looking very pleased. "Magnolia. I'm so happy you changed your mind."

I couldn't think of anything to say. Everything I'd planned on the way here had fled my brain.

"Would you like a drink?" he asked. "Gemma made some lemonade earlier."

"No, thank you," I said, moving toward a leather chair. "I'm fine."

He sat on the sofa and watched me take the chair, and it occurred to me that I'd spent the afternoon in the living rooms of two murdering co-conspirators. It was as if I were making Sunday social calls in hell.

"What made you change your mind?" Bill asked.

"My mother is in the hospital," I said. "She's dying from cancer."

He sat up, looking alarmed. "Magnolia, I'm sorry. I had no idea."

"No one did. She kept it to herself. But it's made me miss Daddy even more," I said, the words tasting bitter on my tongue. If Daddy really was alive, I'd probably spit in his face if I saw him again. But I wasn't about to let Bill James know that. Not yet.

"Your father was a good man. But sometimes good men get caught up in bad things."

I looked Bill square in the eye. "*Was* he a good man, Mr. James?"

His smile faded. "Call me Bill, and what do you know?"

What was I going to confess to? Though it was the most benign of all the accusations I could level, it stung horribly. Especially with Momma lying there in that hospital room. "I know he had an affair."

Bill held up his hand in protest. "He regretted it, Magnolia. It killed him that he was weak."

"I know he slept with Rowena Rogers." The thought of my father sleeping with that vile woman made me want to puke. "However, I don't know many details other than that it supposedly didn't last long. I want to know more."

"It's true. It didn't last long. Maybe a few months. It was when you and Roy were young. You were probably seven or eight, although they had been skirting around it for years." He paused, sympathy in his eyes. "I caution you against hearing more, Magnolia. What good will it do?"

"I want to know the truth."

"Contrary to popular opinion, the truth doesn't always set you free."

"No, but sometimes a person needs a hard dose of reality. I'm not a child anymore."

He studied me for several seconds, then held up his hands in surrender. "What do you want to know?"

He was confusing me. Despite Brady's news, I'd been so certain Bill was the serial killer, but why would he be treating me so kindly if he intended on killing me? Was it because Gemma was here? Was she his girlfriend? But when I compared his voice to the voice in his office, I was pretty sure it wasn't him.

Then who had been in his office?

I just needed to focus on getting as many answers as I could—and then get out. "I want to know when and how their affair started."

"They met at a fundraiser. We were drumming up clients. We were pretty lean back then, and your father was about to have two babies to provide for. Then there was the house he'd overextended his finances to buy, along with a ballooning-interest mortgage. And Rowena . . . she was beautiful and charming. He was tempted, but he didn't succumb to the temptation until she was part of a business deal that went bad. She understood what he was going through while your mother was simply furious."

"So he was stressed?" I asked bitterly. "That excuses what he did?"

"No, Magnolia. Of course not. But things were bad at home with your mother, and he felt trapped. He didn't want to leave you. When you were born, he built his world around you, but it wasn't enough." He paused. "Rowena made him feel like a man again."

I shook my head in disgust. "Don't you dare make excuses for him."

"I'm not." He sighed and leaned forward. "Nothing will excuse what he did, and he knew it. He never wanted you or your mother to know."

"You said it lasted a few months. Why did he end it?"

He hesitated. "She ended it. She was in a loveless marriage, and she loved your father. She gave him an ultimatum, thinking it would work, but she underestimated how much he loved you and your brother."

"So that's why she hates me so much?"

His eyes widened. "You've met her?"

"Yes. A few times."

"I would like to think she doesn't hold anything against you personally, but she's capable of petty jealousy, so I wouldn't be surprised if she does."

"Did my father also have an affair with Shannon Morrissey?"

He grimaced. "Honestly? I don't know."

"You told the police he did."

Bill linked his fingers together. "I regret that now. *I* succumbed to gossip." This was contradicting everything Rowena had said. Who was I to believe?

"So if he didn't run off with Shannon Morrissey, what happened to him?"

"I suspect Geraldo Lopez killed him."

"But why?"

"I think we've all heard the same thing from the police. Your father, Walter, Chris, and Geraldo conspired to embezzle from Steve Morrissey, and your father was about to go to the police. Geraldo stopped him and used it as a warning to the others."

I looked Bill in the eyes. "But that's not what happened, is it?"

His demeanor shifted. "Why would you say that?"

Rowena Rogers had nearly destroyed my family and hated me because my father had—at least once—tried to do the right thing. I decided to throw her under the bus. "Rowena thinks Max Goodwin and Neil Fulton were involved with Shannon Morrissey's death."

His face paled.

"Did Max and Neil try to kill my father?"

"Why would they do such a thing? Winterhaven was at least five years behind us. Water under the bridge." He frowned. "I take it you spoke to Rowena." When I nodded, he said, "Consider the source, Magnolia. She wants to hurt you."

"I want the truth, Bill."

"Bill," Gemma said from the doorway. "I'm sorry to interrupt, but Mitch Kennedy is on the phone. He insists you take his call."

Bill looked conflicted, but he shook his head and stood. "I'm sorry, Magnolia, but we'll have to pick this up later. Maybe we could meet for dinner next week. Let's eat here so we can talk discreetly. Gemma will cook."

"Yes," I said, standing, trying to sound amicable so he would talk to me again if the need arose. "Of course. Sorry to interrupt your day."

"No," he said, walking over and pulling me into a loose embrace. "You are always welcome in my home. I tried to be more of a presence in your life after your father left, but your mother . . ." He grimaced. "Let's just say she never forgave me for your father's indiscretions."

It took everything in me not to cringe when he touched me.

"I never had children," he said as he walked to the doorway. "I know I'll never be your father, but I'd like you to know someone is here for you. Especially after your mother . . . passes. Let's just say I've already assumed that role for your brother. I'd be honored to take it on with you."

"Thank you," I said in genuine shock. What game was he playing?

Bill turned to Gemma, who was still standing in the hallway. "Be sure to schedule a dinner for me and Magnolia this week before she goes."

She nodded. "Yes, sir."

Yes, sir? Were they into some kind of dom-sub thing? The thought of Bill James as a dom . . . *disgusting*.

"Which night would work better for you, Magnolia?" Gemma asked as Bill went up the staircase.

"Uh . . . I'm not sure," I said honestly. "My mother's in the hospital."

She gave me a worried look. "Can I pencil you in for Thursday? You can cancel if need be. He told me to schedule a dinner, and if I don't . . ."

"Yeah," I said in attempt to calm her. "That's fine."

"Thank you." She hid her face, looking embarrassed.

Was she in an abusive relationship like Belinda? That might explain the whole *taking Roy under his wing* thing. "How long have you and Bill been dating?"

Her face jerked up, her mouth open in surprise. "Oh. We're not dating. I'm his personal assistant."

"Oh," I said, scrunching my brow. "I thought he had a girlfriend." When she shook her head, I added, "I could swear Roy told me he was on a date Wednesday. It sounded like things were getting serious." So I had changed Roy for Brady . . .

"Oh, no," Gemma said. "Bill hasn't dated for months."

Gemma seemed clueless about maintaining his alibi. Who was the woman who claimed to have slept in Bill's bed? If it weren't true, he might not have an alibi at all.

Or was Brady lying? I wasn't sure I could entertain this idea, yet it burrowed in my brain anyway.

As soon as I got into the car, I pulled out my phone, turned off the recorder, and texted Colt.

I'm fine. False alarm.

He called within seconds.

"What the hell, Magnolia? I looked up that address. You went to see Bill James. What were you thinking?"

"It turns out Bill James had an alibi the night Emily died—well, maybe—so I figured there'd be no harm. I needed answers only he could give."

"What kind of answers?"

"About my father."

He was quiet for a moment. "What did he tell you?"

"Who are you working for?" I countered.

"Dammit, Magnolia."

"There you go." I looked out the window at Bill's house and noticed a figure in the window. It stepped back into the room, but not before I recognized Bill's face. He wasn't on a phone call. "I have to get back to Momma and figure out a dress. But I'll be there, eight thirty. We'll find out who wants the gold and then figure out where to go from there." I pulled away from the curb.

"You don't have to worry about that part, Maggie. I've got it covered. Just stay safe. We can't be the most beautiful couple in Williamson County if you get killed before you show up tonight."

I smiled at his statement; then I hung up, giving myself plenty of time to mull over everything I'd learned in the last hour and a half. I had more information than ever, but I had a feeling that I *still* didn't know what really happened fourteen years ago.

A half hour later, I was back in my mother's room, but she wasn't alone. Belinda sat in the chair next to the bed, reading out loud. It took me five seconds of eavesdropping to figure out she was reading Tina Fey's memoir. I couldn't help smiling. Momma would have hated it if Belinda had been reading a classic like *Pride and Prejudice*.

"Hey," I said softly when I walked into the room.

Belinda glanced over her shoulder. A frown tipped her mouth as she bent over and picked up her purse.

"You don't have to go because of me," I said, hating this new distance between us.

"It's okay," Belinda said as she stood. "I need to get ready. Are you still going tonight?"

I cast a worried glance at my mother, suddenly having second thoughts. "I've been gone for a few hours. I think I should stay."

"You're going," Momma said with her eyes still closed. "I want to see pictures of you two girls together."

Relief washed through me that she was awake. That she was still here with us.

"But I don't have a dress."

"I brought you one," Belinda said, gesturing to the long garment bag hanging in the corner. She gave me a half-smile. "And also a pair of shoes. I guess I got to pick it out after all."

"Belinda . . ." I reached for her, but she took a step back.

"I just need a little more time, okay?" But she didn't just look hurt. She looked nervous. Maybe she thought she was pushing me away too much to get back to being friends.

I nodded, grateful she wasn't writing me off forever. "Okay."

She kissed Momma on the cheek. "You stay strong, Lila."

"You girls need each other," Momma said, her eyes narrowed to slits as she turned her head to face us. "Magnolia, will you please give us a moment?"

I blinked in surprise. "Okay." But right or wrong, after I walked into the hall, I pressed my ear to the crack.

"Belinda," Momma said. "Give up whatever silly feud the two of you have going on. I know Roy hasn't treated you right, and I should have stepped in."

Belinda gasped and I heard horror in her voice. "Lila, you . . ."

Momma continued, sounding stronger than she had for the past couple of days. "I only have so much energy, so I'm not gonna waste it arguing with you over the facts. I'm a wise old woman, although some might question the wise part, but sometimes I actually know things. I know this: Roy isn't right for you, but Magnolia is. She's goin' to need you when I'm gone, Belinda. Can I count on you to be there for my girl?"

My mother was guilt-tripping my sister-in-law into babysitting me? I was beyond humiliated. But then it hit me: this was my mother's way of telling Belinda goodbye.

My eyes began to sting, so I pried them wide open. I had to keep it together.

"It's not that easy," Belinda said.

"Bullshit. Do you love Roy?"

"Of course I do," Belinda said, but she sounded unconvincing.

"We both know that's a lie, and I don't have time for lies right now, Belinda. You don't love him. It started out that way, but something happened a couple of years ago. He turned mean and you lost part of yourself. You've been biding your time, although for the life of me, I still haven't figured out why. I know it's not money. Gold diggin' is beneath you."

Belinda released a short laugh. "Thank you...I think."

"I love you, girl," Momma said in a rough voice. "You brought joy back into my life, and when you welcomed Magnolia, despite knowing Roy would punish you for it, you gave me a gift I could never repay."

"I didn't do it for you, Lila. I did it for me. I wanted a friend. Magnolia has been that."

"She's more than a friend, she's an ally, and you're gonna need her when you leave that fool son of mine."

"Lila . . ."

"Supposedly, dying women get to make requests, so here's mine for you: leave Roy."

"*Lila.*"

"You know I'm right. You can count on Magnolia. She's stronger than I ever gave her credit for. I know you've got your feelings hurt over something, but things are about to get tough, so you need to get over it quick, do you hear me?"

I heard Belinda sniffle. "I hear you."

"I love you like a daughter, girl. You are the very best thing Roy ever gave me." Momma coughed. "Now send Magnolia back in here before I take another twelve-hour nap."

I heard footsteps and I moved away from the door, pretending to be staring down the hall.

Belinda walked out the door with her purse hanging from the crook of her arm, swiping a tear from her cheek with the back of her free hand. She stopped and stared at me for a moment. "I love you, Magnolia. I just need more time."

My throat burned. "I know."

"Your mother is saying her goodbyes." Two fat tears rolled down her cheeks. "I just thought I should warn you." Then she turned around and walked toward the elevator.

I took several deep breaths before walking back into Momma's room.

"You changed from what you had on earlier," Momma said. "You look like you went to a business meeting."

"Yeah, of sorts." I stopped next to her bed, resting my hand on the metal rail. "I called Tilly earlier and offered to work in your place tonight, but she said they were doing just fine."

"She would never let you work tonight. Tilly's a romantic at heart. For what it's worth, she prefers Colt to that Brody, but she's always had a soft spot for the boy."

I grinned and moved next to her bed. "It's *Brady*. And which one do you prefer?"

Her eyes opened. "The one who makes you happy. The one who makes you laugh and cry."

"You think I should date a guy who makes me cry?"

"If you don't cry when you have a fight, then he's not worth stickin' around for. You don't love him enough."

"Enough for what?"

"Enough to make it work when times get tough, because Magnolia, they'll get tough, no matter how strong your love is."

All I could think about was my father cheating with that terrible woman. Obviously his love hadn't been strong enough.

"Oh." Momma's voice was heavy with disappointment. "You found out."

She couldn't possibly guess what I'd learned. "Found out what?"

"That your father had an affair."

I tried to hide my reaction. "People only think he slept with Shannon Morrissey. They were *rumors*, Momma. We both know they weren't true."

"Not her," Momma said. "The other one."

"What other one?"

"Don't play stupid, Magnolia," Momma said, sounding irritated. "I know you were listening in when I talked to Belinda." My eyes widened, but she shook. It was a small movement—barely an inch either way—yet there was no denying it. "I know you, my girl. I'm not angry. I was counting on it. But since you were listening, don't waste what little time I have left with lies and half-truths." She paused and some of her fire faded. "You know damn good and well there was another woman. Rowena Rogers."

"You knew?"

"Of course I knew. I'm not stupid either."

"But Daddy didn't think you knew."

"And where did you hear that? Let me guess, Bill James." Understanding filled her eyes. "So that's where you went, huh? You always did like to play with fire." She took several breaths before continuing. "Your father was a smart man, but stupid at relationships. He knows I nearly kicked him out, and I'm sure he never cheated again. Not even with that Morrissey woman."

"Why didn't you kick him out?" I asked. "How could you stay with him after that?"

"Oh, Magnolia, you're still so young and idealistic. I stayed because I still loved him. I stayed because you worshipped him. I stayed because I liked our house and our lives and it would have ripped everything apart to leave. So maybe I was strong to stay . . . maybe I was weak. But I warned him there would be no second chances."

"I had no idea."

"And your father and I wanted to keep it that way, but I should have known better. No secret stays buried forever." She took several breaths. "Your father loved you.

It's important you know that. I suspect he loved you more than me, but that's okay, because I channeled my love into Roy . . ." Her voice faded and her eyes closed. "One mistake . . . one mistake can lead to another and another until you're buried under an avalanche of them. I'm suffocating under my mistakes, Magnolia. I'm so damned tired of trying to climb out."

I picked up her hand and held tight. "You don't have to climb out, Momma," I said in a broken voice. "I brought a great big bulldozer and cleared out a path."

Her eyes squinted open and tears escaped from the corners, rolling down into her pillow. "And I love you for that." Her voice barely a whisper, she asked, "Do you remember the dress you wore to your senior prom?"

"Of course," I said with a laugh while I brushed away my tears. "But I'm surprised you do. You were working that night."

"I know, and I've regretted it for most of my life. It was so important to you, and I just dismissed it."

I smiled through my tears. "It's okay. Remember that bulldozer?"

She fumbled for the remote on her bed, then pushed the call button.

"Momma?" I asked, trying not to panic. "Are you okay?"

"I'm about to be."

Ten seconds later, a nurse walked in and stood in the doorway. "Do you need something, Mrs. Steele?"

Momma turned her head to face her. "I've changed my mind. Let's start that antibiotic."

The nurse broke into a big smile. "Yes, ma'am. I'll be right back to hang the bag."

Tears clogged my throat. "You said you were done. What made you change your mind?"

"You may have bulldozed my mistakes away, but I've got plenty of makin' up to do, starting with tonight. I know you're probably still thinking about skipping that ball, but I want you to go. I want to see you all dressed up like the night I missed your prom, but I know you'll never go if you're worryin' about me. If I start that antibiotic, it's one less worry for you," she said. "At least for tonight."

chapter
twenty-eight

As soon as I opened the garment bag, I understood why Belinda had insisted on choosing my dress. Not that it wasn't beautiful—it was the most gorgeous dress I had ever seen—but the quality of the fabric told me it had cost Belinda as much as a wedding dress.

The champagne-colored sleeveless dress had a fitted top with a plunging neckline that wasn't too deep and an open back that stopped at my waist. (Thank goodness it had built-in cups because there was no way to wear a bra.) The skirt fell in long chiffon folds, and Belinda had sent a rhinestone belt and champagne-colored, iridescent heels to add more sparkle. I planned on taking it back to her first thing in the morning. But tonight I would wear it and love every minute of it. I might even wear the gold masquerade mask she'd included. It was the small tiara that I balked at.

"Belinda insisted you wear it all. Tiara included," Momma said, as if reading my mind. "It's a masquerade ball. The one place you can get away with it."

Denise Grover Swank

One of the nurses had a curling iron in her locker, so I curled my hair, and another nurse styled it in an elaborate updo to showcase the tiara. When I stepped out of the bathroom, I had to admit that I felt like a princess, which was utterly ridiculous since I was far too old to play the part.

But my mother oohed and ahhed—and even insisted the nurses take photos of me with her phone. I asked her if the IV antibiotic had made her high, but she just laughed, a sound it felt immeasurably good to hear, and told me to get used to it.

A month ago, I would have run from this. Now I reveled in it.

But at eight thirty, as I stepped out of the Uber with my mask in my hand, I was a mess of nerves. Colt and I had a purpose for coming to this ball, and I had no idea how it would end.

I scanned the sidewalk outside Savannah House, the only true house in Franklin big enough to hold an event of this size. But all thoughts of murders and gold flew out of my head the moment I saw him.

Colt Austin was a good-looking man, but tonight he looked like a Greek god in his form-fitting black tux. His blond hair was freshly cut, though God only knew when he'd had the time, and his blue eyes sparkled when he saw me. I finally understood what people meant when they talked about seeing someone across a crowded room and the whole world disappearing.

I stopped in my tracks, but Colt continued his path toward me. When he reached me, a smile lit up his entire face. "You're beautiful."

"It's Belinda's dress," I said, feeling an uncharacteristic blush rising on my cheeks. "I think it turns into a pumpkin at midnight."

"It's not the dress." Then his smile changed into a sexy grin. "But as long as I'm the only one there to watch the transformation, I'm good."

I laughed. "I had no idea you had a pumpkin fetish, Colt Austin."

He leaned over and kissed me with a mixture of tenderness and possessiveness, a kiss that matched the man who gave it to me. "I had no idea you would be so perfect."

I narrowed my eyes. "What does that mean?"

His bad-boy grin was back. "I've heard about you since the first day I walked into Southern Belles Catering. I expected a diva, which is definitely not what you turned out to be."

"I'm going to take that as a compliment," I said in a mock-offended tone.

He laughed, but then the humor slipped away. "You make me believe everything will work out."

I turned serious too. "It has to. I'll accept nothing less."

"Do or die," he said. I expected him to grin like he was teasing, but he didn't.

"Colt," I said, fear snaking in my gut. "Where's the gold?"

He scanned the crowd, avoiding eye contact. "Hidden."

"What's your plan?"

Looping his arm through mine, he led me to the entrance. "We're denying a whole room full of people the chance to see the most beautiful woman in the world. I'll perform this one act of selflessness and share you for a few hours." He shot me a sexy grin. "But when this dress turns into a pumpkin, fair warning—I plan to take advantage of your naked body."

I gave him a demure grin, but my eyes were full of mischief. "You're just full of promises tonight."

His hand tightened over mine. "And I intend to keep every one of them."

We joined the line of people entering the building, and I noticed several women eyeing Colt with looks of appreciation and lust. There were whispers of my name. Of his.

"Where's your mask?" I asked him.

He grinned. "In my jacket pocket. I'm in no hurry to put it on."

Colt's name was on the guest list, along with a table number, and while I expected to be seated at a table on the edge of the room, we were close to the dance floor. Two older couples who reeked of money were already seated, and a purse lay in front of another spot.

"This table had to cost a fortune," I whispered. "How did you get the tickets?"

His answer was a grin.

We were forty minutes late by the time we got inside, and the event was already in full swing. An orchestra was playing a waltz. While I expected Colt to make fun of it, he surprised me by throwing his mask down on the table. "I'm not putting this on tonight, and you're not putting yours on either. No more hiding. Not anymore." He took the mask out of my hand and tossed it next to his. "Let's dance."

"You know how to waltz?"

"I'm a man of many talents," he teased. "I'll be happy to demonstrate them all, but the X-rated ones will have to wait until later."

I rolled my eyes, ignoring the heat his words had spread through me. Before answering, I dug my phone out of the clutch Belinda had sent for me to use and checked to see if I had any messages. None.

The small gun made the purse look bulky, but it made me feel safer to have it.

I looked up at Colt, the gravity of the situation weighing on me. "How will we know when we're supposed to meet whoever it is we're supposed to meet?"

Colt took my phone and tucked it into his jacket pocket. "I'm the one in charge of communicating with criminals tonight." Then he took my purse and dropped it on the floor under the table. "We don't want anyone stumbling across that."

No kidding. Especially since I didn't have a concealed carry permit.

He put an arm around my back and ushered me onto the dance floor. Only a few other couples were dancing, but I could hardly focus on what was going on around us. Colt's comment had struck a nerve. "What do you mean you're the one communicating with criminals *tonight*?"

His eyes narrowed. "It means I'm checking the messages. I'm serious, Magnolia. I want you as far removed from this as possible." His expression softened and his voice lowered, filling his words with plenty of playful innuendo. "Now let's dance. I finally get to show you my moves."

I found myself laughing despite the fact I was becoming more nervous by the minute.

He pulled me into his arms, and true to his word, not only could he waltz, but he was good. He whirled me around the dance floor, my skirt billowing around me.

"Breathe, Maggie," he said softly, searching my eyes. "Just breathe. It's going to be okay."

"What are you going to do? What's the plan?"

A grin lit up his face, but I could tell he was nervous too. "I thought you didn't care about the gold."

"I don't . . . mostly. But I'm not too happy about turning it over to a blackmailer either."

His jaw clenched. "Me neither."

"So what's the plan?" I repeated.

"The plan is for you to stick close to Belinda while I'm gone."

"Why?" I asked, getting defensive.

He remained silent for a moment, but something seemed to click for him. Reaching up to tuck an errant strand of hair behind my ear, he said, "I think Roy's going to make a move. We both know how much he hates you. He'll think nothing of sacrificing you to get what he wants."

"Sacrificing? What do you think is going to happen?"

He lowered his voice. "I think several people have somehow found out about the gold, and a lot of them will do anything to get their hands on that much money."

"I don't understand why you're here," I said, looking out at the people sitting at the tables. "You have the gold.

The Colt I know wouldn't have come to this thing, but here you are, about ready to potentially give up a lot of money in exchange for . . . me. It doesn't make any sense."

He laughed, but the sound was short and tight. "Are you saying you think I'd just let them kill you?"

"No," I said, watching him closely. "I'm saying that one, you wouldn't have come at all. And two, you would have tried to talk *me* out of coming."

His brow lowered. "Are you saying I'm knowingly putting you in danger?"

"No, I'm saying you're acting uncharacteristically."

I thought he might be insulted, but instead he flashed me a cavalier smile. "For the record, I did try to talk you out of it after our scare at the industrial park—a couple of times if I recall—but despite the rumors, I'm not all beauty and no brains. You're a stubborn woman, Magnolia Steele, and I'm smart enough to know there's no talking you out of something you want to do."

"You're not stupid, Colt," I whispered, searching his face. That was the second time he'd defended his intelligence. It occurred to me that he and I *were* a lot alike. How many people had assumed I was empty-headed because they thought I was beautiful?

His smile faded. "At this very moment, that could be debated."

Something was wrong, but I knew he wasn't going to come out and tell me. Whatever he was wrapped up in had him too spooked. I'd have to find another way.

"For the record," he said, "you're here so I can keep an eye on you."

"You think *I'll* do something stupid?" I asked without any heat.

"No. I'm terrified someone else will do something to you." He searched my eyes. "No matter how this all goes down tonight, you need to know that you're my biggest priority. It didn't start out that way, but that's how it ends."

I shuddered. "Don't say ends, Colt. You're scaring me."

The music stopped and he placed a soft kiss on my lips. "Let's get a drink."

He slipped an arm around my back, and we pushed through the crowd toward a bar—where we came face-to-face with Brady.

How had I forgotten he was going to be here?

But there he stood in a black tux, his face expressionless. "Magnolia," he said, using his detective voice. "I thought you were with your dying mother."

I supposed I deserved that.

"Sorry if I borrowed her for the night," Colt said, but his hand remained in place on my hip. "But I invited her last week . . . before you become Bragnolia."

I shot him an annoyed glance, then turned to Brady. "My mother made me come."

"And did she make you kiss Colt on the dance floor?"

Shit. "No."

He turned and walked away.

"Hey," Colt said, tugging on my hip. "You okay?"

I glanced up into his worried face. "As much as I can be, although I think I might have to kill you for coining the term *Bragnolia*."

"What?" he said, pulling me a couple of steps closer to the bar. "It's a good one, although I'm much more partial to Molt."

I couldn't help laughing. "Molt? Isn't that what lizards do when they shed their skin?"

He winked. "So maybe it needs more thought."

"You've given us a couple name?" I asked, hating the question in my voice.

He turned serious. "I told you that you're my number one priority."

The couple in front of us moved out of the way, and—much to the confusion of the bartender—Colt ordered a club soda and coke and a glass of white wine. I gave him a questioning look when the bartender started filling his glass, but he gave me a tight smile. The club soda was to make it look like there was liquor in his drink, and the wine was probably to help take off my edge.

"When did you eat last?" he asked, steering me toward the buffet table. When I didn't answer, he said, "That's what I thought."

I was too nervous to eat much, but I put a few of my favorites on my plate. I never could pass up Tilly's bacon-wrapped shrimp.

Colt leaned into my ear. "You didn't make those shrimp puffs, did you? I want to get one, but only if they're safe."

I shoved my elbow into his side as I shot him a grin.

His eyes twinkled. "So that means they're safe?"

We headed back to our table, and just as I was about to take my seat, I realized someone new was sitting at our table.

Ava Milton.

That explained how Colt got the tickets, and I had no doubt she wanted me here. Why?

"Magnolia," Ava said with a regal air. "You look lovely tonight." She was wearing a taupe brocade dress with long sleeves and a scooped neckline.

"Thank you," I said, not wanting to play her game.

Colt sat down next to me and put a reassuring hand on my thigh under the table. I covered it with my own and then looked up and gave him a smile. Relief filled his eyes.

Ava had something on him. I was sure of it.

If Ava had picked up on Colt's concern—and I didn't doubt she had—she ignored it and turned to the couple to her left to strike up a conversation about the library bond. Colt and I ate our food, although I picked at mine.

Colt took advantage of her distraction and leaned into my ear. "The best way to get her goat is to pretend she's not getting to you. I need you alert, and you can't drink that wine on an empty stomach."

He was right, of course.

I picked up one of Tilly's shrimps and took a bite as I surveyed the room. I found Belinda at a table in the middle of the room. Her gaze caught mine, and a sweet smile spread across her face before she turned to the woman sitting to her left. She was in full-on social mode.

My brother sat to her right, and it was like looking at my father in the past, back when he'd attended functions like this one. Roy was a handsome man, but he had a rough edge I'd never noticed in my daddy. Or had it been there and I just hadn't noticed?

The greasy bacon made my stomach churn.

I turned to Colt and whispered, "I have to go to the restroom."

"I'll come with you."

"Don't you think that will look odd?"

"Who's going to know? We'll make it look like we're circulating the room. I don't want you wandering around on your own." He grinned, but it looked forced. "I want to make sure no other man tries to steal you away."

We both knew that was a lie, or at best a partial truth.

I grabbed Colt's glass and took a drink. "I'm okay. But let's move around anyway."

"Good idea." Colt reached under the table, then handed me my purse.

I picked up my wine glass to bring as a prop, and then noticed Ava's intense gaze.

"You're supposed to be wearing a mask," she said authoritatively.

"I don't see you wearing one," I said.

"I make the rules, my dear. I'm not obligated to follow them."

I picked up my mask and then purposefully dropped it on the table. "Funny, I was about to say the same thing."

Since I was feeling full of piss and vinegar, I headed toward my brother's table.

"You shouldn't have done that, Magnolia," Colt said as he caught up with me. "You do *not* want to make an enemy of Ava Milton."

I stopped and looked up at him. "Who said I was making enemies? I think it's best if she and I both know where the other stands."

Colt didn't look so convinced, but I didn't give him time to answer. I was bound and determined to talk to my brother.

Roy looked up at me, his mouth parting when he realized it was me.

"Roy, we need to talk."

"I'm listening."

"Privately."

He glanced around the table at his supposed friends, then back at me with a sardonic smile. "I'm not going anywhere." Belinda had gotten up from the table sometime between when I saw her and started my march.

The people at his table squirmed and glanced down at their plates or around the room, anywhere but at the two of us.

"Fine," I said. "If that's what you prefer . . . Momma has changed her mind and is now on IV antibiotics, so you can call off the lawyers who are trying to overrule her wishes."

His eyes widened in surprise. "What . . . why did she change her mind?"

"She admitted that our father preferred me over you, and that she in turn doted on you, making you spoiled and cruel. She decided she wanted more time to make up for it."

The look on his face proved I'd caught him off guard. I felt the zing of victory, and I wasn't even halfway through.

"Of course, Momma probably resented me a little, since apparently I was the reason our father stayed in their marriage after having an affair—and not with Shannon Morrissey, someone else entirely."

Colt's hand rested on my shoulder in warning.

"This was all new information for me," I said. "So I thought you might want to know too."

"This is not the time or place, Magnolia," my brother spat through clenched teeth.

"Just remember that I preferred to have this conversation in private, but you insisted."

I spun around, only to find myself looking directly into Colt's stunned face. Grabbing his hand, I headed for the back of the room.

"Jesus," Colt said. "You're burning bridges right and left tonight."

"I'm tired of being a pawn. Aren't you?"

"Yes." Anger hardened his eyes, and for a moment I thought he was pissed at my question. Then I realized his reaction was directed at someone else.

"I don't need Ava," I said. "I can find another place to live. And I sure as hell don't need Roy. I'm tired of kissing people's asses. I'm done. And you should be too."

He grabbed my elbow and escorted me out of the room and into a hallway. "It's not that easy, Maggie. Not for me, and definitely not for you. You can't afford to set Roy off, especially not tonight, and Ava has her hands in everything in this town."

"Why can't I set Roy off *especially* tonight?"

Frustration and a hint of worry flashed on his face. "Because we have bigger things to worry about. We don't need the distraction."

"No. You know something. You said Roy would sacrifice me tonight and that I should stick to Belinda. What do you know?"

He swallowed but didn't respond.

He knew more than he was telling me.

He reached into his pocket and pulled out his phone. "Shit."

"What?"

He took my phone out and handed it to me. "Go back inside the room and wait for me there. You can hide in plain sight."

"No. Not until you tell me what's going on."

He ran a hand over his head. "Magnolia. *Please*. I'll tell you everything after this is done, but I need to make sure you're safe."

I had two choices: trust Colt to handle this or possibly risk both our lives. "Okay."

He grabbed my arms and gave me a hard kiss on the lips. "Keep your purse and your gun with you. Keep your phone in your hand. I'll let you know when it's safe."

"Colt. Be careful."

"I will. Now go out back inside." He guided me back to the opening to the room, and I let him push me inside.

My phone buzzed in my hand, and I looked down to see I'd gotten a text with a photo.

The photo showed my magnolia necklace in the foreground, and there in the background, sitting at a table here at the fundraiser, was me.

No words. The photo was enough.

The serial killer was here. I had to find Brady.

I scanned the room and spotted him sitting next to an older woman. But before I could push my way toward him, I came face-to-face with Belinda.

"Magnolia," she said, her usually sweet countenance gone. "We need to talk. Now."

chapter twenty-nine

I let her lead me back into the hallway, and then we started up a set of back stairs to the second floor. "Belinda, the serial killer is here."

"Not now, Magnolia."

"But—"

"*Not now.*"

She was scaring me.

"Are we supposed to be up here?" I asked when we were halfway up the stairs.

"No one will stop us," she said, but it sounded flat.

"Thank you for the dress," I said nervously. "It's beautiful, and I want you to know that I'm planning on returning it first thing tomorrow."

"Shh," she said as we reached the top. It was only then that I noticed the small gun in her hand.

"Belinda?" I asked, my voice tight with fear. "What are you doing?"

"I need you to hurry."

She hurried down the hallway full of doors, half of which looked like offices. The floor was covered with carpet, muffling the sound of our heels. She stopped about halfway down the hall and opened a door with a key. "We're going down here."

"What?" I glanced through the door and realized the dark room was actually a four-by-four closet that contained a spiral staircase. "No."

"Yes. Go." She gave me a tiny shove.

I was determined not to lose it, yet hysteria was bubbling up inside me anyway. "Are you going to kill me?"

"No, of course not. But I need you to cooperate. You'll understand when it's done."

"Why does everyone keep saying that?" I asked. "Tell me now, goddammit."

"I love you like a sister, Magnolia, but I've sacrificed the last two years for this moment, and I'll be damned if I let you screw it up for me."

"What is it? What are you going to do?"

"You'll find out, but we need to go. *Now.*" She grabbed my wrist with her free hand and pulled me into the closet stairwell, shutting the door behind us and plunging us into darkness.

"I can't, Belinda. I can't. The killer . . . the basement . . ." I struggled to catch my breath.

"What?" Belinda asked, her voice softening. "What are you talking about?"

"The serial killer . . . ten years ago . . . I saw him kill someone. He knows who I am. He just sent me a photo."

"Okay, slow down," she said, cupping my cheek in the darkness and sounding much more like herself. "Are you saying you've seen the man who killed Emily and Amy?"

415

"And several other women," I said, feeling a small sliver of control return.

"Is it Bill James?"

"I don't know. I couldn't see his face. He hurt me . . . I think I had a concussion and kept drifting in and out of consciousness. He killed a woman and gave me a scar so I'd never forget. And he's here *tonight*, Belinda." I grabbed her arm. "We have to tell the police. I have to tell Brady."

"That's why you ran away?"

"Yes. Let me go tell Brady."

"We'll tell him together after this is done, but we have to go *now*."

"Go where?"

"The basement."

I violently shook my head even though I knew she couldn't see me. "I can't, Belinda. I get panic attacks. I'm having one now."

"No," she said firmly, bringing my face close to hers. "You can do this, Magnolia. Don't give that man any more power over you than he already has." She paused. "If Bill James really is the serial killer, this is your chance to take your life back."

"What are you talking about?"

"I'm about to confront him, but I need you to cooperate. If I promise not to hurt you, will you promise me to play along?"

"Play along with what?"

"Good. It's better if you think it's real, but we have to move." Her hand slipped into mine and squeezed tight. "I won't let go. You're safe with me."

I wanted to tell her that her gun wasn't making me feel very safe, but then I realized that between the two of us, we had two guns. The serial killer wasn't likely to get the better of us tonight.

I closed my eyes and held the railing with one hand and her hand with the other. Since it was dark, I couldn't see anyway, and closing my eyes somehow made me feel more in control.

We seemed to descend forever, but Belinda never loosened her hold on my clammy hand, and we finally reached a concrete floor at the bottom of the steps. I opened my eyes to a space much like the one above us, only there was light pouring through the bottom of the door.

Belinda cupped my face again. "I love you, Magnolia. No matter what happens, I won't really hurt you. I need you to remember that."

I shook my head. "What are you talking about?"

She opened the door, grabbed my upper arm with her left hand, and pulled me out into a small wine cellar. There was another door at the end of the small hallway—presumably the entrance to the larger part of the cellar. I heard muffled voices on the other side.

"Who is—?" I started to whisper.

Belinda clamped the hand holding the gun over my mouth, her eyes widening with fright. "The element of surprise is very important. Okay?" She'd whispered the words so quietly I could barely hear them.

I nodded, panicking again. Belinda may have sworn she wouldn't hurt me, but she was freaking out herself, which made her extremely dangerous with a gun in her hand.

Lowering her hand, she tugged me closer to the opposite door. The sound of Colt's voice sent a jolt through me. "It's here. All of it. I need your guarantee you'll leave Magnolia alone."

"I never touched her," a woman said. Her voice sounded . . . familiar. "But from the cameras I had installed in her apartment, it sure looks like you have." When Colt didn't answer, she became more insistent. "Does *he* know?"

"No." Colt sounded defeated.

"He's not going to be happy." Her voice hardened. "Where is he?"

I realized who *she* was. Colt was talking to Rowena Rogers. But who was the *he* she kept referring to?

"I don't know," Colt said. "He hasn't been in contact with me since Lopez's death," Colt said. "But Maggie doesn't know anything. If you're going to kill anyone, kill me. I've been working for him. I'm the guilty one."

My eyes widened with fear, and Belinda shot me a warning look.

"Who said anything about killing anyone?" Rowena asked, but she sounded amused.

Were they talking about Bill? But if so, why would Bill care whether I lived or died?

"I see you lurking in the shadows, Bill," Rowena called out. "Show yourself, or I'll be forced to shoot."

Had she mistaken Belinda and me for Bill? Could her bullets penetrate the wooden door separating us? The fact that we could hear their conversation so well led me to believe it was pretty thin.

"You always had a penchant for the dramatic, Rowena. What is this nonsense?" Bill asked, his voice getting louder. He was walking closer to them as he spoke.

"Just getting my share of the money your partner stole, plus a nice amount of interest." There was a hitch in her voice when she spoke again. "Where is he?"

"I haven't seen or heard from him for two years," Bill said. "The last time was when he came back and dealt with Ava Milton. He slipped out of my grip then, but he won't this time. You have to trust me."

Oh. My. God.

I glanced over at Belinda to see if she was making the same leap, but she was completely intent on the conversation. It was like she was listening for her cue.

I gasped as I remembered how Colt had insisted that I stick close to Belinda. From Rowena's questions and his own vague admission, he wasn't an innocent victim in this. He was complicit in something, but what he was complicit in remained to be seen. Still, I refused to believe he was part of Belinda's crazy scheme, whatever it was.

"I trusted you before, and look what it got me," Rowena said, growing impatient. "*Nothing.*"

"We're close," Bill said. "But this stunt is going to set us back. Now just go back to the party or your hideaway or wherever you crawled out of and be patient."

"I'm done being patient," Rowena snapped. "If the gold isn't enough of a draw, then Magnolia will do. Colt, go get her."

"*No.* Leave her out of this."

"Bill," Rowena said. "Go get your partner's daughter."

"Rowena," Bill objected. "Colt's right. Leave her out of it."

"Obviously he needs an added incentive."

And that, it would seem, was Belinda's cue. Her hand shook before she tightened her hold on my arm and pushed the door open, dragging me with her. "Ms. Rogers is right. Here she is."

Horror and panic washed over Colt's face when he saw us, which made me feel slightly better. I would have bet my life he wouldn't hurt me, and it looked like I was right. Too bad I hadn't expected the danger to come from Belinda.

We were in a large, unfinished basement with rock walls and an uneven, crumbling concrete floor. The ten-foot ceiling was covered in cracked plaster, and the few bare light bulbs providing shaky light cast eerie shadows in all directions. At roughly twenty-by-twenty, the room was obviously only a portion of the huge house overhead. In addition to the door behind us, there was an open doorway directly opposite me that led to a dark space. There was a third (closed) door on the wall to my right, along with a large open window that looked like a pass-through to a dark kitchen. Two stone pillars in the center of the room braced the ceiling—Colt stood next to the pillar closest to Rowena Rogers, and there was a man I didn't recognize to my left. Bill James stood directly in front of me.

Who was the stranger? I had a sneaking suspicion he might be the man we'd encountered in the industrial park. He stood behind Rowena with a gun in his hand. He was obviously her henchman.

Rowena squinted in confusion, and she glanced toward us. "Who are you?" She turned to Bill. "Is she with you?"

"She's Roy's wife. *Belinda*," Bill said in disbelief, "what are you doing?"

"I have the bait. Now where is he?"

Bill shook his head, his eyes wide with confusion. "Belinda, I know Lila's illness is upsetting, but you need to put down the gun and let Magnolia go. Roy has this under control."

Roy had *what* under control? This was like watching a foreign movie with only some of the subtitles.

"No." Belinda's fingers dug into my arm. "I don't need Roy. Not anymore. I'm doing this on my own."

I was a total pawn in this situation, desperate to regain some sort of control. The best person to get on my side was the woman next to me. "Belinda," I turned to her, pleading, "let's just—"

She gave my arm a violent shake. "Be quiet, Magnolia!"

My mouth dropped open in disbelief.

She glanced from Bill to Rowena with wild eyes. "I know he's around. He's been watching her. *I saw him.* Magnolia did too."

Oh, my God. Was she talking about the serial killer? Because I still couldn't let my mind believe the other idea running through my head was true.

"*Belinda*," Colt snapped. "Why are you doing this? Let Maggie go. This has *nothing* to do with her."

Belinda stiffened. "I know you're in regular contact with him, Colt. Text him."

Colt shook his head and held out his hands. "What are you going to do to Maggie? She's your friend, Belinda. You don't want to hurt her."

Belinda lifted the gun to my temple. "*Text him!*"

Colt, obviously panicking, took a step toward us before he stopped himself. "Okay. Okay. *Please*. I'll text him. But I want you to swear to me you won't hurt her!"

Belinda didn't answer, and at that moment I wasn't sure I believed her earlier promise that I was safe.

"I'm getting out my phone," Colt said. "Okay?"

"Don't try anything, or I'll kill her, Colt."

"I believe you. Just tell me what you want it to say." He slowly reached into his jacket pocket and pulled out his phone.

"I want to see the text before you send it," she said. "Tell him that he has ten minutes to show up or Magnolia dies."

"Text?" Rowena said, sounding disgusted. "Why doesn't he just call?"

"Because he doesn't answer the phone," Belinda said. "*Does* he, Colt? He hides behind his blocked number."

The blood rushed from my head. Was *he* the serial killer? My knees started to buckle, but Belinda jerked my arm, helping me regain my senses.

Bill looked confused. "How do you know that, Belinda?"

She didn't answer.

Colt had already been tapping on his phone and held it up. "Here. It's ready, but he might not be close enough to meet the deadline. I promise you he'll come. You know she's important to him, but he might be too far away."

Belinda shook her head. "No. He knows this is going down. He'll be close. In fact, I suspect he's closer than any of you realize." She nodded to Colt. "Send the text."

He looked up at me with fear in his eyes as he pressed the screen.

"Now that that task has been accomplished," Rowena said in a satisfied voice, "I'll need the bag of gold, Mr. Austin."

Colt slowly backed up, moving partially behind the pillar before he reemerged with the small canvas bag we'd taken from that basement in Chattanooga. It looked heavy from the way the straps strained against his hand.

"Set it down in front of Kent," she said, gesturing to the man at her side.

Colt did as instructed, then slowly backed up.

After handing his gun to Rowena, the henchman squatted in front of the bag and searched through it.

"Is it all there?" Rowena asked.

"It appears to be," he said. Sure enough, I recognized the gravelly voice from that rainy night at the industrial park, but I wasn't so sure it was the man in Bill James's office.

"You got your gold," Colt said. "So go."

"No," she said with a tight smile. "I'll wait to greet our special guest." Then her grin spread.

Lord only knew what would happen then. There was nowhere to hide if it turned into a gun battle.

Colt's gaze landed on the purse still tucked under my arm.

He had a gun, and from the look on his face, he would do whatever it took to protect me. I suspected that included shooting Belinda if he thought she was going to kill me.

"Belinda," I said, trying to keep my voice calm and soothing. "Colt sent the text. He'll show up. You can put the gun away now and wait."

"Do you even know who he sent the text to?"

Tears filled my eyes, but I shook my head. "No."

Her chin quivered. "He killed my parents, Magnolia. Him and these two"—she gestured to Bill and Rowena—"and the others. They killed my parents."

Her words split something inside of me. Was she talking about *my father*? I'd learned a lot of terrible things about my father, but was he capable of murder too?

"I didn't kill anyone!" Bill protested.

"What about those poor women?" Belinda asked. "What about Emily and Amy?"

"*You* were the anonymous tip?" Bill asked in disbelief. "I didn't kill those women, Belinda!"

"Then why were those files about Emily and Magnolia on your desk?"

"A week ago, I got an anonymous email telling me Emily, you, and Magnolia were in danger. I knew Emily had been Magnolia's attorney, but I hired a PI to find out more information about her."

"Why wasn't there a file for me?" she asked.

"Because I know all about you, Belinda. Or I thought I did."

"Did you know my parents invested in the Jackson Project?" she asked.

Bill's face drained of color. "No."

She shot him a glare. "Brian Steele talked my dad into investing everything he owned. My dad even borrowed money to put into it. To say he didn't take the loss very well is an understatement. He was an alcoholic, and when he lost everything, he got depressed. He and my mother were killed in a car accident—a head-on collision that killed the man in the other car. My father had been drinking, but the police called it a murder-suicide. I was five when I was sent to Mississippi to live with my impoverished, invalid grandmother."

"Magnolia didn't do that to you," Colt said in desperation. "She's done everything in her power to help you. Why would you hurt her?"

Belinda started to cry. "I want to hurt him like he hurt me."

"Then use Roy," Colt pleaded. "That bastard has hurt you more times than either one of us can count. Use *him*."

"Because he doesn't love Roy like he does Magnolia. She's the only one who can draw him out." She turned to me with teary eyes. "I thought Bill was the serial killer too. I'm sorry."

"Why are you sorry?" Colt asked.

"I promised she could get her revenge. For what Bill did to her ten years ago."

"What?" Colt gasped. Then his eyes turned murderous. "What did you do to her?"

Bill's eyes widened. "I never hurt you, Magnolia. I swear to God, I never hurt you."

"I know," I said, trying to figure out how to defuse this situation. "I know it wasn't you."

If my father was about to walk through that door, I didn't want him to walk in on this—on me being held at gunpoint by the person I'd considered my best friend. And I sure didn't want her to get shot.

"Belinda. I need you to look at me," I said.

She turned her attention to me.

"Now listen to me. Are you listening?"

She nodded.

"You need to put that gun down. You're going to get hurt, and I've lost too many people to lose you too."

"But . . ."

"*No.* Give it to me, and we'll deal with my father together."

She hesitated.

"Colt's already sent the text. My father thinks I'm in danger, so if it's going to work, the trap has been set. We just have to wait. Together. Now, *please.* Give me the gun."

Her shoulders slumped as she handed the gun to me, and then she collapsed into my shoulder.

"Colt," I called out, unsure I could hold her up.

He gave me a look of hesitation, so I said, "She was never going to hurt me."

Belinda dropped to her knees as Colt took two steps in my direction.

A gunshot went off, ricocheting off the concrete as Rowena shouted, "Everyone stay where they are. Magnolia, toss the gun on the ground, or Kent will shoot Colt."

Colt looked furious. "Don't do it, Maggie. I'm sick to death of taking orders."

Pure evil filled Kent's eyes. I believed him capable of killing Colt, if for no other reason than because he was bored. But if I tossed the gun, we would be completely unarmed—at least as far as Rowena and Kent were concerned. But maybe that could be to our advantage.

I tossed the gun to the ground, and it bounced, skittering close to Colt.

"Don't even think of picking that up, Mr. Austin," Rowena said. "Or Magnolia's forfeiture of the gun will have been for naught." Smiling, she lifted her own gun and pointed it at me. "And if I'm going to shoot someone, I have someone else in mind. Like Magnolia said, you already sent the text."

"No!" Colt shouted.

Several gunshots went off. I automatically dropped to the floor, and my upper arm began to burn as if on fire.

Kent had fallen to the ground, and Colt leaped toward Rowena, tackling her from the side.

I looked down at my bicep in disbelief, watching blood ooze from the wound on my bare skin.

"Maggie?" Colt called out in panic. "*Maggie!*"

"I'm okay."

I glanced around, looking for Bill, but he was gone.

"Magnolia!" Belinda gushed as she helped me to a sitting position against the wall. "Colt, she's been shot."

"I'm okay," I said, but my peripheral vision was getting dark.

"We have to get out of here. *Now*," Colt said in a tight voice. "Rowena and her goon are dead." He paused. "And the gold is gone."

"Bill must have taken it. What are we going to do?" Belinda asked, looking back at Colt. "We have to call the police."

"No, wait." Colt gently touched my arm and lowered his voice, but it sounded strained. "It's superficial, Mags. It just grazed you." Colt shrugged out of his jacket and then started unbuttoning his shirt before he gave up and ripped off the buttons. "Belinda, don't let her blood drip on the floor. Keep it on her dress." He quickly rolled up the shirt, lifted my arm, and wrapped the shirt around it several times before knotting it.

Pain shot through my arm, and I gritted my teeth to keep from crying out.

"Who shot them?" Belinda asked in disbelief. "Bill didn't even have a gun."

"I have an idea and we're not sticking around to find out. Belinda, get your gun off the floor. We can't leave any trace that we were here."

She did as he asked while he picked his jacket up off the floor and slipped it on.

"Maggie, look at me," he said, squatting in front of me. "We have to go. No police, okay?"

"I trust you." I lifted my gaze from my arm up to his naked chest peeking through his jacket, then up to his face. "I lied."

He squinted. "You lied about what? You don't trust me?"

"Your chest. I told you I didn't want to see it. I lied."

He gave me a hard kiss on the mouth and grinned. "You have the worst damn timing." He turned more serious. "Can you walk?"

I nodded. "I think so."

He helped me to my feet. My knees wobbled, and he slipped an arm around my back to steady me. The pain made me dizzy. "Belinda, can we go out the way you came in? I take it that it's discreet?"

"Yes, but what about Magnolia?"

"Can you climb the stairs?" he asked me.

"That's not it," Belinda said, sounding more like herself. "She freaked out in the stairwell."

"Her claustrophobia," Colt said as though upset he'd forgotten.

"Her experience with the serial killer," Belinda corrected.

"What the hell are you talking about?" Colt asked in a tight voice.

Belinda grabbed my left hand. "God, Magnolia. I'm so sorry."

"I can do it," I said. "I have to get out of here." There were two dead bodies less than ten feet from me, and I was close to freaking out. "Let's go."

Belinda opened the wine cellar door with the skirt of her dress. Colt and I followed her in, and we both watched her open the door to the spiral staircase.

Colt gave me a worried glance, then looked up the stairwell. "Can you do this?"

"Yes." I shoved him to the side with my good elbow. "Get out of the way."

"And . . . she's back . . ." Colt muttered, but he sounded rather pleased.

Now we just had to get out.

chapter thirty

Getting out took more effort than I'd expected. There was a fair amount of blood on my dress, which was bound to draw suspicion.

"Colt, get your truck," Belinda said in a brisk tone when we reached the second floor. "Drive behind the house, and I'll bring Magnolia to you, out of view."

Colt shot me a look as if to make sure I was okay with this plan.

I nodded, trying to hide how badly my arm hurt.

He turned to Belinda. "Will you tell Roy you're leaving?"

"I'm staying."

I started to protest, but she held up her hand. "No. Think about it. Once the bodies are discovered, it will look odd if all three of us are gone. I'll say you two left because you couldn't keep your hands off each other. I'll be the eyes here to find out what's going on."

"Belinda . . . I can't leave you," I choked out through a throat thick with tears.

"You can and you will." She looked up at Colt. "Why are you still here? Go."

Colt took off toward the front, and Belinda and I headed to the back staircase. We stayed silent until after we'd slipped through a back door to the garden.

"You have to leave Roy, Belinda," I said. "You accomplished your goal. It's time to leave him."

"I didn't accomplish anything. Not really." She shook her head. "I can't believe I thought it would work. I can't believe I put you in danger."

"You think my father really cares?" I asked. "He's a selfish asshole. Pack a bag when you get home and then come to Momma's house. She's going to need help when she comes home, so that's where I'll be from now on. If you need physical backup, call Colt."

"Why are you being so forgiving?" she asked.

"We're family. Family sticks together."

We pushed through a hedge to reach the street behind the house. Colt's truck was already rounding the corner.

"Belinda, why did you take me to Bill's office? What did you hope to find?"

"I really *did* think he might be the serial killer, and if your father thought his partner was after you . . ."

If Bill wasn't the killer, then who had we overheard in Bill's office that night? Who had burned down the house? That person now had the necklace Brady gave me. The *real* killer.

"You were trying to lure him out. He never showed up tonight. See?" I said. "He doesn't give a shit."

"You're wrong," Belinda said softly. "He cares more than you know. He was there tonight." She paused. "Magnolia. He's the one who killed Rowena and her guy."

My mouth dropped open as Colt pulled up to the curb. How?

Belinda opened the door and pushed me in. "Take her to Lila's. I'll let you know when I hear something."

She shut the door, and before I could say anything at all, she was already hurrying back toward the house.

***

Colt studied my face. "On a scale of one to ten, how much trouble am I in?"

There was no doubt he cared about me, but there were so many unanswered questions. But when I thought about them, the trauma of what just happened hit me full force. My voice broke as I said, "I can't talk about it right now."

He wrapped an arm around my back and pulled me close. I leaned my head into the crook of his arm.

Fat tears leaked from my eyes, which pissed me off. I needed to keep it together.

Colt tilted my head back and searched my eyes as he whispered, "It's going to be okay. I promise."

I shook my head slowly. My world was imploding. My mother was dying. My sister-in-law had held a gun to my head. I'd just seen two people murdered. Maybe by my father. Who, by the way, was alive and apparently keeping tabs on me by using the man I was falling in love with. How could things be okay?

"Let's go to Lila's and we'll get your arm cleaned up. Then we can talk," he said softly.

I nodded. "Okay."

Tears continued to roll down my cheeks as Colt pulled away from the curb. If Belinda was right and my father had killed Rowena and Kent, where had he been hiding?

The kitchen. He'd been there the entire time.

I wasn't sure I could handle the betrayal.

Colt unlocked my mother's front door and guided me into the house. "Sit down at the kitchen table, and let me take care of your arm."

"I just want to change," I said, closing my eyes with exhaustion.

"You can change after I get a bandage on it."

I sat down at the table while he opened up the pantry and pulled out the first-aid kit. He unwrapped his shirt and cleaned up the wound with alcohol, which had me jumping out of my chair and crying out in pain.

"I'm sorry," he murmured, looking distressed. "If we don't get it clean, it will get infected."

"Do what you need to do," I said through gritted teeth.

He'd just wrapped the bandage around my bicep when my phone started buzzing in my purse on the table. I nearly dumped out the gun in my clumsiness to get it out. Colt picked up the phone and gave me a worried look. "It's the hospital."

I sat upright, my heart racing as I took the call. "Hello?"

"Magnolia, this is Vanessa at Vanderbilt. I know you're at your big party, but your mother's taken a turn for the worse. I think you should come back as soon as you can."

I nodded, unable to speak.

Colt took the phone from me and said, "We're on our way."

He practically carried me out to the truck and then raced to the hospital, driving well over the speed limit. It still took us twenty minutes, and my heart was beating like a rabbit's the whole time.

The nurses were waiting when I rushed off the elevator, and they didn't seemed bothered by the bandage on my arm or the spots of blood on my dress.

"Momma?" I asked.

Vanessa, the nurse who had helped me with my hair, walked around the desk. The look on her face sent my heart straight into my throat. "We started giving your mother a round of antibiotics before you left, but as you know, she was already weak from her chemo and the infection. Her body was worn out." She paused, holding my gaze. "Magnolia, your mother passed ten minutes ago."

"No," I said calmly. She was mistaken. "Momma changed her mind. She wanted to spend more time with me."

"I'm so sorry," Vanessa said.

Colt had put his arm around me at some point, and he pulled me closer. "Maggie, let's go sit down."

"*No*," I said more insistently as I pulled away from him. "She said she was going to spend more time with me."

Tears filled his eyes. "She wanted to, Mags. I know she did."

The elevator doors opened, and I knew without looking that my brother had gotten out. "What's going on with my mother?"

"I'm alone," I whispered, overwhelmed by the concept. I'd been alone while I was living in New York, yet it had been a different type of alone. I'd always known my mother was only a phone call away if I needed her. I was as good as an orphan.

"No, Mags," Colt said, holding me close to his side again. "I'm here."

The first sob ripped from my chest. "She left me. I can't believe she left me alone."

Belinda hugged me from the other side. "No. We're family. Family sticks together. You're not alone."

"Belinda," Roy barked. "What are you doing? Get away from her. Magnolia made her choice when she left ten years ago."

"Roy." The name dripped off her tongue like it was poison. "Go fuck yourself."

I gasped and turned around to face her, completely stunned. I'd never even heard her utter more than one damn. I started to laugh.

"What the hell's so funny?" Roy asked. "I'm not kidding, Belinda. Come over here now."

Belinda gave him a condescending glare.

"This is your last chance, Belinda. You either come over here or don't come home."

"Roy," Belinda said in a softer tone. "You're really screwed up if your mother just died, and your biggest concern is that I'm comforting your sister."

Roy turned around and punched the elevator call button.

"I want to see her," I said. "I want to tell my mother goodbye."

"She's already gone," Roy shouted, still facing the closed elevator doors. "She's not there."

"You need to see her too, Roy," I said, feeling stronger with Colt and Belinda beside me. "You need to tell her goodbye."

He leaned his head into his arm on the wall, and his shoulders began to shake.

The elevator door opened again, and Tilly rushed out, panic on her face. She searched me out. "Maggie?"

I walked toward her and shook my head.

Tilly burst into tears and began to collapse. Colt helped me hold her up, and we led her to the waiting room to sit down and let the news sink in.

I looked up to check on Roy, only to realize he'd already left.

Tilly continued to cry, sitting between Colt and me, and Belinda knelt at her feet.

"I'm so sorry, Tilly," I said through my own tears. "You didn't get to tell her goodbye."

She shook her head. "There was nothing left unsaid. It's a lot more than most people get. I'm grateful for that." Glancing around at us, she released a laugh through her sobs. "Why are you all hovering around me? You should be takin' care of Magnolia."

"They already are," I said.

"That still doesn't explain why you're hovering around me."

"It's just like you told Roy," I said. "You loved her the longest." Then I added what I'd always suspected. "You loved her the most."

Her chin trembled and fresh tears fell down her cheeks. "Oh, Magnolia. She was all I had."

"No, Tilly," I said grabbing her hand. "You have me."

"And me," Belinda said, putting her hand on top of mine.

"And me," Colt added.

Turned out I wasn't alone after all.

chapter
thirty-one

My mother was buried on a warm Monday afternoon in April.

I stood by her grave and looked up at the clear blue sky, feeling the sun on my face.

"It's a good day for a funeral," Tilly said. "Your mother would have loved it."

Colt laughed. "She would have made fun of you for saying that."

The minister gave us dirty looks, but I didn't care. He obviously hadn't known my mother.

As per my mother's instructions, she only had a graveside service, which lasted less than ten minutes, also per her instructions. Roy had a fit, but the funeral home insisted Momma was very specific. I watched her coffin lowered into the rectangular hole, but I knew she wasn't there. She wasn't in the clouds either. She was in Tilly and Belinda, and even in Colt. She was in my fresh-brewed coffee and the coffee cake I'd made that morning without a single screwup. She was in her once again impeccably clean house. She was in Tilly's laugh, Colt's protectiveness, and Belinda's goodness.

I had my father's looks, but I had my mother's practicality, a trait that would last me years longer than my beauty. I realized she'd spent her life preparing me for the real world, even if I hadn't known it. I didn't need a goodbye, because she wasn't really gone. She was still here, looking over my shoulder and yelling at me for filling shrimp puffs with buttercream frosting. She was whispering in my ear to be brave. That I was a strong, capable woman. That I would survive this loss.

When the service was over, Roy stood to my right ignoring me as we greeted the mourners. I shook hands for nearly an hour, realizing for the first time how many people were there.

Roy left first. When I saw Brady approaching me, I sent Tilly and Belinda to the funeral dinner, telling them I would catch up. Colt saw Brady and gave me a questioning look.

"I need to talk to him. But I'd like you to wait."

He nodded and walked toward the back of the chairs that had been set up.

Brady stopped in front of me. "I'm truly sorry for your loss, Magnolia," he said, casting a glance toward her grave.

"Thank you."

"I'm not sure if you've heard the news, but Bill James has disappeared."

My mouth gaped. "I haven't."

"Two bodies were found in the basement of Savannah House," he said, watching me closely. "The night of the ball."

I feigned surprise. "Oh, my goodness."

"An old associate of your father's was murdered. Do you know anything about it?"

"An associate? I didn't know Daddy had any left."

"Rowena Rogers. And someone we presume was working with her."

"Do you think that's why Bill James left?"

He lifted an eyebrow. "Who said he left?"

I narrowed my eyes. "Are you really interrogating me at my mother's graveside, Detective Bennett?"

He looked flustered at that. "I'm sorry. But we need to talk soon." He leaned closer. "And we need to take a walk out in the woods behind your mother's house." He took a step back. "I'll be in touch. Once again, I'm sorry for your loss."

"Thank you," I murmured and watched him walk away as someone else approached me.

The last of the mourners went on their way, and finally Colt and I were alone next to Momma's open grave. We'd been too busy with funeral preparation and my grief to address his betrayal, and I knew he sensed it was only a temporary reprieve. The reckoning was coming.

"How long?" I asked, knowing he'd know what I meant.

"Three years." He sounded relieved to finally address the cloud that had been hanging over us.

"How did it happen?"

"He came to me in jail. I'd been arrested for robbing a store, but honest to God, Magnolia, I didn't do it, although I'd done my share of shady shit in the past. Looking back now, I know it was a setup, but at the time I was scared. It seemed like the deal was too good not to take. He said if I'd work with him on a special project, all charges would be dropped, but if I ever stopped fulfilling my end of the arrangement, I'd end up back in jail. Of course I agreed, and somehow the charges were miraculously dropped, even though he wasn't an attorney and had nothing to do with the police.

"After I got out, I met him at a restaurant in Nashville. He told me my job was to keep an eye on your mother and your brother. I didn't find out about you until I started working at the Belles. I was supposed to give him reports every week through email. I was also supposed to keep tabs on Bill James and Belinda.

"I knew you were coming home before you ever showed up at the Belles. Before you showed up on your mother's doorstep. He told me to watch you closely."

"The best way to do that was to become my friend."

He looked down at his shoes. "Yeah. So I stuck close and reported daily, but it didn't take long for me to realize that I wouldn't leave you. Not even if he told me to quit looking out for you." He looked up at me. "I had no idea who he was until I'd been reporting to him for a year. He wasn't actively involved in much until you came back. He came to town and told me to watch you. As you started to uncover the past, I realized he was hoping you would. I think he was counting on you to flush out the gold."

"Why didn't he look in the garage?" I asked. "It's been there for two years."

"When I asked what had become of his office, your mother told me everything had been seized or tossed out. He was sure Bill James had taken the gold. But when we found it, I didn't tell him, Maggie." His eyes pleaded with mine. "You have to believe me. I took it to my friend and had him research it. I wasn't sure what to do when I realized he'd stolen it."

"Why didn't you tell *me*?"

"You worshipped the guy. I wasn't going to be the one to take that away from you. I wanted to be with you, any crumb you would toss my way. I . . . I couldn't bring myself to jeopardize that. I've already lost enough people in my life. How would you have reacted if I'd told you?"

"Honestly? I don't know."

"When things started to get dangerous for you, I started to get paranoid. Do you know I slept on Ava's front porch several nights so I'd be there if you needed me? And knowing you went to Bennett's killed me, but what better place for you to stay than a cop's?"

I closed my eyes to center myself—and took a breath before opening them again.

He searched my face. "I kept falling deeper and deeper into this pit, and I didn't know how to get out of it. I was determined not to let anything happen to you." He paused, looking defeated. "I don't want to lose you, Maggie."

"Are you still reporting to him?"

"I stopped the day after Emily died."

"Why?"

"Because I was scared he was the one murdering those women."

"*Why?*"

He shrugged. "Paranoia? Bodies seem to pop up whenever he comes back. Merritt disappeared when he came back to hire me. I wanted to protect you."

I knew I should write him out of my life, but while he'd started out pretending to be my friend, he'd proven himself to be that and so much more.

"Was Belinda right?" he asked quietly. "Did you really leave town because of a serial killer?"

"Yes."

"The one who killed Emily and Amy?"

"And at least a half dozen more. It wasn't my father. At least those murders weren't." I had to believe that.

"Oh, my God. Are you safe?"

"For now." But he'd come for me soon.

"What's Bennett doing about it?"

"Everything he can." Or at least I hoped he was.

"Can you forgive me, Maggie?"

I thought about what Momma had said about choosing the right man. How I should pick the one who made me laugh and cry. Colt had given me both. I searched twenty-eight years for anything to compare it to, but I came up empty. I wasn't willing to throw it away.

"Don't you screw me over again, Colt Austin. I won't be so forgiving next time."

He pulled me into his arms and kissed me as though he hadn't seen me in a month. "Are you ready to go?" he asked.

"I need a few minutes alone with Momma first."

"Okay. I'll walk up to the road and wait."

"Thanks."

He looked back at me every few steps as he walked away. The staff had started folding and stacking the wooden chairs they'd set up, and the director walked over to me.

"Magnolia, the men said someone left this. I wondered if it belonged to you, or maybe someone meant to give it to you and forgot."

The magnolia necklace Brady had given me was dangling from his hand.

The killer had been at my mother's funeral.

I took it from him with shaking fingers. "Thank you."

"If there's anything else we can do for you, just let us know."

"Thanks." I turned my back to him, clasping the pendant in my hand tight enough for the metal points to dig into my palm. I cast my eyes toward a small grove of trees, looking for the figure that had been hidden there for most of the service. He was still there, on the outside looking in. Exactly where he belonged.

"You have no right to be here," I shouted at my father, certain the men behind me thought I'd lost my mind. "You made your choice fourteen years ago, and I want you to stay gone."

He continued to watch me.

I turned my back on him and walked toward Colt, who had heard me shouting and was already halfway back to me.

"Are you okay?" he asked, glancing toward the trees.

"Everything is fine." At least for today.

Tomorrow would bring the curtain call.

Curtain Call
Magnolia Steele Mystery #4
October 17, 2017

To find out more about Denise Grover Swank's releases and to have access to bonus content, join her newsletter!
www.denisegroverswank.com/mailing-list/

About the Author

Denise Grover Swank was born in Kansas City, Missouri and lived in the area until she was nineteen. Then she became a nomadic gypsy, living in five cities, four states and ten houses over the course of ten years before she moved back to her roots. She speaks English and smattering of Spanish and Chinese which she learned through an intensive Nick Jr. immersion period. Her hobbies include witty Facebook comments (in own her mind) and dancing in her kitchen with her children. (Quite badly if you believe her offspring.) Hidden talents include the gift of justification and the ability to drink massive amounts of caffeine and still fall asleep within two minutes. Her lack of the sense of smell allows her to perform many unspeakable tasks. She has six children and hasn't lost her sanity. Or so she leads you to believe.

For more info go to: DeniseGroverSwank.com